THE STERLING UNIVERSITY SERIES

COMPLETE 3-NOVELLA SET

REBECCA HEFLIN

AWARD-WINNING AUTHOR
REBECCA HEFLIN
She says it's all about the chemistry.
STERLING UNIVERSITY
THE SERIES
BOOK ONE
He says it's all about the romance.
Romancing Dr. Love

ROMANCING DR. LOVE

Copyright © 2016. All rights reserved.

REBECCA HEFLIN

Cover Design by The Killion Group, Inc.

This book is a work of fiction. The names, characters, places, and incidents are the products of the author's imagination or are used fictitiously. Any resemblance to actual events, business establishments, locales, or persons, living or dead, is entirely coincidental.

All rights reserved. No part of this publication may be reproduced, stored in a retrieval system, or transmitted in any form or by any means (electronic, mechanical, photocopying, recording, or otherwise) without the prior written permission of both the copyright owner and the publisher. The only exception is brief quotations in printed reviews.

The scanning, uploading, and distribution of this book via the Internet or via any other means without the permission of the publisher is illegal and punishable by law. Please purchase only authorized electronic editions, and do not participate in or encourage electronic piracy of copyrighted materials.

Your support of the author's rights is appreciated.

Published in the United States of America by:

Rebecca Heflin Books, LLC

www.RebeccaHeflin.com

ACKNOWLEDGMENTS

To my ever-faithful beta readers, Yvonne and my hubby, Ron. Thank you for your continued guidance, patience, and support.

For my introduction into the world of sports analytics, I'd like to thank Will Pantages with the University of Florida. His discussion on how collegiate sports teams collect and utilize statistics was invaluable. I did, however, take some creative license, so any inaccuracies are purely my own.

And to my editor, Paul, your keen eye and indepth knowledge of all things grammarly are much appreciated. Your skill allows my stories to shine.

"How on earth are you ever going to explain in terms of chemistry and physics so important a biological phenomenon as first love?"

— Albert Einstein

1

"No, no, no. This isn't happening. This isn't happening," Samantha Love muttered as she gently banged her head against the steering wheel.

She turned the key again. Nothing. Not even a wheeze. This was the icing on the cake of her otherwise craptastic day.

A bead of sweat trickled down her back. And another one between her girls. God, she hated boob sweat.

When she'd taken the research and teaching position at Sterling University in North Georgia last fall, she'd never have guessed the summer would be so hot.

Throwing open the door of her car to let in even more stifling heat, she searched for the lever to pop the hood. Finally locating it, she pulled it, then walked around to the front of the car. As if she knew what to do.

Just as she leaned under the hood to jiggle some wire thingies, she heard, "Dr. Love? Do you need some help?"

She let out a startled squeak hitting her head on the underside of the hood. "Ow!" Rubbing the offended spot, she turned and saw Ethan Quinn standing there looking all adorable. Not to mention manly.

Dammit. Why did it have to be him? "No. I'm fine." Yeah, right. For all her parents' preaching on women and self-sufficiency, she didn't know a dipstick from a spark plug when it came to cars. She turned back to the mystery parts under the hood.

"You need a jump."

"I beg your pardon?" She spun, hand on her hip.

"Your battery." He pointed in the direction of her open hood. "It probably needs a jump."

"Oh. Right." Of course he meant her battery. What else would he be talking about?

"I have jumper cables in my car. I'll have you going in a few minutes."

"He'll have me going in a few minutes," she mumbled under her breath as she watched him walk to the far corner of the parking lot. Tall, athletic build, dark-wash jeans, white button-down shirt. And that hair. Tousled espresso-brown waves just brushing the top of his collar. "He's already got me going," she said to herself.

He tossed his messenger bag in the car and climbed in. And, of course, *his* car started. Because that's what cars did. They started when you turned the key. Then they blew cold air, so you didn't have to stand in the mid-July Georgia heat. Unless they dated back to the Stone Age like hers. Another bead of sweat trickled between her breasts.

She released a wistful sigh. Bet the AC felt good.

He pulled his recent model American-made car around to face hers and then got out to pop the hood. Walking around to the trunk, he opened it and grabbed a set of jumper cables, looking like he knew what he was doing.

Good thing somebody around here did.

"It's a hot one today," Ethan commented, as he connected one of the clamp doohickeys to what she assumed was the car battery. His sleeves were rolled up over his forearms, displaying muscles with a light dusting of hair.

Clamping the other end of the cables to his own battery, he then returned to her car. When he walked past her, his cologne wafted to her nose, temporarily erasing her angst at being in his presence.

Then he touched his hand to her back. And the anxiety returned tenfold. "Stand clear." He leaned into the gaping mouth of the car and attached the remaining clamp, throwing a spark.

"All right. Let's see if we can get this baby going." He climbed into the driver's seat of his car and turned it on.

"Give her a try," he hollered over the din of his car's running motor.

Sam dropped into the front seat and turned the key. The older-than-dirt engine tried but couldn't work up enough energy to turn over.

"Hold on," Ethan called, then revved his car. "Okay, try her again."

Her car wheezed then reluctantly cranked a couple of times before coming to life.

Ethan was at her door, leaning over, hands braced on the roof. "Great. Let her run a bit, then I'll disconnect the cables." A bead of sweat trickled down his temple. "My AC's on full blast. Why don't you sit in my car until yours is ready to go." He stepped aside to give her room to get out.

Sam felt as wilted as week-old lettuce, so against her better judgment she took him up on the offer.

He opened the front passenger door of his shiny black Lincoln MKS—such a gentleman—and she sank into the leather seats and stuck her face in front of the vent. God, it felt good. The door closed with a solid *thunk*. Resisting the urge to wipe away the boob sweat, she settled for drying the perspiration on her face and neck.

The car dipped as Ethan took a seat on the driver's side before shutting the door and closing out the rest of the world. Music played softly in the background—something popular. The intimacy of being alone in the car with Ethan washed over her.

"I'd offer you something cool to drink, but I don't have anything."

She realized she hadn't said a word in the last five minutes. "Thank you."

"No thanks necessary. You'd do the same for me."

"No, I wouldn't." She smiled. "I don't know a thing about cars."

He nodded as a grin split his face. "Well, from the looks of your battery, you're going to need a new one. I can follow you to Burt's Automotive. He can have a replacement installed in fifteen minutes."

She shook her head. "Thanks, but I don't want to put you out in any further."

"It's no trouble. Besides, if you go straight home, I don't think she's going to start for you in the morning."

"Oh." That would not be good.

"She should be juiced up enough to get you to Burt's. Stay here until I unhook the cables." Ethan got out of the car and set to work.

She'd steered clear of Ethan Quinn since the day she was introduced to the rest of the college faculty. The moment they shook hands she'd felt a connection. And from the look on his face, he'd felt it too. That flood of adrenaline, dopamine, and serotonin one feels when there is a strong physical attraction.

Relationships were complicated, but getting situated at a new university was already complicated enough.

No. Being in close proximity to Ethan Quinn was a bad idea. So as much as she hated to leave the cool comfort of his car, she jumped out and got in her rolling oven before he could say otherwise.

~

HIS LUCKY DAY, Ethan thought. Burt's was a little backed up, so they were looking at a turn-around time of half an hour to forty-five minutes.

"How about a cold drink over at Ruby's?" he indicated the town diner across the street.

"You don't have to wait with me."

"My father always taught me never to leave a woman in distress."

She laughed. "I'm hardly in distress, Dr. Quinn."

"Just Ethan, and no, you're not in distress, but a cool drink would do us both good. Jumping off car batteries in the middle of July is thirsty work." He touched his hand to the small of her back as a subtle indication that he wasn't taking no for an answer. A gentle nudge, and Samantha relented.

After settling in at the diner's lunch counter, he ordered two sweet teas with lots of ice, each with a sprig of mint and a slice of lemon.

He glanced over at Samantha to see her eyes closed, enjoying the blissful feel of the AC as she fanned the collar on her white blouse. When he'd seen her bent over the hood of her car, her snug skirt lovingly hugging her luscious derrière, he'd almost swallowed his tongue. "Have dinner with me this weekend." *Well, that just popped out.* But now that it was out there, he'd go with it.

Her eyes flew open as she shot him a confused look. "What? Why?"

"Why? Why does a man ask a woman out? I like you." He shrugged.

"You like me? You don't know me." She shook her head, taking a generous gulp of the sweet tea the waitress set in front of her before pressing the cool glass to her forehead.

He took a swig from his own. Ruby new her way around southern sweet tea.

"Well, maybe I don't know you that well, but I like what I see." He studied her face a moment before continuing. "I like how you move when I see you at college gatherings. I like how when you talk to someone you make them seem as if they are the only person in the room. Even Dr. DeHaven," he added with a smile.

"He's a lonely old man who just wants to be valued, acknowledged," she said with a shoulder lift.

Dr. DeHaven was the former dean of their college. Somewhere between seventy-five and ninety-five years old, he wore a lamentable toupee and ill-fitting false teeth. And he smelled like licorice.

"I like how you wear that gorgeous red hair of yours in ponytail, and the way you dress—simple, straightforward, and sexy. And I like how your green eyes light up when you receive a compliment. Like they did just now."

Her cheeks filled with color as she glanced down at the bar. "Thanks, but I don't think so."

He wouldn't tell her about the betting pool at the college on who she'd go out with first. He hadn't participated, though he knew his name had been tossed in by some of his colleagues—his secretary Melinda for one. "Because?"

"It's not a good idea. We're in the same college . . ."

"But not in the same department, and neither of us reports to the other. We wouldn't be breaking any rules."

"Maybe not university rules."

"What then, your rules?"

"I don't think dating colleagues is sensible. Ever hear the phrase, 'Don't dip your pen in the company ink?'" she asked, a single brow lifted in challenge.

Ethan snorted. "Around here we say, 'Don't get your honey where you get your money.'" He drained the last of his sweet tea.

"Same difference," she muttered. "Besides, I don't have time. I'm working on a research project that requires my full attention."

He turned his body to face hers. "Your research is on love, is it not?" he asked with a raised brow. "What better way to conduct primary research than by going on a date. Put your theories to the test."

This time she snorted. "I only have one theory: This thing you call love, and I call compatibility, is nothing more than a chemical reaction."

"I agree there must be chemistry." He waggled his finger between the two of them. "We have it. In spades."

She let out a sardonic laugh and shook her head.

"But there's much more to love than just chemistry."

"Like?" she asked, skepticism clear in her voice.

"Romance."

"Romance? All those novels and poetry you teach gone to your head?"

"Perhaps. But romance is more than words on a page." He thought about his parents' long, happy marriage. "Romance is the little things you do to show someone you love them. Holding hands in the movies, a piece of chocolate on her pillow at night, an impromptu dance in the kitchen."

She propped her chin in her hand and studied his face. "You really are a hopeless romantic, aren't you?"

"Well, I don't know about hopeless."

Her phone buzzed with an incoming text. Pulling it out of her bag, she read the screen. "Car's ready." She stood up and began digging in her purse again.

"I've got it." He tossed some bills on the counter.

"Thank you. I owe you."

"Then have dinner with me, and we'll call it even."

She held up her index finger. "One dinner. My treat. And no romance."

Tossing her keys onto the kitchen counter, she opened the fridge and reached in for a cold bottle of water. She felt a twinge of guilt for the environment as she turned down the thermostat in her townhouse. Kicking off her shoes, she checked her voice messages. Nothing interesting. Some telemarketers, a researcher at NYU she planned to meet up with at a conference later this year, and her mother.

Padding barefoot into the living room, she dropped onto the sofa. What a day. She'd lost a promising graduate assistant who'd decided to move back to Los Angeles to be closer to her boyfriend, she had issues with data for a study she'd hoped to be closing soon, and another study hadn't been selected to receive a grant she'd been counting on.

Then there was the whole car fiasco. And the too-sexy-for-his-own-good—and hers—Ethan Quinn.

Propping her feet on the coffee table, she looked around.

She really needed to finish unpacking the boxes that were lining the dining area wall.

She'd taken the associate professor position at the small, private university because she needed a change of pace. Especially after Craig dumped her. *After* he'd cheated on her with one of his students.

Her parents had been appalled that she would leave a secure teaching position at NYU to move to what amounted to rural Georgia in their eyes. But Sterling University was well funded, had a strong commitment to academic freedom, a manageable-sized student body, and was considered one of the Southern Ivy League schools, on par with universities like Duke and Vanderbilt. And, more importantly, they were interested in taking her discovery to market.

Nestled in the hills of Northeast Georgia, the town of Sterling owed its existence to two things: granite and knowledge. Granite because it held some of the richest granite quarries in the world. If it was made of granite, it probably came from Sterling.

Knowledge, because Sterling University educated almost fourteen thousand students inside its hallowed halls, and sent them out into the world to share that knowledge.

Founded in 1835 by wealthy granite quarry magnate and town-founder, Samuel Sterling, who endowed the university with one million dollars and three hundred and fifty acres of land adjacent to the family home, the university's arts department even offered classes in granite carving. When the last of the Sterling line, Victoria Eliza Sterling-Pickard, died in 1974, she left the family home to the University for its use as its main administration building, aptly named Sterling Hall.

If you lived in or around Sterling, you most likely either

worked for the university, or for one of the many granite quarries or monument makers.

Frankly, after the fast-paced life of New York City, she found the college town to be rather charming. It allowed her to focus on her work and held few distractions—unless you counted Ethan Quinn.

Her phone chimed with an incoming FaceTime call. Her mother, no doubt.

She rose and walked to the kitchen where she'd left her phone. Swiping her finger across the screen, she took the phone with her back to the sofa. Her mother's face came into view.

"Hi, Mom."

"Samantha, don't you look like something the cat dragged in. Don't let small-town living turn you into a slob."

Sam heard her father's startled laugh in the background. "Mom, I've had a rough day. My car wouldn't start after work. And it's hot here."

"I don't know why you don't get yourself a new car."

"For the same reason I've told you a thousand times: I don't make enough money yet." She'd already strapped herself with a mortgage and bought new furniture, since Craig kept theirs when she moved out. She didn't need a car payment to top it off. Not that she would ask for their help, but her parents were of the belief that a child needed to make her own way in the world. So, her wildly successful parents would not be offering to put her in a shiny new Mercedes anytime soon.

"I don't know why you don't join me and your father in our field," her mother admonished for the umpteenth time, her face disappearing from the screen as she reached for something. Ah, her daily intake of Scotch.

Sam cringed. *Working in sex therapy with your parents. Like that wouldn't be awkward.*

"I don't know how your father and I managed to have such a sexually repressed daughter," she continued, the highball glass poised for a sip.

Her father's disembodied voice said, "I don't want to know about my daughter's sex life, repressed or otherwise."

Her mother sighed. "World-renowned sex therapist shy about sexuality? It's a perfectly normal human function, as you very well know."

"So is my daughter's digestion, but that doesn't mean I want to talk about it."

"I'm not sexually repressed," Sam muttered. *Okay, maybe a little sexually* insecure. Once men discovered whose daughter she was, they assumed she was loose. Or really good in bed. Neither could be further from the truth.

The only daughter of the Masters and Johnson research team of the twenty-first century, Drs. Vincent and Katherine Love, she grew up in a home where sex was candidly discussed. She spent her teenage and college years living with the stigma that, since her parents were sex therapists, she must be a nymphomaniac. Guys pursued her with this —and *only* this—in mind. As a result, she'd had little to do with the opposite sex. Until Craig, that is.

His engineer's brain worked a lot like hers. She had thought that he understood her. Until he'd broken up with her saying she was frigid.

She wasn't frigid. She just wasn't . . . passionate. *Sue me.*

She thought about Ethan's comment, *Romance is the little things you do to show someone you love them.*

Her parents' relationship was more like a business enterprise, especially since their divorce. There had never been any romance, none of the subtle gestures Ethan had referred to. She thought she'd had the same no-nonsense relationship with Craig. Comfortable. Steady.

Minimalistic.

Or . . . clinical, even.

No, the Drs. Love, name and careers notwithstanding, were not the best role models for Ethan's romantic philosophy.

"Of course, what does it matter? What could you possibly find in that town to stir even the slightest of desires?"

"Mom."

"Well, you've cloistered yourself away from people your own age, your own marital status . . . I don't know how you expect to meet someone with whom you have anything in common. Someone who'll be your life partner. Like your father and me."

"But you're divorced."

"Pfft. We're still partners."

"Yeah, who live in the same house and date other people."

"It works for us. Now back to you. You've sentenced yourself to this celibate existence, and all because Craig didn't know what he had in you," her mom continued. "That's all I'm saying on the subject."

Right. *For now.* "Look, Mom, I've got some papers to grade. I'll talk to you and Dad soon."

"Bye, Samantha." The screen went blank. Tossing her phone on the sofa beside her, she leaned back and closed her eyes. Her thoughts returned to Ethan, and his brown eyes, the way his hair fell across his forehead. His contagious laughter.

What had she been thinking when she'd agreed to go to

dinner with him? He'd caught her at a vulnerable moment. He'd helped her out, and she felt like she owed him.

So she'd pay her debt, and that would be that. No romance needed.

That should be easy. She didn't know how to do romance anyway.

2

After following Samantha home, Ethan took the main road to the other side of town, and the origins of his blue-collar roots. His mom had asked him to dinner—fried chicken, homemade mashed potatoes, green beans fresh from the garden, and apple crisp. That was an invitation he couldn't pass up.

Since his father's sudden death six months earlier, he'd been worried about his mother. His parents had been married almost forty years, and she'd all but built her life around him.

His father, Thomas, had loved reading, but never had the money to pursue an education. It was his love of reading that infused his son with the desire to study literature. Thomas had been employed by the Sterling Granite Quarry since he was old enough to work and was eventually promoted to foreman. Ethan's mother, Margaret, had been a housewife, raising their two kids, Ethan and his older sister Charlotte, on their father's modest income.

Charlotte couldn't wait to get out of Sterling. She went away to college in California and never looked back. She now lived in Vancouver with her husband. The last time he had seen her was for their father's funeral.

Ethan had stayed in Sterling out of guilt over leaving his parents alone after his sister left. He'd attended Sterling University, playing baseball on a full scholarship—the only way he could have afforded an education, and after earning his Ph.D., he'd stayed on to teach, later becoming chair of the Literature and Creative Writing Department for Sterling's College of Arts and Sciences.

Arriving in the section of town known as Graniteville, for its proximity to the many successful granite quarries in Sterling, Ethan stopped at the pedestrian crosswalk in front of Parker Monuments, and waited for two boys to ride their bikes across the street. Not much had changed in Graniteville since his boyhood. Parker Monuments was still the largest headstone and monument maker in the region, the granite quarries and factories still offered the almost five-thousand permanent residents gainful employment, the high school football stadium still featured the granite seats installed in 1961, and his mom still lived in the same house he'd grown up in.

Pulling into the driveway of the modest red brick house, he switched off the ignition. Just like the town, his childhood home hadn't changed. His father's 1965 powder-blue Chevy pickup sat in the yard off the driveway, while his mother's 2000 Chevrolet Impala sat in the carport.

His mom couldn't bring herself to sell the truck yet, even though its pristine condition would fetch a nice price.

The narrow front porch still boasted the metal mint-green and white glider. Some folks would call it retro. He just called it old. It had been his grandparents' before they'd passed it along to his parents.

He'd spent many a summer night on that glider trying

his hand at romance. In fact, his first kiss was on that glider, with Alyssa Gartner, the prettiest girl in his eighth-grade class.

The front door opened and his mother stepped out, wiping her hands on a towel.

Climbing out of the car, he returned her wave. "Hi, Mom."

"What are you doing sitting in the car?"

"Oh, just reminiscing." He climbed the steps then leaned down to kiss her cheek. Margaret Quinn still bore the beauty of her youth. Dark-brown hair with a smattering of gray, smooth creamy skin, and warm brown eyes that lit up when she laughed.

He knew it was far too soon, but he hoped she would find love again someday. She had so much to give, and she had a lot of living left to do.

Dinner already graced the family dining table. What had once seated four, and on many occasions a couple more of his friends, was now set for two.

"Smells great, Mom. And biscuits!"

She patted his cheek. "Your favorite—cheddar drop biscuits."

They talked about the happenings in Sterling, the upcoming fall semester at the university, and Charlotte and her husband Drew's upcoming vacation to Europe. Charlotte's art gallery had recently had a successful show, and Drew's car dealership had posted some good numbers lately, so they were splurging.

After gorging on his mom's handiwork, he settled back with a fresh glass of tea. There was a certain subject he wanted to broach with her.

"Mom, have you thought about getting a job? Just something to get you out of the house?"

"A job? But I don't have any skills."

"Of course you do. You took care of the household finances for years, you volunteered at the public library, and you helped with the books for the gift shop at the hospital. You were PTA treasurer for three years. You've got skills."

"But a job?" She shook her head. "I don't know. Where would I find a job?"

"It just so happens the Department of Social Sciences is looking for a part-time receptionist, three days a week."

"Ethan," she admonished, "I don't have a resume or anything."

"Don't need one. I already spoke with Penny Dawson, the chair's assistant, and she wants to meet you on Wednesday."

She stood from the table and picked up their plates. He knew that tactic. She was thinking about it. She just needed a little nudge.

"You're bright and personable, you're organized, and you like people. You'd be perfect for the job."

He could practically see the wheels turning as she rinsed dishes at the sink.

Carrying the platter of chicken and the half-empty bowl of potatoes over to the counter, he began filling saver dishes with the leftovers. "We could even have dinner on the nights you work."

His mom glanced over her shoulder, a smile playing around her mouth. "I'd like that."

"Me, too." He took a dishtowel out of the drawer and began drying. "At least say you'll talk to Penny, then see how it goes." He gave her a slight hip check, and she laughed.

She patted his cheek as only a mother can do. "I'll think about it."

~

"WANT to catch a movie over in Carlyle tonight?" Delaney Driscoll asked, as Sam waited for her to shut down her computer. They were about to head over to Ruby's for lunch.

Delaney, a creative writing professor, and Sam had hit it off immediately despite their disparate outlooks on life. They'd met at a campus meeting for the American Association of University Women a week after Sam had moved to town and went for drinks that same night. Delaney already felt like the sister Sam never had.

"Can't. I have plans," she said, trying to put on a poker face.

"What kind of plans?" Delaney pressed, as she stuffed papers into a tote bag that read IF A WORD IN THE DICTIONARY WERE MISSPELLED, HOW WOULD WE KNOW?

Dammit, now she'd have to fess up. "I have a date."

"A date? With who?" She cringed. "Not that guy in archaeology who talks about dead people all the time?"

She hesitated, biting her lip. If she didn't tell Delaney who her date was with, she'd never hear the end of it. "No, um, it's with Ethan Quinn."

Delaney dropped the bag on her desk and grabbed Sam's shoulders. "Shut. Up! Ethan Quinn? Dreamy literature professor, Ethan Quinn?"

"Why? Do you know another Ethan Quinn?"

"Do you know how many women—and even a few men —would kill for a date with Ethan Quinn?"

"I suppose," Sam replied, shrugging noncommittally.

"Okay, how did this happen? I need details," Delaney prodded, then returned to the task of stuffing her tote.

Sam didn't really feel like sharing details. She shrugged. "I had a dead battery. He helped me out."

"He jumped you off?"

Sam cringed. "Why do people use that phrase? It's so . . . sexual."

Delaney snickered. "Now, why would you think that?"

"He gave my battery a jumpstart."

"And that's when he asked you out?"

"Well, no. He followed me to Bart's—"

"Aww. How chivalrous."

Sam rolled her eyes.

"Then he asked you out?"

"No. Bart's was busy so we walked over to Ruby's for a drink."

"And that's when he asked you out?" Delaney pressed on.

"Do you want me to tell the story or not?"

"Fine," Delaney said, indicating that Sam should continue.

"So, we were sitting at the counter and he asked me out."

"And?"

"And that's it." Sam tucked a lock of hair behind her ear and tried to look nonchalant.

"Some storyteller you are. No 'he said this,' and 'you said that,' no 'he touched my hand and my heart skipped a beat.' No descriptions, nothing. You'd flunk my beginners' creative writing course." Delaney wore a disappointed expression on her face. "Did he kiss you?"

Sam released an uncomfortable laugh. "No. Why would he do that?"

"Because he couldn't resist your pouty lips."

"You read too many romance novels."

"And you, my friend, don't read enough of them," Delaney suggested.

"I don't read *any*."

"My point exactly." Shouldering the bag, Delaney glanced around the office then headed for the door, Sam on her heels, hoping the conversation was over.

"What are you wearing?" Delaney asked as she flipped off the lights. "Wait, where are you going?"

"Some restaurant and marina north of here." Sam pulled the door closed behind her and came alongside Delaney as they walked down the corridor.

"Dave's. Okay, so it's not exactly swanky, but it could be fun. You should wear something that says fun and breezy, but not too sleazy."

"What?" Sam choked out a laugh.

"You know, a sundress with some cute strappy sandals maybe."

Sam shook her head. "I don't have a sundress and cute strappy sandals. What's wrong with what I'm wearing now?" Sam glanced down at her navy pencil skirt, pale ivory blouse, and Sam Edelman ballets.

Delaney stopped, took a step back, a dubious expression on her face. "That? No, that won't do. You look too . . . buttoned up. This isn't New York." She checked her watch. "We have time."

"For what?"

"A little post-lunch shopping excursion."

ETHAN PULLED his car up in front of Samantha's townhouse and slid it into park. Grabbing the bouquet of multicolored zinnias off the passenger seat, he got out and walked to her door.

The red-brick townhouse was in Georgetown Square, one of the newer neighborhoods that had sprung up around the university campus and had quickly become a favorite of faculty and administrative staff for its proximity. The townhomes' Georgian-style architecture, with its classical proportions, black shutters, and white trim, fit the town of Sterling. A rich glossy red front door on Samantha's place added impact.

Ringing the bell, he looked around at the neighborhood, appreciating the quiet, tree-lined streets, thinking it would be a great place to raise a family.

The door opened, and he turned to see a vision that rendered him momentarily speechless. Samantha stood in the doorway wearing a soft floral sundress in shades similar to those of the zinnias he held—rich reds, smoky pinks, and deep violets. Her flaming-red hair floated around her in soft waves. Sexy, feminine, and flirty.

He couldn't help himself, a whistle escaped before he could give her a proper greeting. "Hi."

"Hi," she said, the corners of that full mouth tugging upward.

"You look . . . incredible."

"Thanks." She glanced at the flowers. "Are those for me?"

"Oh, yes." He held out the bouquet. *Smooth, real smooth, Quinn. Come on, man, it's not like it's your first rodeo.*

Confusion furrowed her brow. "No one's ever given me flowers," she muttered.

"Well then, shame on them." *How is it that this beautiful woman had never received flowers from a man?* "Are you ready?"

"Yes. Let me, uh, go put these in some water. Come in." She left him to make his way inside.

To the left was a tidy living area furnished with modern pieces upholstered in what looked like a soft taupe leather. To the right was a study, the black lacquer desk scattered with papers. Straight ahead through the foyer, on the other side of the stairs, he spied the kitchen.

Samantha stood at the sink filling a colorful hand-blown glass vase with water. A stack of boxes on the other side of the kitchen caught his eye.

"Yeah, I haven't finished unpacking yet." She laughed, sounding a bit nervous. "I guess whatever's in those boxes isn't a necessity, because I haven't missed anything." She dropped the flowers into the vase, loosely arranging them. "There. I guess that's all they need, right?"

"They'll be fine."

Carrying the flowers out to the living room, she breezed past him, leaving a subtle fragrance of jasmine behind. As she placed the vase in the center of a black lacquer coffee table, he took the opportunity to explore the space. Along the wall opposite the sofa stood a bookcase filled with books, mostly psychology tomes with a few mysteries thrown in for good measure. French doors opened onto a screened back porch, with a modest backyard beyond that.

"Can I get you something to drink?" Sam asked, as she turned toward him.

"I thought we'd head out to dinner."

"Sure." Picking up a handbag and sweater, she led the way to the front door, giving him a view of her bare back. Smooth silky skin he knew would be warm to the touch beckoned him. *Slow down there, Quinn.* Yes, it had been a while, but he wasn't the caveman type.

Following her out, he walked around to the passenger

side of his car to open the door for her. When she sat in the seat, the hem of her dress slid up to reveal a smooth thigh. Swallowing hard, Ethan tore his eyes away from that irresistible skin and closed the door.

Holy hell. He only hoped he could keep his hands off her long enough to have dinner.

~

THEY ARRIVED AT DAVE'S, a sprawling ranch-style building with a metal roof and a wraparound porch. Behind it, a large tree-lined lake dotted with boats served as scenery in the late-afternoon sun. To the right, a sidewalk led to a marina where more boats, everything from smallish fishing boats to larger pontoon boats, bobbed at their moorings.

Before Sam could get out of the car, Ethan had walked around to open her door. She glanced up at his handsome face—an errant lock of hair fell over his forehead, resulting in a devil-may-care look with his dark-wash jeans and green button-down shirt. Taking her hand, he helped her from the car. Tingles danced along her arm in response to his touch. Oh yes, they definitely had chemistry!

She knew from her research that hormones and neurotransmitters worked together to help humans find love. But she also knew that chemistry only arises when two people were being themselves. Unlike smiles, chemistry wasn't something you could fake.

Each stage of love, from attraction to romance to attachment, had its own set of hormones that were activated. And right now, the attraction hormones were giving her a buzz much like a cocaine high. A buzz that had been conspicuously absent with Craig.

Withdrawing her hand left her feeling bereft. Lonely.

Not good, Sam thought. Not good at all. She didn't need this kind of complication in her life right now. She had a patent to pursue. A license agreement to negotiate. She didn't need a man to pursue. Or a relationship to negotiate.

And relationships inevitably led to sex, and sex often led to disappointment.

She headed in the direction of the restaurant.

"We're not going there," Ethan said. He held out his hand, indicating that they were going to the marina.

"But I thought we were having dinner." So I could pay my debt and move on, she thought.

"We are, but not here."

Placing his hand on the small of her back, he directed her along the sidewalk to the marina. Picking her way carefully along the boards of the dock, she silently cursed Delaney and her strappy-sandals idea. Any moment now, she expected one of her heels to take a dive into one of the cracks between the boards, and she'd take a header into the lake's dark waters.

"Here we are," Ethan said.

They'd stopped in front of one of the many pontoon boats docked at the marina.

"Is this yours?" she asked.

"Belongs to a buddy of mine." Taking her elbow, he helped her aboard. "Have a seat," he said, indicating the padded seats along the front railing of the boat. "And while those heels are sexy as hell, they aren't practical on a boat." He knelt at her feet, and taking her ankle in his hand, slipped off first one shoe and then the other. The electricity that shot up her legs could have lit the city of Atlanta for a week.

His warm brown gaze shot to her face. He'd felt it, too.

"Um, thank you." She broke the stare and bent down to

slide her shoes out of the way. There had been something unsettlingly sexy about watching Ethan remove her shoes. As if *she* were the *voyeur*.

Ethan stood and moved around the boat, clearly at home, untying ropes and checking gauges before starting the engine. Steering the boat out of its covered slip, he headed out.

The craft looked to be about twenty-four, twenty-five feet long, with two wraparound seating areas in the bow and a captain's chair at the controls. Beneath a green-and-white-striped awning over the stern stood a table set with a red-and-white-checkered plastic tablecloth clipped to the table's edges, presumably to keep it from blowing off. Beyond the table sat a large cooler.

The sun slid behind the trees, taking most of the day's heat with it, making her glad she'd brought a lightweight cardigan.

As they picked up speed, she glanced back at Ethan, standing legs-apart against the bouncing of the boat, looking like he belonged on the water. Aviator sunglasses framed his eyes, and the wind blew his dark-brown locks in disarray, plastering his shirt to the broad chest and flat stomach underneath. A shiver ran up her spine, and it had nothing to do with the now-chilly breeze.

Turning her face into the wind, she gazed out at the lake's vast expanse. There were people on Sea-Doos, others waterskiing, and still others fishing along its shore.

She assumed from the partially set table and the cooler that they would be dining on the boat. Just the two of them. All alone. Her stomach did a slow roll, nerves setting in.

It had been a while since she'd been on an actual "date." She and Craig had lived together for almost two years, and she couldn't recall any time during those two years ever going on what most people would consider a date.

As the boat slowed, Sam's nerves did the opposite, kicking up her heartbeat and pulse, making her wonder why she'd ever agreed to go out with Ethan Quinn.

3

Ethan steered the boat around a bend to a cove surrounded on three sides by white pines, mountain laurel, and sugar maple. Cutting the engines, he moved to the back of the boat and dropped anchor. The boat bobbed on its own wake before the waves dissipated along the shore then settled into a gentle rocking motion.

"Now that we're anchored, I can play the proper host." Opening the cooler, he took a bottle of Veuve Clicquot from its nest in the ice. Then lifting the backseat, he plundered in the under-seat storage compartment for two disposable champagne flutes.

"I hope you like champagne," he said, as he popped the cork. Setting the flutes on the table, he poured the bubbly. Holding one out to her, he indicated that Samantha should join him in the stern. As she rose, the breeze flirted with the hem of her dress, flashing him with a silky thigh.

When he'd slipped off those sinful heels, he hadn't missed the warmth of her legs beneath his hand, the velvety skin, or the rich red nail polish on her toes. He loved a woman who pampered her feet, especially when she slid those pampered feet along his bare legs. Even her legs had smelled like jasmine.

She walked toward him with some hesitation.

"I won't bite, you know," he said, then took a sip from his drink. "Unless you want me to."

Her forward progress stopped, and he laughed. "Come on. I promise, no teeth."

Passing her the champagne, he gazed at her over the rim. "To soft summer nights," he toasted. She tapped her flute to his and turned it up.

"Mmm. Delicious." She licked her lips, and his brain momentarily malfunctioned. Where was he? *Who* was he? *Damn.* She'd been at the university since last fall, and now he was asking himself why he'd waited so long to ask her out.

"Are you hungry?" God knew he was, but not for food. "We have a chilled supper of crab salad followed by a peach gazpacho and cold poached salmon for the entree. And for dessert, bittersweet chocolate mousse."

She laughed, a bright, sparkling sound. "You have all that in the cooler?"

"Yep. But I can't take credit for any of it. Dave prepared the food."

"Dave? As in Dave's Restaurant?" She pointed in the direction of the marina, hidden behind the trees, then shook her head. "I thought it was more of a fish shack than fine dining."

"Oh, it is. But Dave is CIA-trained."

"Then . . . Why?"

He shrugged. "It's the family business. His father, David Lawrence, Sr., started the restaurant back in the sixties. It's been very successful, and you don't mess with success."

He watched as several expressions flitted across her face.

Bemusement, amusement, and then understanding.

He refilled her glass and then set about the business of serving dinner. Retrieving white disposable dinnerware from the storage compartment, he set salad and dinner plates on the table, followed by flatware and napkins.

"Ma'am," he held the back of a chair. As she moved past him, her hair brushed his shoulder, and he wondered how those glossy strands would feel sliding across his bare chest.

Taking a seat, she placed the napkin in her lap. He gazed down at the bare skin and couldn't resist. Grazing his fingertips across her shoulder, it was all he'd expected and more. Smooth and warm. Her sharp intake of breath at his touch sent heat straight to his groin.

Step away from the sexy woman, his brain said. *Grab her and kiss her senseless*, his body said. His brain won out. *Damn brain.*

Glad to have something to occupy his hands, he plated the salads and opened a bottle of chardonnay, then took the chair opposite the lovely professor and poured the wine into cups.

The sun had set, ushering in dusk, so he lit a citronella candle he'd found in the storage compartment for both light and mosquito control.

"*Bon appetit*," he said, picking up his fork. He watched with pleasure as she tasted the delicate crab salad, a look of delight on her face. *Talk, man, talk. Get your mind out of the gutter.* "What brought you from NYU to the hills of Northeast Georgia?"

"Sterling University is expanding its Department of Social Sciences, so they contacted me about joining the faculty." She paused to sip her wine and looked as if she were going to say something else then changed her mind. "It was an offer I couldn't refuse. How did you end up here?"

"I grew up in Sterling, went to school here." He shrugged. "Then took a position here."

"You spent your entire college career here? All three degrees? That's unusual."

"I suppose. But I like it here. My parents were here. Sterling is an excellent university, and the town has a lot to offer. So why would I leave?"

"Were?"

Surprised she'd caught that, he hesitated. "Well, my mom is still here, but my dad passed away six months ago." The kick in the gut those words still delivered left him breathless.

Her eyes softened as she gazed at him with sympathy. "I'm so sorry. I'm sure that's been difficult."

"It has, especially since it was so sudden." At her questioning look, he explained, "Heart attack. What about your parents?"

She made a face then laughed, a nervous one this time. "My parents are still alive and living in upstate New York."

Her response was vague, but he let it go. He knew who her parents were. Everyone at the university knew. It was one of the juvenile reasons for the betting pool. "And, as we determined the other day, Dr. Love, your research is on . . . love. A fitting topic for you given your name."

"Yes, well. I wouldn't say my topic is love, but rather compatibility. What brings two people together and what makes them stay together."

He shrugged. "Love."

She shook her head. "Sometimes love isn't enough. Just because you 'love' someone," she put air quotes around the word, "doesn't mean you'll be compatible. Compatibility is all about biology. Chemistry."

"Yes, so you said the other day."

"And you said there was more to love than chemistry."

"Yes, I did." He thought about his parents. "Romance."

She shook her head again and laughed that cynical laugh he'd heard in Ruby's Diner the other day. "And why the air quotes?"

"Around the word 'love' you mean?" At his nod, she continued, "I don't believe in love."

Reaching across the table, he took her hand, his thumb brushing along her skin. "What, or should I say who, Dr. Love, has made you so cynical when it comes to matters of the heart?"

"MATTERS OF THE HEART?" She snorted, as she withdrew her hand. She didn't consider herself cynical. Just practical. "That's a romantic notion perpetuated by jewelry stores, florists, and chocolatiers. True biological compatibility has nothing to do with the heart and everything to do with evolution and survival of the species."

He scoffed. "Anyone can reproduce. Two complete strangers can ensure the perpetuation of the species. But it takes a strong relationship to see the couple, and their family, through good times and bad."

"Well, at least we agree on something. But love has little to do with whether a couple has a strong bond."

"Right." He rose from the table and took away the salad plates. Taking two small containers out, he removed the lids, and as he set them on top of the dinner plates, he continued, "You contend it's just chemistry."

She looked up into his brown eyes that held a challenge to her theory. "Yes," she said, brow lifted, accepting that challenge.

Before he took his seat, he walked up to the bow of the boat and retrieved her sweater. "You look chilly." He draped it around her shoulders then rested his hands there.

The thoughtfulness of the gesture touched her, and the warmth of his hands penetrated the light knit material. "Thank you." He squeezed her shoulders then walked around the table to his chair, his expression smug. *Oh, no you don't, Dr. Quinn.* "I see what you did there." She picked up her spoon and wagged it at him then dipped into her gazpacho. Sweet peaches, mild cucumber, and bright cilantro teased her tongue.

"What did I do?" he asked, looking innocent.

"You're trying to prove your point by doing something thoughtful."

"No, I'm trying to keep you from catching pneumonia."

Sam snorted. "Right. Pneumonia in July. And you know as well as I do that you don't catch pneumonia from being chilly."

"Even so, you said thank you."

"I was just being polite."

"Uh-huh. Like when I gave you the flowers. Admit it, you were touched."

She shrugged. "It was nice. No one has ever given me flowers."

"Which reminds me, how is that even possible? What kind of men have you been dating?"

This was a road she didn't intend to go down. "Practical, educated men."

"But not very smart, if you ask me."

"Craig was an MIT-educated engineer." As soon as the words were out of her mouth, she wished she could take them back. She hadn't planned on discussing Craig.

"Craig? Since you referred to him in the past-tense, and you're here with me, I'm assuming the relationship is over."

She set her spoon in the now-empty container and placed her hands in her lap. Upbringing notwithstanding, the soup had been so good she yearned to turn up the bowl and drink the little bit that remained. "Yes."

"And how long did Craig last?"

"Almost two years."

"Two years, and the man never brought you flowers?"

"No."

"As I said, dumbass."

"Our relationship wasn't like that. We were . . . partners . . . helpmates—"

Ethan snorted. "Doesn't sound like a relationship at all. Sounds more like roommates."

Sam bristled, then calmed. The truth hurt. "And you, Casanova, how long was your last relationship?"

He rose from the table, removing the containers. "About the same as yours."

"And did you bring her flowers?"

"Of course."

"Didn't seem to have solidified your relationship." She turned in her chair to watch him. She liked the way he moved. He had an economy of motion—efficient, but graceful.

"No, I suppose it didn't. But bringing her flowers made me happy, and she seemed to enjoy them."

Taking a platter out of the cooler, he removed the cellophane to reveal two beautiful salmon steaks with a creamy dill sauce, dressed with slender asparagus spears. He plated the entrees in silence, and she let his comment go, focusing instead on the delectable salmon, the crisp chardonnay, and the sounds of nature.

The night sky had gone purple, creating silhouettes of the trees and setting the stage for a chorus of frogs and crickets. The candle in the center of the table flickered, casting shadows and light across Ethan's face.

He'd clearly worked hard creating a scene most women would melt over. She didn't want to appear ungrateful. "Dinner is delicious. Dave is wasting his talents."

"Perhaps, but family is important to him. He does have plans to open a second restaurant in Sterling. Something casual, but offering upscale food." He stabbed an asparagus spear, bringing it to his mouth.

"Sounds like you know him pretty well."

"We went to high school together."

Sam didn't know what it was like to have long-term relationships. Not just with guys, but with girls, too. Her parents moved around a lot. Chasing careers in academia sometimes meant moving from institution to institution. They rarely stayed for more than two or three years before some other prestigious institution came calling offering bigger lab space, more support staff, and more money. They'd been at Cornell the longest—five years now.

"So, you must have research that backs up your theory," Ethan said, interrupting her thoughts.

"I do. It's the reason I'm here. Sterling University is very interested in this research."

"Why is that?"

"Because it's groundbreaking, and because I brought patent-ready IP for a blood test."

Ethan sat back, set his fork on his plate, and wiped his mouth with his napkin. "A blood test? What kind blood test?"

"I call it a compatibility assay. It can determine who your match is."

"You mean like an organ donor?"

"Yes, but for relationship compatibility."

"All right, I'll bite. How do you determine someone's compatibility with a blood test?"

"I can't give you details, since my patent application is still pending, but I *can* say that there are certain chemicals in the blood that indicate who will be a good biological match."

Humans are often attracted to people who possess a particular set of genes called major histocompatibility complex, or MHC. MHC plays a critical role in the ability to fight viruses. Mates with dissimilar MHC genes produce healthier offspring with broad immune systems.

Sam had discovered a blood chemical, which she called MHC-P1 that predicts MHC, and through her current research, she'd proven that couples whose MHC-P1 were on opposite ends of the spectrum, indicating their MHC genes were dissimilar, not only had healthier, more productive children, but they also had longer, happier relationships.

"And you've proven this how?"

"My research studies. By taking blood samples, conducting interviews with, and administering compatibility questionnaires to, happily attached couples who have been together twenty years or more."

"Compatibility questionnaires? You mean like the ones online dating services use?"

"Correct. I have a control group of some five thousand couples married for at least twenty years. I've given them the questionnaire and taken blood. A statistically significant percentage of those who report that they are happily married—or otherwise attached—show strong chemical compatibility, similar to that of the questionnaires."

"I also have a cohort," of which she was one, but she

didn't tell him that, "of some forty-eight hundred single or divorced men and women who have taken the same questionnaire and blood test. When I take blood, I run the tests against those individuals in the database, and when I find matches, I compare the chemical compatibility to the questionnaire compatibility."

"A statistically significant percentage of the time, the blood chemistry inversely matches, and the compatibility questionnaires match as well."

Once she completes her research, and the university obtains the patent, SoulMates.com, a popular online dating service, was very interested in licensing her "compatibility assay," which they would like to offer their users for an additional fee.

"Impressive." He sat back and crossed his arms over his chest. "You've taken love, with all its mystery and beauty, and reduced it to something as romantic as a cholesterol test."

"I'd prefer to think I've removed all the barriers, pitfalls, and heartaches people encounter on the road to finding a lasting relationship."

"Sign me up then." He sat up and slapped the table with his hand.

"Excuse me?"

"Are you still enrolling people in your single-slash-divorced cohort?"

"Yes."

"Then sign me up. Take my blood. Give me the compatibility questionnaire."

Holy crap. He was serious.

SHE HAD A DEER-IN-HEADLIGHTS LOOK. "OKAY." Then she blinked. "Are you sure?"

"I can come by your lab on Monday around three-thirty, after my last class."

"I'd have to check my schedule." She bit her lip. "I think that should work."

"Good. Now that that's settled, how about some dessert?"

She nodded, still appearing stunned by his request to join her study. She'd become animated when she talked about her research. The glow of pride looked good on her.

Ethan rose from the table and, opening the cooler, reached in for the two parfait glasses filled with creamy chocolate mousse and topped with shaved dark chocolate.

Handing her a glass and a spoon, he reassumed his place across from her. "More wine?"

"No, thank you." He watched as she took a bite of the sweet mousse with the bitter dark chocolate shavings then closed her eyes in ecstasy. "Mmm. Oh my! Talk about patents! Dave should patent this dessert." She opened her eyes and pointed her spoon at the glass.

He'd felt that hum of pleasure all the way to his groin, but he knew what she meant. The sweet and bitter collided on your tongue, creating an explosion of tastes.

"Yeah, this is his specialty. It's the one thing he added to the restaurant's menu, and it's been a big hit." He took another bite, his gaze focused on her mouth, where a morsel of dark chocolate rested. Before he gave it any thought, he stood and, leaning over the table, licked the chocolate from her mouth. The spark he felt when his tongue met her lips might have come from sticking his tongue in a light socket.

He retreated, gazed into her surprised green eyes then advanced once more. This time he pressed his lips to hers, a soft caress, before diving in. His tongue parted her lips to tangle with hers, tasting the chocolate. No other part of their bodies touched, just lips and tongues, and the headiness of it raced through his blood, pooled low in his belly, and made him dizzy with want. *Sweet Jesus.*

This wasn't just chemistry. This was a conflagration.

Her spoon clattered to the boat deck, and her hand found its way into his hair, as she moaned low in her throat. Reaching down, he groped his way around until he found the glass of mousse she still held in her hand and set it on the table before it followed the fate of the spoon. Lifting her hand, he pulled her from her chair and up against him, no longer content with just their lips touching.

Grasping her hips, he held her against him, where she could feel every inch of what she did to him. Her other hand wrapped around his neck, playing with the hair at his nape, sending shivers along his spine, as she groaned and tried to get closer still. His leg slipped between hers as he drew her up his body.

Sliding his hands up her ribs, he broke the kiss and pressed his lips to the pulse in her neck, fluttering like a hummingbird's wings. The gentle rocking of the boat intensified his arousal.

He had to stop this before he dragged her down to the deck, ripped off that sundress, and buried himself deep inside her.

One last nip at her neck, then a flick of his tongue over her lips, and he stepped back. Her eyes flew open, and the look of desire he saw in them almost swept his resolve.

A flash of lightning and a rumble of thunder in the distance spurred him to action. "We'd better head back."

Her hand rose to her lips, lingered there. "Right." She wore that dazed look again, but for a different reason this time. His male pride gloated a little.

At least the ride back to the marina would give him a chance to lose the screaming erection he had. He just had to think of something unappealing. Like the time he'd walked in on his grandmother in her underwear. Yep. That should do it.

"THANK YOU FOR DINNER. I had a nice time," Sam said, hand on the car door latch, ready to bolt.

"Don't run away, little girl." In the dark car interior, Sam could hear the laughter in his voice. "What kind of gentleman would I be if I didn't walk a beautiful woman to her door. Especially when that beautiful woman neglected to turn on her porch light."

"Bulb's burned out," Sam responded. "I can't reach it without a stepladder. Which I don't have."

"Then it's a good thing I'm here to ensure the bogeyman doesn't get you."

He opened the door and made his way around the front of the car to open Sam's door.

"I'm quite capable of opening my own door," she said as she took his hand. "And getting out of the car by myself."

"No one said you weren't. Just gives me an excuse to hold your hand." He winked, making her glad he held her hand to steady her as her knees threatened to give way. His hand now at the small of her back, he followed her up the walk.

When she reached her door, she fumbled with the keys, hoping to unlock the door and get inside the house before he had an opportunity to kiss her again. Something about his kisses switched off all higher-functioning parts of her brain, leaving only her reptilian instinct in control —a little like leaving a teenager at home without adult supervision. For an entire weekend. With a cabinet full of liquor.

Just as she thought she was free, Ethan stepped up behind her, his hands settling at her waist, his lips pressed to her bare shoulder. An involuntary shiver coursed down her spine.

"Samantha, I'd really like to see you again."

"Hmmm." She lowered her chin, giving him easier access. He nibbled his way around to her ear, and she leaned against him for support. Her legs had suddenly turned to a quivering mass of Jell-O. And the unsupervised teenager just invited all her friends to a house party.

He turned her to face him and captured her mouth with his, and she knew she'd lost the battle. His tongue touched hers, and her fingers found their way into the front of his shirt, grasping onto it like a life preserver in a stormy sea. The scent of fresh air, soap, and full-blooded male assaulted her senses.

Her blood hummed through her body like electricity through a powerline. Never. It had never been like this. She wanted to wrap herself around him, feel the heat of him, the taste of him. He pressed her back against the door, trapping her between his delicious heat and her erstwhile escape route.

When he released her, disappointment swamped her. A chill crossed her body in the absence of his warmth, leaving her bereft.

"Good night, Sam," he murmured against her ear. "I'll see you Monday."

Too dazed to speak, she let herself into her house and closed the door behind her, slumping against it. Ethan Quinn should be on the FBI's Most Wanted list. With kisses like that, he was armed and dangerous.

4

———

Whistling a happy tune, Ethan parked in front of Granite Fitness. His evening with the smart, beautiful, and slightly uptight Samantha Love had gone swimmingly. He couldn't have written a better script for romance.

And the kiss good night? Well, let's just say he'd spent a good ten minutes in a cold shower after he'd gotten home.

After retrieving his gym bag from the trunk, he headed into the center where he was meeting Nash Taylor, his best friend from high school and Sterling Bobcats head football coach. Sterling University's fledgling NCAA Division I program had proved to be an upstart in only its second year. With Nash's third season coming up, fans had high hopes for the Football Championship Subdivision.

After checking in, Ethan spotted Nash running on the treadmill, wiping his face with a towel. Nash still had the physique of an NFL player, but a season-ending injury his fifth season as a highly drafted starting quarterback for the Denver Broncos forced him to treat his body with a kinder, gentler workout, a far cry from the training he'd done as a pro. Not that most people would notice the difference.

"'Bout time you got here, Quinn."

"You almost finished?"

"Just getting warmed up. I thought I'd kick your ass in a little bench-press competition this morning. Think your college-professor form can handle it?"

"Bring it on." Ethan climbed onto the StairMaster next to Nash, punched in his preferences, and started climbing like it was the final approach to the summit. Feeling Nash's eyes on him, he looked over. "What?"

"Someone ate their Wheaties this morning."

"Just feeling good."

"Hiya, Nash," one of the local gym bunnies called out. Nash waved, but Ethan knew Nash preferred women with a lot more upstairs. And he wasn't talking about boobs.

Single, and some not-so-single women, went crazy over Nash's blond hair, all-American face, and disarming smile. He could've had his pick of any one of them, but he chose to keep his distance.

"We'll see how good you feel after I'm done with you." Nash slowed the treadmill to a crawl before stepping off. "I'll see you in the weight room."

Ethan welcomed the time alone with his thoughts. And his first was about Sam. He really liked her. He'd been giving more thought to settling down lately. Maybe having a couple of kids. He knew his mom wanted grandkids, and since his sister didn't appear to be in any hurry, it looked like it might be up to him to pass on the Quinn genes. Besides, he'd sowed enough wild oats already.

He wanted what his parents had had. Someone to come home to, someone who understood his world and wanted to share it. And Samantha Love more than fit the bill.

MONDAY AFTERNOON, Sam set out everything she needed to enroll Ethan in her study and to take a finger-stick blood sample. She straightened the consent form and pen, lined up the lancet, alcohol wipe, and capillary tube, then huffed out a breath of exasperation. Her nerves jangled like she was going on a first date.

And speaking of first dates, her date with Ethan had sent her into a tailspin. She couldn't get that good night kiss off her mind. Every time she tried to concentrate on the data she was analyzing, she'd see his warm brown eyes that crinkled at the corners when he laughed or recall the taste of his lips on hers.

Generally, kissing for her held the same level of interest as vanilla ice cream—she could take it or leave it. But kissing Ethan was like indulging in cookies 'n cream ice cream with extra chocolate sauce on top. And white chocolate sprinkles. Decadent. Sinful.

No kiss had ever rocked her world like that.

After her run yesterday, she'd come home to find a folded stepladder leaning against the wall and a pack of bulbs at her front door with one missing. His thoughtfulness touched something that she'd kept buried deep. No one ever took care of her. She always took care of herself, even if that meant calling a repairman. And that had been the second time he'd come to her aid.

She glanced at her watch. Three-fifteen. She really needed to find something to occupy her mind besides Ethan's kisses for the next fifteen minutes. She was a busy woman—surely she could find *something* to do.

A knock sounded on the doorframe of the open lab door, and she nearly jumped out of her skin.

"Hey there. You looked like you were in deep concentration." Delaney stood in the doorway. "What's up?" she asked, as she stepped into the room.

"Nothing. Nothing's up, why?"

Delaney chuckled. "Nervous much?"

Sam clasped her hands in front of her. "I'm not nervous."

"Okaaaay. This is the first chance I've had to see how your date with Dreamy Dr. Quinn went." Delaney's eyes sparkled with mischief.

"Fine. It went fine."

"Fine? Just fine?"

"It was nice." Sam waved her hand as if dismissing Ethan's soul-altering kiss.

"Nice? Sheesh." Delaney pulled up a lab stool and perched on it, and Sam groaned inwardly. "That sounds disappointing."

"I, uh, I have a research subject coming in," she glanced at her watch again, "five minutes."

"Okay. Chill. I'll leave when the subject gets here." Sam could feel Delaney's eyes on her face, and the longer she stared the hotter Sam's face felt. "Did he at least kiss you good night?"

A full-on flush swept over Sam as she thought back to that moment.

"Oh, yeah," Delaney said, wagging her finger at Sam. "I can tell by that blush that he did. And even more, you liked it. A lot."

"Knock, knock. I'm a little early. Am I interrupting? Is this a good time?"

Oh, for the love of chemistry—did he hear their conversation?

Delaney gasped, but Sam willed herself not to glance her way.

Ethan stood filling her doorway, his light-blue dress shirt open at the neck tucked into dark gray slacks, and hair looking tousled and sexy. A grin split his face. Clearly he'd heard.

"No. I mean, yes, this is a good time. Come in," Sam said with as much dignity as she could muster. Ethan moved into the room, glanced at Delaney and nodded, "Dr. Driscoll."

"Dr. Quinn," Delaney said on a sigh, then apparently came to her senses. "I'll just be going. Got some papers to grade." She hopped off the stool and gave Sam a look that said they'd talk later.

Ethan came around the lab desk to stand next to Sam, filling her vision. "I had a really nice time Friday night."

God, he smelled like heaven. "Yeah, me too. But I still owe you for helping with my car. And now the light bulb." *Now why did she have to say that?* She could have just let it go and been done with the all-too-attractive Dr. Quinn.

"Why is that?" He leaned a hip on the counter, bringing him within a couple of inches of touching her. Her pulse stuttered.

"I thought the plan for Friday was for me to buy you dinner." She stepped back. "That didn't happen."

"Well, if you insist on repaying me, go out with me tonight." He inched toward her again. "I'll even let you buy this time."

"I can't." She couldn't take another onslaught like Friday night. "I'm having dinner with Delaney." She pointed to the door where said scapegoat had exited only moments before. And now she'd *have* to have dinner with the scapegoat, *er,* Delaney, so she wouldn't be a liar.

Which meant Delaney would give her the third degree about Friday . . . and today. The lesser of two evils—or in this case, rock meet hard place.

"Tomorrow then." He inched closer. Every move she made away from him, he made up the distance. And she didn't have a lot of room in her ten-by-ten lab.

"Our department has a cocktail party to welcome the new anthropology professor." Retreat.

Advance. "Then you name the day."

Retreat. "I'm busy—all week."

Advance. "You're the one who feels the need to pay me back."

Retreat. *Damn.* She'd bumped into the lab stool that Delaney had just vacated and had nowhere else to go. "Fine. How about lunch?" Lunch would be safe. No good-night kisses. Or kisses across the table in broad daylight. "Wednesday?"

"I can do that." Advance.

With no other choice, she stood her ground. "Good. It's a date. I mean, I'll put it on my calendar."

Before he could say anything else, she said, "So, before I take your blood, I'll need to get your written consent to participate in the study." She picked up the paper form and handed it to him. "I explained the study to you Friday night." On the boat. Where you kissed me senseless. "But let's go over it again."

"Whatever you say, Dr. Love." He leaned over her shoulder to read the document, his scent nearly driving her mad. She had the sudden urge to bury her face in his neck and inhale.

She pointed out the salient points of the study as he drew closer and closer. She glanced up at him with annoyance then realized her mouth was only inches from his. *Crap! Look away from the delicious lips.* She cleared her throat and returned her attention to the form.

As the researcher for the study, she owed him, the

research subject, a clear and concise explanation of the study, but in a moment of self-preservation, she stepped back and said, "Please read the consent form and feel free to ask me any questions you might have before signing it."

She moved around him and busied herself with some nonsense just to get some distance.

"Done."

She turned around, saw his signature on the form, then lifted her eyes to his. "But you didn't even read it. Don't you have questions?"

"I trust you, Dr. Love." His face was earnest, but his eyes sparkled. Those eyes lowered to her mouth, and her legs wobbled.

∼

"BUT YOU REALLY SHOULD READ DOCUMENTS BEFORE you sign them," she admonished, her brow furrowed in confusion.

"I'll take my chances here. Now you have to stick my finger, right?"

"Yes." She gathered the lancet, an alcohol wipe, and a small glass collection tube.

"Will it hurt?" he asked, feigning fear.

"You'll feel a quick stick, but it hurts no more than a pin prick."

He chuckled. "I think I can handle it, Dr. Love." She looked so professional . . . and hot in her white lab coat, light-gray blouse, and dark-gray pencil skirt. The killer heels she wore put her mouth just below his. He only had to lean forward an inch or two to claim it.

"Have a seat," she said, interrupting his thoughts. She pulled on a pair of gloves, while he perched on the lab stool.

"You'd be surprised how many people get light-headed

from a little finger stick. Give me your middle finger."

He presented her with his right middle finger and flashed her a flirtatious grin.

She blinked but tore open the alcohol wipe, then bent over his hand and swiped the fingertip. Picking up the lancet, she gave his finger a quick jab then set about filling the glass tube. Her hands were warm through the latex gloves as she worked efficiently to complete her task.

Her hair slipped over her shoulders, brushing the back of his other hand where it rested on the countertop, and that flowery perfume filled his nose. He reached up, tucked her hair behind her ear, and her gaze lifted to his.

Green eyes with long dark lashes stared into his. Her lips parted, then her brow creased, and she returned her attention to his finger.

Finished with her collection, she opened a Band-Aid and wrapped it around his finger.

"So what happens next?" he asked.

"If you'd read the consent form, you'd know." She moved to a counter behind them that was lined with equipment.

"True enough. But I'd rather hear it from you." He turned on the stool to watch her.

"Now, I'll mix the blood with a stabilizing reagent, and the mixture will incubate at room temperature for two hours." She picked up a glass tube about the size of a large Tylenol capsule, then pipetted a clear fluid into the pellet along with the blood. Sealing the pellet with a tiny black cork, she then placed it in a stand.

"When will I get my results?"

"You won't. I mean, not until the study is closed and only if both you and your match chose to be notified. Again, if you'd read the consent form, you'd know that." She skirted around him, began picking up the debris, then turned to toss it into a red biohazard trash can. Stepping on the lid opener, she tugged off the gloves and tossed them in with the trash.

His gaze traveled up from her stilettos, along her calves, and up her legs where they disappeared beneath her skirt. "Your results go in my database and are used to prove my assay." When she turned again and tried to step around him, he caught her, hands at her waist, and pulled her in between his legs.

"Ethan," she admonished.

"Samantha," he replied in the same tone. "Now, what shall we do to pass the time while my blood incubates?"

"*We* will do nothing. *I*, however, will do some data analysis for another study." She tried to move from his grasp.

"I like you. I like kissing you. I like being with you."

"Ethan, I'm very busy."

"Yes, busy reducing the mysteries of love to numbers in a database when I'm trying to show you what romance is."

"Rom—"

He pressed his lips to hers, testing, tasting, gathering his own form of data. Attempting to replicate his experiment from Friday night. Her lips parted and her hands found their way to his thighs, settling there, their heat penetrating the fabric of his pants.

She tasted exactly as he'd remembered, and with the tightening in his groin, he knew he'd replicated the experiment. Perfectly. His methodology had proven their chemical reaction resulted in a hard-on of epic proportions.

She gripped his thighs and moaned into his mouth. Skimming his hands along her ribs, he stopped just beneath her breasts. Swaying into him, she became pliant. *Sweet Jesus.* He'd better put a stop to this. A student or another professor could walk in any minute, and while the university didn't have a policy prohibiting fraternization among the faculty and staff, he was pretty sure the administration would frown on sexual activity on university property. Like lab countertops.

Hands back at her hips, he broke the kiss and pushed her away. "Samantha. Not here." Her eyes, hooded with desire, gazed back at him, as if she'd momentarily lost track of time and place. Her lips, wet and swollen from the kiss, parted. Her breasts rose and fell with each pant. God, she was the most beautiful thing he'd ever seen. That glazed look suddenly cleared, and she took a step back, glancing around as if to orient herself.

ATTEMPTING to gain some control over her erratic heartbeat, Sam took a deep breath. How did he do that? How did Ethan Quinn make her forget where she was and what she should—and shouldn't—be doing?

And made her want things she didn't typically want. Like hot, sweaty sex. On the countertop in her lab.

"You started it," she muttered. Her gaze darted to the bulge in the front of his pants, then lifted to his face. His warm brown eyes stared back.

Giving herself a mental shake, she said, "I almost forgot. You need to log on to this website and take the compatibility questionnaire." She handed him a card. "This card has your unique code and password. Once you've completed the questionnaire, hit submit. Your responses will automatically upload to my database with your unique code so I can match it to your blood-test results."

"Sam." Ethan shoved the card in his front pants pocket,

then winced. "I don't need a blood test to prove we have chemistry. I feel it every time we're in a room together. Every time our eyes meet. And when we kiss—holy hell—it's like an atom bomb detonating."

Sam shook her head. She couldn't let this happen. She couldn't get tangled up with Ethan. Or anyone. She had her work. Her career. And she didn't plan to stick around Sterling University forever. Besides, now he was one of her research subjects.

While she might not be looking for a long-term relationship, she wasn't looking for a fling either—far from it. In fact, she wasn't looking for *anything* but advancing her career at the moment. "No."

"No?"

"No. Look, Ethan. I like you, and yes, we have chemistry, but it's purely physical."

"And?" He stepped closer, and she held up her hand.

"And, Sterling hired me to bring this assay to market, and that's what I have to focus my time and my attention on." It even sounded lame to her own ears.

Ethan chuckled. "Whatever helps you sleep at night, sweetheart."

He picked up his copy of the consent form then said, "I'll see you Wednesday." He grazed her lips with his, and she forced hers closed like he was trying to feed her liver and onions. This only elicited another chuckle from him. "See ya, Dr. Love."

She released a sigh as soon as he'd cleared her door. That was one frustrating, sexy, hot-blooded male. And she needed to stay the hell away from him.

She'd buy him lunch on Wednesday, paying off her debt, then avoid him thereafter. Even in a small college town, that couldn't be too difficult, right?

5

---

than strode down the corridor to his office. He'd
ducked into the men's room near Sam's lab and
waited for ... things ... to deflate. Not an easy task,
given the taste of Sam's mouth was still on his lips and
tongue.

He stopped by his assistant's desk. Melinda handed him
a stack of messages, three of which were from a helicopter
parent of one of his students. She'd been upset over the
grade he'd given her son on his paper on Thomas Hardy's
women. He'd compared them to the Kardashians.

"Guess what?" Melinda interrupted his fantasy of telling
the mom her son would never be the next Tom Wolf and
that she should just give up.

"What?"

She handed him a stack of mail, a Cheshire Cat grin
adorning her face. "I won the pool." At his confused frown,
she continued, "You know, the one about who would date
Dr. Love first?"

He rolled his eyes. "And how did you win?" He
thought taking Sam to Lake Ketchum and bypassing

Dave's would be clandestine enough to avoid the gossip. Apparently not.

"Stan Gillespie saw you and Dr. Love walking out to the marina on Friday night. She was dressed up, and you had your hand on her back. That was a date, right?"

Ethan heaved a heavy sigh. "Clearly I don't keep you busy enough. Yes, it was a date." He took his stack of mail from her, shuffled through it. "I hope your bet was worth it."

"You bet it was. I won five hundred dollars."

"Five—Je-sus! You people really need to get a life." He shook his head and walked toward his office. Five hundred dollars over who'd be the first to take Samantha out. *Good Lord.*

He nodded to Frank Carson, the ancient contemporary-lit professor, as he passed, then unlocked his office door.

Once inside, he picked up the phone to call his mom. She'd relented on the possible job, and her interview with the Department of Social Sciences had been that morning.

"Hello."

"Hi, Mom. How'd the interview go?"

"Good, I think. It's been so long since I've had an inter-view, I have little to compare it to. But they said they'd let me know by the end of the week."

"And what did you think about the people you met?" That was just as important as them liking her.

"They were very nice. And Tiffany Hannon, the chair's executive assistant, is Marilee Hannon's daughter-in-law. You remember Marilee? You met her at your father's funeral. She works in the administrative offices of Sterling Granite."

"Yes, I remember her." Marilee liked to talk about her husband's gout—*ad nauseam.*

"Well, I'm glad you liked everyone." He was trying to

stay out of it, but he was sorely tempted to walk to the other side of the building and ask Tiffany if she thought his mother had a chance. "I'll come over for dinner tomorrow night."

"Good. I'll make that pork tenderloin you like so much. You know, the one with the mustard-bourbon glaze."

"Sounds good. Love you." He hung up the phone and sorted his mail, tossing the junk, stacking the academic journals for future reading, and opening the letters. One was from a literary journal, accepting his article on the economy and romance poets. Another was from his publisher. He was compiling and editing a book on nineteenth-century poetry.

The last one was from a headhunter. A prestigious university in Boston was in the market for a dean for their College of Arts and Sciences.

While he had a career goal of becoming a dean, he preferred to stay right here at Sterling.

Tossing the mail aside, his thoughts drifted back to the lovely professor and her theories on love. Or, to use her word, compatibility. He knew in his bones they were compatible. He just needed to prove his own theory to her. Everyone needed a little romance in their lives. Especially sexy college professors who thought it was overrated.

"I'M STUFFED," Delaney said, as she stretched out her legs on one of Sam's two sofas, a glass of plum wine in her hand.

Sam joined her on the opposite sofa. Who knew Asian-Southern fusion could be so good? In keeping with her alibi, they'd ordered takeout from Bubba Buddha and dined on egg rolls stuffed with turnip greens and pulled pork, egg-drop gumbo, spicy Hunan catfish, and buttermilk fried-chicken lo mein.

True to form, Delaney had pumped her for the details on her date with Ethan, including the toe-curling kisses. But Sam wasn't one to kiss and tell, no matter how much Delaney begged.

"You know, a really good friend would give her currently celibate friend some details. I've hit a dry spell, so I need to live vicariously through you."

Sam shook her head. "Let it go."

Throwing her head back in dramatic fashion, Delaney groaned. "You are one cruel doctor, Dr. Love." She tipped up her glass, draining it.

Unlike Sam, Delaney over-shared the intimate details of her love life—that is when she had one. Her last exploit involved a visiting chemistry professor, but that had fizzled like day-old soda.

Sitting up like she'd been prodded with a red hot poker Delaney said, "So! Ethan's in your study. How'd that happen?"

Sam lifted a shoulder, trying to appear nonchalant. "He asked me about my research and wanted to participate." She didn't say he considered it a challenge.

"Mm-hmm. And tell me, was there any hanky-panky in the lab after I left?"

Sam could feel the heat creep into her cheeks—one of the downfalls of being a fair-skinned redhead.

Delaney pointed, a big grin on her face. "There was! Do tell."

"What gave you that idea?"

"Oh, I don't know, maybe it's the nuclear reactor flush in your cheeks."

"It could be the wine." Sam ducked her head, hoping to hide the flush as it intensified.

"It could be, but in this case it's not."

"Fine. He kissed me." She waved her hand as if it were inconsequential when it was anything but.

"Oh, oh!" She leaned forward. "Was their groping involved?"

Sam recalled his hands sliding up her ribs, her hands gripping his thighs. "No. No groping."

"Well, darn. Maybe next time." Delaney poured another glass of wine and settled back on the sofa.

The doorbell rang.

"Who could that be?" Sam set her glass of wine on the table and made her way to the front door. Peering through the peephole, she saw a human, but she couldn't tell if it was male or female, holding a bouquet of the largest sunflowers she'd ever seen. Thinking they had the wrong house, she opened the door.

"Samantha Love?" the disembodied voice asked.

"Yes."

"These are for you." Hands shoved the vase of flowers at her.

"Um, thank you." Taking the vase, she watched as a young man ran down the steps back to his delivery truck.

Entering the house, she took the flowers to the coffee table.

"What's this?" Delaney touched the bright yellow petals. "Aren't they beautiful?!"

Finding the card amid the bright yellow petals, Sam opened it.

"Each kiss a heart-quake . . ." Lord Byron,
Don Juan

I look forward to more heart-quakes.
Yours,
EQ

Delaney peered over her shoulder. "Look at you, Sam. You've got a boyfriend."

ETHAN WALKED alongside Sam back to campus after lunch at Bistro Café, heavy clouds providing a welcome respite from the sun, if not the humidity.

True to his word, he'd let her pay, even if it went against his upbringing. "Thank you for lunch." Ethan slipped Sam's arm through his.

She in turn disentangled herself, frowning. "Now we're even."

"Even?"

"Yes. For helping me with my car. And thank you for the flowers, by the way," Sam said, while he let her previous comment sit for a moment.

"You're welcome." He tried to take her hand, but again, she escaped.

Crossing her hands in front of her, she continued, her body language unmistakable. "Please don't send me anymore."

"Why? Are you allergic?"

"No." She shook her head. "It's just not necessary."

"Of course it's not *necessary*."

Sidestepping the newspaper stand in front of Dink's Corner Drugs, Ethan asked the question her earlier response evoked. "Why is it so important for you to 'pay your debt'?"

Sam shrugged. "I don't want to be beholden to anyone. I need to stand on my own two feet and rely on myself."

"And why is that?"

"It's what my parents always expected. I guess it stuck."

"Well, Dr. Love, did you know that giving a gift gives as much pleasure to the giver as to the receiver? That regularly performing good deeds increases longevity? And feeling indebted is not only unnecessary, but is often unwanted?" He glanced over at her to see if his words had had any effect. "So sit back and take it like a woman."

She smiled and shook her head. "Are you always this frustratingly obstinate?"

Sticking his hands in his pockets, he grinned. "Kettle? Meet pot."

"Point taken, but I have my reasons—"

"You don't like romance."

"It's difficult to like something you don't believe in."

"I don't know about that. I like the *idea* of Santa, even though I don't actually believe a corpulent bearded man delivers gifts to kids all over the world on Christmas Eve. Not to mention, I like the whole naughty-and-nice thing. Tell me, Dr. Love, are you naughty or nice?" He waggled his brows at her.

She stopped and looked at him. "You . . . I . . ." She threw up her hands in exasperation.

"Left you speechless." He grinned. "My work here is done."

THE FOLLOWING WEEK, Sam strode into her department chair's suite. "Oh, hi." Sam smiled at the woman sitting at the reception desk. She didn't recognize her. "You must be new. I don't believe we've met. I'm Samantha Love, I have a meeting with Dr. Carmichael."

The woman stuck out her hand. "I'm Margaret Quinn. I just started yesterday."

"Quinn?"

Before Sam could form a coherent question, Margaret replied, "Yes. Ethan is my son." There was no hiding a mother's pride in her voice. "And you're Dr. Love. My son has told me about you."

Uh-oh. She wondered what Ethan had told his mother about her. "Really?" She recalled that Ethan's father had passed away. She didn't know whether to bring it up or not. "Well, welcome to the department."

Mrs. Quinn appeared the quintessential Southern woman. Polite, nicely dressed, but unlike many of the ladies Sam had met, she wasn't made up to within an inch of her life. Her brown shoulder-length hair, similar in texture to Ethan's, was sparsely streaked with gray and worn in soft layers around her face. Ethan had clearly gotten his warm brown eyes from her.

"Dr. Love?" Tiffany asked. "Dr. Carmichael will see you now." She indicated the chair's office down the hall.

"Thanks, Tiffany. It was nice to meet you, Mrs. Quinn."

"Margaret, please."

"Margaret."

Sam walked through the hushed atmosphere of the chair's office. Just the sound of phones ringing in subtle tones, fingers flying across computer keyboards, and the hum of voices.

Dr. Carmichael wanted an update on her patent application. Growing his department required money, and getting a percentage of the royalties from her assay would go a long way toward making that goal a reality.

Unless a university waived their intellectual property interest in faculty inventions and discoveries, the university held the patent, took royalties from any license agreements it negotiated, and paid the inventor a portion of those royalties. Some of that money could also trickle down to the faculty member's home department.

NYU had had no interest in her compatibility assay, which is one of the reasons she'd left. Well, that, and Craig. Bringing an invention to market took money and time she didn't have. She wanted the support of a university with experience at filing patent applications and negotiating licensing deals. Even with the percentage of royalties the university would keep, it was worth it for her to bring her blood test to market.

Fifteen minutes later, pleased with the discussion, Sam left Dr. Carmichael's office then stopped short when she recognized a voice.

"Where would you like to go to lunch?" he asked.

"Oh, Ruby's is fine," his mother answered.

Her heart squeezed a little in her chest. He was taking his mother to lunch. How thoughtful was that?

She debated whether she should hide until Ethan left, then thought better of it. Continuing down the hall, she entered the reception area.

"Well, if it isn't Dr. Love," Ethan said, giving her an appreciative once-over.

"Dr. Quinn." She nodded, keeping things on a professional level.

"We were just going to lunch. Why don't you join us?"

Before she could refuse, his mother blurted, "Yes. Won't you?"

Quick, think of something. Lunch with Ethan twice in the same week would set a bad precedent. And with his mother, no less. "I, uh, I have an experiment running in my lab, and I need to get back." Okay, not a total lie. She did have his blood in the chemical analyzer.

"How long will it take? We'll wait," he prodded.

"Oh, I wouldn't want to keep you."

"It's no problem," his mother said.

Sam looked into Mrs. Quinn's sweet face and couldn't say no. *Crap!* "Okay, why don't I meet you at Ruby's in fifteen minutes?"

"Perfect." Ethan indicated his mother should precede him through the door. "It will probably take that long to get a table anyway." He winked as he passed.

Sam groaned. For all her no-nonsense science, she was a sucker for a sweet face. And Ethan's mother had it in spades.

~

ETHAN HAD JUST DIRECTED his mother to the booth when he saw Sam walk through the door where a small crowd waited for a table.

Ruby's did a brisk lunch business during the week, especially when Ruby dished up her Thursday special, chicken and dumplings with fresh homemade biscuits, white acre peas, and peach cobbler.

He raised his hand, getting Sam's attention. As she made her way through the busy restaurant, he took a moment to appreciate the subtle sexy that was Sam. She'd abandoned her standard blouse and pencil skirt for a dress that fit like a glove, stopping just below the knee. Her red hair, which hung loose today, stood out against the cobalt-blue of her dress.

"Please." Indicating that Sam should slide into the

booth, he gave her no option but to sit next to him. He slid in beside her, their thighs bumping beneath the table.

"Hi, Ethan. Mrs. Quinn," the waitress greeted them as she approached their table.

"Mellie, how's your mom?" Mrs. Quinn asked.

"She's hanging in there, thank you for asking."

Mellie handed out menus and took their drink orders. Melanie Grooms had been in Ethan's class from first grade all the way through high school. She'd had dreams of moving to New York and auditioning for Broadway, but then her mother was diagnosed with MS, and being the only girl, Mellie felt it her obligation to stay behind and take care of her mother.

After she left to get their drinks, Ethan set aside his menu. He knew what he wanted—Ruby's Thursday special.

"Isn't this nice?" Mrs. Quinn said, gazing across the table at him and Sam.

"Very nice," Ethan replied, intentionally knocking his leg against Sam's.

When she glanced his way, he grinned. For some absurd reason, he liked yanking Sam's chain. For one thing, it was easy. For another, it was entertaining. She always appeared so buttoned-up. So in control. Except when he poked at her. He enjoyed getting a rise out of her.

And then, there were those kisses. Buttoned-up Sam quickly became unbuttoned Sam. And he liked unbuttoned Sam. A whole lot.

"Ethan tells me you study love."

She threw Ethan a look. "Oh, well, not love so much as relationships and compatibility."

"Love," his mother returned, matter-of-factly, and Ethan chuckled.

"We've had this discussion before, Mom. You'd have a

better chance getting Sherman to say the burning of Atlanta was an unfortunate accident than you would getting Samantha to say her research is on love."

Mellie returned to take their orders, postponing Samantha's inevitable rebuttal.

Orders placed, Ethan returned to the discussion. "Samantha doesn't believe in romance."

His mother joined the fray. "Oh, honey, romance is what makes relationships last. It's that hug for no reason. That cuddle when you first wake up in the morning. And that kiss good night before you fall asleep. It's what shows your partner that you're thinking about him or her. It's what made me fall in love with Ethan's father."

Seeing the melancholy expression on his mother's face made him regret his line of discussion.

"Ethan's father and I were married for almost forty years. And they were the happiest years of my life because we never let a day go by without making each other feel loved and appreciated."

Ethan waited for Sam's response.

"Mrs. Quinn—"

"Margaret."

"Margaret, my research doesn't negate the need for respect between partners. It simply provides a basis to find the *right* partner. And if you find the right partner, there's no need to spend money many people don't have on flowers and jewelry to keep that partner happy. Your chemistry tells you you're meant to be together."

"Honey, not to disparage your research, but chemistry doesn't mean much when you're both so sleep-deprived from your newborn child's upside-down sleeping schedule that you don't know which end is up. It's your husband's offer to get up with the baby even though he's got to go to work the next morning. It's when he takes you in his arms and sways to your favorite song, even after he's been on his feet all day. That's what love is. That's what makes for a happy relationship."

Ethan looked across the table at his mother's face. Memories of his father pulling his mother into his arms and dancing around the kitchen with her as she giggled like a schoolgirl swept through him.

Mellie returned with plates piled high with food and slid them across the table. Ethan frowned at Sam's salad. "You passed up Ruby's chicken and dumplings for a salad?"

She snorted. "Yeah. Delaney and I had Bubba Buddha's last night."

He chuckled. "Enough said."

Just as he took a big swig of his iced tea, his mom chimed in.

"Well, I may not agree with your theories, but I'm happy you're dating my son."

Oh shit. He coughed as the tea went down the wrong pipe. So much for subtle.

∿

"YOU LOOK SHELL-SHOCKED," Delaney said, as she walked into Sam's lab. "What's up?"

"Nothing." She'd returned from lunch to evaluate her latest test results. "I, uh, I ran the latest blood I collected through my assay, and I have a match." Sam sat in front of her computer staring at the results on the screen. She'd checked and rechecked them, certain there must be a mistake. First, his mom's comment about them dating, and now this.

"Ooh, is it mine?" Delaney leaned against the lab counter, eager for the results.

"No. It's mine."

"Shut the front door!" She popped up like she'd just been goosed. "Who's the lucky guy? Or gal?"

"Subject 7645. Ethan Quinn." *Crap.* If only she could hit rewind. She shouldn't have disclosed his name.

"Ethan Quinn? You've got to be kidding me!" She came around the counter and gave Sam a nudge. "That's good isn't it? Isn't that good?" She bent over and studied Sam's face. "You don't look like that's good."

"It's not."

Straightening, hands on her hips, she continued, "Why isn't that good? I got some pretty hot vibes off you two the other day when he was in here."

Sam had looked at their compatibility questionnaires as well. Same results. Groaning, she buried her face in her hands. She didn't *want* a match. She didn't *need* a match. If Craig Sinclair had taught her anything, it was that she didn't need a man, and she certainly didn't want one. "Well, don't."

"Don't what?"

She turned and pointed her finger at Delaney. "Don't get any hot vibes off me and Ethan."

"Sister, I've got news for you, the hot vibes coming off you two could melt *Iceman.*"

"Iceman?" Sam looked at Delaney in confusion.

"Yeah, you know, X-Men? Marvel Comics? Hunk Shawn Ashmore?"

Sam shook her head, clueless.

"You really need to get out more. And don't try to change the subject. Why is this a problem?" Delaney threw up her hands. "You're dating him."

"No. No, I'm not dating him." Sam wagged a finger in

Delaney's face. "And because it is. Because I don't *want* a man. Especially a man like Ethan Quinn."

"You mean a sexy man? A smart, educated man? A man that loves his momma but doesn't live with her? That kind of man?" She threw her hands up in the air again. "No. I mean, what woman in her right mind would want *that* kind of man?"

Sam rested her head in her hand and sighed. Why had she enrolled him in her study? Why had she told Delaney about the match? Now what? He'd opted to learn if he had any matches after the study closed. *Gah!*

Delaney placed her hand on Sam's shoulder. "Are you going to tell him?"

She sat up. "No. Absolutely not. The consent form tells participants they will not receive their results."

"Until the end of the study. Did he opt for that?"

"Yeah. He did." Unfortunately. *That* part of the consent form he read.

Delaney took a deep breath, then released it. "Okay, look. I know you're a scientist, and you need to do the ethical thing here, but the consent form doesn't say that you *can't* tell him before the end of the study. So, really, what harm could come of telling him you two are a match?"

What harm? Where should she start? Him thinking it's a tacit admission that she has feelings for him. Him thinking she's after an engagement ring and a white dress. Him believing they have a future together when they don't. Sterling was just a steppingstone in her career, and he clearly had deep roots in the community. Whereas she had shallow roots.

She was the rolling stone to his Rock of Gibraltar.

"Hey, wait a minute." Delaney pulled up a chair across from Sam. "If you believe in your science, doesn't it follow that you should believe he's your perfect histocompatible mate? And that, according to your research, histocompatible mates make the happiest relationships?"

Sam knew where Delaney was going with this, and she didn't like it. Not one bit. She closed her eyes against the reality of her situation then reopened them to see Delaney, deep in thought, now pacing the small confines of the lab.

"And if you don't believe he's your perfect mate, doesn't that bring into question your research? Your compatibility assay? Your reputation. Your very *career*?" Delaney stopped, looked Sam right in the eye. "Wouldn't that make you a hypocrite?"

6

———

Ethan threw out the first pitch, a slider, then removed his cap and scratched his head and, at the catcher's signal, adjusted for a change up.

The Sterling Nads faculty intramural team was playing Elberton Technical College in a rivalry match. Sterling won the last two, and the Elberton Exabytes were out for blood.

Two strikes, one more to go. He shot a glance over his left shoulder toward first base, where Nash guarded the bag. The runner's body language spoke volumes, and it said 'steal.' Ethan spun and whipped the ball to Nash, catching the runner unaware. Nash tagged him out to home-team applause.

As the sun slid below the horizon, players and fans alike breathed a sigh of relief. The heat this summer had been brutal, with only a few afternoon thunderstorms to provide relief. Maybe the predicted strong storm system that promised to dump record rains on the area would bring some relatively cooler temperatures.

In the meantime, Ethan had a batter to strike out.

Turning for the windup, a pair of sexy legs in shorts

caught his eye. The red ponytail was unmistakably Sam's. He watched her making her way up the stands and grinned.

He'd just started to wind up the pitch when she bent over to pick up something. The ball slipped, catching the batter on the ankle, sending him to first base.

"Damn!" *Get your head back in the game, Quinn, and stop ogling Dr. Love's behind.*

Stepping off the mound, he pretended to take a break. Pulling his cap lower over his eyes, he looked up into the stands again. In those shorts, a tank top, and sunglasses, Sam could have been at home at a pool party or on the lake. Thoughts of a refreshing swim led to thoughts of skinny-dipping, which lead to thoughts of—"Shake it off, man."

"Hey, Quinn, you gonna pitch or do we need to call in a reliever?" Rich Davis, the ump called from behind home plate, as the catcher rose.

Ethan flagged off his catcher and walked back to the mound with an uncharacteristic case of performance anxiety.

SAM FOLLOWED Delaney up the home-team bleachers toward the top, a perspiring diet soda in her hand. Damn, it was hot, even though the sun had already set.

Delaney selected a spot and took a seat, clapping her hands with a shout, "Let's go Nads!"

Sam rolled her eyes. "The Nads? Geez, whose idea was that?" Opening a bag of peanuts, the only reasonably healthy thing she could find at the concession stand, she offered one to Delaney.

"Probably Dr. Trotter's—he likes to talk about man bits."

Delaney pried open the peanut, removed the nuts, and tossed the shell.

Sam took a sip of her soda and found Ethan on the pitcher's mound where he'd just hit the batter.

"That's the second batter Ethan's hit since we got here. Wonder what's up." Delaney leaned back, elbows on the empty bleacher behind her. "What better way to spend an evening than watching a bunch of hot guys in tight pants flex their muscles and display their athletic prowess?"

"Is that all you ever think about?"

"No. I also think about hot guys in swim trunks. Hot guys in wet T-shirts. Oh, and hot guys in nothing."

Sam laughed and shook her head. If only she could be that open and honest about sex. Setting aside her cup, she tilted her head to admire Ethan's backside. Delaney was onto something with the whole tight-pants thing. Ethan filled out his pair nicely.

But fine behind aside, she'd vowed to avoid him. She didn't have a poker face, so keeping her secret from Ethan was going to be tough enough without running into him on campus. And she would not get tangled up with him and his romantic notions. The best thing for both of them was to steer clear of one another.

Feelings of guilt flickered through her. As a scientist, she'd promised the results to those who'd opted for them. It was part of her promise to those who took the time to participate in her study. Ethan Quinn was no different than her other subjects.

She snorted. Right. If you didn't count the fact that their chemistry was off the charts.

"Swing batter, batter, batter!" Delaney hollered.

After a pop fly, Ethan struck out the next batter and headed for the dugout. Moments later he came out, bat in hand, took a few warm-up swings, then approached the batter's box.

"Ethan's one of our best hitters," Delaney said, around a bite of soft pretzel liberally slathered with mustard. "He pitched for Sterling in undergrad." She gestured with her soda cup to another batter warming up outside the dugout. "And Nash, first baseman and Sterling's hunky football coach, is right behind him."

Ethan stepped into the batter's box, got in position, and swung.

"Ste-rike!" the ump called.

"Come on, Quinn," Nash called.

The pitcher released the next pitch, and PING! Ethan threw the bat aside, loping to first base as he watched the ball sail over the fence. Home run.

She had to admit a little pride in that.

His teammates waited at home plate, where high-fives, fist-bumps, and ass-pats welcomed him. Just shy of the dugout, he turned in Sam's direction, saluting her with his cap and a big smile. Heads turned in her direction as a flush crept up her neck.

Delaney gave her a shoulder-nudge. "Aww. It must be love."

ETHAN SLUNG his bag over his shoulder and headed in the direction of Sam and Delaney. Delaney smiled and laughed with the third baseman, Steve Kirkland from engineering, while Sam looked . . . uncomfortable.

"Sam," Ethan said, as he sidled up next to her. "Did you enjoy the game?" They'd won again by two runs in the bottom of the ninth.

"Yeah. You, uh, you looked pretty good out there."

"*Pretty* good?" He shook his head and laughed. "Well, all right then. Way to stroke a man's ego." Steve pulled Delaney away to introduce her to his kid brother. "Want to go grab something to eat? A few of us are heading over to Ruby's."

"Oh. Thanks, but no. I promised Delaney we'd go to that new pub in Carlyle." She frowned over her shoulder at Delaney as she flirted with Steve.

Sam's hair had curled around her face in the humidity, and she had a fine sheen of perspiration on her arms and chest. He wondered what it would be like to shake loose that ponytail and make her sweat for a different reason. *Head. Gutter. Out.*

Disappointed, he said, "Maybe next time then. Hey, when do you think you'll have the results from your love assay?"

"Compatibility—"

"Whatever."

"Soon. I've been distracted in my search for another grad assistant. But you won't know the results until the study closes. You'd know that—"

"Yeah, yeah, if I'd read the consent form," he finished with a grin.

"Oh, Ethan!" He winced at the sound of his name and turned.

"Hi, Jackie."

Jackie Ledbetter winnowed in between him and Sam. "You were awesome tonight!" She laid her hand on his forearm. "That home run! And that catch!" she gushed.

A single mom, Jackie was on the hunt for a new daddy for her five-year-old son. Little Jack was a good kid as far as he could tell, but he had no desire to become Jackie's next prey, *er*, husband.

Jackie was a firm believer in the idiom, 'The higher the hair, the closer to God,' and wore enough goop on her face to rival the rock band Kiss.

"Awesome, huh?" Ethan grinned over Jackie's head into Sam's eyes. "Some people thought my performance tonight only pretty good."

"Pretty good? Why, who on earth would say that?" Jackie asked in astonishment.

At least *someone* liked to stroke his ego. He flashed a grin at Sam, who narrowed her eyes in return.

Remembering his manners, he introduced the two women.

"Love." Jackie tapped her chin in thought. Her eyes widened, and she pointed her finger at Sam. "You're the one with that blood test. The one that tells people who their soul mates are. I saw your flier in Dink's Corner Drugs the other day."

Ethan glanced at Sam in time to see her cringe.

"I wouldn't say soul—"

"Sign me up." She nudged Ethan, as she stuck out her arm as if ready for a blood draw.

"Oh, well . . ."

Jackie patted Ethan on the belly and smiled up at him. "You never know, Ethan, maybe we're soul mates."

Now it was Ethan's turn to cringe.

"Just, uh, call the number on the flier and schedule an appointment to come to my lab."

Jackie clapped her hands and looked back at Ethan.

Oh, joy.

"Good night, Ethan," Sam said.

The last thing he saw over Jackie's high hair was Sam grabbing a reluctant Delaney by the arm and hauling her toward the parking lot.

~

To say Sam dreaded her next research subject like she dreaded a root canal would be putting it mildly. No sooner had she taken the consent form out of the file when in walked Jackie Ledbetter of the high hair.

"Well, hi there, Dr. Love." Her cheerful expression was all Southern charm, but Sam felt the woman's scrutiny of her like an opponent assessing her rival.

"Ms. Ledbetter." Sam nodded.

Jackie giggled and waved her hand. "Oh, please. Call me Jackie."

Sam hadn't seen that much hairspray since, well, since she saw the *Hairspray* revival on Broadway.

"Well, Jackie, I'll review the consent form with you, and then I'd like you to read it thoroughly and ask me any questions you might have before signing it."

While Jackie read over the document, Sam finished setting up for the blood test.

"Wait—you mean I won't find out if I have any matches?" Jackie asked, looking up from the document, the distress clear in her voice. "What's the point then?"

"You will learn if you have any matches once the study is closed, and only if your match also consented to it."

A scowl marred Jackie's make-up-slathered face. "When will the study be closed? I mean, I'm not getting any younger here."

"The study will likely close within the next month or two."

"Oh, good! I'm hoping for Ethan. Ooh, or Nash Taylor. Has he signed up for your study?"

"I can't say."

"Oh, right. That would violate the psychologist-patient privilege."

Sam didn't bother to explain that there was no psychologist-patient privilege involved in this context. Just her promise to her subjects not to reveal any confidential information about them without their express consent.

Jackie scrawled her signature on the document and handed it back to Sam.

As Sam prepared her finger for the stick, Jackie continued, "I'm a perfect match for Ethan. He just doesn't see it. Yet." She winked at Sam, and the sharp knife of jealousy stabbed Sam in the heart just as she jabbed Jackie's finger with the lancet. Just a *tad* harder than was necessary.

"Ouch! That hurt!"

"Sorry. Didn't I mention that part?"

Jackie grimaced, but continued, "Even so, I'm not opposed to Nash either."

After filling the collection tube, Sam wrapped a Band-Aid around her finger as Jackie prattled on. "I would never do to Ethan what his last girlfriend did to him."

Sam frowned but took the bait. "What did his last girlfriend do to him?"

"Well, rumor was that he popped the question, and not only did she say no, she left for another job in New York." She paused. "Or was it D.C.? Anyway, somewhere up north. She was always a little too high and mighty if you ask me. North Georgia was never going to be her home. Too . . . what did she say? Oh, yes, too backward." Jackie snorted in contempt and rambled on.

Sterling wasn't exactly New York City, but Sam had known that coming into this job. When she left, it would have nothing to do with the size or sophistication of Sterling. It would have everything to do with taking the next step in her academic career.

"Don't you agree?" Jackie asked her.

"Hmm?"

"I said, men often don't know what's good for them. They need to be taken in hand by a good woman."

She didn't think Ethan, or most other men she knew, wanted to be "taken in hand." That is, unless you were talking about foreplay. "Oh. Well. I wouldn't say that. But my research shows that couples whose MHC-Pi are on opposite ends of the spectrum—indicating their MHC genes are dissimilar—not only have healthier, more productive children, but they also have longer, happier relationships."

Jackie blinked. "I don't know what you just said, but," she shrugged, "if it means Ethan is my match, I don't care."

SAM HAD BEEN AVOIDING HIM. His phone calls and messages had gone ignored. He didn't know what he'd done or said, but as his father had taught him, apologies worked wonders. Especially when accompanied by flowers.

Determined to confront her, he checked her office hours on the university's digital directory. Flowers in hand, he strode toward her wing of the building.

Hearing a conversation, he stood outside the door waiting. He hadn't waited long when a student with a backpack that looked as if it were filled with bricks instead of books nearly collided with him.

He knocked on her door.

"Come in."

He stuck the flowers in the doorway. "Delivery for Dr. Love."

When he stepped into her office, Sam looked up and the smile she wore froze. "Ethan."

"So, you do remember my name."

"What does that mean?" She set her pen down and folded her hands on top of the desk.

"Well, you've been avoiding my phone calls and text messages as if I were a telemarketer."

"I've just been," she waved her hand, "busy."

"Not buying it. Why are you avoiding me?" He scrubbed his hands through his hair. "Was it something I said? Something I did?"

Appearing uncomfortable, she could barely look him in the eye.

She shrugged. "What reason would I have to avoid you? Or to seek you out? We're colleagues. Either we see each other on campus or around town or we don't."

"Colleagues is it? Do you often have your colleagues' tongues down your throat?"

"That was a mistake."

"Well, that's news to me."

"Ethan, I can't have a relationship with you."

"Can't, or won't?"

"Both."

"I think I at least deserve to know why."

Picking up her pen again, she gripped it like a lifeline. "We've talked about this before. I need to focus. On my career. On my patent. On my goals."

"You know, your career and our relationship aren't mutually exclusive. Couples the world over manage to have successful careers and relationships—at the same time."

She narrowed her eyes. "Couples? Ethan, we aren't a couple."

"Not yet. But we could be if you would just give it a

chance." He had a sick feeling in the pit of his stomach. When she didn't respond, he prodded, "What are you afraid of?"

Biting her lip, she looked away. "Who says I'm afraid?"

"It's written all over your face." Seeing her expression made him ache for her, and made him wonder if Craig had put that fear there.

Her expression turned obstinate, and he knew nothing he could say would change her mind. "So this is it then?"

"I'm sorry if I hurt you, but yes, this can't go any further. I'm just trying to be fair to you."

"How about you? Are you being fair to yourself?"

Sam rose from her chair, hands on her desk. "I have to go. I have a potential subject coming to my lab in ten minutes."

Ethan strode over to the desk and laid the flowers on top of her papers. "Well, I hope you and your career are very happy together."

7

"Severe weather is headed our way later tonight," the local weatherman said. "Be sure to have your weather radio next to you and plenty of candles or a flashlight handy."

"Great," Sam muttered, as she sat on her sofa with a Lean Cuisine in her hands.

"Expect high winds, heavy rain, potential flash floods, and possible hail." As if to punctuate his words, a low rumble of thunder rolled across the area. "Stay tuned for updates throughout the evening."

Sam hated storms. Living in New York the last few years, she'd dealt with snowstorms—even some thunder snow— but nothing like the violent summer storms here. This was something new and frightening.

Finishing up her dinner, she tried to settle her nerves as a crack of thunder shook the house, rattling the dishes in the cabinet. Lightning followed close on its heels, along with another loud boom.

Between breaking up with Ethan and now this, she was a bundle of nerves. She snorted. Breaking up? Where had that come from? How do you break up with someone you never had a relationship with in the first place?

She hadn't lied when she'd told Ethan she needed to focus on her career. But that wasn't the only reason for discouraging his interest in her.

He'd asked her what she was so afraid of.

Disappointment. Not hers. His.

Relationships meant intimacy—sex. Not one of her talents, as Craig had so callously informed her when he'd dumped her. If she couldn't please someone as dispassionate as Craig, how could she ever hope to please someone as passionate as Ethan?

Thunder rumbled overhead, closer than before. She needed a distraction—from Ethan, and from Mother Nature's fury.

Until her new grad assistant started, she had papers she should grade, but what she needed was a good book. Too bad she didn't have one of Delaney's fluffy romance novels. Going to her bookshelves, she selected a mystery. It would have to do. As long as it didn't start with 'It was a dark and stormy night.'

She'd barely opened the book when her cell phone rang. "Hi, Delaney."

"You okay?"

"So far," she said with a shaky laugh.

"Listen, I can come over if you'd like."

"No. Don't be silly. You don't want to come out in this." KA-BAM! "Holy shit!"

"I know, right?" Delaney commiserated. "I grew up in Tornado Alley, so I'm used to this, but if you get scared, just call me and I'll come over."

"Thanks, but I'll be fine. I'm a big girl." Sort of.

"If you change your mind, you know where to find me."

She ended the call, released a shaky sigh, then picked up her book. Just as she opened to the first page, the lights flickered, then went out.

ETHAN PACED HIS LIVING ROOM, while the weather alert scrolled across the television screen. He'd persuaded his mother to stay at her neighbors so she wouldn't be alone. Now his concern turned to Sam.

The storm had the potential for downed trees and power lines, not to mention flash flooding. He tried to call Sam but got no answer.

When the meteorologist came on and said residents of Georgetown Square should take cover, Ethan made up his mind. After grabbing his chainsaw, he pulled on his rain jacket, picked up his keys, and he headed for his car.

The heavy rain and wind made the drive across town treacherous. When he'd arrived, Sam's neighborhood was pitch black. In his headlights, he could see some limbs and other debris strewn along the street, and finding Sam's townhouse in the dark was no easy task.

Placing a ball cap on his head, he pulled the hood over his head before dashing through the blinding rain. Hail the size of marbles began to pelt him. "Ow! Jesus." He reached the front door and hammered with his fist, afraid otherwise she wouldn't be able to hear him over the onslaught.

The door flew open. "Ethan!" Then Sam wrapped herself around him like kudzu. "I'm soaked," he said, as he wrapped his hands around her waist.

"I don't care." She clung to him, even as he carried her into the dark house.

"Why on earth don't you have any lights?"

"The power's out."

"I know that. I mean where's your flashlight? Candles?"

"I, uh . . . probably still in those boxes I haven't unpacked." She gestured toward the dining room.

"Jesus, Sam." He set her away from him and shed his jacket. Pulling his phone out of his back pocket, he found the flashlight app and turned it on. She looked like she'd just walked out of a horror movie, fear written all over her face. "Where is your phone? I tried to call you."

"Battery died and I couldn't charge it."

Lightning flickered and Sam winced. He wrapped his arms around her and she fell into his embrace. "How? Why did you come? You shouldn't have been out in this. It's too dangerous."

He released her, and she stepped back. "I was worried about you. You're trembling."

"I don't like storms."

In the dim light of his phone, he could see she was wearing some sort of pajama bottoms and a T-shirt that read, IF LOVE IS THE ANSWER, WHAT WAS THE QUES-TION? Her hair was pulled up in a messy ponytail, and her feet were bare. She'd look adorable if she weren't so scared.

"Come on." He took her hand and pulled her into the living room. "Do you have anything to drink?"

"There's a bottle of Scotch in the cabinet by the fridge."

"Good. You sit here and I'll be right back." He left her on the sofa and made his way to the kitchen. He found the bottle of Scotch then, after some searching, came up with two glasses.

Thunder shook the house as a gust of wind blew some-thing against the window. From the sound of it, hail still clattered against the roof.

Pouring two fingers of Scotch into each glass, he carried

them into the living room. "Here." He placed the glass in her hand and settled down next to her on the sofa. Wrapping a hand around her waist, he pulled her next to him. "Drink up. It'll take the edge off." He tapped his glass to hers. "To Mother Nature's fury."

~

Sam lifted the glass to her lips and drank a healthy serving, coughing as the liquid burned its way down her throat. But, after a moment, the heat it delivered relaxed her.

When she'd opened the door and saw Ethan standing there, she'd never been so glad to see anyone in her life.

Lightning flickered in the darkened house like a strobe light, illuminating Ethan's strong profile, casting his face in eerie light and shadow. He'd come through this hellish storm to check on her, even after the way she'd treated him. She didn't know what to say, so she simply said, "Thank you."

"For what?"

"For doing something stupid like driving in this storm to make sure I was okay."

He chuckled. "You're welcome, even if you think it was stupid."

She snuggled closer, enjoying the feel of his warmth and the security of his arms.

"Feeling better?"

She nodded against his shoulder.

"Good." He pressed a kiss to the top of her head, and her heart did a slow roll in her chest at the tender gesture.

The wind shook the house as if trying to knock it from its foundations, while the hail did its best to pierce the roof shingles. But none of it mattered. Ethan made soothing circles on her bare arm as they polished off their drinks.

"Why are you so afraid of storms?"

"The storms here in Georgia are so violent. Unlike any storms I've ever experienced."

"You're safe. I won't let anything happen to you."

How soothing those words were. To know someone had your back.

Suddenly exhausted, she closed her eyes and nodded off for a moment.

"Hey." Ethan took the glass from her hand and set it on the coffee table. "Let's get you to bed."

Too tired to resist, she let him pull her to her feet, then he scooped her up and carried her up the stairs. She knew she should resist. In her Scotch-, fear-, and fatigue-fogged mind, she knew his game. Rescue frightened damsel in distress, then said rescued damsel would be so grateful she'd take him to bed. Only to have him end up dissatisfied. Still, she couldn't muster enough indignation.

He placed her in bed and pulled the covers up before kissing her forehead. "Good night, Sam. Sleep well."

Her eyes flew open. "You're leaving?"

"I'm not leaving you alone. I'll just be downstairs."

"But . . . don't go." She grabbed his hand. "Don't leave me up here alone."

❧

"SHH. I'LL STAY." The fear in her voice broke his heart.

He laid down on top of the covers next to her and pulled her into his arms. As if the covers would be a barrier to her soft, warm body—and his almost painful need for her.

She snuggled against him, her breath against his neck.

Sweet Jesus. Spending the night here would be pure torture.

"Ethan, why did you come here tonight?" The wind blew something against the window, and she flinched.

"Because I was worried about you."

She lifted herself up onto one elbow, and he felt her gaze on his face in the pitch darkness. "But, after everything I said—"

"Doesn't matter. When you care about someone, you want to help them. Protect them. No matter what."

"You care about me?" she whispered.

"I thought that was evident."

"I thought all that was just to prove a point."

"And that point being?"

"That flowers, candlelight dinners, and coming to my rescue—romantic gestures—would make me fall for you."

"Is it working?" He held his breath waiting for her answer.

After what seemed like an eternity, she finally said, "Yes."

"Thank God." He rolled her over and took her mouth with his. One hand fisted in his shirt while the other hand tangled in his hair. *Sweet. So damned sweet.* His tongue danced with hers, their breath mingling, converging. Deepening the kiss, he cupped her face, holding her there so he could drink his fill of her mouth.

Changing the angle, he slid his hand along her neck, and she sighed into his mouth. Continuing his exploration, his fingers skimmed her shoulder, traveling down her arm to where she was still grasping his shirt. From there, he found her hips and pressed her against him so she could feel the heat of his erection, groaning when their bodies made contact.

Her fisted hand pushed against his chest. "Wait."

~

"I'm not good at this," she panted.

With nothing more than the gentle pressure she applied against him, he withdrew, giving her space to think. To confess.

God, she wanted him. With every fiber of her being. Every nerve ending in her body was attuned to him. To his touch. His kiss. His heat. But, she needed him to under-stand. To know what he was getting. Or in this case, what he wasn't.

"Good at what?"

"This." She gestured between the two of them.

"Kissing? Oh, I beg to differ."

"No." She cleared her throat. "Sex."

"First, unless they've changed the rules, we're currently not having sex. Second, why would you say that?"

"Look." She sat up, shoving her hair out of her face. "Just because my parents are world-famous sex therapists doesn't mean—you know—I'm some kind of expert in the bedroom."

He took her shoulders, looked into her eyes. "Sam, this isn't some sort of competition. You're not being graded or anything."

"I just don't want you to have any expectations."

"Sam?" His finger drifted down her cheek to her mouth. "Yes?"

"Shut up and let me make love to you."

His reassuring gaze never left her eyes as he patiently waited for response. She knew if she said no, he'd accept it and not pressure her. That alone made her want him all the more. "Yes." She turned, took his finger into her mouth, elic-iting a caveman-like growl.

Dragging his finger from her mouth, he replaced it with his tongue, while the wet finger found her pebbled nipple through her shirt. Arching into him, she gasped. Electric. His touch sparked lust, greed, wantonness.

His mouth followed his finger as he captured her nipple through her T-shirt.

"Naked," she gasped as she tugged on his shirt hem. "I want you naked."

He chuckled low in his throat, and she felt it against her breast. Sitting up, he yanked the offending shirt over his head and tossed it behind him. Then made short work of her own T-shirt. When he laid back down, she hissed at the searing contact of skin against skin. Ten atomic bombs couldn't create this much heat.

Greed took over her hands. She wanted to touch every inch of his skin. His stomach quivered as her hand glided over him. The hard ridges of his abs, the smattering of hair on his chest, fueled a desire she never knew possible. Slipping lower, her hand encountered his erection, and she stroked it through his jeans.

He grabbed her wrist, groaning. "Slow down, sweetheart, or I won't last long. First things first."

Bringing her hand to his mouth, he kissed her wrist, then her palm, before releasing her. Settling her back against the bed, he lathed one nipple with his hot tongue, sending fire through her already-melting veins. Showing the same attention to her other breast, his hand grazed her bare stomach before slipping beneath her pajama bottoms.

She'd already almost reached the pinnacle, and with one touch she splintered into a million pieces.

~

HE KISSED HER TEMPLE, waiting until the last tremor dissipated. "How are you doing, sweetheart?"

"Good. I'm really . . ." she sighed, "good."

Cupping the back of his head, she lifted her mouth to his, biting his bottom lip. Her other hand was busy popping the button on his fly before unzipping his jeans. Plunging her hand in, she wrapped her fingers around him, making him draw in a breath.

Gritting his teeth, he let her explore him until he couldn't take anymore. Rising, he grabbed his wallet out of his pocket and pulled out a foil packet then dropped his jeans to the floor. He feared this wouldn't last long.

Rolling on the condom, he knelt on the bed and slid her pajama bottoms off. On the way back up, he grazed between her thighs with his fingertips, stirred by the moan that escaped her, and gratified by her waiting arms when he settled himself between those silky legs.

Positioning himself above her, he entered her in one long, slow glide. Holding himself in check, he reveled in the feel of her. Taking her mouth, he began to move with unhurried thrusts, getting to know what she liked. She wrapped her legs around his backside and arched to meet him.

"Ethan," she breathed, as her fingernails clawed at his back.

"I've got you, sweetheart." He picked up the pace, meeting her thrust-for-thrust, driving them higher and higher. The howl of the wind, the rumble of thunder, and the relentless onslaught of the rain faded into the background. Only the sound of their labored breathing, the moans of their mutual pleasure, filled the room.

With one last deep thrust, his soul tore in two, and when the pieces reunited, a part of hers was intertwined.

8

<hr>

Shattered was the first word that came to mind, transcendent the second.

"Sweetheart, why would you ever think you weren't any good at sex?" She lay curled up against his side, while his hand made gentle circles on her back.

She shrugged, the only movement she had the energy for. She didn't want to tell him that Craig had called her frigid.

He nudged her. Sighing, she finally responded. "Let's just say my past, um, partners, said I wasn't passionate."

"Well, then they must have been doing it wrong."

She giggled. He had that way about him. He shot through all her insecurities and made her laugh.

Disentangling himself, he propped himself up on one elbow and looked down into her face. "If you were any more passionate, the sheets would have caught fire."

She felt the flush creep up her chest and into her face. Ducking her head against his arm, she shook it.

Rolling her unto her back, he kissed her so sweet and slow, she felt her bones dissolve. Retreating a millimeter, he spoke against her lips, "That was, without a doubt, the best experience of my life. Not just sex. Experience."

Wide-eyed, she gazed into his face, as her heart filled with . . . something. "Me, too." Chalking it up to an oxytocin overload, she covered by asking if he was hungry.

Kissing her nose, he said, "Starved!"

"I think I can scare up some cheese and crackers, maybe a bottle of Pinot."

"A meal fit for a king," Ethan exclaimed. "Be right back." Sam could just make out his silhouette as he headed for the bathroom, and what a silhouette it was.

As soon as he returned, he turned on the flashlight app on his smartphone and shrugged into his jeans, sans shirt and shoes, while she wrapped herself in a silk robe, tying it at the waist.

Leading the way to the stairs, Ethan said, "Careful." Taking her hand, he guided her down the dimly lit staircase.

After laying out the crackers, cheese, some olives, and sliced prosciutto, ravenous, they fell upon it like it was manna from Heaven.

She'd unearthed a scented candle that Delaney had given her as a housewarming gift, so they ate by candlelight at the dining-room table. Though it still rained buckets outside, the storm had expended most of its energy, leaving behind only the occasional flicker of lightning and distant rumble of thunder.

Around a bite of provolone, Ethan asked, "Why the love assay?"

"Compatibility."

He winked. "Tomato, tomahto."

Rolling her eyes, she considered his question a moment because, honestly, she didn't know if she had an answer. It was really something she'd stumbled upon in her dissertation research about what makes some marriages or relationships last, and others not so much.

"My parents divorced when I was fifteen. And while they remain professional partners to this day, I always wondered why they couldn't stay married."

"Wait. Your parents, world-renowned sex therapists, aren't married?"

"No. They've kept it very quiet. They insist that they're an inseparable team when it comes to faculty positions. They still work together every day, write articles and books, even live together, but they're divorced. They see other people from time to time, but neither one has been in a relationship."

Ethan scratched his chin, the sound of the day-old scruff sending delicious little shivers down her spine. "Huh."

"Yeah, I know. Weird." She sighed, took a sip of her wine, then continued. "So, I guess that's why my research took the turn it did." She lifted a shoulder. "Call it intellectual curiosity."

Ethan reached out and laid a big, warm hand over hers. "Or the little girl inside the woman trying to understand why her mom and dad don't love each other anymore."

Their divorce had always bothered her more than she'd let on. If two people so seemingly suited for one another, with identical interests, couldn't stay married, what hope did any couple have? Then there were Ethan's parents, whose marriage ended tragically. What was the formula for a long, happy marriage? To her mind, it all came down to chemistry.

But she began to wonder if Ethan, and his parents, weren't onto something. Her parents had the same professions, the same goals, the same tastes in music and art, food and wine, yet their marriage had failed. Was it simply because they didn't believe in romance? Because they took each other for granted? Would chocolates and flowers, a tender gesture, or a kind word have made a difference?

Confused and uncertain, she chose to change the subject. "Your turn. Why literature?"

~

"NICE DEFLECTION, DR. LOVE."

"Guilty as charged." A soft smile lifted the corners of that delectable mouth. "But I really want to know," she finished softly.

"My dad loved reading but never had the money to pursue an education. It was his love of reading that made me decide to study literature." He topped a cracker with a slice of prosciutto and a piece of cheese, handing it to her.

"When I was too young to read, he would read *Oliver Twist*, *Robinson Crusoe*, or *Gulliver's Travels* to me at bedtime. When I was older, we'd read books like *A Tale of Two Cities*, *Tom Sawyer*, and *Huck Finn*, and we'd discuss them at dinner. Much to my sister's dismay." He chuckled, remembering Charlotte's protests.

She popped an olive into her mouth. "And your mom? Was she a big reader?"

"She loved Austen and Brontë, but she didn't venture far from romantic fiction."

"How old was your father when he died?"

"Sixty-four."

"Young."

"Too young." And it was his fault.

"You said it was a heart attack."

"Yeah." He scrubbed a hand over his face. How did they wind up talking about this?

"You don't have to talk about it if you don't want to."

She'd shared her sexual insecurities with him. Maybe he should share his feelings of guilt with her. "We were fishing out on Lake Ketchum. I'd talked him into it. He said he wasn't feeling well, but he'd been working a lot at the granite quarry, and I thought he just needed some fresh air and relaxation. Turned out I was wrong. What he'd needed was a trip to the hospital."

She stroked his cheek with her hand. "You couldn't have known that."

"I couldn't save him," he whispered. "No matter how long I did CPR, I couldn't keep him alive."

"Oh, Ethan." Sam rose from the table and knelt by his chair, her hands resting on his thighs. "You did everything you could. I'm sure your mom knows that. And you should, too."

Intellectually, he knew she was right. But, emotionally .. . well, that was another matter.

God, she was beautiful on her knees looking up at him, her eyes soft with compassion.

Draining the last of the wine from his glass, he rose and lifted her to her feet. Leaning over, he blew out the candle. Safety first. Then pulled her along behind him.

"Where are we going?"

"Bedroom."

"Wait."

"For what?" He stopped short, and she bumped into him in the dark.

"This." She grabbed his face and pulled his mouth down to hers, where she proceeded to lick and nip him like he was an ice cream cone.

Turning so that her back was to the stairs, he lowered her until she sat on the third step, and opening her robe, he proceeded to do the same to her. All the way down her sexy body until he reached her pearly gates.

"Talk about nice deflection," Sam said later—much later —as Ethan drew her up against him so they were spooning.

He chuckled, his breath tickling the back of her neck. "I aim to please, Dr. Love."

"Thank you. Again."

"Well, you don't have to thank me for the orgasms. That's just awkward."

She snorted. "I'm thanking you again for driving through the storm to see if I was okay."

"Oh. That." He kissed her neck. "You're safe, Dr. Love. Get some sleep." His arms tightened around her.

Should she tell him about the results? she wondered. No. Then he'd think she was after more than just sex.

That's what this was, right? Just sex? And what amazing sex it was! She wasn't frigid after all. Nor was she sexually unresponsive. She'd discovered her sexual mojo. And it felt . . . awesome!

Problem was, she may have discovered something else, too. Romance.

The next morning, Ethan surveyed the damage from Sam's living-room window. The beautiful tree-lined neighborhood had taken quite a hit. He took a sip from the coffee he'd managed to brew on Sam's gas range. His phone buzzed in his back pocket. Checking it, he saw a text from his mom saying all was well.

The power in the area was still out and likely would be for some time, and the house was already getting stuffy without AC.

It had taken every ounce of willpower to crawl out of Sam's bed so he could check on things. What happened between them last night had left him shaken. Off kilter. Their union had touched something deep inside his soul. Something inexplicable. He ran a palm down his face. And talking about his dad; well, that had been surprisingly . . . cathartic.

He'd gotten little sleep last night. And neither had Sam. Not because of the storm outside, but because of the storm inside. Her bedroom to be exact. Oh, and the staircase on their way back from the kitchen after their late-night snack. They'd burned a lot of calories last night.

It was early yet, and Sam hadn't stirred. He'd let her sleep.

The tree limb lying across her driveway would require a chainsaw to clear. Good thing he'd tossed his in the trunk of his car just in case. He'd thought he might need it to just get to her house last night. But now it would come in handy.

Finishing up the coffee, he set the cup in the kitchen sink and headed out just as the rip of a chainsaw down the street broke the post-storm silence.

SAM SIGHED as memories drifted across her consciousness. Ethan carrying her up the stairs, placing her in bed . . . then . . . nirvana. She sat up with a start.

The bed was empty. The pillow next to her revealed an indentation from where Ethan had slept. Alone in her bed, she didn't know how she felt about last night.

Physically, she was loose, relaxed. And satisfied. Most-definitely satisfied. All thanks to Ethan and the flood of the hormone DHEA in her system.

Before she could give her emotions more than a cursory analysis, the growl of a chainsaw ripped through the morning. Throwing back the covers, she drew on her robe as she walked over to the front window. Ethan stood, chainsaw in hand, arm muscles flexing, as the machine bit into wood. The limb was huge! Almost the size of a tree. And where had Ethan found the chainsaw? Certainly not in her tool-barren garage.

Grabbing a pair of jeans and a T-shirt, she dressed in a rush, brushed her teeth, and de-snarled her hair before pulling it up into a messy bun. Taking in her kiss-swollen mouth, her radiant complexion, and her silly smile, she high-fived herself in the mirror with a giggle.

As she headed down the stairs, the aroma of coffee had her detouring to the kitchen. Bless him, Ethan had made coffee. Cup in hand, she moved to the front window. Brow furrowed in concentration, Ethan attacked the downed limb with the skill of a lumberjack.

Thank goodness she'd parked her car in the garage, otherwise it would've been toast. On the other hand, if the tree limb *had* flattened it, she'd have a new car. Sighing at the injustice, she polished off the last of her coffee then went out to help.

Ethan looked up as she walked down the front steps. He shut off the chainsaw and lifted the safety glasses from his eyes. "Morning."

Damn, but he was a beautiful man! "Morning." He wore the same silly grin she'd observed on her own face.

"It's a mess, but we'll get it cleared."

She nodded. "What can I do?"

"You can start dragging some of the smaller limbs to the curb."

"Sure."

The chainsaw roared to life again, and he turned his attention back to the task at hand while she began clearing away what she could.

They worked in the still, humid air, the sound of chainsaws echoing around them. Sam surveyed the results of Mother Nature's temper tantrum up and down her street and wondered when power would be restored.

A half-hour later, Ethan had tackled the tree limb and stacked the wood along the curb next to her pile. He'd stacked some of the smaller pieces in the garage for use in her fireplace for the winter.

"I'm going to walk the neighborhood, see if anyone else needs help."

And her heart gave a little squeeze.

"You have anything else in the fridge that needs to be eaten before it spoils? If so, I could use something to eat."

She tilted her head and raised her hand to her forehead as the sun came out. "I think I can scare up something."

"Be back in a little while." He flashed her a grin then walked off up the street, carrying the chainsaw like a modern-day knight in shining armor. And that's when it happened. For the first time in her life, her heart—not her head—sat up and took notice.

ETHAN STROLLED BACK DOWN the street toward Sam's, his arms and back aching, his shirt covered with wood chips and saw dust. He'd seen the power company crew earlier, so power should be restored within a couple of hours. He knew one thing: he needed a shower. And some lunch. And not necessarily in that order.

The sun had come out, heating up the atmosphere, creating an outdoor sauna. So much for the cooler weather.

Wiping sweat from his forehead with his hands, he swiped it on his pants. He looked at his T-shirt and grimaced. Filthy hand prints, some tree sap, and was that a smashed bug?

"Ethan? I thought that was you!"

He glanced over to his left, across the street from Sam's, and saw Dr. Snyder's wife. The town's biggest gossip. "Mrs. Snyder." He nodded.

"What brings you to Georgetown Square?"

"Just helping out."

"Well, aren't you handy? Is that your car parked at Samantha Love's place? I saw it there last night."

Great. "Yes." He'd just leave it at that. "Everything okay at your place? You and Joel need any help?"

"No, no. We're good. Just waiting for the electricity to come back on."

"Glad to hear all's well." Hoping she'd go back in the house, he stopped to tie his shoe, but no such luck. The old bat would stand there and watch to see if he went to Sam's.

Wondering how long it would be before the story made the gossip train, he popped his trunk, laid the chainsaw in it, and headed up the walk to Sam's door.

SAM OPENED the door to see where Ethan was and almost jumped out of her skin when she saw him standing on her front stoop. "Everything okay?"

"Yep."

"Lunch is ready, and I made some lemonade."

"I can't come in like this. Do you have a hose?"

"Around back. I'll bring lunch out to the screened porch."

He nodded and walked around the side of the house.

A few minutes later, she heard the screen door slam and glanced out the French doors. Fumbling with the pitcher of lemonade, she stopped in her tracks.

Ethan stood, wet T-shirt clinging to him, his hair dripping down his neck. *Holy*—That was as far as that thought got before the circuits in her brain short circuited.

"Hey, Sam! Can you bring a towel?" Ethan hollered from the porch.

Towel. Yeah. I can do that. Towels would be in the linen closet. Which is at the top of the stairs. *But you actually have to stop staring in order to go get them. Right.*

She came back through the kitchen and skidded to a halt again.

This time, he'd stripped off his shirt.

His muscular chest tapered to a hard flat stomach, and his damp jeans hung startlingly low on his hips, revealing the navy waistband of his underwear. Things it had been too dark to see the night before. But she'd let her fingers do the walking. Body Braille. Now, in the full light of day, she could see just how beautifully he was made.

He opened the door, spurring her into action.

"One towel."

"Thanks." He reached out for it, and his jeans slipped a little lower. Any lower and she'd probably faint. "I didn't want to track debris on your porch. Plus, I was damned hot."

Oh, you're hot all right, and no amount of cold water will change that. For either one of us.

As he scrubbed the towel over the hard planes of his

chest, she wondered if she should check her mouth for drool. Giving herself a mental snap-out-of-it slap, à la *Moonstruck,* she pondered those nascent feelings of lust.

The ceiling fan spun to life.

"The power! Thank goodness." Lifting her overheated face—for more reasons than the outdoor temperature—to the cooling breeze of the fan, she admonished herself for her fanciful thoughts.

Opening her eyes, her gaze found his, a sly smile on his lips. *Busted.*

Why not go for it? Lifting a brow in invitation, she asked, "Can I interest you in a shower?"

The corner of his mouth lifted. "I thought you'd never ask."

The following Wednesday, as Ethan strode down the hall for his meeting with Dr. Cosgrove, the dean of the college, he straightened his tie and tugged his shirt cuffs down.

He had an idea why Dr. Cosgrove had called the meeting.

After ushering him in to the dean's office, the receptionist asked if he'd like something to drink.

"Water. Thanks, Stacy."

"Ah, Ethan." Dr. Cosgrove entered on the heels of his assistant's departure. "Good to see you." He held out his hand to shake Ethan's. A tall, imposing man, Dr. Cosgrove had a head full of white hair, a ruddy complexion, and a ready smile. He'd been the college's dean through two presidents. Quite an accomplishment, considering the political jockeying that occurs when a member of university administration turns over.

Stacy returned with a bottle of water then quietly closed the door behind her. Dr. Cosgrove took a seat in the cozy leather chair adjacent to the sofa across from his desk.

"I understand congratulations are in order in the hiring of Dr. Danica Harding. Good job."

"Thank you." Ethan took pride in a job well-done, and he knew Dr. Harding's position with Sterling University was a feather in the department's cap, as well as in the college's.

Dr. Cosgrove clapped his hands together. "But that's not why I called this meeting."

Ethan raised a brow.

"I wanted you to be the first in the college to know that I'm retiring. Candice and I are ready to spend more time with the grandkids."

He hadn't seen that coming. "Congratulations. You've earned it."

"That I have. And I think you're in the market for a deanship."

Oh. Well. "I guess I've been pretty transparent."

"That, and I've always known you were dean material. Sterling would be crazy to let you slip out the door. So I'm recommending you as interim dean, and I strongly suggest that you put in for the position when it's posted."

Stunned, Ethan didn't know what to say. "Thank you. I'm, well . . . I'm speechless."

"A professor who's speechless. That's a first."

If Ethan were to get the job, it would create a problem with Sam. Sterling had a nepotism policy, and as dean of the college, her department would report to him. It would also create a problem with his mother's job, which he'd talked her into, and which she'd come to love.

"If you don't mind, I'd like to give it some thought."

"Of course. Would a week give you enough time?"

"Yes."

"Dr. Love! Sam!" At the sound of his voice, Sam picked up her pace heading for her car. *Ethan!*

When he'd left the afternoon after the storm—and her first experience with shower sex—there had been no promises. No plans. And she was okay with that. She wasn't looking for a relationship. It was just sex, right?

She'd never had a purely sexual relationship because, well, given her sexual hang-ups, she hadn't really seen the point. Now, she didn't know how to behave. What was expected of her. And what she should expect. *Like, oh, I don't know . . . communication?*

No phone calls, no text messages, nothing. Not even a smoke signal. And she hated that the lack of communication bothered her.

She opened her car door, tossed her bag in the front seat then faced him, her hand on the top of the door, her blood boiling. "What?"

"Hi."

Damn! Why did he have to smile like that. Why did he have to look at her with those warm brown eyes? *Do not say it!* "Why haven't you called?" *Dammit. You had to say it, didn't you?*

"I'm sorry. I've been in negotiations with a prospective faculty member. You remember, I told you? The one who would bring with her a Nobel Prize in literature?"

Yep. He'd told her. She'd just forgotten. Her anger dissipated. But then he hadn't told her he would be *incommunicado*. Her anger returned. She leveled him with a glare.

"What? Are you mad?" He chuckled, which only raised her ire. Then he stepped into her, invading the space between the car door and the passenger compartment. His hands went to her shoulders, as he gazed into her eyes.

She glanced around, uncomfortable with his close proximity in public. She didn't want to start any tongues wagging. Unless it was theirs. In each other's mouths.

"I'm sorry. I should have called. Forgive me?"

Geez. Just one touch from him and she was ready to melt into a simpering puddle of womanhood. She nodded.

"Good. Listen, it's my mom's birthday on Friday, and I'm having dinner with her. I'd like you to come with me if you're free."

Dinner with his mom? She didn't know what to make of that. Apparently wariness was written all over her face because he cajoled, "Come on. You'd make us both very happy."

"Um, sure. What time?"

"I'll pick you up at six."

She nodded.

"I've got to run. Department meeting. I'll call you later." He tried to kiss her on the mouth, but she turned her cheek. They'd already put on quite the spectacle in the faculty parking lot. And she didn't do spectacle.

"So, let me get this straight. It's your mom's birthday, but she's cooking?" Sam asked from the passenger seat.

"That's correct."

Sam shook her head and Ethan chuckled. Flipping on his blinker, he turned into his childhood neighborhood. This is just what he needed—a distraction from the pros and cons of the job as interim dean colliding in his head. "She loves to cook. And when it comes to cooking for those she loves, she couldn't think of anything better."

Driving down the street, he passed Nash's childhood home, where his father still lived. Then Suzy Stringfellow's house on the right. Her parents finally put it on the market —planning to retire to Florida. Young couples were invading the modest neighborhood looking for affordable first homes. His mom and Nash's father were the last holdouts.

Pulling into the driveway, he threw the car into park. "This is it."

Sam took in the manicured front yard with its beds of colorful petunias, the trimmed boxwoods lining the sidewalk to the front door, and the porch with its hanging baskets of Boston ferns. "You grew up here?"

He nodded. "Me and my sister."

"I like it." She opened the car door and stood a moment, looking around the neighborhood.

"It's small, but it's home." Ethan came around the car and took her hand. "There's Mom now."

His mom stood on the front porch, dishtowel over her shoulder, a smile on her face. Hard to believe today was her sixtieth birthday. Patting the little box in his jacket pocket, he guided Sam up the walk.

"Hi, Mrs. Quinn," Sam greeted her.

"Margaret, remember?"

"Of course."

"Don't you look a picture?" his mom said, as she took Sam's hand and kissed her cheek.

And his mom was right. Sam did look a picture. Her red hair back in a ponytail, an emerald-green sundress flirting with her matching eyes, and sexy little sandals with those Jezebel-red toenails.

"Come on in. I hope you're hungry. We've got pot roast, green beans, roasted potatoes, and homemade apple pie for dessert."

~

AFTER EATING what amounted to enough food for a week, Sam took Margaret's refusal of help in the kitchen as an opportunity to peruse the photos displayed about the tidy living room.

The red-brick fireplace mantel held photos of Ethan as a boy, alongside photos of a girl who must be his sister. Ethan in a football uniform, kneeling, his helmet under his arm, another of him, a baseball bat on his shoulder and a cap pulled down low over his eyes. Finally, one of him in a cap and gown, apparently his high-school graduation picture. He wore the wry grin she'd come to recognize. The one that said, *Yeah, I'm just as surprised as you.*

On the bookshelf next to the fireplace stood photos of his parents—wedding-day photos, picnics, birthdays. Their mutual respect for one another clear in every snapshot. How she would have loved to have had them in her study.

Margaret and Ethan had shared stories over dinner about family vacations, nothing extravagant, just fishing and camping trips, s'mores by the campfire, swimming in the lake. Simple, meaningful experiences.

Her parents didn't take vacations. They took sabbaticals and were usually holed-up in some Italian villa or French chateau working on their latest bestseller. She had no photo albums filled with memories. No one with whom to reminisce. Shaking off her maudlin thoughts, she returned to her exploration.

Below the photos, the shelves were stuffed with books. The very ones Ethan said he and his father had read together.

Hands rested on her waist, and Ethan leaned in to kiss her shoulder then rested his chin there.

"You have an amazing family." She settled back against him as if it was the most natural thing in the world.

"Yeah, I do. Even my sister, Charlotte, has her moments." He turned Sam to face him, "What about you? Any brothers or sisters?"

She shook her head. "No. Just me."

"Cousins?"

"No." Being an only child had never bothered her, but for some reason her answer left behind an unfamiliar ache.

"Well, you can share mine." He pointed to a group in a photo—kids and adults, young and old. "The Quinn family reunion the summer before my grandmother died. Thirty-two of us in all."

"Wow. How do you remember all their names?"

"I'm not sure I do. Mom," he called into the kitchen, "who's the guy in the John Deere cap with the pipe in his mouth?"

"That's your late Uncle Arty. You know, Aunt Zelda's husband?"

"Oh, yeah."

"Dessert," his mom called back.

"None of my clothes are going to fit after this meal," Sam said, as she ran her hands down her stomach.

"Then I guess you'll just have to go naked. Such a pity."

SAM WAS quiet on the drive back into Sterling, but it was a companionable silence. Ethan liked that they could just be in each other's company and not feel the need to fill it with chatter. He reached over, took her hand, and received a soft smile in return.

He'd been giving it a lot of thought. Work complications

notwithstanding, he'd like to take this relationship to the next level—exclusivity. Not that he'd been seeing anyone else. And as far as he knew, neither had she. But he'd like to make it official.

Not only was Sam beautiful, she was smart and funny. And while she said she didn't believe in romance, her actions spoke differently.

He'd seen the wistful expression on her face when his mom spoke of his dad. He'd observed the tender touch of her fingertip as she'd skimmed it along his parents' wedding photo. The way she'd reacted to the bouquet he'd brought to her. She'd been surprised and touched.

Maybe she said she didn't believe in romance because she'd never *experienced* it. He just needed to show her; then she'd believe.

And while she might declare otherwise, even to herself, she yearned to belong. To a family. To someone who would cherish her. Someone with whom she could make memories.

While he'd stood at the sink drying dishes after dinner, his mom had told him how much she liked Sam, not so subtly hinting that she was daughter-in-law material.

He wasn't ready to walk down the aisle yet, but a relationship? Yeah, he could do that. And who knew? Maybe one day they would take that walk down the aisle. Make those memories she so clearly craved.

But first, he'd set the mood with some romance of his own, then he'd tell her how he felt about her.

∾

As Sam walked up the sidewalk to her front door, her hand clasped with Ethan's, she thought again of the pretty little necklace he had given his mom for her birthday. A custom arrangement of birthstones—hers, his, his sister's, and his late father's. Such a thoughtful gift. His mother had cried as he placed it around her neck. Happy tears, she'd said.

There was no arguing that, with him, it was the little things that counted.

She hadn't exactly been engaging on the ride home, but only because she'd been deep in thought, and oddly, a little envious of Ethan's childhood.

By all accounts, he'd grown up in a warm, loving home, maintained long-term friendships with the kids in his neighborhood, like his best friend, Nash Taylor. He'd lived in the same town, the same house, until he was eighteen years old. Whereas, she'd pulled up stakes every two or three years at the whim of her parents' careers.

Delaney was the closest thing she'd ever had to a best friend, and they'd known each other less than a year. Ethan and Nash had known each other since grade school.

What would it be like to have someone know you inside and out, and like you despite your shortcomings?

What nonsense. Must've been the walk down memory lane that Ethan and his mother had taken over dinner that left her feeling bereft. If she wanted to reach the pinnacle of her career, she'd be pulling up stakes in another year or two to move onward and upward.

"Would you like to come in?" Sam asked, as she unlocked her door.

"Sure."

She'd barely closed the door behind them when he'd snagged her around the waist and covered her mouth with his. Dropping her purse where she stood, she raised her arms, wrapping them around his neck. Ethan Quinn had turned her into a nymphomaniac. She'd been thinking about getting him back in her bed all evening.

"God, I've been dying to do that since I picked you up three hours ago," he murmured against her lips.

Walking her backward into the living room, they fell back on the couch, his long, lean body covering hers. Relishing the weight of him on her, she tugged his mouth down to hers. Tongues circling, breaths mingling. Such poignant sweetness.

He sat up, gazed down at her, his hair mussed from her frantic fingers. Lifting her head, he freed her hair from its tie, spreading it across her shoulders. "So beautiful."

Reaching up, she began flicking open the buttons on his dress shirt, tugging it free from his waistband. She spread her hands along his rib cage. "You're not too bad yourself, Dr. Quinn."

He sucked in a breath as her fingers grazed his stomach, heading south. "Take me to bed, Ethan."

"Your wish is my command." Scooping her up, he threw her over his shoulder in a fireman's carry.

She barked out a laugh at his unexpected action. As he climbed the stairs, he smacked her ass. She yelped, then dissolved into a fit of giggles.

Sex had never been so much fun.

"You think that's funny, huh?"

"Yes," she choked out.

He dropped her onto the bed and tossed the skirt of her dress up, covering her face. Her giggles died the moment he shoved her panties aside and covered her with his mouth.

STRETCHED OUT NEXT TO ETHAN, his warm hard body

against hers, she sighed in contentment and thought about what she'd been missing all of her adult life—incredible, breathtaking, mind-blowing sex.

Ethan rose, propping himself up with his elbow, and gazed down at her. He brushed his fingertips along her cheekbones. "You know, I can't help the rush of male pride in the post-sex flush in your cheeks."

She rolled her eyes but blushed all the same.

Settling his hand on her stomach, he continued. "So, I received some interesting news the other day, but it's not for public consumption."

"Didn't anyone ever tell you that pillow-talk is confidential?" She reached up and ran her fingers through his hair.

"Now that you mention it . . ." he replied with a grin. "Dr. Cosgrove is retiring."

"Oh. That's nice."

"And he's not only recommending they appoint me interim dean, but also that I apply for the permanent position."

"That's incredible, Ethan. Congratulations." She couldn't help the smile that stretched across her face.

"Too soon for congratulations. It's not a done deal yet."

Then she recalled the conversation they'd had in Ruby's Diner the day her car battery died, about why they shouldn't date: the university's nepotism policy. His argument had been that neither one reported to the other. That wouldn't be the case anymore.

Now, when she'd put aside her reasons for avoiding any kind of relationship with him. Now, when she'd begun to crave his company. So would he be the one to end this? Or should she end it before she descended any deeper into this . . . whatever it was?

"I see the wheels turning in that pretty head of yours," he said, as she sat up and shoved her hair out of her face.

"That means—"

He cradled her face in his warm hand. "I know. But I'm working on it. There has to be a solution."

"And what if there's not? What if—"

"You think too much." He touched his lips to hers, as his hand skimmed down her neck and along her shoulder.

"But—"

He pressed a finger to her lips, effectively shushing her. Anger surged through her as she prepared to tell him exactly what she thought about being stifled. Then his lips replaced his finger and his hand cupped the back of her head, easing back down on the mattress. Her head said "resist," but her heart and body said "surrender." Sighing, she raised the white flag.

10

"So, you and that pretty new professor, Dr. Love . . . ?"

"How'd you know?" Ethan huffed out as he and Nash took an early-morning run.

Nash lifted a sweaty brow. "Did you forget where you live?"

Right. The gossip train of Sterling was a well-oiled machine. He should have known it was only a matter of time, especially after Mrs. Snyder caught him. He let that go, as the sound of their feet struck the pavement. "Who told you?"

"Colleen Dukakis told Ginny Decker, who told Grady Morgan, who told me."

Great. Even Nash's coaching staff got in on the fun.

"When were you planning to tell me?" Nash lifted the hem of his ratty Denver Broncos T-shirt and wiped his face.

"Sorry, *Dad*, I didn't know I needed your permission to date someone."

Nash snorted. "Not just someone. Samantha Love,

daughter of the famous 'Love Doctors.' And subject of the dating pool your assistant won."

God, would he ever live that down? "And your point is?"

"My point is, apparently this has been going on a few weeks. Is it serious?"

Was it serious? For him it was. He wasn't sure about Sam. She played her cards close to her vest. "Maybe." It was the best he could do.

"Just watch yourself. Don't get hooked on this woman if she doesn't plan to set down roots. I know you like a brother. You'll never leave this area. I just hate to see you get hurt again."

By hurt, Nash meant Julie. If she'd stayed, they would have been married a year now. She might've even been pregnant. But then again, no. She didn't want the interruption to her career. "I'm good." He felt Nash's eyes on his face. "Really."

They ran in silence a few paces, just the sound of their feet against the pavement and their labored breathing, in tune with one another as if blood brothers.

"There is something I want to talk to you about, though," Ethan said.

"Sounds serious."

"This is confidential."

"Goes without saying."

"The dean of my college is retiring. He's recommending they name me interim. He's also recommending I apply for the permanent position."

"Man, that's the best news I've heard all day!" Nash slapped him on the shoulder. "It's what you've wanted for so long."

"Yeah, but there's a problem." He took a swig from his water bottle, wiped his mouth.

"Your mom."

"And Sam."

"Look, Ethan. It sounds like you and Sam are pretty serious, but you haven't put a ring on her finger yet, so don't put your career on hold. You owe it to yourself to explore this. Take the interim position. Who knows? It might really suck," he said with a grin. "Problem solved."

～

STROLLING OVER TO UNCOMMON GROUNDS, the campus coffee shop, later that day, Ethan pulled together the perfect plan to raise the subject of a serious relationship with Sam.

He'd ask her if she'd like to go to the annual Founder's Day Parade and Fair two weeks from Saturday and then catch dinner and a movie in Carlyle afterward. A lot of handholding, a little ice-cream sharing, very subtle romance. Then when the moment was right, he'd bring up the idea of an exclusive arrangement.

What he didn't have a plan for was what to do about their relationship while he was interim. Or, what's more, if he went after it and got the permanent position.

Well, at this point he didn't know if she would say yes. He'd cross that bridge when he came to it.

The little bell jingled when he opened the door and stepped inside the welcoming cool of the AC. Spotting the subject of his musings standing in line, he couldn't stop the grin that spread across his face.

She juggled a tote bag, a handbag, and a smartphone. Her fiery red hair was in an intricate braid, and the silky white blouse and navy pencil skirt hugged her subtle curves. Sensible flats graced her feet.

He stepped up behind her and whispered in her ear, "Just who I was looking for."

She gasped and turned toward his mouth, and he quickly leaned in to take advantage, pressing a kiss to those lovely lips. She swayed toward him for the briefest moment, before remembering their public surroundings.

"You were looking for me?"

"Yeah. That, and a little iced caffeine."

She shrugged her tote bag back up on her shoulder.

"Give me that." He slipped his hand beneath the strap and slid it down her arm then threw it over his shoulder. "Why women carry tote bags and handbags the size of small cars is a mystery to me."

"We have a lot of stuff, and I was coming from my last class."

Next in line, she gave the barista her order then tucked her smartphone into the voluminous bag that served as a purse.

Before the barista could ring up Sam's order, Ethan ordered an iced coffee. "I've got hers as well." Taking a twenty out of his wallet, he handed it to the tattoo-decorated girl.

"You didn't have to buy my coffee."

"I know I didn't."

"But thanks."

After receiving their orders, they proceeded out the door. "Where are you headed?" Ethan asked.

"Back to my office."

"Perfect. I'll walk with you."

A sidewalk wound its way through a particularly lovely section of campus, where moss-covered oaks offered a welcome respite from the hot sun. In spring, the azaleas and dogwoods wore showy flowers, and in fall, the Japanese maples sported leaves in shades of red and purple.

Students sat at picnic tables scattered beneath the trees. Others sat on the ground, computers in their laps, while still others used their backpacks as pillows and stretched out for afternoon naps.

Ethan loved the energy of the campus. The debates, the intellectual discourse. And, spying a couple nuzzling one another behind a giant live oak, the romance.

He glanced over at Sam. "What are you doing on August twenty-fifth?"

A frown creased her brow. "Why? What's August twenty-fifth?"

"It's Sterling's Founder's Day. There's a parade followed by a fair with food and craft vendors. It's a pretty big deal."

"A big deal, huh?" She smiled at him, and his heart stuttered in his chest. He'd never grow tired of that smile. The way her green eyes sparkled. The dimples he wanted to kiss. "Well, then I guess I'd better go."

"Yeah. You don't want to be labeled a pariah by the locals for failing to pay tribute to our benefactors."

"No. I wouldn't want that." She tucked an errant lock of hair behind her ear. "But who would I go with?" she asked with a wry grin.

"Hmm. That's a good question." He tapped his chin with his finger. "I suppose I could take you. You know, to save you from the scorn."

She nodded, her expression serious. "A selfless deed then?"

He shrugged. "I'm nothing if not selfless."

"Then I accept. After all, I wouldn't want your noble sacrifice to go unappreciated."

"Thank you." He gave her a shoulder bump. "And if I'm not mistaken, Dr. Love, you're flirting with me."

"I don't flirt."

"If you say so."

GIVING instructions to her new graduate assistant, Lisa Reynolds, Sam handed her a stack of student papers. "I'll need the grades entered by tomorrow, noon."

"No problem," Lisa said, then gathered her backpack. "Anything else?"

"Not at the moment."

"See you tomorrow then."

What a relief to finally have a new assistant. Now maybe she could get caught up.

Her phone buzzed with an incoming text.

GOOD MORNING, DR. LOVE. I HOPE YOU SLEPT WELL.

Sam snorted. He knew very well how she'd slept.

I GOT VERY LITTLE SLEEP.

Momentarily, her phone buzzed again.

COMPLAINING?

She smiled as she thumbed her response.

NO, BUT I NEARLY FELL ASLEEP DURING MY OWN LECTURE.

Seconds later.

IT'S NOT MY FAULT YOUR TOPIC IS BORING.

"Humph."

YOU MUST BE CONFUSING MY LECTURE WITH YOURS.

His reply arrived shortly.

OUCH! HOW ABOUT LUNCH LATER? YOU CAN PULL THE KNIFE FROM MY HEART.

Smiling, she contemplated her reply. She'd like to go, but . . .

Can't. I'm meeting with a student. See a doctor about that knife wound.

She waited, wondering if she'd really hurt his feelings. Her phone buzzed.

There's nothing to cure what ails me. I'll call you later. XOXO

She stared at her phone, a no-doubt goofy smile on her face.

Okay, enough of that. She had a backlog of blood samples to run through her assay. Setting aside her phone, she rounded her desk and headed for her lab. Word had spread, and every unattached female, and a few attached ones, were flocking to her lab to sign up for her study. Most were disappointed to learn they wouldn't get the results until the study was closed, and only if their match had also agreed.

But given the recent influx, she'd reached her enrollment goal for females, and she only needed a few more men. Then, she could close the study, and run the final data analysis. With Sterling's access to a super-computing facility in Atlanta, the number-crunching wouldn't take long. The program had already been written and tested.

When she got to her lab, she noticed that the results from her latest batch had popped up on her computer screen. Pulling the code key, she began running the data to match it to the questionnaires. Of the twenty new blood tests she'd run against the existing database, two were matches.

And she recognized one of the identifiers: Subject 7645. Ethan Quinn.

~

"Are the rumors true?" Melinda asked Ethan as soon as he walked into the office from his meeting with the dean. The provost agreed to the interim dean appointment and strongly encouraged Ethan to put his name in for the permanent position.

He frowned, thinking she was talking about him and Sam. "What rumors?"

Handing him his mail, she leaned forward and whispered, "Dr. Cosgrove is retiring and you're going to be dean."

No matter how hard you tried, there was no such thing as secrets in academia.

"I don't know what you're talking about," Ethan lied, as he shuffled through his stack of mail.

"So, it *is* true."

At his lifted brow, she smirked. "You don't lie very well."

Melinda had been with him too long. "Come into my office."

She rose with alacrity and followed him into his office, shutting the door behind her.

He tossed his mail onto his desk then perched a hip against it. "Dr. Cosgrove is retiring. I have been asked to take over as interim until the search for a new dean is completed."

She rubbed her hands together in delight. "And you're applying, right?"

Ethan sighed. The woman was irrepressible. "Yes."

"Yes!" she said, with a fist-pump.

"Now, don't get the cart before the horse. I'm not a shoe-in."

"I beg to differ. I'd be willing to bet—"

He groaned. "Don't tell me there's another pool."

"No. Not yet, anyway," she said with a grin.

"Look, I'd appreciate it if you'd keep this between us."

"You know me better than that." She drew herself up, clearly affronted. "I may like to listen to the gossip, but I don't participate."

Sighing, he rubbed his face. "I know."

She turned and headed for the door, but stopped short, her hand on the knob. "What happens to your relationship with Dr. Love if you become dean?"

Good question. Too bad he didn't have an answer.

STILL REELING from her latest results, Sam headed out her front door for a much-needed run. She craved the distraction, not to mention the endorphins. Escaping campus as soon as her meeting was over, she'd avoided bumping into Ethan.

Ethan was the first person in her database to have a duplicate match. Of course, it was bound to happen. People are compatible with more than one person, right? A widower finds companionship again after his first wife dies. It's a wonder this is the first double-match.

But why Ethan? And Jackie Ledbetter, of all people! And why did she care? She didn't even want to be his match. She didn't want *any* match. Right? Right.

Picking up her pace, she ran up a hill toward a nature path she'd discovered last week. The peace and solitude of the woods would do her good.

"Jesus!" A squirrel darted in front of her, startling her.

This whole thing with Ethan had been ridiculous from the start. Him and his romance. Well, he could romance Jackie Ledbetter. She seemed willing enough.

She'd let the ever-charming Ethan Quinn get into her head, not to mention her bed. He'd helped her discover her passionate side, but he'd also become a colossal distraction. And one she could ill-afford right now.

It was time to put the brakes on and refocus her energies on her work. Her career, her professional reputation, were more important than a fling with a sexy colleague.

LATER THAT AFTERNOON, relaxed after her run and confident in her decision, Sam stood in line at the Piggly Wiggly, unloading her shopping basket when she heard her name.

"And he spent the whole night at her house the night of that big storm."

"Oh. No. He. Didn't!"

"Oh. Yes. He. Did! Marjorie Snyder saw him cutting up downed limbs the next morning. *After* seeing his car there all night."

One line over, two clerical assistants from her college gossiped over their grocery carts.

"I bet thunder wasn't the only thing rattling the house."

"And you know who her parents are?"

The other girl snickered. "The *Love* Doctors."

"No wonder he's sniffing around her. She probably knows her way around in the bedroom."

More giggling.

Sam felt sick. So much for the endorphins. Cortisol flooded her system as they continued their gossip.

"Well, I saw them in the faculty parking lot the other day, and the body language—let me tell you, she is all into him."

"And I heard he'd invited her to his momma's house."

"And you know what that means . . . no Southern gentleman brings a girl home to momma unless it's serious."

"Uh-huh. You got that right."

"'Course, what did you expect, after Melinda Wilson won that pool?"

A pool? What kind of pool? A swimming pool? What did that have to do with her and Ethan?

"She figured he'd be the first to take her out. After years as his assistant, seems to me that's what you'd call a sure thing."

"She won a boatload of money, too!"

A betting pool? There'd been a betting *pool over* her? Her blood began to boil. Was he in on the pool? Was this all just a game to him?

One of the women giggled. "I wonder if there was a bet on how long before he slept with her."

What the—

"Didn't take long," the other woman responded.

Sam gasped.

"Ma'am? Ma'am?"

Sam realized the clerk was talking to her. "I'm sorry?"

"That'll be $45.56."

"Right."

Ethan Quinn, you're dead meat.

11

"I really need to get a housekeeper," Ethan muttered to himself as he ran the vacuum over the carpet. He'd sent Sam a text earlier asking her to dinner at his place, and although she hadn't texted back yet, he got a jump on making his home presentable. He'd paid special attention to his bedroom and bath. Clean sheets and towels, a candle on the side of the big soaker tub he never used. Maybe that would change tonight.

He'd run out to the store later for a couple of steaks, a nice bottle of Merlot, maybe run by Connie's Confectionaire for dessert.

He'd been spending a lot of time at Sam's place, but he wanted her in his home, in his bed. Maybe the caveman in him wanted to show her he could provide the basic human needs: food, shelter, and romance.

Putting away the vacuum, he couldn't recall having been happier.

Sam could be prickly, sure. Especially when she retreated behind that reserved professional guise. But he'd seen her open and warm, laughing, those green eyes sparkling like emeralds. He'd also seen her scared and vulnerable, like the night of the storm. No, Sam may come off as aloof to people who didn't know her, but the woman behind the façade was anything but.

SAM KNOCKED on Ethan's front door, steam escaping from her ears.

The door flew open. "Sam! You're a little early for dinner." A smile lit his face, but it quickly turned to a frown when he read her facial expression.

"I need to talk to you."

Ethan had on workout shorts that hung low on his hips and a holey T-shirt that read LIT HAPPENS. Dammit, why did he have to look sexy no matter what he wore? *Focus.*

"Sounds serious. Come in."

Although this was the first time in his house, she put her curiosity on hold as she tore into him. "Was this all just a game to you?"

"What are you talking about?"

"Do you go around romancing every new female professor on campus, betting you'll be the first to go out with her. To *sleep* with her?"

"Whoa." He raised his hands. "Wait a minute. Are you talking about the pool?"

"Damn right, I am." She poked him in his chest. *Ow.* His very hard chest. "How could you? How could you make me think you were Mr. Romance, when really, all you are is Mr. Get-In-My-Pants? How dare you?"

"Sam, I wasn't involved in that pool. I didn't start it, I didn't put my name in it, and I certainly didn't put any money in it."

He took her by the shoulders and leveled her with a look. "Sam, I can't control what other people do. I don't deserve the blame for someone else's actions. I'm sorry I didn't tell you about it, though. I should have."

She pulled free and paced into his living room, her nerves humming with anger and frustration.

"Did you know we're the subject of gossip?"

From the look on his face, he did. "Sam, when you work and live in a small college town, gossip is part of the package."

She pointed in the direction of the grocery store. "I was standing in line at the Piggly Wiggly, my name being bandied about like some town slut." Tears clogged her throat. She would not cry. "My personal and professional reputations are of utmost importance to me. Professionally, I've had to work hard to separate myself, and my work, from that of my parents. And given my chosen field, I often have to defend myself to skeptics who don't take my science seriously."

"Sam—"

She held up her index finger. "I'm not done. Personally, because first boys, and then *grown* men, assumed I was loose, I've strived to maintain an impeccable reputation, seeking to avoid adding fuel to the fire. Even with my carefully protected reputation, I still deal with the snide remarks about my parents' work and my own sexuality."

Ethan stepped into her, settling his hands at her waist, making it difficult for her to continue her tirade. "Sam, people only gossip when you're behaving as if you've got something to hide. So, let's come out of the closet. Take our relationship public. That will stop the gossip mill."

"I don't want a relationship with you." She threw her hands up in the air. "What else do you want me to say? I don't really see the point anyway, Ethan. If you become dean, we *can't* have a relationship . . . unless I leave, and while Sterling is just a stopover in my career, I'm not willing to sacrifice my career for the sake of yours."

ETHAN RUBBED HIS CHEST, where it felt as if he'd been kicked by a horse. Taking a mental step back, he searched her face, and what he saw there was fear. Putting his hurt aside, he approached her again. "Sam, where is this coming from? Why do you keep retreating behind this wall of fear?"

"Where is what coming from? I've been trying to tell you all along that I didn't want this, but you were bound and determined to prove me wrong."

"I wasn't trying to prove anything."

"Weren't you?" She narrowed her eyes, which currently spit green sparks. "You saw me, and my science, as a challenge. Not something to be respected, but something to be refuted. I can't be with someone who doesn't respect me, or my work."

Okay, that was a low blow. He held up his index finger to make his point. "I never once said I didn't respect you or your work. I may not agree with your theories, but disagreement doesn't equate to disrespect."

She folded her arms across her chest and turned her back to him.

Closing the mile-wide gap between them, he placed his hands on her shoulders. "Sam, tell me what's holding you back. Tell me what you're so afraid of."

Shrugging off his hands, she said, "Nothing. I'm not afraid of anything. I don't want a relationship with you, or with anyone, for that matter. Why can't you understand that?" She stalked over to his door, yanking it open. "I'm asking you to please just leave me alone."

Walking through the front door, and out of his life, Sam closed the barrier between them with a final soft click.

Ethan stood in the middle of his living room wondering what the hell had just happened. He'd gone from happiness to despair in the time it took to boil an egg.

He released a mirthless laugh. "Well, guess that solved the nepotism issue."

TWO WEEKS after Sam broke up with him, Ethan dropped into his desk chair and scrubbed a hand over his face. He should be elated. He'd at least attained an interim dean position. But instead, he just felt empty. Not only did he not have someone to share in his accomplishment, the accomplishment itself had lost its appeal.

He'd done it again. Placed his heart in the hands of a woman who had no intention of staying in Sterling. No intention of putting down roots.

He'd seen Sam from across the parking lot that morning, gathering her things from the backseat of her POS car before heading into the building. She'd never once looked in his direction. Either she didn't see him, or she was ignoring him.

Melanie entered, a stack of messages in her hand. "Congratulations, Dean Quinn—"

"Interim," he corrected.

She shrugged. "That's only temporary." She frowned. "What's wrong? I thought you'd be . . . I don't know, happier?"

"Nothing. Just a lot on my mind."

"Like Dr. Love?"

He held back a retort. "No. That's . . . over. And I sure as hell hope there was no pool for that."

Melanie crossed her arms over her chest, her mouth a thin line. "Should I arrange for the movers?"

"No. I'll stay put until the search for a permanent dean is concluded."

"But—"

"No. I don't want to move twice if I don't have to." And now he wasn't even sure he wanted the job.

"Suit yourself then." She turned to leave then stopped before she reached the door. "I'm sorry about Sam."

No sorrier than he.

SAM HAD FINALLY RECEIVED some good news: The patent application had been granted. Now the university could finalize the license deal with SoulMates.com.

The final study data was remarkable actually. She'd received a voice message from the company CEO to give him a call. Probably just wanted to talk about the deal, maybe offer some words of congratulation.

She'd moped around long enough. It was time to get her head back in the game and focus not only on the TED Talk she'd been asked to give but on her latest theory. Clearly, Ethan's double-match indicated her test was not infallible, but she had some ideas for refining the testing.

Taking a deep, calming breath, she picked up the phone on her desk and dialed Perry Childers, SoulMates.com's CEO.

"This is Perry."

She was momentarily dumbstruck. She'd expected an assistant, not the man himself.

"Hello?"

"Oh, Mr. Childers, this is Dr. Love. I'm returning your call."

"Dr. Love. What a fortuitous name. Thank you for calling me back. I'll get straight to it. I love your assay—no pun intended—I'm impressed with the results of your study, and I'd like to make you my VP of Research."

If she could see her expression right now, she knew it would be one of shock and awe.

"Dr. Love? You there?"

"Um, yes. Yes, I'm here. Sorry, I . . . Well, I wasn't expecting that." She pressed her hand to her stomach, hoping to calm the riot of butterflies there.

"I'd love to fly you out. First class, of course. Take you on a tour of our campus, show you what we have to offer. What do you say?"

She scrubbed at the lines she knew were forming on her forehead. What did she have to lose? "I . . . Sure. That would be wonderful."

"Great. I'll have my assistant, Isabel, contact you with a detailed itinerary."

"Thank you, Mr. Childers."

"I look forward to meeting you. And, please, call me Perry."

GRABBING a to-go lunch from Ruby's, Ethan saw Delaney at a booth with some other professors from her department. Approaching the table, he nodded to everyone.

"Hi, Ethan." Delaney offered him a sad smile. *Great. Just what he needed—sympathy from the jilter's best friend.*

"Can I talk to you a minute?"

"Um, sure." Delaney rose from the table and followed him over to a quieter corner of the diner.

"Have you seen Sam? I've been looking all over for her, and she's not answering my phone calls or text messages." He really needed to meet with her. He didn't want any awkwardness between them now that he was interim dean. It was important that their previous relationship not affect the morale of the college.

Delaney gnawed on her lower lip, a look of uncertainty on her face. "She didn't tell you?"

His gut clinched. "Tell me what?"

"Sam is in San Francisco meeting with the online-dating service who licensed her assay about a job."

If she'd told him Sam was getting married, he couldn't have been more shocked. When Sam had said Sterling was just a rung on her career ladder, she wasn't kidding. But even so, he didn't expect her to leave so soon. And to leave academia for private industry.

Delaney touched his arm. "You okay?"

"I'm fine." His free hand clenched into a fist. Some time in the gym with Nash and a punching bag was in order.

Delaney's concerned gaze made him uncomfortable. "I've got to run to a meeting." He nodded then strode out of the diner, handing off his lunch to a student walking by. "Here. I've lost my appetite."

"Thanks, dude!"

Thunder rumbled overhead as he made his way through town back to campus. Just as he passed beneath the main gates, the clouds opened up. "Sure. Why not," he muttered.

WITH A GLASS of champagne at her elbow, Sam sat back in her luxurious first-class seat and sighed in satisfaction.

She hadn't expected to fall in love with a job, but that was before she'd spent an amazing two days at SoulMates.com's Silicon Valley campus, touring the facilities, which reportedly rivaled that of Google. Employee cafeteria that served only organic, locally-sourced foods. A dry cleaners, medical clinic, hair salon, state-of-the-art fitness center, and daycare right on the grounds.

Perry and his executive team had wined and dined her. They had big plans for her compatibility assay, and for her, if she liked the job. And what wasn't to like?

The research staff who would report to her were top-notch. Her office had a spectacular view of the Santa Clara Valley, and the salary and bonus package were off the charts.

A real-estate agent had shown her some properties in the Bay Area, and with the salary they were offering, she could actually afford them. She'd pay off her student loans, buy a new car . . .

It had all happened so fast.

She hadn't given Perry an answer, telling him she'd like to mull it over, but she was leaning heavily in favor of it.

She'd have to put her place up for sale. Or maybe rent it out. Delaney really liked the place. Maybe she'd take it.

Delaney. She closed her eyes. In her excitement, she didn't think about leaving her best friend. The only one she'd ever had. Delaney had been very excited but also apprehensive and disappointed at the possibility of losing her best friend so soon. But Delaney could always come out to visit, right?

And then there was Ethan.

Who was she kidding? *You broke up with him, remember?* It was the right decision, she told herself for the umpteenth time. Then why did it hurt every time she thought about him?

Even if she wanted a relationship with him, which could never work, of course, he'd never leave Sterling. And a long-distance relationship with the entire continental U.S. between them would never work. And if she stayed, there was the insurmountable nepotism issue.

With time and distance between them, she wondered why she'd said the things she did. Anger? Hurt? Or, as Ethan had said, fear?

Maybe her parents' career moves weren't the only thing to blame for her lack of close friendships. Which circled her thoughts back to Delaney. Could their friendship last, or would they drift apart, phone calls and emails growing more infrequent, until the only communication they had was birthday and Christmas cards?

Her head began to ache, along with her heart, as the initial enthusiasm turned to anxiety, and the pleasure of success turned hollow.

12

───────

Ethan threw a punch at the bag Nash held, catching him unawares and knocking him off balance. Nash replanted his feet. Ethan would have preferred a good old-fashioned brawl without any protective padding– maybe the pain from a well-delivered punch would replace the pain in his chest where his heart used to be before Sam ripped it out and stomped on it. But the last thing Nash needed was to have his brains bouncing around inside his skull like a pinball.

Even so, Nash egged him on, and it didn't take much for Ethan to light into the bag. A few punches later and Nash released the bag and threw up his hands in surrender. "Damn. You trying to give me another concussion?"

Guilt washed over Ethan. "Sorry man."

"What's eating you, anyway?" Nash walked over to the bench where they'd dropped their gym bags.

Ethan followed him over and sat while Nash helped him remove his gloves. "Nothing."

"Bullshit."

Ethan picked up a bottle of Gatorade and guzzled it. Wiping his mouth, he replaced he cap then tossed the empty bottle into the trashcan across from them.

"The last time you hit the bag like that Julie had just left you." Nash narrowed his eyes. "Shit. She didn't?"

Ethan sighed. That's what happened when you'd been friends since grade school. You could read each other's minds.

"Where's she off to?"

"San Francisco." Ethan wiped the sweat off his face and neck with a towel then opened his gym bag for some water.

"Well, hell. Nothing like moving across the country to put a damper on a relationship."

"Even if she wasn't leaving, she said she didn't want a relationship with me." Tossing back the bottle of water, he took several gulps.

"Ouch. Did she say why? Not good-looking enough? Not great in the sack?"

Ethan held up his middle finger. "Asshat."

Nash chuckled and slapped him on the shoulder. "Let's go grab a beer and you can tell me all about it."

THE SUN HAD JUST SET when Sam drove past the Sterling City Limit sign. Releasing a breath, some of the tension gripping her neck and shoulders most of the drive from the Atlanta airport dissipated at the sight of Sterling University's red brick clock tower. Passing the main entrance to campus, she thought about how beautiful the school was. Collegiate gothic buildings surrounded by ancient oaks. In spring, dogwoods, redbuds, and azaleas put on a show. And when she'd arrived last fall, the trees welcomed her with their brilliant red, orange, and yellow foliage.

Look at her waxing poetic. She shook her head. Jet lag.

She thought about the frenetic three-day weekend. Certainly, San Francisco was a city-dweller's paradise. The performing arts, the museums, the food, the diversity. She'd never lack for entertainment. But she'd had all that and more in New York City. How many shows did she go to in the five years she'd lived there? Maybe three. And how often did she visit the Museum of Modern Art or the Whitney? Embarrassed to admit it even to herself, she only visited MOMA once, and she'd never gone to the Whitney Museum.

Driving down tree-lined Main Street, she slowed at the crowd standing outside Ruby's waiting for a table, as usual. And the Bistro Café's outside tables were full despite the heat. Sterling might roll up its sidewalks early during the week, but its citizens flocked to the antique stores, gift shops, boutiques, the bakery, and the restaurants on the weekends.

Her vision blurred as she came to the four-way stop on the corner of Main and First Street. *Damn.* A tear trickled down her cheek and into the corner of her mouth. When did she get so attached to this town? Was it the town, or was it Ethan? Or Delaney? Or maybe all of the above?

Thinking about pulling up even her shallow roots hurt far more than she'd ever expected.

∼

ETHAN GLANCED at the caller ID on his phone. His mom. Guilt poked at him. He'd been avoiding her.

"Mom."

"Ethan? I haven't heard from you. Are you okay?"

"Yeah, Mom. Sorry. I've just been busy."

"The new position?"

"Yeah." And sulking over Sam's breakup and impending departure.

"Why don't you and Sam come over for dinner on Friday? I'll make a big pot of beef stew."

He rubbed his hand over his face. He'd been hoping to avoid this topic, at least until the hole in his chest had mended. In which case he might never speak to his mother again. "Mom, I don't think Sam can make it."

"Oh, well, it doesn't have to be Friday."

He sighed. "Mom, Sam's likely leaving."

"What? Where's she going?"

"She's got a job offer out in California."

This revelation was met with silence.

"Mom?"

"Have you told her how you feel about her? That you love her?"

Love? Did he love Sam? Had it really happened that fast? He rubbed the ache behind his ribs. Yeah. It had happened that fast. "Mom—"

"I saw how you looked at her. And how she looked at you."

"Let's not go there. It's over."

"Maybe if you told her. Maybe she doesn't know—"

"Mom. It won't make a bit of difference. Listen, I'll come pick you up on Friday and take you to that restaurant in Carlyle, the one with the Bananas Foster."

"All right, sweetheart. I love you."

"Love you, too." He hung up the phone. I love you. Three

little words that held so much meaning. And caused so much pain when they were left unspoken.

AFTER A FULL AND busy day on campus, Sam walked into her townhome. Guess there was no need to unpack those boxes in the dining room after all.

Kicking off her shoes, she set her purse, tote bag, and keys on the table in the foyer. Before she could even get a drink of water, her doorbell rang.

She opened the door to find Delaney standing there, hands on her hips, an annoyed expression on her face. "You were supposed to come by my office and tell me about your trip."

Sam opened the door wider, inviting Delaney in. "Sorry. It's been a rough day." She'd told her department chair about the job offer, which had gone over like a lead balloon. He'd been speechless, then cajoling, followed by a dose of annoyance. Guess she couldn't blame him. They'd gone to a great deal of trouble to bring her to Sterling.

Grabbing two diet sodas from the fridge, she handed one to Delaney. They settled in the living room, and Sam described her visit to San Francisco, the SoulMates.com campus in Silicon Valley, and the job offer, minus the salary and bonus numbers.

"I'm happy for you, if it's really what you want, but I can't believe you're leaving. You just got here." Delaney's blue eyes filled.

God, this was hard. Sam swallowed around the lump that had formed in her throat. "It's an offer I'd be crazy to refuse."

"I guess. But—"

Sam's phone rang. Her mother launched into her before she could say hello. "Is it true? Your dad just told me you're moving to San Francisco—"

Wincing, she interrupted, "Hi, Mom, how are you?"

"Don't be fresh with me," her mother reprimanded. "Well, at least you're getting out of that backwater town. But industry? How can you sell out like that?"

Sell out! Sell out? This from a woman who'd made a small fortune on the bestselling couples self-help books she and her father had written.

"Mom, I have a friend over. Can I call you back?"

"A male friend?"

"Bye, Mom." Sam hung up the phone and tossed it onto the couch.

"And what about Ethan?" Delaney flung at her before she'd even recovered from her mother's barrage.

She was getting it from all sides today. "What about Ethan? What's he got to do with this?"

"How can you leave him like this when you're in love with him?"

"Love!" Sam threw up her hands with a mirthless laugh. "Where the hell did that come from?" Her heart beat a staccato against her ribs at the mention of love and Ethan in the same sentence.

"Really, Sam? And Denial is a river in Egypt."

"Denial? I'm not in denial."

Delaney snorted in disgust. "You've heard the phrase, 'physician, heal thyself'? How about 'psychologist, psychoanalyze thyself'? You're in total denial." Delaney rose, stalked over to Sam. "To the point that you're even denying your own research. Your own science."

Sam recoiled from the vehemence in Delaney's words.

"What are you so afraid of?"

That's the second time someone accused her of being afraid. "Nothing." Her voice sounded small. "I'm not afraid."

"You're running away from two people who love you." Delaney said, just above a whisper, as her eyes filled again.

"I'm not running—and Ethan doesn't love me."

"For someone who is supposed to be an expert in 'compatibility,'" she made air quotes around the word, "you don't know shit about love."

"And you do?" Sam threw back.

"Just because I haven't found Mr. Right doesn't mean I don't know how to love." Delaney grabbed her purse and tossed it over her shoulder heading for the door. "At least I don't run away every time things get difficult." Before walking out, she turned. "Just be damn sure this is what you want." She slammed the door so hard the windows rattled.

Stunned by her friend's violent departure, Sam sank back into the sofa. She'd been pissing off a lot of people lately. Why couldn't they see how important her career was to her?

Flopping back on the couch, she threw her arm over her eyes where tears threatened.

The doubts that had plagued her on the flight home returned.

When she'd decided to take the job at Sterling, there had been no doubts. She'd relished the opportunity the offer presented and looked forward to the challenge. This time, not so much. But if she were completely honest with herself, it wasn't just the job.

What are you so afraid of?

Were Ethan and Delaney right? Was she afraid?

Delaney had said she was running away from two people who love her. Did Ethan love her? Even more important, did she love Ethan? She missed him desperately. His laughter, his warmth, his sincerity. The way he made her feel, like she was the center of his universe. No one had ever made her feel so special.

And how had she repaid him? By accusing him of playing her, of disrespecting her and her work.

Wrapping her arms around herself, she buried her face in a pillow and cried. This pain and regret could only mean one thing—she was in love with Ethan Quinn.

EARLY THE FOLLOWING SATURDAY MORNING, Sam closed the lid on the last box. Looking around her now-empty lab, she breathed a sigh of relief. Done. The study was completed and she'd be moving next week. She laid the folder holding the final results on top of the box.

A lot had happened in the week since her visit to the SoulMates.com campus.

A few days after she'd told her department chair about the job offer, he'd called her into his office and offered her the moon to stay. Fast-track to tenure, an associate professor position immediately, more money, and even more importantly, a bigger lab.

She didn't tell him that she'd already made up her mind. About a lot of things.

Glancing at the results folder, she gnawed on her lip. She had several couples in the town and surrounding areas that she needed to inform, and she'd had another double-match. Jackie Ledbetter. One with Ethan, and another with Irwin Dumwilder, a nerdy physics professor, *a la* Sheldon Cooper. But there was one person she needed to give the results to first.

Setting the box on the moving cart, she picked up the

folder and, flipping off the lights, headed for downtown Sterling. She had a parade to attend.

THE STERLING VOLUNTEER FIRE DEPARTMENT threw candy to screaming kids from atop their fire truck, as Ethan walked along the parade route looking for a vantage point.

The Founder's Day Parade was in full swing by the time he got there. A blazing sun beat down on the parade-goers and turned ice cream cones into puddles of milk on the sidewalk.

Alone at the parade; this is not how Ethan had envisioned the day. He hadn't seen Sam at all, not even around campus. She was probably looking for a place to live in California.

He waved to Melanie and her husband then spotted Delaney standing on the corner, a ball cap pulled low over her eyes. He scanned the crowd thinking maybe Sam was with her, but there was no sign of her.

Give it up, man. She's moving on.

"Hi, Ethan!"

Gazing down, he saw Jackie Ledbetter's son. "Hi, Jack."

Where he was, his mom was sure to follow. A hand touched his arm from behind. "Why, Ethan! I wondered where you've been."

Yep. Jackie.

"Just been busy."

"I heard! A big congrats on the new job! Dean!"

"Interim," Ethan muttered.

The Sterling Equestrian Society cantered down Main Street.

"I can't see!" Jack hollered.

"Oh, Ethan, would you mind?" Jackie asked, her hand on his chest.

Ethan stepped back from her touch. "Sure." Leaning down, he lifted Jack onto his shoulders so he could see.

"Cool!" Jack said.

Jackie stepped closer, standing on tiptoes and leaning against Ethan for support. *Holy hell.*

"Isn't this fun?" Jackie giggled. "And maybe we can get some ice cream after the parade."

"Yeah!" Jack agreed.

"Sure." *Juuust shoot me.* No. This day was not turning out at all liked he'd planned.

∾

SAM COULDN'T BELIEVE the crowd on Main Street. Ethan wasn't kidding when he'd said Founder's Day was a big deal. Red, white, and blue bunting decorated businesses, and the town's flag flew from the Victorian light posts lining the street.

The high school marching band played a Sousa march off key, while the cheerleaders waved their pompoms. Small Town, U.S.A.

Searching the crowd, she spotted a little boy, head and shoulders above everyone. The man who held him turned, and Sam's knees quivered. Ethan. And he was standing next to Jackie.

Jealousy, hot and sharp, knifed through her. Didn't take him long to get over her, she thought.

Feeling a little sick, she stopped and leaned against a light post. So much for her plan. She glanced down at the folder in her hand, tempted to toss it onto the overflowing trash can.

Turning, she headed back toward Ruby's. Her head hurt, and she could use some of Ruby's sweet iced tea.

With the parade in full swing, the diner only had a few patrons who'd given up on the heat and sought cooler climes. Taking a seat at the lunch counter, Sam dropped the folder onto the countertop and ordered her drink.

What did she expect? She'd broken up with Ethan. Of course he'd moved on. And with his other match. Made perfect sense.

That didn't make it any easier to take. She'd been such an idiot. She'd denied her own science, refusing to accept that Ethan was her histocompatible mate. But more than that—refusing to believe in love, when she'd clearly fallen helplessly in love with Ethan.

Taking a gulp of her iced tea, she relished the cool, soothing liquid. Then she pressed the glass to her cheek.

The bell over Ruby's door chimed, and someone sat in the empty seat next to her.

Turning, she gasped when she saw Ethan. Glancing behind him, she didn't see Jackie or her little boy.

"Hi," Ethan said.

"Hi," she breathed. God, how she'd missed him.

She slid the folder over to him. It's now or never. And he deserves to know.

"What's this?" Picking up the folder, he looked at her.

"Your results."

"My results from the love assay?"

She didn't bother to correct him this time. "Uh-huh."

"May I?"

"Of course. You said you wanted to know the results." She held her breath as he opened the file.

He stared at the paper with his two matches, saying nothing.

"You have . . ." She cleared her throat and continued, "You have two matches."

"Is that even possible?"

"It's not *impossible*, obviously."

Still nothing but a blank expression on his face. Well, she'd done what she needed to do. Throwing a five on the counter, she rose from her seat.

"Wait." He put his hand on her arm, and her skin tingled like she'd touched a live wire. "You mean to tell me you and I are a match?"

"And you and Jackie."

"And you've known you and I were a match since . . . when?"

Taking a deep breath, she replied, "Since July twenty-eighth." He still didn't mention his match to Jackie.

"You and Jackie are a match, too," she repeated. She would understand if he chose Jackie. *But it would still kill me.*

"Well, there would have been no contest." He waved his hand in the air as if it were a foregone conclusion.

No contest? What did that mean?

"You decide to give me this now, when you're leaving?" he continued, anger coloring his tone.

"You asked me what I was so afraid of." She blinked back tears. "Being wrong." She drew in a deep breath. "I was afraid of being wrong." A mirthless laugh escaped. "And, God, I've been wrong about so many things. And this job is just the latest."

"What other . . . things have you been wrong about, Dr. Love?" He set his hands on either side of her barstool, and her breath shallowed as his warm brown eyes searched hers.

"Relationships. Romance." She licked her dry lips. "Love."

"Love? Are you saying . . . ?"

"Yes. I'm saying I believe in romance now. And love."

He lifted a brow.

"My whole career I've denied the existence of love. That it's our chemistry, not our hearts, that determine who our best mates are. How could I admit that everything I'd built my professional life on was wrong?"

"Sam, your relationship theories and mine are not mutually exclusive."

"But, you said—"

"I know. I said I didn't agree with your theories. But what if we're both right? What if long, happy relationships are part chemistry, part romance? It's the chemistry that brings two people together. But it's the romance, along with mutual respect and love, that *keeps* them together."

His face blurred as her eyes filled. "I love you, Ethan."

"Did I just hear you say the 'L' word?" he asked, his voice incredulous.

"Do I need to say it again? I love you, Ethan, but I understand if you don't feel the same, especially after the way I've behaved . . . the things I've said." She held her breath, waiting.

His eyes softened, and his gaze moved to her mouth, then back up to her eyes, as his thumb captured the tear that rolled down her cheek. "I love you, too, Sam."

He loved her! She closed her eyes, and more tears spilled over.

"But, what about San Francisco?" Ethan asked, his voice rough with emotion.

"I turned them down. I'm not leaving."

"But—"

"I don't belong in industry. I belong in academia. I don't belong in San Francisco. I belong right here in Sterling." Closing her eyes, she drew in a deep breath, then opened them and looked into Ethan's warm brown eyes. "And according to our chemistry, I belong with you, if you'll still have me."

"Dr. Love, that's the most romantic thing you've ever said to me."

EPILOGUE

A month later, Sam walked into the main administration building for an appointment with the Provost, Dr. Chamberlain. Smoothing her skirt and adjusting the sleeves of her jacket, she gnawed on her lip. She and Ethan were finally being called on the carpet for their relationship.

Ethan's offer letter for the dean of the College of Arts and Sciences was on hold until the nepotism issue was resolved. She didn't want to leave Sterling, but she'd been secretly researching positions with universities in Atlanta and Athens. She could get an apartment and commute home to Sterling on the weekends. Not ideal, but she and Ethan could make it work if it meant the deanship he had worked so hard to achieve.

Drawing in a deep, calming breath, she approached the provost's receptionist. "I'm Dr. Love. I have a two o'clock meeting with Dr. Chamberlain."

"Right this way, Dr. Love."

She followed the young woman down the carpeted hallway and waited for her to announce her arrival to the provost. Sam halted in the doorway when she saw Ethan. How humiliating. The two of them called into the provost's office like two high-school kids called to the principal's office for kissing in the hallway. Ethan nervously wiped his hands on his pants.

Oh boy. Not good. Not good at all.

"Dr. Love," Dr. Chamberlain said, as he stepped forward. "Thank you for meeting with me today."

Like she had a choice. "My pleasure."

"Please, have a seat."

Unsure what to do—sit next to Ethan on the sofa or take a seat in the chair—she finally opted for the chair.

Ethan cast a confused glance at her, and she subtly shook her head.

"So," Dr. Chamberlain clapped his hands together, taking a seat across from them, "I understand the two of you are a couple."

Sam and Ethan answered together, "Yes."

"And Dr. Quinn is the final candidate for the dean of your college, if we can eliminate the nepotism issue. Otherwise . . ." Dr. Chamberlain shook his head, "we may need to hire the runner-up candidate."

Sam shot a look at Ethan, licked her dry lips, then spoke, "Dr. Chamberlain, I am prepared to—"

"If I may interrupt you," Dr. Chamberlain said, hand raised. "I believe I may have a solution."

Confused, she turned to Ethan. "The only solution I see is my departure from the university."

Ethan sprang to his feet. "No!"

"Now, Dr. Love, let's not be hasty. I think I have another possible solution. You see, we have two other couples in the university whose relationships raised similar issues. I convinced the university trustees that we could resolve the situation by permitting the reporting employee to report directly to me, thus bypassing the issue of reporting to his or her spouse."

Sam felt a glimmer of hope. Maybe she wouldn't have to leave Sterling.

"Of course," Dr. Chamberlain continued, "those couples were married, so there is a critical distinction between their circumstances and yours. I'm not sure I could persuade them to agree under the current circumstances," his voice trailed off.

"But if we were married," Ethan filled the silence, "that would solve the problem."

"Yes. I think it's safe to say that the trustees would accept the change in your reporting structure if you were married."

Coercing Ethan into marriage? No, this would not do. She would resign before she backed Ethan into that kind of corner.

Before she could speak her mind, Ethan walked over and took her hand. Dropping to one knee, he pulled a little turquoise box from his pocket and held it out to her.

Sam didn't know what to think. Pressing a shaking hand to her mouth, she looked over to see Dr. Chamberlain grinning from ear to ear. This had been a setup!

"Samantha, I've waited my whole life for you. Please say you'll be my wife so I can spend the rest of my life making you happy." Opening the box, he presented her with a brilliant pear-shaped diamond ring.

She laughed, and tears spilled down her cheeks. "How can I refuse my perfect histocompatible mate?"

REBECCA HEFLIN

She's benched
her heart.

His is on
injured reserve.

Winning Dr. Wentworth

WINNING DR. WENTWORTH

Copyright © 2017. All rights reserved.

REBECCA HEFLIN

Cover Design by The Killion Group, Inc.

This book is a work of fiction. The names, characters, places, and incidents are the products of the author's imagination or are used fictitiously. Any resemblance to actual events, business establishments, locales, or persons, living or dead, is entirely coincidental.

All rights reserved. No part of this publication may be reproduced, stored in a retrieval system, or transmitted in any form or by any means (electronic, mechanical, photocopying, recording, or otherwise) without the prior written permission of both the copyright owner and the publisher. The only exception is brief quotations in printed reviews.

The scanning, uploading, and distribution of this book via the Internet or via any other means without the permission of the publisher is illegal and punishable by law. Please purchase only authorized electronic editions, and do not participate in or encourage electronic piracy of copyrighted materials.

Your support of the author's rights is appreciated.

Published in the United States of America by:

Rebecca Heflin Books, LLC

www.RebeccaHeflin.com

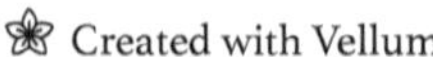 Created with Vellum

ACKNOWLEDGMENTS

As always, I must thank my beta readers, Yvonne, and my hubby Ron. Thank you for your continued guidance, patience, and support.

I also owe a big thanks to Will Pantages for his insight into the world of sports statistics. Any error in my portrayal of sports analytics is my own.

And to my editor, Paul, thank you once again for catching and correcting my errors. I couldn't publish my stories without your keen eye.

"Boys love football, girls love football players,
and some girls love football and football players."

– Unknown

1

---

urphy's Law ruled her life.

Shelby Wentworth tossed her backpack across the console onto the passenger seat of her car then dropped into the driver's seat and slammed the door shut. Closing her eyes, she took a deep, cleansing breath. At least, she *tried* to take a deep breath. After the contentious conversation with her ex-husband, the pain in her chest made it difficult to breathe.

Would she ever be able to leave the past behind and focus on rebuilding her career? Her life?

Pressing a hand to her sternum, she counted to five as she inhaled, held her breath for another five-count, then exhaled. The breathing exercise slowed her racing heart and calmed her. "That's better," she murmured.

Starting the car, she threw it into reverse and backed out of her spot in Sterling University's faculty parking lot.

And right into a solid object.

The sickening *crunch* set her heart racing at warp speed this time.

Glancing behind her in horror, all she saw was a big gray behemoth.

With trembling hands, she put the car in park and jumped out to find a late-model dark gray Suburban, it's rear passenger-side fender crumpled, but little damage otherwise. Her old Honda Civic, on the other hand, hadn't stood a chance against the tank she'd backed into. The trunk was crumpled, and her bumper hung off the passenger side in a lopsided grimace.

Out of the corner of her eye, she saw a tall, athletic man stride around the back of the SUV.

Fear swamped her, and she covered her mouth with both hands. "Oh my god, I'm so sorry! Are you okay?" Bracing herself for the tirade, she backed away from him, holding her hands out in front of her.

"No harm done."

What? That's it. No yelling? No name-calling? No threats?

He adjusted his red Sterling Bobcats ball cap, leaning down to assess the situation then scratched his chin and stood up. "Okay. Maybe a little harm done," he said with an easy smile. "Question is, are you okay?" He removed the aviator sunglasses he wore and directed his concerned gaze right at her.

"Nash?" The instant she saw those electric blue eyes, she recognized him. Butterflies took flight in her stomach, and not from fear this time.

He'd been powerfully built in high school, but that had been just a preview to the powerfully built man he would become. And although he'd left the NFL, he hadn't lost his quarterback build. The son for former NFL quarterback, Carl Taylor, Nash had been destined for greatness.

They hadn't seen each other since the day they'd gradu-ated high school. But, despite her broken heart, she'd secretly followed both his college and pro football careers.

She'd been watching the day of the NFL draft, five years earlier, when the Denver Broncos called his name and he'd gone down on one knee and proposed to his college sweet-heart, Stephanie Cummings, further adding to her heartbreak.

She'd also been watching the Broncos versus the Raiders the day he'd taken the hit that had ended his career.

And finally, she'd witnessed the press conference when Nash Taylor stood, tears in his eyes, as he gave up the sport he loved at the young age of twenty-seven, his beauty-queen wife noticeably absent.

It wasn't long after that news of their divorce hit the headlines.

"Shelby?" he asked, his surprise evident in his expression.

"You remember me?" she couldn't help asking.

"Of course." He frowned. "Why wouldn't I remember you? We were best friends back in the day."

Were being the operative term.

A flush crept up her neck and into her face as she recalled her first kiss in the backseat of their best friend's car. But the flush turned to heartache at the memory of Nash's later betrayal.

"I thought your mom moved. Are you here visiting the university?" he asked.

"No. I, uh, I took an assistant professor position in the College of Arts and Sciences." A step down for her, but she'd been lucky to get even *that*. She toed a piece of her car's bumper that had fallen off in the collision.

"No kidding?" He rocked back on his heels. "How long have you been back?"

"I moved two weeks ago. I'm surprised I haven't seen you before now." She knew he'd moved back to his hometown of Sterling after he'd left the NFL and became the head coach of the newly formed Bobcats football team. It was the one of the reasons she'd hesitated in taking a job she'd so desperately needed. Being in the same town—and a small one at that—as Nash would be a constant reminder that she'd never really gotten over her high school crush.

"I've been . . . out of town." He shoved his hands into the front pockets of his jeans.

"Oh." She nodded as if she understood, but really she didn't. Clearly there was more to that statement. An awkward silence fell.

"Look, I know the new police chief. Let me give him a call so we'll have a report for the insurance companies." He pulled a smartphone from his back pocket.

"Oh, but—" She'd really rather just pay for the damage than deal with the insurance . . . and have them raise her already-too-high rate. "Can we just handle it between ourselves? Of course I'll pay for the repairs."

"You sure about that?" He paused in tapping out the number.

"Yeah." A nervous laugh escaped. She'd just add it to the long list of bills she currently struggled to pay. Maybe Nash would take it in installments for old times' sake. "Why deal with all that paperwork?"

"I can't let you do that."

~

SHELBY WRAPPED her arms around herself, the body

language unmistakable. She nodded. "I'll get my insurance information." She turned back to her car.

"No. I mean I can't let you pay out of pocket. And don't worry about the insurance. The deductible is probably more than what it would cost to repair the damage." He could think of a better way for her to repay him. "How about you buy me dinner instead and we'll call it even?"

She looked good, Nash thought. Better than good. The pretty tomboy had grown into a beautiful woman. She'd cut the long, light brown hair that as a teenager she'd worn almost exclusively in a ponytail, so that it just touched her shoulders, and she'd filled out in all the right places.

The shy smile was still there, although he didn't miss the sadness in her amber eyes. Or the fear when he'd first approached her.

"What?" Confusion skittered across her face.

No surprise there, considering he was just as confused by his offer as she was.

He grinned. "You know, the meal you have at the end of the day? In the South we call it supper, in case you've forgotten."

She'd lost some of that innocence he'd found so appealing so many years ago. Along with her accent. Guess that's what happened when you received an Ivy League education.

She looked away and then back at him. Her eyes narrowed. "I just nailed the back end of your car, and you want me to have dinner with you?"

He had an all-consuming urge to gather her in and hold her close until the tension in her shoulders, and the sadness and fear in her eyes, retreated. But he doubted she would accept his sympathy. After they'd both left for college, he'd tried to hold onto their friendship despite the distance, but she never answered his emails or phone calls.

He knew he'd hurt her in high school when he took Leandra Lucas to prom instead of her, but he'd made a promise to a friend, and he didn't break promises.

"Yeah, why not? Catch up. It's been, what, eleven years since I saw you?" The day they'd graduated in fact. Him with decent grades and a football scholarship, and her as class Valedictorian. She'd headed off to Brown University for an accelerated program in mathematics the following week, and he hadn't laid eyes on her since. Not even for their ten-year reunion last year.

She bit her lower lip then drew it into her mouth, and his eyes locked on like a heat-seeking missile. The memory of the sweet, hot kiss they'd shared in the back seat of Ethan's 1993 Ford Mustang assaulted him.

"I don't think that's a good idea."

She was probably right. He just nodded. Clearly, she hadn't forgiven him for what he'd done. Not that he could really blame her. He should have been upfront with her then. She would have understood. Maybe.

"I should probably give you my number so you can get me the repair bills for your car if you change your mind," she said, returning his attention to the present.

"Right." She stepped close and a light, clean scent tickled his nose. Like lemons, only sweeter. He tapped the number into his phone as she rattled it off to him, all the while wondering whether she wore perfume or if it was her shampoo. "But I won't. Change my mind, I mean."

"Okay. Well. Again, I'm really sorry about . . ." Her voice trailed off as she indicated the fender-bender.

"It's just a car. Nobody got hurt, and that's the important thing."

"I'll see you around." Shelby rounded her car and climbed into the open driver's side.

Realizing she couldn't leave until he moved his car, he turned to do just that, but couldn't help but wonder what twist of fate had brought Shelby Wentworth back into his life.

SHELBY PULLED up in front of her apartment building and exited her damaged vehicle, slinging her backpack on her shoulder as she walked to the front door.

Her wrecked car would have to stay that way for now. Glancing back at it, she contemplated the lopsided bumper. First, she had to ensure that Nash's would be repaired, despite his assurances to the contrary. And come up with the money to pay for it.

After years of being publicly berated for her mistakes, Shelby had expected the same from the guy whose car she'd just smashed. Once she'd recognized Nash, though, she knew better. His calm, cool demeanor in the face of a defensive blitz was one of the reasons he had been an NFL first-round draft pick.

The polar opposite of the man she'd spent the last five years with.

Of course she'd run into Nash at some point. After all, with a population around sixteen thousand—and that included the university students—Sterling was no Atlanta. She just didn't expect to *literally* run into him.

She stopped by the mailbox, dreading what she'd see— more bills she couldn't pay. Thumbing through the pile, she almost considered putting them back in the box.

What a day! A hot bath, a glass of cheap wine, and a

juicy romance novel were at the top of her Friday night to-do list. And since Sterling didn't offer much in the way of nightlife—unless you were a twenty-something college student—it was a safe bet she wouldn't be missing much.

Nestled in the hills of northeast Georgia, the town of Sterling owed its existence to two things: granite and knowledge. Granite because it held some of the richest granite quarries in the world. If it was made of granite, it probably came from Sterling. And knowledge because Sterling University, one of the Southern Ivy League schools, educated almost ten thousand students each year inside its hallowed halls, and sent them out into the world to share that knowledge.

Established in 1835 by wealthy granite quarry magnate and town founder Samuel Sterling, the university's arts department even offered classes in granite carving. And of course its geology program was one of the country's best. Sterling had endowed the university with one million dollars and three hundred fifty acres of land adjacent to the family home.

When the last of the Sterling line, Victoria Eliza Sterling-Pickard, died in 1974, she left the family home to the university for use as its main administration building, aptly named Sterling Hall.

If you lived in or around Sterling, you most likely either worked for the university or for one of the many surrounding granite quarries or monument makers.

Which meant everyone knew everyone else's business.

Just as she stuck her key in the lock, her neighbor's door opened.

"Oh, hi, Shelby!"

Delaney Driscoll had been her first new acquaintance since coming back to town, not that they'd done anything other than exchange pleasantries at the mailbox, but Delaney was warm and friendly.

"Hi, Delaney. Heading out for the evening?"

"Yeah, I'm meeting a friend." She locked her door then looked up. "Hey! Why don't you join us? I mean, I know you already know people in town, but Sam's really terrific. I think you'd have a lot in common since you're both big-time researchers."

Big-time researchers? Well, maybe Delaney's friend was, anyway. She glanced longingly at the door that led to peace and solitude. And another evening filled with self-recriminations and figuring out how to pay the bills she currently held in her hand. "I don't know. I wouldn't want to impose .. ." Not to mention spend money.

"It's no imposition. Come on. It'll be fun."

Teetering on the edge of saying no, she reversed course. Why not? Maybe some girl time would do her good. She'd been holed up in her apartment since moving in. Not because she was busy unpacking—she'd left with little more than a few personal belongings, just what would fit in her car—but because going out meant potentially running into former high-school classmates that still called Sterling home.

Which meant questions about what she'd been doing and why she was back. Questions she wasn't up to answering yet, if ever.

"Okay. But should I change?" She glanced over at Delaney's bombshell figure, flatteringly displayed in a red silk blouse, black skinny jeans, and sky-high stilettos, then looked down at her own blue jeans, rust-colored blouse, and serviceable ballet flats.

"Nah." She waved her hand. "You look great." She

shrugged, "We're just going to McGinty's Pub. Burger and beer night."

"Let me drop off my stuff and I'll be right out."

"Sure. Hey, what happened to your car?" Delaney asked.

"Don't ask."

2

———

Forty-five minutes later, Nash walked into the locker room at Granite Fitness, wiping sweat off his face with a towel, and came face-to-face with his best friend, Ethan Quinn.

As the new dean of the College of Arts and Sciences, Ethan already had his plate full, but he always managed to squeeze in a workout.

"You done?" Ethan asked as he threw a towel around his neck, his sweat-free appearance a clear indication he hadn't worked out yet.

"Yeah. You just getting started?"

"Yep. Sam and I had an appointment with the florist."

"The florist? Damn, she's got you wrapped." Ethan and his fiancée, Dr. Samantha Love, were tying the knot next spring, and wedding plans had just begun.

"Yeah, she does. And I wouldn't have it any other way," he said with a grin and a wink.

Nash had never seen Ethan so happy. And why shouldn't he be? He had the deanship he'd worked so hard for, he had a smart, beautiful woman in his bed every night, and his latest book was due out next month. The man was living under a lucky star.

"Hey, did you know Shelby's back?" Ethan asked as he bent over to tie his shoe.

"Yeah, I just ran into her. Or, should I say, she ran into me? Literally."

At Ethan's puzzled look, Nash told him about the fender-bender with Shelby.

"She okay?"

"She's fine." Oh, so fine. But hurt—at least emotionally. "Hey, what about me? I'm the innocent bystander here," he said, tongue firmly tucked in his cheek.

Ethan snorted as he stuffed a pair of jeans into his gym bag and stuck it in a locker. "You took hits from three-hundred-pound defensive linemen for a living. I think you can withstand a tap on the bumper of that tank you drive."

Nash pulled his sweaty T-shirt over his head, and began drying off with the towel, recalling Shelby's fear. "What do you know about the reason for Shelby's return?"

Shrugging, Ethan said, "Only that her ex-husband and former mentor had falsified research data. There was a big investigation resulting in journal retractions, his termination from Stanford University, and prohibition from any future research involving federal dollars."

"Damn." No wonder Shelby was gun shy. "And Shelby?"

"She was innocent but decided a change of scenery would be best, so she resigned from Stanford and took an assistant professor position here—a demotion for her. But, it's going to take some time to shake off the taint of her ex-husband's betrayal."

"She's essentially starting over," Ethan continued as he

rose. "She has no articles or papers to her credit, except her dissertation. A death knell to anyone seeking tenure." Ethan filled his water bottle from a dispenser. "It would be like you trying to get into the NFL draft without your college stats."

Why did life have to kick the shit out of people like Shelby? Good people. People who worked hard, told the truth, and trusted their fellow man?

Like she'd trusted him, only to have that trust betrayed. He winced. "Why did you hire her then?"

"She deserved a fresh start."

Yeah, that was Ethan. Although it probably didn't hurt Shelby's chances that she and Ethan had been best friends back in the day too. The three of them had been as thick as thieves growing up.

"Sam's going to dinner with Delaney tonight," Ethan interrupted his musings. "Got any plans?"

"Nope." Especially since Shelby turned him down. "What do you have in mind?" Toeing off his athletic shoes, he dug around in his gym bag for a bottle of shampoo.

"Burger and beer at McGinty's?" Ethan offered.

"Sounds good. I'll wait for you, and we can walk over together. I've got some new plays I can review while I wait."

"Works for me. I won't be long. Just going for a quick run on the treadmill," Ethan said as he headed out to the gym. Stopping before he reached the door, he asked, "What about tomorrow?"

"Nothing, other than taking my car over to Mac's Body Shop in Carlyle for an estimate." With the Labor Day weekend, he'd given the team the day off after practicing hard all week. He wanted them fresh and ready for next week's home-opener against Cornell.

"Sam and Delaney are driving into Atlanta to go dress

shopping, so it only seems fitting that I take my best man to Atlanta to look at tuxes."

Nash held back his groan. After all, how many times would his best friend get hitched? He pointed at Ethan, "In that case, you're buying tonight."

"Deal."

~

"Oh. No. He. Didn't!" Samantha said, her eyes wide with shock.

"Oh. Yes. He. Did!" Delaney replied, a look of disgust on her face. She'd just regaled them with the details of her latest blind-date-gone-wrong—with the new middle school principal from Sterling's exclusive all-boys private school. Delaney crossed her fingers over her heart, "God's truth."

"What did you do?" Sam asked as she scooped the olive from her martini.

"I told him, in no uncertain terms, that I did not want to go back to his place to see his . . ." she shuddered, "iguana."

Sam snorted. "Is that what they're calling it these days?"

Shelby couldn't stop giggling. She really needed this. More than she'd realized. Sipping on an ice-cold Cosmo, nibbling on fried pickles and cheesy nachos, and dishing with two smart, funny women.

She wouldn't think about the hit to her wallet from the cocktails, appetizers, and entree she'd ordered. Just add it to the rest of her debt.

She really liked Sam. A psychology professor in the same college as Shelby and Delaney, she'd recently hit the news with her latest discovery the press called "the love test"—a blood test that determined compatibility. One of the largest online dating services in the U.S. now offered it as part of their premium package.

Sam was everything Shelby wasn't. Polished, confident, beautiful.

But the best thing about Sam and Delaney—they didn't know anything about her Great Career Suicide or GCS for short, so she had nothing to prove to them. They had no preconceived notions about Sterling High School's Valedictorian, voted Most Likely to Succeed.

And she'd missed female camaraderie. When she and Charlie had been married, they'd rarely socialized, and when they did it was usually with another group of researchers, most of whom were men. Charlie didn't approve of girls' nights out. Or alcohol. Or fun, for that matter.

It was true that you can't judge a book by its cover. Charlie had a nice cover, but once you flipped through the pages, he was nothing but a poorly written villain.

Delaney flagged down the waitress and ordered another round before happy hour ended. Shelby could already feel the delightful effects of one Cosmo. She polished off her drink and licked her lips. At this rate, they'd need to take a cab home. Wait. Did Sterling even have cabs now? Or Uber? Not that she could afford either one. Last resort, she could always walk the five blocks to her apartment.

"Okay. Enough of that." Delaney drained the last of her margarita. "It's time to talk wedding." She rubbed her hands together with glee. "What have we got?"

The bride-to-be lifted several thick bridal magazines from the bench seat next to her and set them on the table. Colorful tabs fanned out from the pages marking things that interested her.

She turned to the first tabbed page and spun the magazine to face Shelby and Delaney. They both released collective sighs. Shelby hadn't had a traditional wedding. She and Charlie married at City Hall because Charlie thought weddings were a waste of time and money. She'd never thought of herself as a bride—couldn't even remember what she wore.

Suddenly she wished for the opportunity to wear something so beautiful when she married the man she loved.

Which was utterly preposterous since she'd never place her heart, her trust, and especially not her career, in the hands of a man again.

"Do you like it?" Sam asked, her well-manicured hands folded beneath her chin, a hopeful expression on her face.

"What's not to like?" Delaney asked as she ran her fingers over the glossy photo and read the description. "'A floor-length ecru silk ottoman dress, bateau neck, with lush overskirt.' It's so . . . you."

Although Shelby and Sam had just met, she completely agreed with Delaney. The gown was simple, elegant, and tasteful.

"And I can remove the chapel-length overskirt for the reception." She pointed to the photo on the facing page of the simple sheath dress beneath the overskirt.

"It's perfect." Delaney's eyes looked suspiciously moist.

"Hello, ladies."

Gasping, Sam slammed the magazine shut and hugged it to her chest.

Shelby looked up into Ethan Quinn's smiling brown eyes. Even more handsome with eleven years added. He'd thrown her a lifeline when he approved hiring her in his college. Behind him stood Nash, looking every bit the former NFL quarterback in his worn jeans and Bobcats sweatshirt. Living in Small Town, USA, she knew she was bound to run into him, but twice in one day?

❧

To say Nash was surprised to see Shelby at McGinty's Pub with Delaney and Sam would be an understatement. And, as people often liked to remind him, he was the master of understatement.

Shelby looked adorable with a lopsided smile, giving away her slightly inebriated state.

"Tell me you *did not* just see my wedding dress," Sam whispered to Ethan.

Ethan's eyebrows shot up. "You've already picked one out?"

"Yes, but if you saw it, it's a no-go."

He leaned down, stared into her eyes, and said, "Sweetheart, I didn't see a thing. Cross my heart."

Sam sighed as her eyes glazed over like she'd had her bell rung by a defensive lineman.

Nash shook his head at the two lovebirds. But also felt an unwelcome longing. His ex-wife had put his heart on injured reserve, but maybe it was time to get back in the game. His gaze found Shelby again.

"You boys want to sit down?" Delaney asked as she pulled Shelby toward her in the booth, leaving space for Nash to sit next to Shelby.

"Sure." Ethan slid in next to his bride-to-be, and they shared a tender kiss. "But only for a minute. We have man things to discuss," Ethan said, indicating Nash.

Man things? What the hell were *man things*?

With nothing else to do but join the group, Nash sat down, bumping his thigh against Shelby's. They shot a glance at each other at the contact, and her face registered her surprise at the sudden heat.

Yeah, they still had it. Question was, did she still want it? Because he'd discovered maybe he did.

"What kind of man things?" Delaney prodded.

"Oh, you know," Ethan shrugged, "Saturday night's match-up between Georgia and UNC, whether the Braves are going to get into the World Series, and world peace."

"Given Georgia's new five-star QB, I'd say they'll beat the Tarheels. Six-five, two-fifteen, one hundred twenty-five career TD's, six hundred fifty-nine completions, and total passing yards just shy of ten thousand . . ." Shelby shook her head. "He's a force to be reckoned with. And with the Braves' pitching staff ERA of three-thirty-five, sixty-nine wins, six hundred one strikeouts, and ten shut-outs, they should easily route the teams in the remainder of the regular season. As for world peace, well, statistics aren't in your favor there," Shelby finished with a sigh, her chin propped in her hands.

Nash sat speechless, Delaney's mouth hung open, and Sam's eyes widened.

"Damn, Shelby, you're still keeping up with Georgia sports?" Ethan asked.

Shelby shrugged. "I like sports, and I like statistics. Sue me." She popped a fried pickle into her mouth.

"You're a walking sports statistics encyclopedia." Ethan chuckled, picked up Sam's glass and took a gulp before swallowing and making a face. "Gah! How do you *drink* that?"

"What's wrong with a dirty martini?" Sam shot back.

"You mean, other than the dirty and the martini?" He signaled their waitress and ordered a whiskey on the rocks. Nash ordered a cold beer and stretched out his legs, settling in for what would clearly be longer than a minute.

"So, you and Delaney are off to Atlanta tomorrow to hunt for dresses?" Ethan asked as he helped himself to some nachos.

"Yes," Sam replied, another dreamy look on her face.

"Good. Nash and I are headed to Atlanta to look at tuxes. We can meet up for dinner before heading back."

"We can?" Nash asked, surprised.

"Sure, why not? There's a new eclectic restaurant in Buckhead I'd like to check out."

"Hey, Shelby," Delaney said, nudging her none-too-gently, "Why don't you join us?"

Shelby's brow furrowed, "Oh, no. I wouldn't want to intrude."

"You wouldn't be intruding, would she, Sam?"

"Of course not. The more opinions the better."

"It's settled then," Ethan said. "We'll meet you ladies at New Leaf at seven. That give you enough time?"

"Perfect," Delaney responded for them.

The waitress returned, her tray filled with drinks. Nash lifted a brow when she handed Shelby what looked to be another Cosmo.

Shelby raised the glass to her mouth and took a healthy pull.

"You're not driving tonight, right?" Nash leaned over and asked. Big mistake. Her warmth and scent enveloped him, turning his thoughts to driving her straight back to his place. Now.

Giving himself a mental shake, he realized it had been far too long since he'd been with a woman.

"No." She pointed to Delaney.

He looked across Shelby to see Delaney suck down a good third of her Margarita. "You're not driving tonight either, right?" he directed at Delaney.

"Not if I'm not safe. Uber." She popped a fried pickle slice into her mouth and broke into a stupid grin.

Definitely not safe, Nash thought.

He sighed, guess his boys' night out was turning into Nash's Taxi Service. No more alcohol for him, as it appeared he'd just become the designated driver.

3

———

Just as they all dug into their dinner, a voice from the past made Shelby cringe.

"Well, well, well. If it isn't Miss Most Likely to Succeed. Or should I say Mrs. Ingram?" Tonya Jordan raised her hand to her mouth in a fake show of chagrin. "Oh, that's right. You're divorced now, aren't you? Tsk, tsk. Such a shame."

Nash's body stiffened, and Shelby felt the heat of embarrassment in her cheeks. News travels fast in a small town. The glint in Tonya's eye reminded her why she'd been hiding out in her apartment since she moved back.

"Hi, Tonya," Shelby murmured.

"And that would be *Dr. Wentworth*," Ethan interjected, correcting both Shelby's title and her last name.

Tonya rolled her eyes. "A doctor? Is that what it's called when you play with numbers all day?"

"Don't be bringing that nonsense around here. We've got plenty of our own." Delaney wagged her finger at Tonya.

Tonya snorted.

"How's married life treating you, Tonya? Still playing the

trophy wife?" Nash wore a pleasant grin that didn't reach his eyes.

"Well!" Tonya gasped. "I never!"

"And you never will either," Ethan said, giving her a pointed look.

Tonya turned on her heel and left.

"Wow, what a beyotch," muttered Delaney.

Nash and Ethan had had her back since fourth grade. And apparently still did. The thought assuaged some of the humiliation, but Nash's rescue also confused her. Why would he leave her hanging senior year but stand up for her now?

"She's got no business throwing stones," Nash muttered as he plucked a fry off his plate and popped it into his mouth.

Shelby snorted. "She's the daughter of one of the richest men in town. Of course she can throw stones."

Ethan reached for the ketchup. "You've missed a lot in your eleven-year absence. Tonya's and her mother's lives took a turn for the worse when Mr. Jordan died."

Before Shelby could ask why, Ethan continued. "Turns out Mr. Jordan was in hock up to his eyebrows from keeping Mrs. Jordan and his daughter in the lifestyle to which they'd become accustomed."

"Not to mention a gambling problem," Nash added.

"The family sold the quarry," Delaney supplied. "And Tonya married the new owner out of desperation. A man twenty-five years her senior."

"Mr. Helsinger is closer to her mother's age than her own." Sam wiped her mouth with her napkin. "And is much tighter with the purse strings than Tonya's father."

"Karma's a bitch," Nash said.

"She sure is," Ethan echoed with a grin.

NASH POLISHED off the last of his fries and cast a glance at Shelby. The color had returned to her face. When she'd looked up and saw Tonya standing there, it was like watching a balloon deflate. Shelby had collapsed into herself.

Some people just didn't know how to be nice, not that Tonya would know "nice" if it came up and bit her on her now-fat ass.

As the conversation around the table turned to wedding talk, Nash recalled the day he first saw Shelby—the first day of fourth grade. He and Ethan had been engaged in a little friendly competition on the monkey bars when Nash noticed that Tonya and her four-feet-tall henchgirls had Shelby backed up against the chain link fence that enclosed the school playground.

Shelby had been the new kid in school, painfully shy, and rail thin.

One thing Nash and Ethan agreed on—bullies would not be tolerated, regardless of their gender or socioeconomic status. And Tonya Jordan was a bully.

He'd brought the situation to Ethan's attention and the two headed over to intervene.

Turned out Tonya was making fun of Shelby because, unbeknownst to her, she had been wearing one of Tonya's hand-me-down dresses.

He and Ethan had made it clear that day that Shelby was off limits and if either one of them saw Tonya or any of her mean girls so much as frown at Shelby, they'd tell Dirk "The Jerk" Michaels about her crush.

And to ensure nothing else happened after school, they'd walked Shelby home.

Even as Shelby put on weight and grew stronger from her physical activities, she learned to stand up for herself so that the bullies and mean girls were no longer a threat. Oh, they still teased her, but she no longer needed him or Ethan to stand up for her. She stood up for herself. But even then, unbeknownst to Shelby, he and Ethan had reinforced her own defenses with a few well-placed warnings of their own.

Despite her self-reliance, Nash had always felt protective of Shelby. And apparently still did.

From her reaction this afternoon and now, she'd lost her self-confidence somewhere along the way. Seeing her so cowed just made him mad. Mad at her dick of an ex-husband for taking that away from her, because he had no doubt he was at the bottom of this.

Ethan kicked Nash under the table. "You okay?"

"Yeah." With the warmth of Shelby's legs pressed up against his, her arm brushing his, her scent tickling his nose, he was more than okay.

~

THE WAITRESS DROPPED off the check and began clearing away the dishes.

Delaney picked up the folder, removed the bill, and looked at it, rubbing her temple with her free hand. "Oh, man! I can't figure this out. Why didn't we get separate checks?"

"Parties of four or more always get one check at McGinty's," Nash reminded her.

Talk turned to next week's football game, and Shelby watched as Delaney attempted to divvy up the bill. Her lips moved as she ran her finger over the receipt, apparently doing math in her head.

Shelby could've made short work of it, but she was reluctant to offer. She didn't know Sam and Delaney that well, and she didn't dare put herself out there like that yet.

But no one else at the table seemed aware of Delaney's struggle.

Nash finally leaned over, "Got it figured out yet, Einstein?" he asked with a wink.

"I think . . ." Her shoulders dropped. "No, I don't." She sighed.

"I'll figure it out." Taking pity on her, Shelby held out her hand for the bill. She took it from Delaney, quickly scanned it, then told everyone their portion, along with a twenty percent tip.

"Damn, Shelby. You're still a walking calculator too," Ethan said as he pulled some bills out of his wallet and slipped them into the folder.

"How did you *do* that?" Delaney asked in awe. Not waiting for a response, she rummaged around in her purse.

"It's easy." Shelby shrugged, handing Nash some money to cover her drinks, her portion of the appetizers, and the hamburger. This had been an unplanned—and irresponsible—splurge. Looked like a week of ramen noodles and cereal was in her future.

"No." Delaney began placing things on the table as she pulled them from a handbag the size of Shelby's overnight bag. None of which was her wallet. "It's not easy." Smartphone. Sunglasses. Hairbrush. Gum. "Math is not easy." Pack of Kleenex. Several lipsticks. Energy bar. "It's an unsolvable mystery, one that I abandoned after barely passing college algebra." Tampons. Condoms.

Nash chuckled and shook his head. "Interesting combo you got there."

Delaney ignored him and continued to fish around in what seemed like a bottomless pit.

Shelby reached over, her face hot with embarrassment, and pulled Delaney's wallet from the now-empty bag, then stuffed the offending items back in. "You just need the right teacher. I could show you sometime."

Delaney grimaced then swept the remainder of the items off the table and into her purse. "Thanks, but no thanks. I'd rather play with words."

"Come, woman. Let us away," Ethan said, taking Sam's hand and pulling her along behind him. She turned and called to Delaney and Shelby, "See you at eight in the morning."

Nash rose, followed by Shelby. Food had soaked up that second Cosmo and her encounter with Tonya had sobered her up. Unfortunately.

Delaney, however, struggled from the booth then stood, swaying on her feet.

"You okay?" Shelby asked.

"Yep. Never better." She missed her first attempt to scoop her purse from the bench. Then missed her second. Taking pity on her, Shelby grabbed it for her.

Nash chuckled. "You sloshed?"

"Lil bit," Delaney said, then giggled.

"All right." Nash stepped in. "Ladies, your chariot awaits."

"A chariot? I've always wanted to ride in a chariot," Delaney said with a slur.

"Now's your chance." He put his arm around her waist and directed her out the door, leaving Shelby to follow.

Guess Shelby knew who Nash was going home with tonight. Not that she could blame him. Delaney's blond hair, sexy curves and outgoing personality would make her appealing to any red-blooded male. Just like Leandra Lucas.

The burger she ate sat in her stomach like a brick.

The night had grown chilly, making Shelby wish for a jacket. Following Nash and Delaney, she walked out to his damaged Suburban parked across the street. Before Nash could assign seating arrangements, Shelby opened the back passenger door and climbed in, leaving the front passenger seat for Delaney.

"All aboard?" Nash asked, glancing back at Shelby in his rear-view mirror. "Buckle up."

Delaney had some problems getting her seatbelt fastened, so Nash leaned over and clicked it for her.

"Thanks, Nash." Her words ran together as she patted his face.

"She's really drunk," Nash said to Shelby with a chuckle.

U2 came on the radio, and Delaney reached over for the volume, cranked it up, and proceeded to sing at the top of her lungs about a beautiful day, while dancing in her seat.

Mercifully, by the time the song ended, they'd arrived at the nearby apartment complex where she and Delaney lived.

"Can you help me get her to bed?" Nash asked.

"Um, sure." Odd request if he was planning to make a move on Delaney.

While Nash guided a wobbly Delaney toward the bedroom, Shelby walked ahead and pulled back the covers for her friend. After sitting Delaney down on the bed, Nash picked up her feet, slipped off her stilettos, then laid her in bed and adjusted her legs.

"You're suth a nithe guy, Nath." No sooner did her head hit the pillow than she was out.

"Okay. Well, guess I'll head over to my place." Shelby said after pulling the covers up over Delaney's prone form.

"I'll follow you out."

"No. It's okay." She waved him off. "You can stay if you want."

"Stay?" His eyebrows shot up in confusion. "Why would I stay?"

"I—Oh, never mind." Embarrassed by her less-than-charitable thoughts about Nash, she turned to leave.

"You should probably unbutton and unzip her jeans." Nash pointed in the direction of Delaney's waist.

"What?" Shelby stopped short and stared at him like he'd just asked her to join them for a threesome.

"Those jeans are awfully tight. Might not be a good idea for her to sleep all, you know, bound up. Bad for the circulation."

"Oh." Right. Why else would he ask?

Nash turned his back, while Shelby lifted Delaney's blouse and did as he'd suggested.

"I don't know how much good she'll be to Sam tomorrow. She's going to have one hell of a tequila headache," he said as Shelby moved to the front door, with him right behind her.

He turned the lock on the front door knob, making sure Delaney was locked in for the night, then closed the door behind him.

Shelby had her apartment door unlocked and the door open just as he stepped up behind her.

"Shelby." He placed his hands on her shoulders. "You know I don't take advantage of inebriated women. Besides, I'm not attracted to Delaney," he continued, his breath warm on her ear, and she shivered in response. "You're cold. I should let you go in." He released her, leaving her bereft.

"Thanks for bringing us home, Nash." She didn't turn around. She couldn't look into those blue eyes and not make a fool of herself. She'd already done plenty of that today. The resentment she'd been harboring all these years crumbled like a dry biscuit.

"See you tomorrow night." She heard his footsteps along the sidewalk.

Tomorrow night. Stepping into her apartment, she closed the door and laid her forehead against it. Her fears had been confirmed. Coming home had been a bad idea.

4

———

If Nash never looked at another tux, it would be too soon.

Waiting in the bar for the ladies to join them, he took a healthy pull on his craft beer and eyed Ethan like he'd grown another head. Since when had his best friend become such a clothes horse?

They'd looked at tuxes with shawl lapels, notched lapels, and peaked lapels. They'd looked at dinner jackets and morning coats, cummerbunds and vests, bow ties and long ties. And still hadn't selected anything because Ethan wanted Sam's opinion and approval. He pressed a thumb to his twitching eye. Who knew there were so many choices?

Ethan caught his gaze, chuckled, and slapped him on the shoulder. "Too much?"

"No. In fact, let's go look at a few more. I'm sure we missed something in the thousands of tuxedos we looked at today."

"Just wait, my friend. One day, this will be you again."

Not. In. This. Lifetime. Been there, done that. Burned the T-shirt.

Nash had been engaged to his college sweetheart, Stephanie Cummings. It was a match made for a romantic chick-flick: he the star quarterback, she the beautiful cheerleader and homecoming queen.

And they'd been the NFL's perfect couple too.

Or so he'd thought. But Stephanie had only been interested in his star status. When he'd retired early from the NFL, she'd called in an audible, and left him for a teammate.

"You fellows looking for dates?" Sam asked as she wrapped her arms around Ethan's waist. He leaned down to kiss her and came away with a big-ass grin.

Nash nodded a greeting to Delaney. "You're alive."

"Yeah. It was touch and go there for a while," she muttered, then ordered a club soda with lime from the bartender.

Nash's gaze found Shelby, who stood off to the side like she was the fifth wheel. Her hair was back in the ponytail he remembered, and she wore what looked like a simple knit dress in deep green and a pair of flats. She'd never been one for the latest fashions, probably because growing up she hadn't had that luxury. But he liked that about her. Shelby's lack of materialism was the polar opposite of Stephanie.

"What would you like to drink?" he asked, gathering her into the huddle.

"What you're having looks good."

"Another Drafty Kilt," Nash said to the bartender.

"Drafty Kilt?" Shelby raised a brow and looked down at Nash's well-worn jeans. And damned if that look didn't stir a little heat.

"Kilt's at the cleaners," he said with a shrug, taking the glass from the bartender and handing it to Shelby. Their hands touched, lingered over the glass, and Nash had an inexplicable urge to twine his fingers through hers and bring her hand to his lips.

Even when she was out with friends, she carried a haunted look in her eyes. He found himself wanting to make that look a thing of the past. To bring back the Shelby he'd known before she'd taken life's many hits.

"Did you look at as many dresses as we looked at tuxes today?"

"That depends. We looked at approximately eight-point-four million dresses. You?"

"About the same number of tuxes. I lost count at eight million three hundred ninety-five thousand." He drained his glass. "I thought Sam had her dress picked out."

"Me too. But she said she needed to make sure she made the right decision," Shelby said with a shrug and an eye roll.

Sam filled Ethan in on their day, while Delaney nursed her nonalcoholic beverage.

The bar in the trendy new restaurant had become more crowded, the patrons pushing him and Shelby closer together until they were hip-to-hip. Someone bumped Shelby from behind, causing her to make full-frontal body contact with Nash. Breasts to chest, good parts to good parts. Shelby's mouth opened, and a flush tinted her cheeks, as he stared into her startled amber eyes.

Holy hard-on, Batman. He stepped back as if electro-cuted, bumping into the guy behind him, who shot him a dirty look.

"Quinn, party of five, your table's ready," the hostess called over the din in the bar.

Thank God for small favors, Nash thought.

❧

"Man, am I tired," Delaney yawned heavily then eyed the others at the table. She nudged Sam in the chair next to her. "Aren't you exhausted?"

Sam gave her a funny look, glanced at Shelby and Nash, and then said, "Oh. Yeah. I am a little weary." She in turn gave Ethan a nudge. "How about you, babe? You tired."

With a glance at the two of them, and a furrow between his brows, he finally said, "Sure. I'm tired too," and then appeared to wait for some instruction.

They'd already divvied up the check, using Shelby's computational skills, and were just hanging out.

Delaney jumped up, grabbing her monster purse. "Great. I mean, wow, look at us turning into lightweights." She turned to Shelby and Nash. "But we don't want to rush you two." She poked first Sam and then Ethan. "Do we?"

Taking the not-so-subtle hint, Ethan stood and pulled out Sam's chair.

"Oh, but—" Shelby stood.

Placing her hands on Shelby's shoulders, Delaney pressed her back down in her seat. "No, no. Don't get up. We'll see ourselves out." With that she shooed Sam and Ethan ahead of her.

"What was that all about?" Shelby asked, totally confused.

Nash smirked. "I can only guess. Anyway, it looks like I'm driving you home."

"But it's so odd. Delaney and I live right next door to each other," Shelby insisted. "It's illogical to go home in different cars, not to mention inconvenient for both you and Ethan." She chewed on her lip, worried he would think she'd set this up. "God, Nash. I'm so sorry."

"Shelby, Sterling isn't that big. Besides, I live southeast of town. It's on my way. You ready?"

"Uh, sure." With no choice, other than a budget-breaking taxi ride, she rose from her chair and gathered her handbag.

Nash followed her out, his hand on the small of her back, warm and protective. She recalled the feel of his body against hers when she'd been pushed into him. His lean, hard body.

And now she had a nearly two-hour ride back with him all alone in a dark car. The man who'd unapologetically broken her heart. And yet, she couldn't stay away from him.

NASH HAD CARRIED the conversation while he'd made his way out of the congested Buckhead area, chatting about the sports teams he remembered Shelby following, where some of their classmates were now, and how she'd liked living in, first, New England, then California, after growing up in Sterling. But about fifteen minutes outside of Atlanta, Shelby finally spoke without being spoken to.

"You said you lived southeast of town. I thought that was mostly rural still."

"It is. I bought the old Brooks' place." He had the remaining ten acres of what had been a hundred-thirty-acre farm, but on it sat the sprawling white farmhouse and barn. He kept a couple of horses, a rescued jackass named Duke, and a barn cat. One of these days he'd add a golden retriever or two to the menagerie.

"That house must be at least ninety years old," Shelby said.

"Ninety-two to be exact, and, yeah, it needed some work. I spent the first six months having the plumbing and electrical brought up to code and putting in modern kitchen and bathroom facilities."

Shelby laughed.

"What?"

"You. It needed *some* work, but it took six months on electrical and plumbing alone." She shook her head. "Sounds like it needed a *lot* of work."

He laughed and shook his head. "You're right. It needed a shitload of work. But it turned out nice. You should come see it sometime." Stephanie would have hated the house. Too old-fashioned and welcoming. Which made him love it all the more.

"In fact, I'm having a cookout at the farm on Monday. Mostly my coaching staff and their wives and kids, but there will be some people there you know, like Sam and Ethan, Delaney . . . oh, and Grady. You remember Grady Morgan? We were in social studies together? He's my special teams coach. He married Amanda Gibson—she graduated a year behind us."

Shelby glanced his way, the reluctance on her face lit by the Suburban's interior lighting. "Thanks. Can I let you know?"

"Sure."

They rode in silence for a few miles.

"What made you return to Sterling?" Shelby finally asked.

Nash thought about it a minute. He thought about his dad, alone since his mother died three years ago, and his father's health problems. He thought about Ethan. They'd stayed in touch throughout Nash's college and NFL careers. Ethan even made it to a few games. "Family. Friends. The job. And I guess I never stopped thinking about the town. It's a great place to live."

"Yeah, I guess," Shelby muttered noncommittally.

He didn't know if she was ready to go there, but he asked anyway. "And what about you? Why did *you* return to Sterling?"

~

How was she supposed to answer that? To run from her mistakes? To lick her wounds? To get as far away as possible from her ex-husband and still live on the same continent? Because it's small enough to hide away from her small-knit research community? All of the above?

But, of course, she knew the answer: It was because Sterling University was the only academic institution willing to give her a job after the scandal involving her husband's research misconduct. She owed Ethan big time for that.

"Oh, you know, you can take the girl out of Sterling, but you can't take Sterling out of the girl." She laughed, and it sounded false to her ears.

"Well, Sterling is glad to have you back," Nash said with a quick look her way, his eyes warm in the vehicle's dim interior.

Her heart squeezed.

She couldn't go there again. Not with anyone, and especially not with him.

She leaned her head back, closed her eyes. Maybe if she pretended to be asleep the polite conversation would end.

She didn't want to go too far down the road of whys. The fact that her career was in shambles wasn't a big secret, but her role in the downfall was, and she'd like to keep it that way for as long as possible.

"I'll see you to your door." Nash's voice startled her in

the quiet confines of the car. She must have fallen asleep in earnest.

"Oh, you don't have to do that." She unfastened her seatbelt.

"I'd like to just the same," he said as he opened his door.

Shelby walked up to her apartment, Nash by her side, his stride relaxed.

She unlocked her door.

"Shelby?"

"Yes?" She turned to find him close, so close she could feel his warmth.

Without answering, he gazed into her eyes, then lifted his hand to cup her cheek. Nash was going to kiss her, she thought. But she couldn't let him. Yet like Mowgli falling under the snake Kaa's spell in the *Jungle Book*, she couldn't move. And the resentment she'd been trying her best to hold onto dissipated like fog on a sunny morning.

Nash leaned in, his gaze dropping to her lips, which had suddenly gone dry. Then his lips caressed hers, soft and gentle, their warmth welcome in the cool night air. A whimper rose in her throat just as his mouth released hers.

"I've wanted to do that since you backed into me in the faculty parking lot."

"You have?"

He nodded and licked his lips, as if he wanted to taste her again, and it was the sexiest thing she'd ever seen. Her knees, already weakened by his kiss, threatened to give way.

He dropped his hand from her face and took a step back.

"I hope to see you on Monday. I'm firing up the grill around noon."

"I'll let you know."

"Goodnight, Sassafras."

She had to laugh at her old nickname, even as her lips still burned from his kiss. And her heart still ached for his unrequited love.

5
____

Late Sunday afternoon, Nash pulled up in the driveway of his modest childhood home. Not much had changed in the years after he left for college, and then for the NFL. Since his mother died three years ago, the colorful profusion of flowers was absent from the beds. Just shrubs flanked the house now, tidy and trimmed thanks to the monthly lawn maintenance Nash paid for.

His dad couldn't keep up with the house anymore, but he refused to move into an apartment, so Nash hired out for necessary repairs, painting, housekeeping, and lawn care.

Many wondered why the son of a former NFL quarterback would grow up in a three-bedroom, two-bath brick house in a lower middle class neighborhood rather than one of the mansions in the wealthier neighborhood of Sterling Hills.

Easy. Bad investments and reckless business decisions.

Sighing, Nash gripped the steering wheel, wondering what version of Carl he would get today.

He climbed out of his SUV then reached in the backseat

for the bag of groceries he'd bought. Steaks for grilling, potatoes for baking, and ingredients for a simple salad. Man-food—his dad's favorite.

Juggling the bag, he inserted a key into the lock on the front door, calling out as he entered, "Dad, it's Nash."

Nothing.

The house was dark, the blinds closed, making the interior particularly dim after the bright sunshine outside.

"Dad?" He made his way to the back of the house and into the kitchen. "Jesus." The house was a mess, clothes strewn about, and in the kitchen, dirty dishes filled the sink. An open loaf of Wonder Bread sat on the counter, along with an empty Coca-Cola bottle and a knife with what looked like dried mayonnaise on it.

Clearly the once-a-week housekeeper wasn't enough.

Swearing under his breath, he cleared a space for the bag, then opening the fridge and peered in. Practically empty. Looked like another trip to Piggly Wiggly was in his immediate future.

He heard a toilet flush and then the sound of shuffling feet along the laminate floor. "Who's here?"

"Dad, it's Nash."

His father rounded the corner, looking unkempt in a dirty T-shirt and boxer shorts, at least two days' growth of beard covering his face.

But when a smile lit his father's expression, it tugged at Nash's heart.

"I brought steaks, potatoes, and salad for dinner. You hungry?"

Carl rubbed his once-flat belly. "I could eat."

"Good. Why don't you go shower while I clean up in here?" He opened the dishwasher to find a box of cereal.

Scrubbing his hand over his face, he held back a groan. "Dad, cereal goes in the pantry."

Confusion skittered across Carl's stubbled face. "Right."

Nash carried the cereal over to the pantry and was pleased to see that there was food on the shelves. "Why is the house such a mess? Didn't Carlotta come yesterday?"

"I fired that girl."

"Fired?" Nash spun to face his father. "Why'd you do that?"

His expression turned belligerent. "She was stealing."

"Dad, she was doing no such thing." Nash strode over and turned on the faucet then began rinsing the dirty dishes. With dried food stubbornly stuck on the dishes, it'd be a miracle if they came clean.

"She was. I can't find my pocket knife. And the other day the TV remote went missing."

"Dad, why would she steal a TV remote?" More likely his father put the knife and the remote somewhere it didn't belong, like the cereal in the dishwasher. Throwing a dishtowel over his shoulder, he filled the dishwasher, then put a detergent pod in, and turned it on.

"Who knows why that woman does what she does?"

"All right. Go shower, and when you come back out I'll have dinner going." Nash knew that arguing with his father was useless. He'd likely forget this conversation as soon as he got in the shower.

He'd have to make it up to Carlotta and beg her to come back. She'd been the only housekeeper willing to put up with his father's behavior. Her grandmother had Alzheimer's, so the actions of his father were not foreign to her.

His father shuffled back down the hall, and a few minutes later Nash heard the water come on.

Scrubbing the potatoes, he shook his head thinking about how to deal with his dad.

Carl had been a decent quarterback in the NFL, back when the players weren't paid nearly as much. A second-round draft pick with the Miami Dolphins before Nash was born, Carl later signed with the Atlanta Falcons. They moved back to Sterling, his parents' hometown.

Nash put the steaks in a Ziploc along with some marinade, then placed them in the refrigerator.

At only forty-five, his father began showing signs of what they'd thought was early-onset Alzheimer's but now believed was chronic traumatic encephalopathy, or CTE. Now fifty-six, his father's dementia-like symptoms had become more frequent and more noticeable.

Although CTE could not be definitively diagnosed until after death, as many hits as his father took, Nash and the specialist at Cornell felt almost certain that's what it was.

It's one of the reasons Nash left the NFL after his own grade three concussion and why he was so determined to find a new career and move on. He didn't want to follow in his dad's footsteps.

Potatoes in the oven, Nash went out to the back patio to start the charcoals.

He gazed out at the dilapidated tree house while he waited for the coals to heat up.

During the off-season, when Nash was eight years old, his father had built the tree house. Carl was a skilled woodworker, having grown up the son of a carpenter. But one day while Carl was working on the tree house, he'd been distracted—no one knew why or by what—and he'd sliced off two middle fingers from his throwing hand with a radial saw.

Career over.

After spreading out the coals, Nash covered the grill and went back to the kitchen to check the steaks and prepare the salad.

Nash's father had been planning for retirement from his NFL career but never expected it to end so abruptly. Sort of like what had happened with Nash.

When Nash was about three, his father bought into a car dealership in Atlanta that went belly-up due to poor management. Then he invested in a tech company that went down when the dot-com bubble burst. His parents had been lucky the house was paid off, or else they might have lost it.

After his career-ending accident, his father struggled with depression. He'd lost his identity and hadn't known what to do next. It wasn't until the aging owner of a thriving hardware store in Sterling put it on the market that Carl found his answer.

Carl loved do-it-yourself projects, despite the radial saw accident, so the hardware store was a natural choice for him, and he was very successful for the first five years. But life had a funny way of sacking you behind the line of scrimmage.

He began experiencing debilitating headaches and forgetfulness. One day, when Nash was in high school, Dink's Corner Drugs called Nash's mom and told her Carl was in the store but that he was confused about where he was.

He'd finally had to sell off the hardware store when Nash's mom became ill. His mother's eventual death had exacerbated his father's symptoms. If Nash's career hadn't ended when it did, he would have worked with his agent to move to the Falcons, where he'd be closer to home.

Nash sliced tomatoes, cucumbers, and onions for the salad then tossed some croutons in. Carrying the bowl to the kitchen table, along with a couple of dressing choices, he heard the squeaky closet door in his father's bedroom open and close. Carl should be out any minute. Time to put the steaks on.

He was just turning the steaks on the grill when the sliding glass door opened and his father stepped out wearing a haphazardly buttoned Hawaiian shirt, a pair of dress pants, one black shoe, and one brown shoe, his thick salt-and-pepper hair sticking up at odd angles like he'd toweled it off but hadn't combed it.

Heaving a sigh, Nash knew he needed to be honest with himself. It might be time to hire a full-time caregiver.

ON LABOR DAY MORNING, after feeding and watering the equines, Nash set about preparations for the cookout. Ethan would be over later to help move the picnic tables beneath the shade of a heritage live oak behind the house.

In the meantime, Nash had already hauled the steel drum smoker out from the barn and started the coals. On the menu was sweet Silver Queen corn on the cob, barbecue ribs and chicken, and hamburgers and hot dogs for the kids. Guests were bringing everything from coleslaw and potato salad to chocolate cake and peach cobbler.

The cornhole board, horseshoes, and *bocce* ball awaited kids and adults alike for some friendly competition, while Duke the Donkey could be counted on to take some of the kids for a short ride around the paddock.

As he hoisted a couple of two-hundred-quart coolers into the back of his SUV and filled them with ice from the bags he'd bought in town, he thought about Shelby and the goodnight kiss he'd been unable to resist. He nestled beer, sodas, and bottled water in the ice, along with a few bottles of white wine, while remembering the taste of her lips, the little whimper she'd let out when he'd retreated, and the way she'd looked into his eyes, as if he had just opened a door that had been bolted shut for far too long.

It had certainly unbolted a door for him. One that was probably better off closed and locked.

He still hadn't heard from her. He didn't know if she'd accept his invitation or not, but he hoped so. He wanted to see her again. Probably more than he should.

Clearly she had a lot going on and probably didn't need any further complications in her life. But he wanted to be her friend, to remind her that he's had her back since her first day of fourth grade and that he always would. Despite her notions to the contrary.

~

SHELBY FOUND herself driving along County Road Fifty-Seven headed to the old Brooks Farm. She'd been working on a research idea, reviewing some articles, but nothing was gelling, and she was beginning to think her ex-husband's work had been the only vehicle for her research.

She hadn't intended to accept Nash's invitation, but she couldn't take the four walls of her apartment any longer.

Nash had broken her heart, and if she wasn't careful, he'd do it again, but she couldn't make herself stay away from him. Neither could she bring herself to hold a grudge —not where Nash was concerned.

She snorted and wondered if her heart could get any more broken than it already was. Her experience with Charlie had left it in tatters. Or was it just her pride that had taken the hit?

Unsure what was on the menu at Nash's, she'd stopped at the Piggly Wiggly and picked up the fixings for a tossed salad. It would go with anything, and she could put it together when she got to the house. And as far as the cost of ingredients went, it was fairly cheap. An important factor when she was scraping the bottom of her back account.

Drawing a deep breath, Shelby rounded the bend in the road right before the turn-off to the farm. As she turned in, she noted the concrete that covered the once-red clay drive. When she arrived at the house, she counted at least ten cars and pickup trucks parked out front on the lawn.

The house wore a gleaming coat of white paint, and the glossy black shutters stood out in the midday sun. The red-brick chimneys still flanked either end of the house. Beneath a wraparound porch, black rockers beckoned for someone to come and set them in motion. A black swing on one end of the porch faced the front yard. Four lacy Boston ferns hung along the porch, their bright green leaves adding a welcome pop of color to the black and white setting.

The house looked better than she'd ever seen it.

Climbing out of the car, she gazed up at a sky so blue it almost hurt. With temperatures in the mid-seventies, it was a perfect day for one last summer barbecue. Grabbing the bags out of her back seat, she glanced down at her khaki skirt and Keds and wished for a pair of cowboy boots instead.

After picking her way across the yard and around the house to the sound of laughter and the tantalizing aroma of grilling meat, she stopped dead in her tracks when she saw the crowd. She hadn't expected so many people. Just as she considered sneaking away, Nash called her name, waving her over.

Painting a smile on her face, she headed in his direction.

She felt as if all activity had stopped and every eye was on her. Judging. All seeing her for the failure that she was. And a snitch. She rolled her eyes at the ridiculous self-centered notion, as if everyone's life revolved around hers.

"Hi. I didn't think you would come." Nash met her with a broad smile on his handsome face and relieved her of the grocery bags.

"I couldn't stand my own company anymore. I hope salad is okay."

Nash glanced in the bags. "Looks great."

Delaney waved at her, inviting her to take the empty Adirondack chair next to her.

"I'll just go get a big bowl, a knife, and a cutting board and be right back," Nash said. "Grab a drink and make yourself comfortable."

∼

THE ADULTS WERE SPRAWLED in various places beneath the oak tree, some in chairs, some on blankets, while the kids burned off their excess energy with games of chase and dodge ball. Nash glanced around and found Shelby, Sam, and Delaney huddled around an iPad. No doubt the wedding playbook.

Ethan and a few of the coaching staff were battling it out in a game of horseshoes, while some of the coaches' wives laughed over the cornhole board.

What was left of the feast waited on the picnic tables for those with hollow legs who wanted seconds.

Rising from her seat, Shelby headed over to one of the coolers and plucked a diet soda from the icy water. Nash walked over to join her, just as Grady did the same.

"So, Shelby, you doing okay?" Grady asked as he popped

the tab on a Coke. "I heard about your divorce. That's rough."

Ah, dammit.

Shelby's face went white. Grady was a nice guy, but sometimes he didn't have the sense God gave a goose, to borrow a phrase from his late mother.

Before she could answer, Nash said, "Hey, Grady, your boy's calling you." Not a lie. His son, Mikey, was calling his dad to come watch him ride Duke.

"Oh, thanks, man. You let me or Amanda know if you need anything," he said to Shelby as he headed over to the paddock.

Shelby stood, her face a mask of shame.

"Sorry about that. Grady didn't mean anything by it."

She shook her head. "I know. You'd think I'd get used to it by now. I mean, it's not like divorce is uncommon. And in a town the size of Sterling, it's bound to get out." She bit her lip then took a sip of her soda as an afterthought.

"Come take a walk." He headed for the paddock on the other side of the barn. Some time away to compose herself would do her good and Shelby had always loved horses. Nash recalled that she had even worked at Sterling's riding stables in high school. A breeze kicked up, sending her sweet lemon fragrance his way. She looked adorable in a skirt that showed off her still-toned legs.

When they reached the fence railing, Whisky nickered and sidled over, hoping for a carrot or half an apple. Nash held out one of the carrots he'd swiped from the bag Shelby had brought, and the horse snuffled Nash's hand before crunching down on the carrot.

"This is Whisky. And that shy little girl over there is Moonshine."

"They're beautiful. I didn't know you wanted horses."

"Neither did I." He chuckled. "They sort of came with the property." He reached up to rub Whisky's muzzle. "Duke came later." He pointed to the jackass in the neighboring paddock. "Want to see if we can coax Miss Moonshine over for a carrot?"

Shelby smiled, and his heart rolled over in his chest. "Sure."

Nash handed her the carrot, and Shelby clucked to the horse.

Whisky nudged his head in, and Nash pushed him away. "No, dude. You've already had yours."

Feelings hurt, Whisky turned with a flick of his tail and wandered over to the shade of a tree.

Shelby's patience paid off when Moonshine ambled over and hung her head over the rail. She held out her hand and Moonshine took the carrot. While the horse crunched on the treat, Shelby stroked her muzzle. "Yeah, you're a sweet girl, aren't you?"

This was the most relaxed he'd seen Shelby since she'd come home. She'd lost the haunted look and had bright spots of color in her cheeks. And he had a thought. "If you'd like to come out and ride, let me know. You can saddle her up yourself, or we can ride together, either way."

Her hand paused on the horse's muzzle, and she dipped her head, a soft smile on her lips. "Thanks. I might do that."

Well, that was progress.

6

———

The following Wednesday afternoon, Nash reached over for his cup of coffee as he reviewed the previous night's practice video. With the short week, he was beginning to regret giving his guys the Labor Day Weekend off. In the three days off, his defensive line forgot how to run a zone defense, his offensive line forgot how to block, and his QB forgot how to execute a screen play.

All his players were wicked-smart—the future generation of brain surgeons and rocket scientists. College wasn't just a stepping-stone to the NFL for his guys. In fact, few, if any, were headed for a career in the NFL, but they had heart. They played for the love of the game.

Good thing, since this afternoon's practice was going to be a bitch.

His phone chirped with an incoming text. Glancing over and seeing Shelby's name, he picked it up.

I'D LIKE TO TAKE YOU UP ON YOUR OFFER.

His offer? Oh, yeah, his offer. For a second there his mind had darted into the gutter.

He texted her back.

Feel free. The tack is in the room to your right after you walk into the barn.

Damn. He'd love to join her, but that was an impossibility right now.

His phone chirped again.

Thanks.

He snorted. Guess that meant he wasn't invited anyway.

"Hey, Coach. Got a minute?" Matt, his QB coach asked.

"Sure. Come on in." He set aside his phone and turned his attention to Trent.

It was after nine o'clock that night before Nash pulled up in front of his house. He walked out to the barn to make sure the horses were secure for the night. Whisky, Moonshine, and Duke were ensconced in their stalls with fresh oats in their buckets. Moonshine's coat showed signs of recent currying. Shelby hadn't forgotten everything she'd learned working at the riding stables.

He hoped she'd had a good ride.

"Goodnight, equines."

He was bone weary as he walked to the back door of the house. On the stoop sat a container of chocolate chip cookies with a note inside. "Thanks for the therapy session."

Biting into the gooey cookie, Nash smiled. *Therapy session.* He liked it.

On Saturday morning, Shelby answered the knock on her front door to see Delaney standing there, reusable grocery bags in hand. Careful to pull the door to so Delaney couldn't see inside the apartment, she stepped out onto the stoop.

"Hey. Sam, Ethan, and I are going to tonight's football game. Want to join?"

Shelby had been planning to go, if only for the first half, to see Nash in action.

"Sure." She really enjoyed being with Delaney. She was always so cheerful and confident, as if she felt good in her own skin, a feeling Shelby used to know herself. Maybe she could reclaim that feeling again one day.

"Great. We're meeting at Ruby's for an early dinner, then we'll head over. You up for that?"

Shelby smiled at Delaney's enthusiasm. "Of course."

"See you at five-thirty," Delaney said as she headed to her car.

Later that afternoon, after another frustrating day of literature reviews, Shelby gathered a light jacket just in time for Delaney's knock. Making sure she had her faculty ID, which would get her in the game for free, she opened the door.

"You look great," Delaney said with a bright smile. "Walking okay with you? We'll never find a parking spot in town."

"Walking sounds good. I've been sitting all day." Shelby locked up and fell alongside Delaney, all decked-out in team apparel. Shelby needed to hit the university's bookstore for some Bobcats apparel. As soon as she found some spare change, that is. She'd unearthed a Bobcats-red shirt. That would have to do for now.

She still hadn't furnished her apartment. She had the bare necessities: a used kitchen table that doubled as her desk, a mattress and box spring—on the floor—and a book-shelf. For kitchen basics, she'd raided the small storage unit her mom still kept in town after moving to Miami with her new husband.

She owed her divorce attorney money. Then there was the attorney she'd hired during Stanford's research misconduct investigation. And, of course, Nash's car repairs—not to mention her own. At this rate, she might have everything paid off by the time she retired. That is, if she could afford to retire.

"What are you researching?" Delaney asked, interrupting her morose thoughts.

Shelby huffed out a laugh. "Right now I'm researching what to research."

"Oh." Delaney smiled. "Been there, done that, bought the T-shirt."

Delaney pointed to Shelby's car. "Haven't gotten that fixed yet?"

"Oh. No. It's no big deal."

"But, you have duct tape holding up your bumper."

Shelby shrugged, hoping Delaney would drop the subject. "It works for now."

They turned onto Main Street and could hear the marching band up ahead.

"So, what was it like growing up in Sterling?" Delaney asked.

"It was nice, especially after meeting Nash and Ethan." She and her single mom had moved to Sterling from Memphis the summer before fourth grade. She knew her mom had escaped an abusive relationship but never thought to ask what had brought her to a small college town in northeast Georgia.

Delaney gave her a shoulder nudge. "Tell me about it. I love a good story."

"Oh, the three of us ran wild as kids, especially in the

summer. Riding bikes, climbing trees, collecting bugs—all the things kids do in a small town—from sun up to sun down." And because her mom waited tables on the weekends at Ruby's Diner, in addition to her regular job in one of the quarry offices during the week, Shelby often found herself invited to eat with Nash or Ethan's family.

Nash and Ethan lived two doors down from one another. Shelby and her single mom, on the other hand, lived one street over in one of the duplexes in a rundown neighborhood.

"You're such a brainiac. I don't see you catching frogs and skipping rocks."

"Well, when I wasn't running the woods and streets of Sterling, you could find me curled up with a book or solving math and logic puzzles." Shelby shrugged. "I've always had a knack for numbers."

"Clearly," Delaney said with a laugh.

She and Delaney merged with more fans on their way to the university's stadium, some already rowdy from too much alcohol.

Although a tomboy, Shelby hadn't played organized sports growing up like Nash or Ethan because her mom couldn't afford it. But she'd always gone to Ethan's baseball games and Nash's football games, cheering them on all through Little League and Pop Warner, middle school and high school, and keeping stats on their performances for fun.

Their friendship sustained Shelby through the tough times, like when her mom lost her job at the diner and finances got even tighter than they already were, or when she came down with pneumonia and had to be hospitalized.

But one day, when Shelby was fifteen, her relationship with Nash had changed.

She and Nash had been climbing one of the ancient oak trees down by the abandoned gristmill when she'd slipped and landed flat on her back, knocking the wind out of her.

As she lay writhing in agony, trying to get her stunned lungs to draw in a breath, Nash jumped down from the tree and ran to her.

He'd leaned over her, and she looked up into his concerned blue eyes, and that was it. She fell, and she fell hard. Harder than her fall from the tree.

He lifted her to a sitting position. "Relax, Sassafras. Don't panic. You just got the wind knocked out of you. Hurts like hell, but you'll be fine in a minute."

Shelby coughed, painful and hard.

"That's good. Coughing is good. Means your diaphragm is working again." He knelt in front of her. "Sit up on your knees. That's it. Coach says to breathe in through your nose and out through your mouth. That's it. Good." All the while, he ran his hands up and down her back.

She drew in a deep and painful, but head-clearing, breath.

"Anything broken?" he asked as he checked her arms, wrists, and ankles.

She just shook her head no, too mesmerized by his touch to speak.

"Damn, Sassafras. You were lucky. A fall like that should have broken something." He pressed his forehead to hers and gazed into her eyes, and she held the breath just moments before she'd been grateful to take. Was he going to kiss her?

"Come on." He sat back on his heels and held his hands out to her. "Up you go."

From that moment on, Shelby Wentworth had an unrequited crush on Nash Taylor, town football hero.

"You and the guys were good buddies then?" Delaney asked, dragging Shelby back onto Main Street from her walk down Memory Lane.

"Yeah, you could say that." Shelby smiled at the memories.

"Still are from the looks of things."

"Well, things have changed, of course, with Ethan getting married, and Nash . . . Well, it's been a while."

"I don't think that matters to him," she said as she waved to some friends.

"What do you mean?"

"I mean the way he looks at you. Like he'd run through fire to protect you."

Shelby shook her head. She used to think that too. "That's just Nash. He'd run through fire to protect just about anyone."

"Maybe, but for you, he'd run through fire, brimstone, and straight into Hell."

Shelby didn't say anything.

They'd arrived at the fan-packed Ruby's and spotted Ethan and Sam.

"You know, Shelby," Delaney gave her another gentle shoulder nudge, "if you ever want to talk about it, I'm here. And Sam too."

Were her feelings for Nash that transparent? Shelby shook her head. "Thanks, though."

IT WAS STANDING room only when Nash walked into McGinty's later that night. Amid claps on the back and offers to buy him drinks, he made his way to the bar, where people stood three deep. Like the Dallas Cowboys' offense opening a hole for Emmitt Smith, the crowd parted, giving him a clear path.

"What'll it be, Coach?" Hugh, McGinty's owner asked in his deep, booming voice.

"I'll take that amber ale you've got on tap."

Hugh drew the beer and handed Nash a frosty mug. "On the house. Congrats on pulling out a win."

Yeah, by the seat of his pants. He didn't know how the team managed it, but he'd take the win. "Cheers." He raised his mug to the crowd and took a satisfying pull. As he scanned the crowd, his gaze landed on Shelby sitting in the corner with his other running buddies.

She laughed at something Delaney said then tucked a stray strand of hair behind her ear. She'd begun to look more relaxed, losing some of the haunted look in her eyes.

She'd also begun to let down her guard a little more around him. Maybe she'd forgiven him after all.

He should just finish his beer and head home. Well past midnight, it had been a hell of a long day—game days always were—and a hot shower and comfortable bed sounded good. But he found himself making a beeline straight for Shelby.

As he approached the table, Shelby glanced up, and her eyes locked with his. And something clicked, just like it always did when he looked at her. The eleven years apart had done nothing to change that.

"Hey, Coach," Delaney yelled. "Come sit down." She pulled Shelby's arm, indicating she should slide over.

"Great win tonight, man!" Ethan said as he raised his glass in salute.

Nash collapsed onto the bench next to Shelby and felt that *zing* when they touched. She snapped to attention and scooted closer to Delaney, who gave her a look like, WTF?

He couldn't resist. Leaning over, he said, "Hi, Sassafras," right in Shelby's ear and noted her slight shiver in response.

What the hell was he doing? It must have been the adrenalin of a close win. Shelby wasn't the kind of woman a man toyed with. Shelby was for keeps.

"That play at the end of the third quarter . . . brilliant! Just brilliant!" Ethan said, before shoving a fry in his face. "And gutsy. That could have gone south quick."

"Yeah. Thanks." Nash reached over and stole a fry off Ethan's plate and received a kick under the table for his trouble.

No sooner had he sat down than Shelby tapped him on the arm indicating she needed to get up.

He watched her wend her way through the inebriated Bobcats fans on her way to the ladies' room, catching a glimpse of that sweet little ass in her snug blue jeans just before the crowd swallowed her up.

He drained his beer, and it took him two seconds to make up his mind to follow her.

"Where you going?" Delaney shouted above the din. "You just got here."

"I'll be back."

SHELBY WALKED OUT OF THE LADIES' room determined to go back to the table and say her goodnights. Despite her protests to the contrary, she was hungry and didn't want to spend money on food at McGinty's. She'd ordered water to drink while everyone else had beer or liquor. She'd just go home and curl up in bed with a late-night bowl of Cheerios. Dark Chocolate Crunch. Even a broke girl had to have *some* creature comforts.

Rounding the corner, she ran right into a hard immovable object. Nash Taylor.

"Whoa!" He grabbed her shoulders to keep her from falling.

"Nash!" She stepped back out of his reach. "I'm sorry, I didn't see you."

"No harm done."

She stood there for a moment, silent and awkward.

"Want to dance?"

Her gaze shot to Nash's face. "What?" The music wasn't that loud in the hallway they were standing in, but she was sure she'd misheard him.

"You know, shake our booties to the beat?"

Nope. She'd heard him correctly. Why would he ask her to dance when any one of the star-struck female Bobcats fans would gladly oblige? She shook her head. "I think you've had one too many. Besides, I was just leaving."

"I'll walk you home then."

"No. That's okay. Then you'd have to come back for your car."

"I parked in front of your apartment." He shrugged. "It was the only place I could find a spot."

"I'll be fine. You just got here anyway." She started to walk away.

"Shelby, you knew my mom. She'd tan my hide if she knew I'd let a pretty young woman walk home late at night by herself. Especially with these rowdy fans."

He thought she was pretty? She couldn't remember the last time anyone paid her a compliment, especially on her looks.

"Fine," she said with a sigh. "I'll just go say goodbye."

She felt Nash's hand on the small of her back as he

guided her through the sea of red and blue Bobcats fans in various stages of inebriation.

"I'm walking Shelby home," Nash shouted, before she could speak.

"Sure," Delaney replied with a grin. "Ethan will make sure I get home okay, right, Ethan?"

"Uh, yeah. I mean, of course." Ethan responded after Sam nudged him.

Nash followed Shelby out as she stepped into the chilly night air. Fall had finally come to north Georgia.

"You didn't bring a jacket?"

"No. It was warm when we left for the game."

He slipped off his red Bobcats jacket and draped it over her shoulders. She shivered as the warmth enveloped her, and she barely resisted putting her nose to the fabric and inhaling deeply. "Thanks," she muttered. So much for avoiding Nash. "I noticed you had your car repaired. If you send me the bill, I'll pay you back." Somehow. She could always sell her eggs.

"Forget it."

"But—"

"Forget it." This time the edge in his voice made her comply.

Students whooped and hollered. The frat parties didn't show any signs of letting up anytime soon. Clearly, Sterling loved its victories. As if college students needed a reason to party.

"You did great out there tonight." Shelby said as she and Nash strolled side-by-side along the sidewalk. Watching Nash coach had been like watching a maestro conduct an orchestra.

"Thanks. There was a point in the third quarter when I didn't think we were going to come back."

They'd been deep in their own territory with fourth and short. "And then the flea flicker."

He nodded and smiled. "And then the flea flicker." His smile could light up the night, Shelby thought.

This was bad. So, so bad.

"It got the crowd back into the game and gave us the kick in the pants we needed to pull out the win."

"Fourth and short conversions have a sixty-three percent success rate, so you were right to go for it. Not enough coaches do."

Nash stopped, looked at her like she'd just revealed the opponents' secret playbook, and then laughed.

"How do you know that?"

She stuck out her hand. "Shelby Wentworth, sports fan and numbers junkie. Nice to meet you."

He took her hand, and Shelby realized her mistake as warmth spread up her arm and across her chest. His gaze captured hers and held here pinned to the spot.

Closing the distance, Nash lifted her hand to his chest and lowered his head to kiss her. And she wanted him to. God, how she wanted him to.

"Look out!" Nash grabbed her shoulders and pulled her against him just as a guy on a skateboard flew past her, knocking her purse off her shoulder.

"Sorry, dude!" the kid yelled without looking back.

"Idiot," Nash muttered. "You okay?"

The tension between them grew as he stared into her eyes, his mouth just inches from hers. "Yeah." Shelby stepped back, breaking the spell, then they both bent down to pick up her bag and knocked heads.

"Ow!"

"Shit!"

Rubbing their foreheads, they both started laughing.

Deep, belly-shaking laughter. It felt so good. So damn good. Cathartic. Powerful. And long overdue.

Now her stomach hurt along with her head, but she'd take it. Glancing around, she realized they were only yards away from her apartment. Holding out her hand to warn him off, she bent over again and scooped up her purse.

"Thanks for walking me home, Nash." She handed him his jacket.

"Anytime, Sassafras."

With reluctant feet, she turned in the direction of her front door. It was for the best. The last thing she needed was to fall for Nash Taylor. Again. But then again, it may already be too late.

7

Early the next morning, Nash heard a car pulling up in front of the house. Coffee cup in hand, he walked to the front window in time to see Shelby climb out of her car and head for the barn.

Hmm. Well, he had issued her an open invitation to come out and ride whenever she wanted. Good to see she was taking him up on it.

She looked sexy in those snug jeans, but he frowned over her athletic shoes. She needed a good pair of boots to ride in, he thought.

It was a beautiful morning, cool with a hint of coming fall, and a ride sounded appealing.

He'd scheduled the post-game review for later that afternoon to allow his coaches to spend Sunday morning with their families.

Making up his mind, Nash strode through the house, stopped by the kitchen, dropped off his coffee mug, and grabbed a jacket as he passed through the mudroom and out the back door.

When he reached the barn, Shelby had just draped Moonshine's saddle blanket across her back.

"Want some company?"

Shelby gasped and spun to face him, her hand over her heart.

"Sorry about that," Nash said with a grin. "Didn't mean to startle you."

"As my mother would say, you took ten years off my life."

He noted her accent was making a comeback and he liked it. "Well, I do live here, you know."

She returned her attention to Moonshine, adjusted her bridle. "I wouldn't mind some company," she said, her voice so soft he wasn't sure he'd heard her correctly.

"Great. How about we ride over to Pine Bough Creek?" He, Ethan, and Shelby used to swim in the creek in the heat of summer, clothes and all. He remembered the summer Shelby turned sixteen and the way her thin white tank top had done little to conceal her hard nipples when she'd waded out of the water. He and Ethan had talked about that for months on end.

He'd wanted her even then. But he and Ethan had made a pact in sixth grade that Shelby was off limits to both of them. They'd spit and shook on it, and you didn't break promises made with that most sacred of rituals.

He'd held up his end of the bargain, even though years later it had meant hurting Shelby.

"Sure. Although I don't think we'll be swimming today." She slung the saddle up over Moonshine's back and cinched the strap.

Yeah. Too bad.

He smiled over the shared memories. The years between them fell away whenever they were together. They just seemed to pick up wherever they'd left off. And since they left off with him crushing on Shelby and not being able to have her, it wasn't necessarily a good place to pick up again.

SHELBY TOOK a deep breath of the fresh country air, relaxed and contented, if only for the moment, with Nash by her side. Country living suited him.

He'd made something out of his life, and when adversity had taken him away from the game he loved, he'd shifted gears and found another career that allowed him to stay with the sport. She admired that.

She knew she needed to do the same, but knowing and doing were two different things.

"Let's stop here," he said as he dismounted in a sunny patch alongside the lazy creek.

She followed suit, releasing Moonshine's reins so she could graze alongside Whisky.

Nash stretched out on the ground, plucked a late dandelion, and handed it to Shelby as she sat next to him. "Thanks." She smiled at the sweet gesture she remembered from childhood, and tucked the flower behind her ear.

Whisky nickered, then settled beneath a shady tree.

Leaning back on her hands, she crossed one ankle over the other. "God, I missed this place. I didn't realize how much until just now."

"I know what you mean. The things we took for granted as kids mean so much more now."

That might be true of some things, but she'd never taken Nash for granted.

Shelby lay back in the grass, lifted her face to the sun, and closed her eyes, listening to the breeze in the trees, the call of a cardinal, and the breathing of the man next to her. She'd missed more things than Pine Bough Creek.

She felt his gaze on her face, and the heat of embarrassment competed with the heat of the sun. Opening her eyes, she turned to face him. "What are you looking at?"

"You."

A butterfly fluttered in her stomach. How long had she wanted this? How long had she yearned for Nash's notice of her as someone other than a friend?

Rising up on his elbow, he leaned over her, his gaze intense as he lifted his free hand to cup her face, and her heart battered her ribs. "Stop me, Shelby. Tell me no."

"No."

He dropped his hand.

"No." Against her better judgment, she rose to meet him. "I meant, no, I don't want you to stop. I don't want to tell you no."

HE GROANED low in his throat then pulled her beneath him as his mouth took hers. Her lips were warm from the sunshine, and her sweet lemon scent engulfed him.

Her fingers found their way into his hair, stroking, gripping, and he wanted more. So much more.

Their tongues danced, dipping and swaying. He nibbled her lip, reveled in her indrawn breath. He swept a hand along her ribs, the heat of her conjuring images of her in his bed, naked and willing.

Sweet Jesus.

He broke the kiss, nipped his way along her jaw to her ear, sucking her earlobe into his mouth. Gasping, she turned her head, giving him easier access to the tender skin on her neck. He could feel her erratic pulse when he pressed his lips to her, his pulse just as erratic.

When she wrapped a leg around him, he was lost. Lost in the feel, the smell, the taste of her. His fingers found the buttons on her blouse, opening them until he could slip his hand inside. She arched against his hand as he cupped her breast, his thumb working the pebbled peak.

Her breath hitched, her hands glided over his back, and he shifted his weight, settling between her hips, moaning when his erection pressed against her center. If he didn't stop this right now, they'd be naked in no time, for anyone who came along to see. And Shelby deserved better than that.

Calling on a reserve of will power he hadn't needed since the days of NFL training camp, he broke the kiss and rolled off her. "We can't. Not here."

Her brow furrowed, and she raised a shaking hand to her wet, swollen lips. Sitting up, she looked around as if just now aware of her surroundings.

"Come home with me?" His voice was rough with desire.

She nodded.

Pulling her up by her outstretched hand, he then buttoned up her blouse and adjusted her jacket before sending her off to Moonshine with a pat on her butt.

Adjusting himself, he winced. Nothing like a horseback ride with a hard on. But if Shelby welcomed him at the other end of the ride, it would be worth it.

THEY WERE silent on the ride back, giving Shelby some time and space to think about what they'd almost done. God, she wanted Nash. Wanted him in a way the teenage Shelby never could. Wanted him with her heart, her head, and her body.

They watered and fed the horses, and Nash released them into the paddock.

She should leave. She should get in her car, start driving, and never look back. Because this had disaster written all over it.

Nash clasped her hand in his and she caved. "How about something to drink?"

She nodded and headed toward the house with him by her side.

In the kitchen, Nash pulled two bottles of water from the fridge, opened one, and handed it to her, before opening his own.

Her mouth had gone desert dry, and not from the ride. She gulped two swallows before setting the bottle on the granite counter behind her. He followed suit. Then backed her up against that same counter, his blue eyes locked on hers.

"God, Shelby. I know your life is complicated right now, and I don't want to add anymore complications." He skimmed a finger along her cheekbone, and she closed her eyes, leaning into his caress.

"But?"

"But I want you more than I've ever wanted another woman in my life. It's selfish and short-sighted, but there it is."

Her knees trembled, and she suddenly forgot how to breathe.

"Tell me you want me too."

She nodded, the only thing she was capable of at the moment.

He smelled like hay and horses and fresh sweat. He

tilted his head, his mouth honed in on hers, and the antici-pation of his kiss nearly made her drop to her knees. And when his mouth found hers, she felt as if she were coming home.

Capturing her mouth with his, she reveled in the warmth and sweetness. His hands gripped her hips, and his tongue slipped between her lips to tangle with hers. Visions of him hovering over by the creek flooded her brain. The feel of his hard body, the heat of him nestled against her, spurred her on as his mouth continued to plunder hers.

Her hands glided along his shoulders, skimmed along his neck, before she plunged her fingers into his hair.

Sliding his hand down her ribs, she was struck anew by how large his hands were, and she shivered at the thought of those hands on the rest of her body.

His hands brushed her breasts, and she arched to meet them. He undid the buttons on her blouse until he could peel it back. Lifting her, he sat her up on the counter. The feel of ice-cold water cut through the haze of her desire, and as water spilled across the counter and down the cabinets onto the floor, the spike in her adrenalin had nothing to do with arousal, and everything to do with fear.

"Oh my god, I'm so sorry."

Nash almost laughed until he saw the look in her eyes. Fear.

She jumped off the counter and made a grab for the roll of paper towels next to the sink, while also pulling her blouse closed.

"Shelby. Shelby. It's okay. It's just water." He took the roll from her hands, set it on the counter. "And besides, it was my fault. I'm the one who set you on the counter."

"I should have put the cap back on the bottle. I wasn't thinking." Her hands fluttered, looking for something to do. He caught them, held them to his chest. "You couldn't have known."

She shook her head.

He had a sick feeling in the pit of his stomach.

"Shelby, what's this all about? What are you afraid of?"

Moving away from him, she bit her lip and looked away.

His smartphone rang.

Sweet Jesus! Talk about poor timing.

He pulled the phone from his back pocket, glanced at the screen, and stalked into the living room. "This better be important."

"Uh, Coach?" his assistant stammered on the other end of the line.

"Kenny, what the hell do you want? I gave you the morning off."

"I've got the game films ready for you. You said you wanted to come in and review them before the post-game review meeting today."

Nash scrubbed his hands down his face. "Right." He looked down at the bulge in his jeans. "Just load them on the computer and I'll be in later."

"Right, Coach."

Sending his gaze heavenward, he groaned and hung up the phone.

When he walked back into the kitchen, he found Shelby, her hair rumpled, her lips swollen, and her eyes wide. She'd misbuttoned her blouse, and her jeans were wet from the water she'd spilled.

Damn. Guess she was leaving.

"I have to go. We shouldn't be doing this anyway." She strode toward the front door.

"Dammit, Shelby. Don't leave like this." He followed her to the living room.

The closing of the door was the only sound that met his plea.

HER FINGERS GRIPPED the steering wheel as she sped along Country Road Fifty-Seven back toward town. She never should have come out. She never should have accepted his invitation to ride.

The spilled water brought bitter memories flooding back. The time Charlie yelled at her for knocking the bottle of water over on his laptop. Never mind that she hadn't left an opened bottle of water next to a valuable computer—it had been him—but she'd taken the blame. Or the time he berated her in front of their grad assistants when she came in late for a meeting after getting sick in the bathroom from food poisoning.

But, bad memories aside, she should be grateful she'd knocked over the water. It had stopped what couldn't happen. She knew that if she slept with Nash there'd be no going back. At least for her.

It wouldn't be just sex for her. It would be the beginning of the end for her heart.

8

———

That afternoon, Nash and his coaches gathered in the media room to view the tapes from the previous night's game, cups of coffee at their elbows.

Some had writing pads and pens at hand, others electronic tablets, but they all took notes as they dissected the game, play-by-play. Nash tried to refocus his attention after his morning with Shelby and his suspicions about her ex-husband, but the look on her face when she'd left was like a helmet-to-helmet hit. It left him aching for her.

"Grady, work on Hansen's blocking," Nash said, using a laser pointer to indicate the missed block.

"Already noted, Coach."

Nash cringed on the next play when Angelo, their QB, got sacked. "Kevin, what the hell was Drew doing on that play?"

The offensive coordinator, Kevin, shook his head. "We'll work on it, Coach."

Nash's smartphone rang. Normally, he would've ignored

it, but it was his dad. He held up a finger to his staff, indicating he needed to take the call.

"Dad, I'm in post-game. What do you need?"

"Nash? Is that you?"

"Yeah, Dad. *You* called *me*. What's up?"

His father hesitated. "I, uh, I don't remember."

"Okay, well, I'll come by later—"

"No, wait! I remember. There's someone in the attic."

"Dad, there's no one in the attic. Remember? I checked it the other day." Nash could feel the eyes of his staff on him. He rose from his chair and walked over to the corner of the room, turning his back.

"Son, I heard them walking around. They're probably robbing me blind as we speak!"

"Dad, listen." Nash lowered his voice. "No one can get in the attic in the first place, much less steal what's stored up there." When he'd checked the other day, he'd been surprised by all the crap—broken small appliances, old football pads and cleats (his and his dad's), boxes of yearbooks, and other high school paraphernalia.

"Well, I can't sit here and do nothing! I'm going up there to run whoever it is off!"

"No. Dad!" Dammit. He'd hung up. Drawing in a deep breath, he turned back to the group then gave them a stiff smile. "I need to go check on my dad. Kevin, can you take it from here?"

"Sure, Coach."

Avoiding the concerned expressions on everyone's faces, Nash gathered his iPad and keys. "I'll call you later."

Then he got the hell out of Dodge.

~

WALKING past McGinty's on the way to the local drug store on the Monday after her close call with Nash, Shelby spotted a sign in the window. HELP WANTED. WAIT-STAFF AND BARTENDER.

After paying bills and balancing her checkbook that morning, she had just enough money left to buy some feminine necessities like Midol, Tampax, and a pint of Ben & Jerry's Chocolate Fudge Brownie.

Thinking of her ever-insufficient checking account balance and her maxed-out credit cards, she considered the job. She'd waited tables in a respectable restaurant in Providence while she attended Brown University. Thinking of her mom's years as a waitress, she guessed maybe it was in her blood.

She gnawed on her lower lip. But could she bear the stigma of waiting tables at McGinty's, knowing she would be waiting on former high school classmates, her students, even her academic colleagues?

Maybe she should look for something in one of the neighboring towns, somewhere she'd be less likely to see people she knew. She had to do something. Soon. She hadn't been this deep in debt since she'd been a college student.

"Hey, Shelby."

She turned to see Delaney. Even in jeans and a T-shirt, Delaney looked like a walking sexpot.

"Hi, Delaney."

"You thinking about lunch?" She pointed to McGinty's. "I was just thinking about grabbing a quick bite. Want to join?"

Considering her lack of funds, her answer had to be no. *Dammit.* She liked Delaney and wouldn't mind getting to know her a little better. Holding back a groan of regret, she scrounged for an excuse. "Thanks, but I have an appoint-ment. Maybe some other time."

"Sure." Delaney's understanding smile added to Shelby's disappointment.

"I'd better go." Shelby pointed in the direction of the drug store.

"See you later then." Delaney waved as she opened the door of McGinty's.

Even more depressed now than she was when she set out on her mission, she wondered if she had enough to buy *two* pints of Ben & Jerry's.

MONDAY EVENING, Nash stood in the medication aisle of the Piggly Wiggly trying to decide which laxative to get for his father. "Too many damn choices," he muttered. Not to mention embarrassing as hell. Buying Stephanie's Tampax was less humiliating. At least anyone who saw would know they weren't for him. He needed to make a decision before someone saw him.

"Hey, Nash."

Too late. He groaned then pasted a smile on his face and turned to greet Delaney.

"Hi, Delaney."

They chatted a few minutes about the football season, a typical conversation when he ran into folks around town.

"By the way, I ran into Shelby earlier today outside McGinty's."

"That's nice," he replied, still too preoccupied with his escape. Not from Delaney—he really liked her—from his present predicament.

"She was looking at the want ad they had in the window for wait staff."

That got his attention. "Wait. What?"

"Yeah. She acted all nonchalant, but when I asked her to lunch she said she had to run."

"Well, maybe she had something going on." Nash said, waving off her speculation.

"Maybe. But did you know she still hasn't had her car fixed?"

He frowned. He hadn't seen the backend of her car. "Maybe she hasn't had the time to drive up to Carlyle."

"That, or she can't afford to have it fixed."

Nash put his free hand on his hip. "What are you saying, Delaney? That Shelby is having financial problems?"

"I think so. She's looking at a want ad, her bumper is duct-taped to her car, after the first football game, she didn't order anything to eat from McGinty's—"

"Maybe she wasn't hungry."

Shelby leveled him with a look. "She didn't order anything after the football game. Not even a soda. Just water. It all adds up."

Nash considered Delaney's observations. If it was true, Nash new that Shelby would never ask for help. She'd grown up wearing hand-me-downs and eating Hamburger Helper. She wouldn't want to admit she was still living hand-to-mouth.

But she had a good job, so how could that be?

He nodded. But he didn't know what he or Delaney could do about it. It wasn't as if she'd take charity.

"What should we do?" Delaney asked, her eyes filled with concern.

Delaney wore her heart on her sleeve most of the time. It was one of the things he admired about her.

"I don't know, but I'll give it some thought."

"Good. Let me know if I can help."

"Will do."

"Oh, and if you're looking for a laxative, magnesium citrate works best. My grandfather swears by it," she said with a wink.

Juuust shoot me. Nash thought his dilemma had gone unnoticed. The joys of living in a small town.

Nash turned into his driveway the following Wednesday. It was only four twenty, and he should've gone back to his office at the stadium, but after spending the afternoon with his dad at a doctor's appointment, he knew he wouldn't be able to concentrate on work.

The results of his dad's neuro-psych tests were getting worse. Today he couldn't remember his address or phone number.

He spotted Shelby's still-damaged car parked in the driveway and was reminded of Delaney's concerns. Nash had been mulling over a plan, but he'd been preoccupied with his father's continued decline. He had a few more issues to iron out, and then he'd set the plan in motion.

But still, he couldn't understand how a professor—even an assistant professor—could be that strapped. But whatever the reason, he'd always stood by Shelby and would continue to stand by her when she needed him, even if she wouldn't admit it.

For now, he just wanted to get to the bottom of Shelby's reaction to the spilled water the other day.

Entering the house, he grabbed a couple of beers from

the fridge and walked back out onto the porch, settling himself in the swing.

Moments later, Shelby picked her way across the lawn toward her car, jacket slung over her shoulder.

"Want a beer?" He held up the second bottle.

She stopped, hesitated, then glanced his way. "I'm sorry to disturb you. I didn't think you'd be home this early."

"You're not disturbing me, Shelby." God, he hated seeing her like this. Cowed. Unsure of herself. And of him. "Come on. One beer."

She turned her feet in the direction of the porch, and he couldn't help but smile.

Handing her the beer, he patted the swing. "Go for a swing, Sassafras?"

She shook her head, laughed, then sat down next to him, and he pushed the swing back and let it go.

While she took a swig of her beer, he asked how her ride was.

"Good. I rode over to the old gristmill. It's a shame to see it so dilapidated. Someone needs to buy it and give it some tender loving care." She eyed him over her bottle.

"Oh, no you don't. I'm fresh out of tender loving care after fixing up this money pit," he said as he gestured toward the house with his bottle of beer.

They sat in companionable silence for a few minutes, both lost in thought. Or memories.

"Hey." Nash broke the silence. "Remember when you, Ethan, and I used to play Truth or Dare?"

Shelby nodded, then laughed.

"The silly questions we used to ask? 'If you were a super-hero, who would you be?' or the dares like 'Ring Mrs. Colburn's door and run?' How about a game now?"

"You offered me a beer to play Truth or Dare?"

At her reluctance, Nash prodded, "Come on. Where's the Shelby who used to give as good as she got?"

She wouldn't look at him, so he gave her shoulder a nudge. "Truth or dare?"

She waited a beat then said, "Truth."

"All right. If you had to pick the all-time best NFL quarterback who would it be?"

Her gaze shot to his face. Clearly not the question she'd expected.

"You already know."

"You can't say me," he said with a grin.

She snorted. "Wasn't going to."

"Ouch." He rubbed the imaginary wound on his chest.

"Peyton Manning."

"You just think he's cute," Nash teased.

"Hey. Five hundred thirty-nine career touchdowns for a total of over seventy-one thousand yards and a completion percentage of sixty-five-point-three."

"Fine." He threw his hand up in surrender. "Your turn."

"Truth or dare?"

"Truth."

"Did you toilet paper the Kaminsky's yard senior year?"

He laughed. "Yes."

"You sneak! And you didn't invite me?"

"It was past your curfew. Your mom would have tanned your hide."

"That's no excuse."

Still grinning, he asked, "Truth or dare?"

"Truth."

He dropped the grin and looked Shelby in the eye. "Did he hurt you?" he asked, his voice rough with emotion.

She sucked in a breath, and he thought he'd pushed too

hard too fast. Shelby shook her head, picking at the label on her beer. "No. At least not physically."

He fisted his free hand by his side. If he ever encountered her ex-husband, he'd make sure he never hurt Shelby again. Physically or otherwise.

"Okay. Then how?"

She turned her head, her arms wrapped around her, and looked out at the setting sun, gnawing on her lip.

"Talk to me Shelby," Nash entreated her, his voice gentle.

She nodded, hands clinched in a fist. "You have to understand. Charles Ingram was a god in the world of statistics. When I learned he would be my dissertation chair and that I would get to work as his grad assistant, well, it would have been like you being able to train under Tom Brady or Roger Staubach—"

"Or Peyton Manning."

A smile ghosted across her face. "Yeah." The smile evaporated, and she rubbed her arms as if cold. "He was the reason I went to Stanford. We started seeing each other outside of work. He invited me to meetings with researchers who were the rock stars of their fields. I was in awe of him and his friends. One thing led to another, and the next thing I knew we were married."

"But after I married him it went downhill. We argued if I wanted to go out with friends or colleagues. Then he always had some reason why I couldn't fly home to see my mom or why she couldn't come to see me."

"Separating you from friends and family," Nash muttered.

"His control began so slowly that I hardly noticed my transition from a confident, strong young woman to a . . . doormat. He would berate me in front of our grad students, in front of other researchers." She threw up her hand as if in defeat. "I got so tired of fighting that I stopped standing up for myself. I backed down when he pressed me."

"So, the spilled water . . ."

"Yeah. He would have yelled at me, called me clumsy, or worse, stupid."

He set his beer on the ground and took her by the shoulders. A tear trickled down her cheek. "You are light years from stupid, and don't let him or anyone else make you think otherwise. You just need to get your mojo back."

"Right. I'll work on that." She took another pull on her beer.

Taking her free hand, he clasped it in his. "Seriously, Shelby. Don't let that asshole get the better of you. He isn't worth it."

Maybe it was his pep talk, maybe it was the beer, but he saw a little spark in Shelby's eyes. "Truth or dare?" she asked.

He smiled, "Dare."

"Kiss me."

9

N ash felt those words all the way down to his groin.
He cupped Shelby's beautiful face then gently
wiped the tear from her cheek with the pad of his
thumb. Her asshole ex-husband didn't know what he'd had.
Her gaze flickered to his lips, lingering there, and he felt
himself grow hard.

Taking her hand, he pulled her up and walked to the
front door and into the living room. His house was secluded,
but he didn't want to risk someone driving up and seeing
them. And if this went where he hoped it would, the swing
was no place for it.

He gently pushed her down on the couch and covered
her, rocking into her and feeling the rush of adrenalin when
she moaned at the contact.

Making quick work of the buttons, he opened her blouse
then caressed her hard nipples through her bra, eliciting a
throaty moan from her. She wore a simple black bra, no
lace, no bows. So Shelby. But seeing her pale skin in contrast
with the black of her bra made him groan with desire.

Flicking open the front closure of her bra with one hand, he smoothed his other hand along her inner thigh.

When her breasts were bare before him, he devoured her with his gaze. "So beautiful," he whispered. How he'd resisted her all through high school, he'd never know. But he damned sure couldn't resist her any longer. Ever since the interlude by the creek, Shelby had been on his mind.

He had to touch and taste her. Taking a nipple into his mouth, he traced it with his tongue, and he felt a shudder ripple through her. Offering the same treatment to her other breast, his fingers grazed the silky soft skin of her stomach before dipping beneath the waistband of her jeans.

"Oh God, Nash." With her breathy pants and his own labored breathing, they sounded like two horny teenagers making out on his parents' couch. And he loved it! He couldn't remember the last time he'd just made out with a woman.

The house phone rang. *What the hell?*

"Do you need to get that?" she asked in a breathy pant.

"No. Ignore it."

It rang five times then stopped. Now, back to business, he thought. Then it started ringing again. Thinking about his dad, he got up to answer it.

"Oh, for the love of—whoever it is, you're dead meat," he growled as he rose, adjusted himself, and stalked into the kitchen.

"Nash," he ground out.

"Hiya, Coach! Catch you at a bad time?"

Nash bit back an expletive. "What is it Grady?"

"You asked me to let you know when the new tackling dummies arrived, so I'm letting you know."

Closing his eyes, he ground his teeth. "Good to know,

Grady. I'll see them tomorrow." He hung up without waiting for a reply.

When he walked back into the living room, Shelby was sitting up on the couch and had gathered her blouse around her.

"Sorry about that. Good news is my employees do what I ask. Bad news is my employees do what I ask." He didn't know what to do or how to recreate the mood. And he wanted to. God, how he wanted to.

Her gaze landed on his crotch, and she licked her lips. His gut clenched as he held in the groan of desire waiting for some signal from her.

"Truth or dare?" Shelby asked as she lifted her eyes to his face, her cheeks flushed.

Intrigued, he said, "Dare."

"Take me to bed."

That would be the signal. Her request stunned him, but he quickly recovered. "I thought you'd never ask."

Rising, she wrapped her arms around his neck, kissed him, timid and shy at first. He let her lead the dance. Then she gave him a gentle shove, and he fell back onto the couch. When she climbed onto his lap, he almost cried hallelujah.

She deepened the kiss. Turning up the heat, she straddled him as her hands got busy on his fly. Before she could get too far in her endeavors, he wrapped his hands around her thighs and stood up, walking with her to his room and his king-size bed.

Gently lying her on the mattress, he followed her down, covering her. She rocked her hips into him, sending molten heat straight to his already-overheated parts.

Wasting little time, he flicked open her bra again. "Now, where were we? Oh, yes. I believe we were right here," he murmured as his tongue grazed first one nipple then the other.

Shelby gasped when his mouth claimed her breast, his dark skin and stubble in stark contrast to her own pale skin.

Warning bells sounded in her head.

Then his hand slid between her legs, cupping her, and she didn't care. The house could fall down around them, and as long as he was touching her, she wouldn't have noticed. She'd been waiting for what felt like her whole life for this.

"I want to see you, Shelby," he whispered. Undoing the button on her jeans, he pressed a kiss to her stomach, and she arched into him. As he slid the zipper down, his lips followed until he met the top of her panties.

Rising, he pulled her jeans off, taking her panties with them, then stood looking down at her, his heated gaze sweeping across her like fire across a dry plain.

There was no shyness, no shame. He made her feel like the most beautiful woman in the world.

"My imagination doesn't hold a candle to the reality."

His imagination? He'd imagined her naked? She'd imagined him naked too, and she couldn't wait another minute for her reality.

"Your turn." She stood up and ran her hands beneath his T-shirt, along his smooth skin. The muscles of his stomach quivered at her touch. Lifting the hem, she pulled the shirt over his head, standing on tiptoes to reach. Then she stepped back to admire the treasure she'd uncovered.

"Shelby, you keep looking at me like that, and this won't last long."

She smiled. She felt wicked and . . . free. Sex with Charlie hadn't exactly been the stuff of fantasy, and it only got worse as the years passed.

Reaching out, she flicked open his unbuttoned fly and reached in to take him in her hand.

"Je-sus!"

Latching on to her wrists, he pulled her hand free and stepped out of his jeans. He was a work of art. Lean muscles, broad shoulders, hard flat stomach. She wanted to kiss every inch of him.

"No," he said as if he'd read her mind. "Not yet."

He gave her a gentle shove, and she fell back onto the mattress. Making his way up her body, he kissed her inner thighs, her stomach, her breasts, as she writhed in both agony and ecstasy.

His fingers caressed her thigh before giving her what she craved.

Her hips rose to meet his hand, and he took her mouth with his, his tongue stroking and swirling, mimicking the tantalizing movements of his fingers.

And then she was gone. Shattered into a million pieces.

NASH COULDN'T WAIT another second. He reached into the bedside table drawer for a condom. Hovering over her, he tore open the packet and rolled it on, then captured her mouth once more. He entered her slow and easy, clenching his jaw against the strain of holding himself in check.

That restraint didn't last, as she wrapped her legs around his waist and thrust her hips against his.

"Nash," she moaned.

"I've got you. Hold onto me." His thrusts increased,

harder and faster, hardly able to believe that he was inside Shelby at last. Something he'd fantasized about since he was a horny teenager.

Her breathy pants in his ear, he drove into her, seeking release for them both. When she took his earlobe between her teeth, he came undone. A light flashed behind his eyes, and he thrust one last time before collapsing, breathing as if he'd just run the length of a football field. Twice.

Rolling off her and onto his side, he gathered her into him, enfolding her in his arms, as their breathing returned to normal. He stroked her arm, eyes closed, reveling in the feel of her.

Drifting in a pool of contentment, he started when Shelby's voice broke the silence.

~

"GOD, Nash. I saw the play. The hit. I was so scared." She choked up, felt the tears in the back of her throat. She'd held her breath waiting for him to move as he lay there on the field. To give some sign of life. He'd been knocked unconscious and was still out when they'd brought the backboard and cart out to pick him up.

The sickening hit he took had made all the highlight reels and was the talk of the NFL and safety experts for months afterward.

Being with him now only reminded her how close he'd come to a devastating injury, or worse, death.

"Yeah, me too. But, I can't have regrets. I can't think about what could have been. I've got to accept things as they are and keep moving forward."

She could take a lesson from Nash on that.

She hadn't asked and felt bad that she hadn't. She closed

her eyes against the pain of her selfishness then opened her eyes and looked his way, searching his face in the fading light. "Do you have any residual issues from the concussion?"

"I get headaches, and I see a specialist up at Cornell twice a year. That's where I was when you first came back to town." He tucked an arm under his pillow. "I get cognitive function tests, neuro-psych testing, and MRIs. You know, to catch any changes in my brain."

She rolled onto her side to face him. "God, Nash. It's that bad?"

"Well, not yet. Hopefully, it never will be. But that's the point, right? To catch it before it gets bad. Not that there's a whole lot I can do about it."

They were silent a few beats, her heart battering her ribs as she thought of Nash with a neurodegenerative disorder.

"Do you miss it?" she finally asked.

He stroked her cheek. "Well, I don't miss getting hit." He grinned. "But yeah, I miss watching the perfect play unfold, the adrenalin rush when my long bomb is caught for a touchdown, the crowd noise."

"I could see how that would be addicting."

"I still get the rush, but now it's for my guys."

"I watched your press conference. You looked shell-shocked."

He snorted. "Yeah. I don't know which was worse—giving up the game I loved or standing there alone while I did it."

She lifted up on her elbow and looked down at him. "Why was that? Where was Stephanie in all this?"

~

NASH SAT up against the headboard, positioning the pillow behind his back. Shelby followed suit, pulling the blanket up to cover her breasts. Pity.

Sighing, he spoke. "She didn't bother to show up that day. No. Looking back, Stephanie had never been there for the difficult parts."

Shortly after he'd signed with the Broncos, he and Stephanie had moved to Cherry Hills Village, a suburb of Denver and one of the most affluent neighborhoods in Colorado, and he'd given her carte blanche on the house, from picking it out, to furnishing it.

She'd chosen a modern, nine thousand square-foot monstrosity of stone and glass then filled it with sleek, cold, modern furniture of chrome and more glass. Decorated it to intimidate whoever entered. Even him, so it seemed. But she had been enjoying herself, so he let her have at it.

That Stephanie didn't bother to use the degree she'd earned in social work, but chose instead to throw herself into Cherry Hills' active social life, didn't really bother him either.

He focused his energy and attention on becoming the best quarterback the Broncos had ever had, no easy feat given past QB greats like John Elway and Jake Plummer.

Wedding plans were underway for the off-season, a destination wedding on the Caribbean Island of Nevis.

Shifting to a more comfortable position, he continued, "I became friendly with another rookie on the team, Colin Jackson, wide receiver. We both came from small towns, both played for SEC schools, and both were first-round draft picks."

"I remember him. He's with the Raiders now, right?"

"Yeah. For some reason, Stephanie couldn't stand him. Whenever he'd come over for dinner or with some of the other guys for a cookout, she'd ask me why I had to invite Colin. No matter how friendly Colin tried to be, she'd give him the cold shoulder."

Other than that, Stephanie settled into life as the wife of an NFL quarterback. She sat with the other wives at the home games, had the wives over for away games, or joined them at their homes.

"After my concussion and being placed on injured reserve, Stephanie grew sullen and distant, always asking when I would be able to play again. When I decided to consult a specialist in traumatic brain injury at Cornell before making a decision, she flew off the handle. Why? Weren't the team doctors good enough? Didn't I want to start playing again as soon as possible?"

Shelby reached out and took his hand in hers. Just that small gesture spoke volumes. He had no doubt that, if Shelby had been there, she would have stood by his side at that press conference. Because that's what you did when you cared about someone.

"Dr. Ibrahim, the Cornell specialist, told me if I took another hit, even one with less impact than the one that had injured me, I could spend the rest of my life permanently disabled. Continuing to play football would've been like playing a game of Russian Roulette. It would only be a matter of time before the chamber with the bullet fired."

With the CTE symptoms his father was showing, the disease was high on Nash's radar.

The options had been clear: continue to play football and risk death or permanent disability, or leave the game he loved and live a relatively healthy life.

"So, you made the only decision you could and left the game."

With his free hand, he stroked Shelby's arm. "Too bad Stephanie didn't see it the same way."

"What did she do?" Shelby asked, laying her head on his shoulder. Nothing felt as right as they did in that moment.

"She'd been furious that I would just walk away from my career. She bailed on me." He still got angry thinking about that afternoon.

He'd come home to find suitcases by the door and her waiting for him in the cold, impersonal living room.

"She couldn't believe I had given up football. And the kicker in all this? It wasn't about the money. It was about the prestige of being Nash Taylor's wife." He snorted in disgust. "She couldn't understand why I had to walk away from all that."

Stunned by her avarice for the spotlight, if not for the money, Nash had stood and stared at the woman he'd loved. The woman he thought loved him in return, when all along she'd just loved the money and fame of being his wife. Nothing more.

"When the doorbell rang, she said it was her ride. I assumed she'd called a limo service, but when I glanced out the window, I saw a familiar car—a red Maserati Ghibli."

Shelby's brow puckered in confusion. "Whose was it?"

"Colin Jackson's." Turned out his friend's betrayal had hurt worse than his wife's.

"Oh, Nash." As she sat up on her knees to face him, the blanket fell away, leaving her bare. But the only thing he wanted to look at in that moment was Shelby's beautiful concerned face. She cupped his jaw and gazed into his eyes. "What a fool she was." Leaning in, she pressed her lips to his. His hands skimmed up her bare back then drew her into him.

Taking control of the kiss, he swept his tongue along her

lips and into her mouth, her breathy sighs a balm to his injured heart. And when she straddled him, the hurt and the anger that had lingered for the last three years fell away.

He must have dozed off because the next thing he knew he was alone. Sitting up, he looked around for evidence that this hadn't been just another fantasy. He spotted it in the form of a pair of hot pink panties lying on the floor and couldn't stop the grin that spread across his face.

A noise from the kitchen caught his attention. He got up, pulled on his jeans, and walked barefoot through the house. It was dark outside, and his stomach let him know it was dinner time.

Turning the corner into the kitchen, he caught her, bent over, head in the fridge, clearly looking for food.

In his T-shirt, her legs and feet bare, she was a sight. A sight that made him forget his hunger for food and shifted his attention toward another hunger.

He snuck up behind her and grabbed her around the waist.

Screeching, she would have collapsed if he hadn't had his arm around her.

"Jesus, Nash! You scared me!"

He buried his face in her neck and chuckled. "Who'd you think it was?" He ran a hand up her thigh to her bare bottom, enjoying the gasp his touch elicited.

"I thought you were asleep." She panted.

"I was. Got hungry." He nuzzled behind her ear and felt her shiver.

⌒

"I WAS TRYING to rectify that when you snuck up behind me and took ten years off my life."

"Yeah, well, I'm not hungry for food anymore."

She turned in his arms. "No?"

"No."

"Then what are you hungry for?" She lifted a brow in challenge.

Taking her by the waist, he lifted her onto the kitchen island. She squealed when her bare bottom hit the cold granite, and he chuckled.

"I'll show you." Opening her legs, he stepped between them and reached for the wallet still in the back pocket of his jeans. Pulling out a foil packet, he waved it in front of her eyes.

"Well, isn't that handy?" she asked, her voice heavy with sarcasm.

"I live by the Boy Scout oath." He dropped his jeans to the floor, and her hands quickly found his bare ass.

"You were never a Boy Scout." Her gaze dropped to his erection.

"Doesn't mean I'm not always prepared. Now, stop talking, woman, and kiss me."

And she gladly obliged, drawing in a breath when he entered her.

"God, Nash. You feel so good." She dropped her head back and let him take control. His big quarterback hands gripped her thighs, holding her in place as he drove into her, over and over. She felt the tension build tighter and tighter until she thought she might burst with it.

As her release washed over her, he growled in response to his own.

And on the tip of her tongue were the words, *I love you.*

～

LATER THAT NIGHT, Nash lay awake in the dark staring up at the ceiling, trying to figure out if he said or did something to make Shelby run away like her ass was on fire.

With memories of her soft skin sliding against his, his name on her lips, her hands gripping his shoulders as she came, he knew a sleepless night lay ahead.

He rolled over, and her sweet lemon scent rose from the pillow, making him groan. Part of him wanted to change the sheets, and another part of him wanted to bury his face in the pillow and breathe her in.

What the hell was he supposed to do now? He knew this wasn't enough. He wanted her again already.

What would this do to their friendship? And would Ethan sense the change?

And yet, he couldn't regret what they'd done.

He'd had the best of intentions when he'd asked her to have a beer with him. He'd been giving her situation some thought, and he had a plan in mind. Then one thing led to another, and the next thing he knew, they were naked in his bed.

So then he'd made up his mind to ask her to stay for dinner and talk with her then.

But she'd fled before he could ask.

He'd just have to find another time to present his offer. Except now that he'd taken Shelby to bed, his offer had gotten a whole lot more complicated.

10

The following day, Shelby pulled out of the faculty parking lot and drove along Quarry Road past the football practice field. All she had to go home to was a lonely, mostly unfurnished apartment, some leftovers, and an evening poring over want ads on Craigslist for jobs in one of the neighboring towns.

And memories of her night with Nash.

After their kitchen interlude, she'd made some excuse about papers to grade and escaped like the hounds of Hell were dogging her heels.

She knew Nash had been confused, but she couldn't help it. If she'd stayed, they would have ended up back in his bed for a fourth round, and she knew she'd never get through it without saying those three words that she'd never be able to take back.

A few people stood outside the fence watching the undefeated Bobcats practice for this weekend's upcoming trip to face Georgia Southern.

On a whim, Shelby pulled into the lot and threw the car in park.

Tapping her fingers on the steering wheel, she muttered, "Don't do it. Just turn around and go home." Since she'd fled Nash's house the night before, she'd been moping around like a lovesick teenager desperate to see him again.

Heaving a big sigh, she climbed out of the car anyway and walked over to join the other spectators. Dressed in athletic shorts and a Bobcats T-shirt and ball cap, a whistle around his neck, Nash stalked the field as his guys lined up along the line of scrimmage.

Gathering her sweater around her, she wondered how he could wear shorts on such a chilly, overcast afternoon. But she was glad he did. He had the most beautiful legs she'd ever seen on a man.

And the rest of him was pretty damned beautiful too.

Clapping his hands, he approached his starting QB and gave him a helmet slap, followed by a butt pat, then walked over to the sidelines again.

Nash Taylor in his element, Shelby thought. Watching him on the sidelines on Saturdays, anyone could see it wasn't just his love for the game or his skilled play-calling. He loved and respected his players. And clearly the feeling was mutual.

At the end of the play, he blew the whistle. "All right men, let's huddle up."

The players encircled Nash, the assistant coaches and coordinators forming the outer ring. Shelby couldn't hear what Nash was saying, but he definitely had the team's attention. A few minutes later, "Go Bobcats!" rang out, drawing applause from the onlookers. The team headed for the locker room facilities in the new ten-thousand-seat stadium across the street, a gift from a wealthy quarry owner.

Just as she turned to beat a hasty retreat, Shelby heard her name and groaned. Turning, she saw Nash trotting over to her.

"What are you doing here?" he asked when he reached her, a grin lighting his face.

"Thought I'd stop by, see if you needed my expert opinion," she said with shrug and a smile, coming up with a quick cover.

"Funny you should say that." He tucked an iPad under his arm, adjusted his cap.

"What do you mean?"

"I mean, I could use your expert opinion."

"Okay, I think you should run it up the middle on third and short. Not only are they successful sixty-six percent of the time, they're over sixteen percent more successful than passes on third and short."

He snorted. "You may be right. Walk with me." He directed her toward the stadium and presumably his office.

"All right."

"You, uh, okay?"

She knew what he was asking, but chose to ignore it. "Sure. Why wouldn't I be?"

He laughed. "No reason." He cleared his throat and looked straight ahead. "While Sterling's football team is still in its infancy—"

"Yes, I know. You started it just three years ago, but you've done an amazing job. And look at this brand new stadium," she said, sweeping her hands out to encompass the red-brick walls of the building.

"I'm chasing the Division I FCS title this year. And I could use your help."

"I hate to disappoint you, but my kicking days are over."

He smiled, shook his head. "Maybe. I haven't seen you kick in a while, but your statistics days aren't over, Dr. Wentworth."

"Statistics?"

"Yeah. We have a team of grad assistants collecting the stats, but we need someone with experience in analyzing them. Spotting trends. We haven't had a team statistician. Too young to have any significant stats to compare. But now we've got some meat on our bones, and I could use someone who can run the numbers—beyond the basics—on both the Bobcats and on our opponents. You know football. You know numbers. And you know what football numbers matter most, as you just demonstrated with those stats on third and short."

They'd reached his office. Unlocking the door, he flipped on the lights. "Water?" he asked as he walked over to a small fridge in the corner.

"Sure." She looked around his office. Cluttered desk against one wall, side-by-side computer monitors, abandoned coffee mug. He had a big picture window overlooking the practice field, a small sofa, a coffee table, and an end table. Bookshelves along one wall were lined with books on his sport, everything from *Football Scouting Methods* to *The Blind Side*.

She couldn't deny that his request intrigued her. She'd have to do it on the side, along with teaching her classes and finding her groove again when it came to her research.

It meant working with Nash, seeing him on a regular basis. Could her heart handle it?

It also meant no more sex. As a direct report to him, even as a volunteer, she and Nash couldn't have a romantic relationship.

Cart before the horse, Shelby. A romantic relationship

could be the farthest thing from Nash's mind. Maybe for him it was just a one-night stand.

A glass trophy case stood in the corner. In it, his Heisman Trophy, the Davy O'Brien Award, and the Maxwell Award, along with his ESPY for Best College Football Player and trophies from his high school days. His athletic superiority evident in the gleaming white marble, cast bronze, and brass statues.

He'd accomplished some impressive stats in his short NFL career. What he could have accomplished had he stayed, no one will ever know. He might have been one of the most successful quarterbacks in NFL history.

"Here." Nash came up behind her, handed her a cold bottle of water. His spicy cologne mixed with the scent of sweat for a lethal combination.

Taking the water from him, she said, "You're a natural-born coach, Nash."

"You think so?"

"I know so. I always thought that, even when you were playing Pop Warner. You always knew how to get the team fired up."

"Some days I wonder . . ." He screwed the top back on the bottle, set it aside, then put his hands on her shoulders, and her breath backed up in her throat. "What do you say? Will you be my team statistician?"

Her amber eyes wide, her lips parted. God, he wanted to kiss her. Gather her in and kiss her until they were both breathless. Her gaze went to his mouth. She wanted that kiss as much as he did.

And after last night, he knew how electric that kiss could

be. But last night had to be where it ended if she agreed to work for him.

"Coach—oh, I'm sorry, I didn't know you were, uh, with someone."

Nash dropped his hands, turned and gave Grady an eat-shit-and-die look.

Nevertheless, Grady couldn't wipe the grin off his face. Until Nash leveled him with a frosty glare that would make Hell freeze over. "I'll come back later." He turned on his heel to go, and Nash called him back.

"Yeah, Coach?"

Nash looked at Shelby, eyebrows raised in question. She nodded. "Meet our new team statistician."

Grady broke into a big grin and clapped his hands once. "Yeah? Hot damn, we got ourselves a statistician." With that he left them alone, a spring in his step, the Bobcats' fight song floating down the hall behind him.

"Now, let's talk salary—"

"Salary? But, I thought I'd just—"

"Oh, no. I'm not looking to use our . . . friendship," he didn't know what else to call it, "for the benefit of me or the team. Your time is valuable, and I intend to compensate you for that time."

"Nash—"

"No. This is nonnegotiable. You'll have to clear it with your department chair, but as Seth Durden is a huge foot-ball fan, that shouldn't be too difficult."

He threw out a number, and Shelby's mouth fell open.

"Too low?"

"No." She held up her hand. "No. That's plenty."

"Good."

He took a step back, swept his gaze over her. "Also, stop

by the Sterling Bookstore and pick up some Bobcats gear—polos, sweatshirts, a jacket, and maybe a visor or ball cap. Tell them to put it on the team's account." He wanted her to feel like part of the team. He'd reimburse the school for the expense.

"This is too much."

"What's too much? If you're sitting in the booth with my offensive and defensive coordinators feeding them stats, you need to be in uniform."

"The booth?"

"Well, yeah. Where did you think you'd be?"

"But, I thought I would run the numbers, create some graphs, put together a weekly report, and that would be it. Isn't that how it usually works?"

"Yes. But you're not the usual statistician."

He pulled a book off the shelf, tossed it to her—*Moneyball: The Art of Winning an Unfair Game.*

"Did you read the book or see the movie?"

She nodded. "Both."

"Paul DePodesta was the A's secret weapon, and now you're mine."

"I don't know." She shook her head. "This is happening too fast."

"I need a statistician. You're perfect for the job. What's too fast about that?" He put an arm around her shoulder and felt the *zing* of contact. "We're going to make a great team."

STILL STUNNED by the evening's turn of events, Shelby crawled onto her mattress on the floor. Working for Nash, she'd be making over half her annual salary as a professor, and that money would go a long way to helping her pay off her debts and get back on her feet again.

That, and she knew she'd love the job.

But. Two problems.

One. She needed to focus on her research. If she had any hope of moving up to an associate professor position at Sterling, which she'd had at Stanford before the Great Career Suicide, she needed journal articles. And in order to publish journal articles, she needed to do research. And in order to do research, she needed a research hypothesis.

She'd been fresh out of those since this whole trip through Hell had started. *No one's fault but your own.* Her ex-husband's words rang in her head.

Two. She'd be in close personal contact with Nash almost daily. Which meant she'd have to hide her feelings, just like she had when they were teenagers. It also meant she'd be exposed to his warmth, his charm, and his magnetism. Which she didn't think she could resist, especially after last night.

And resist she must. A relationship with him now could cost her professorship, in addition to her part-time job with the team, and then where would she be? The position with the mathematics department had been her only lifeline. That, and her tattered heart couldn't take another blow. From any man, and certainly not from him, especially when that heart still carried the scars from his betrayal eleven years ago.

Which begged the question: Why did she sleep with him? She snorted. Not that there was any actual *sleep* involved. And she'd "slept" with him because she'd wanted to since forever.

She'd already said yes to the job, but that was when she thought her duties would begin and end with charts and reports.

Reaching over for the notepad and pen she kept on the floor by the bed, she drew a line down the center, wrote "Pros" on one side of the line, and "Cons" on the other.

Under pros went "money," and under that she listed all the things she could do with that money. Things like "pay off attorney bills," "pay for Nash's car repairs," and, as she looked around her bedroom at the boxes on the floor and grimaced, "buy a dresser."

Under cons, she listed "time," "career," and "research." Tapping her lip with the pen, she considered other factors.

"Job satisfaction" went in the pros column. Tilting her head, she realized that was something she hadn't felt in a while, even before the GCS. Also under pros, she listed "seeing Nash regularly." This also made it onto the cons list.

Then she added the biggest con yet: No more sex with Nash.

Maybe it was for the best. It would only be a matter of time before he'd be ready to move on. At least this way she had a solid reason to avoid further intimate contact with him.

Heaving a sigh of disappointment, she reviewed the lists.

Even with the cons, the possibility that she could get herself out of debt and maybe have a little to put away swayed her decision. She could always do it for the remainder of the football season and earn the extra cash until Nash found someone permanent.

Surely she could protect her heart for three months. Right?

Remembering last night, the way he tasted, how he

touched her with such tenderness, and then that moment in Nash's office when it looked like he was about to kiss her again, she sighed. The odds were definitely not in her favor.

11

Removing the ringing smartphone from his pocket, Nash frowned at the caller ID. "This is Nash."

"Nash, Sheriff Cole. I, uh, I've got your dad here at the station," he said, hesitation in his voice.

"Jesus. Is he okay?"

A heavy sigh followed. "He's fine, but Nash . . . I had to arrest him."

"Son-of-a—what for?" Nash made an about-face and returned to his car. Combing his hands through his hair, he squeezed his eyes shut momentarily.

"He was removing his clothes in Mrs. Snyder's front yard."

"Damn. How far did he get before you picked him up?" Nash held his breath, dreading the answer.

"He was in his boxers and socks."

"Thank God for small favors," Nash muttered. "I'm on my way."

"Nash?"

"Yeah."

"He's pretty bad. I was thinking of calling 911."

"Don't. Thanks for calling me first."

After six hours in the ER at Sterling Regional Medical Center, then two more in the Emory University Hospital ER, where he'd requested his dad be transferred, Nash pulled into his driveway and released the death grip he'd had on the steering wheel. One o'clock in the morning.

According to the psychiatrist who'd treated his dad, his father had had a psychotic break, hearing voices telling him his clothes were on fire, and he had to take them off.

Shutting off the car, Nash scrubbed his face with both hands, a lump in his throat. Would this be him someday?

Carl was now medicated and safely ensconced in a private room. If he stabilized, he'd be discharged in a few days, which gave Nash some time to figure out what to do next.

He now had a new medication regimen, which included the anti-psychotic risperidone.

He'd need a health care worker to make sure his father followed the new plan. No way could his dad do it on his own.

Tomorrow. Right now, he needed a hot shower, and a soft bed.

Once she'd received the approval of her dean, Shelby wasted no time in getting her feet wet. She dove into the team's stats headfirst. With just two years' worth of stats, she didn't have much depth, but she'd often worked with less.

Most university sports programs hired graduate students to collect and record game stats, while managers or equipment staff kept practice stats and videoed practice. Sterling hired six students who sat in the new stadium's press box. Two acted as spotters: one for all offensive plays for both teams, and one for all defensive plays for both teams. These spotters called out who was playing on that particular down, kept track of whether it was a pass play or a rush. On the defensive side, the spotter called out tackles, interceptions, sacks, etc.

One student served as the inputter, entering all data into a DOS program called StatCrew. In case of a computer meltdown, the team also employed a scribe, who manually kept the data the old-fashioned way—by hand. Finally, there were two participation keepers, who checked players off as they came in and out of the game.

At the end of each game, reports were generated for each team, which were then shared with each coach. Each week, before the next game, the coaches reviewed the last three box scores—the structured summary of the results of the games. Game stats were also posted to the team's website.

Part of Shelby's job would be to take over the staff books generated each week for the coaches. But she wanted to do much more than generate generic reports, and from what Nash had said, he wanted more too. She planned to analyze the data, search for trends, strengths, and weaknesses. Her goal was to gather rich data that could be analyzed to actually inform sideline decision-making.

As she pulled up StatCrew on her laptop to familiarize herself with the software—what its strengths were, what its weaknesses were—she began making notes. Her notes would help her create her own database, which she could use to run reports and perform sophisticated analyses using such methods as basic regression analysis, logistic regression, Monte Carlo simulation, classification, and hierarchical regression.

Her excitement grew. She finally felt as if she'd climbed back onto the horse that had bucked her off. And it was exhilarating.

She'd eventually tinker with her own methods, some of which she'd developed during her ill-fated career at Stanford, to answer questions about game strategy and tactics. Eventually, the data and methods could be used to develop statistical models to measure player value and forecast future performance for use in making recruiting decisions, *à la Moneyball.*

Of course, she'd mastered advanced spreadsheet skills including pivot tables, macros, scripting, and chart customization throughout her career.

If she did her job well, and she intended to, the tool could be used by future statisticians after she stepped out of the role at the end of the current season. The key was to develop a set of analyses and algorithms to run that would keep things consistent and eliminate, or at least minimize, confounding factors.

Of course, the number-cruncher had to understand the sport and the challenges coaches and players needed to overcome in order to win.

Shelby glanced at the clock, shocked to find it was already eleven-fifteen. She'd been working on this for close to four hours. She couldn't recall the last time she'd been so engrossed in her work that she lost track of time.

Rubbing the back of her neck, but satisfied with the progress she'd made on the new database, she packed it in. She had some interesting stats to include in her first staff book.

Intellectually energized for the first time in years, she smiled.

THE MONDAY after her second home game as statistician, Shelby knocked on Nash's office door.

"Yeah?" he called out, then glanced up with a smile. "Shelby. Thanks for coming by. I know you've already put in a full day."

"Sure." She couldn't figure out why Nash wanted to see her.

"Have a seat."

"Why do I feel like I've been called to the principal's office?" She tucked her hands between her knees when she sat down.

"Not at all. First things first." He pulled a large gift-wrapped box out from under his desk. "This is for you."

Shelby froze. "What's that?"

"Consider it an early birthday present," he said with a grin.

"But my birthday isn't until February."

"Okay, then it's an early Christmas gift."

"But—"

"Just open the box, Shelby."

"Fine." Taking the box, she set it on her lap and tore open the paper to reveal a Lucchese boot box. "What the—"

"If you're going to keep riding Moonshine, you at least need to wear a decent pair of boots."

She lifted the lid to see a beautiful, hand-tooled pair of boots in tan. She ran her fingers over the fine craftsmanship. She'd never owned anything so nice. "Nash, I can't—"

"Yes, you can."

Dismissing her objection, he moved on. "Now, the second reason for this meeting—you're doing a great job. I never had my doubts, but I also never expected your freakish number-crunching to have such a direct impact on the outcome of last Saturday's game."

She shrugged, still in awe of the boots, as she lifted them from the box. "It's what I do."

"And oh so well. That's why I want you to come to South Carolina next week."

She practically dropped the boot she'd been holding in her hands. Confused, yet trying to temper her excitement over what he was saying, Shelby asked, "You mean you want me to travel with the team?"

"That's exactly what I mean."

She shook her head. "But, stats people don't usually travel with the team."

"I thought we'd already determined you're not the usual stats person." He rose from his desk and came around to perch a hip on the corner. His hair was sticking up as if he'd been running his fingers through it recently. "You've proven your value to this team after just two home games. Why would I leave such a valuable commodity behind when we're off to play the Citadel, our most difficult opponent of the season?"

"And your staff? They're okay with that?"

"They are. But even if they weren't, I'm the coach, and you're just as much a part of this team as any of the other coaches."

Shelby couldn't contain her excitement a moment longer despite her reservations.

But Nash was a professional. He wouldn't let their recent encounter get in the way of his job. Or hers. In fact, he'd made no more attempts to kiss her . . . sadly.

"I'd love to travel with the team." She would be spending even more time with Nash. And despite his restraint, it was becoming increasingly difficult to keep her hands to herself. And, more importantly, rein in her heart.

A WEEK after beating the Citadel, Shelby gathered her purse, laptop, and keys to head over to the stadium for her meeting with Nash. She'd reviewed their upcoming opponent's stats and found some interesting weaknesses, especially their ineffectiveness against fake punts.

Just as she reached her front door, someone knocked. Peering through the peephole, she sucked in a breath. It was Nash. And he had a pizza box from Momma Michelle's in one hand and what looked like a bottle of wine in the other. What the—

"Shelby, I know you're there. Your wrecked car is still parked outside."

Chewing on her lip, she considered not answering. Maybe he'd think that she had walked or ridden a bike— never mind that she didn't have one—and give up and meet her at the stadium as planned.

"Come on, Shelby. I can practically hear you thinking."

Damn. She opened the door and stepped out like she was leaving, then closed the door behind her. "Nash. I was just on my way out to meet you. You didn't need to pick me up."

"I thought we could meet here. Quieter. More convenient for you. And I know it's a little early, but I brought dinner." He held up the pizza, which smelled like Heaven, especially since she'd skipped lunch.

"Oh, but, I thought we could use the projector in the conference room."

"Nah. Not necessary. By the way, why haven't you had your car repaired?"

"Oh, just busy."

"I see."

She stood rooted to the spot, trying to figure out something else. She couldn't let him in her apartment for two reasons. One, he'd see it was empty, and two, she couldn't be in such close quarters with him again. She worked for him now. Sex with her boss had career-suicide written all over it. Just like marrying her mentor. "Well, my apartment is a bit of a mess. I haven't really finished unpacking." Not a total lie. She was still living out of boxes, but only because she didn't have any furniture to put her things in.

"So what? Come on, I'm starved, and the pizza's getting cold."

Resigned to her fate, she opened the door and stepped aside.

Nash followed her in and stopped short. What was supposed to be the living room held boxes of her books—both academic tomes and pleasure reading—an old desktop PC sat on the floor next to a printer, and the *pièce de résistance*, a small TV sat on a TV tray.

Yep. Home sweet home.

"What the hell? You've been here how long and don't have any furniture? What happened? The moving company lose it or something?"

"Um. No." She dropped her purse on the floor by the front door and set her laptop on a box. "I don't have any furniture."

Avoiding his scrutiny, she took the pizza and wine from him and walked into the kitchen. She could really use a glass of wine about now. Thankfully, it was a screw top, since she didn't have a corkscrew.

Reaching into a cupboard, she took out two mismatched highball glasses—any port in a storm, right?—and poured some wine. Turning, she handed one to him and raised the other to her lips for a mouthful.

"Shelby, where is your furniture?" He took the glass from her and set it on the counter then put his hands on his hips.

"I left it."

"You left it where?"

"In California."

His brow furrowed in confusion. "Isn't California a community property state?"

"Yes."

"So, why?"

She turned and pulled two plates out of the cabinet where the pitiful collection of glasses were and opened the pizza box. "When I left, I just wanted out. I didn't want to haggle over . . . stuff."

"Okay, but why haven't you bought new furniture?" When his response was met with silence, he stepped up behind her and placed his hands on her shoulders. "Shelby?"

"Because I can't. I can't afford it."

Nash turned her toward him, her face a mask of shame and reluctance.

"Talk to me, Shelby." He held up his hand. "Wait." He took the plates, put them on top of the pizza box and carried it to the table, then went back for the wine and glasses, tore off some paper towels from the roll by the sink, and indicated she should join him at the table.

After serving them both a slice of pizza, he said, "Talk."

Shelby took another gulp of wine, which prompted Nash to say, "And eat."

She took a bite of pizza, wiped her mouth with the paper towel, and lifted her gaze to his. "I'm broke," she shrugged, "and I'm in debt."

Delaney had been right about her financial issues, but he never would have guessed how bad those issues were.

"What do you mean you're broke? What about your divorce?" He thought about the money he'd paid to his ex-wife—and *she* was the one who'd cheated—who'd walked out on their marriage. "What about your portion of the assets?"

"What assets? California is a not only a community property state, it's also a community debt state. Debts incurred by either spouse during the marriage belong equally to both spouses. And my ex ran up a lot of debt." She pushed aside her half-eaten pizza slice. "Plus, I still owe my divorce attorney money, and the attorney who represented me for the year-long research misconduct investigation."

"Jesus." He rubbed the back of his neck. "Why didn't you say something?"

"To who?"

"To me? To Ethan? Delaney?"

"And then you'd do what exactly?"

"Help you."

"No. Absolutely not." She folded her arms across her chest. "I'm not taking money from my friends." Then she waved her hand. "Besides, the money I'm making number-ing-crunching for you is starting to put a dent in my debt."

"Let me—"

"No. I mean it, Nash. I'll be fine." She picked up her now-cold slice of pizza. "Can we just eat and get to work?"

Even growing up, Shelby and her mom wouldn't accept help. When her mom lost her job at the diner, he and Ethan's family had offered to help, but the answer had always been no. The best they could do was to invite Shelby to dinner as often as possible.

He didn't want to drop it, but he would for now. He couldn't bear the thought of Shelby living out of boxes with no furniture. He hoped she at least had a box spring and mattress.

He had a moment of discomfort. If Shelby knew the reason he'd given her the job, she'd be pissed. It didn't matter now, though, because while he'd only been trying to help, she'd helped him and the team instead.

After they'd finished dinner, Shelby sat next to him and opened up her laptop to display graphics, including a bar graph and a pie chart. She started rattling off an alphabet of software: SQL and R/S-PLUS, SAS and SPSS.

He had no idea what she was talking about, but he loved seeing her in her element, her amber eyes alight with excitement. Much better than the shame he'd seen in those eyes earlier.

Everything she'd said was Greek to him, but when she boiled it all down, she made it clear and understandable, taking complex statistical analyses and communicating them effectively. She must be some teacher, he thought. For a minute, he let what she said flow over him and just enjoyed watching her, his gaze drawn to her mouth. He wanted to kiss her. No, he *needed* to kiss her. Like he needed to draw his next shaky breath.

Even as she chattered on, he leaned in, until the next word froze on her lips and her gaze slid to his mouth.

"Nash, don't. We can't do this. I work for you now."

"Just one more kiss. Nothing more." He closed the distance between them, slow and easy. Then their lips touched, and she sighed into his mouth.

Need for more than just her lips against his shot through him, hot and sharp. More. He wanted . . . more. Pulling her out of her chair and into his lap, she straddled him, her fingers in his hair. Her sweet lemon scent tickled his nose as her hair fell around them.

The hell with one more kiss! Just as he stood to take her . . . somewhere, he didn't know where, since she didn't have a couch, his phone rang.

Groaning, he looked down at his phone lying on the table, then his heart filled with trepidation when he saw the number. Reaching for the phone, he accepted the call. "This is Nash."

"Mr. Taylor, this is Crystal."

She sounded like she'd been crying. He hoped his dad hadn't hurt her feelings.

"Your dad . . . he's missing."

12

—————

"**M**issing?" The pizza congealed in his stomach. Shelby's gaze shot to his face, and she climbed off his lap. "What do you mean? How long has he been gone?"

"About half an hour. I . . . I went to the bathroom, and when I came out the front door was open, and he was not in the house."

"Shit." He looked up at Shelby and saw concern there.

"I've been looking for him and calling his name, but I can't find him anywhere."

"Okay. Listen, I'm on my way." He pressed a thumb to his right eye where a headache had begun.

"Do you want me to call 911?"

"No. I'll call the sheriff directly." He ended the call and looked into Shelby's concerned face. "My dad is missing. I have to go."

"I'm coming with you." Shelby closed her laptop and headed for the door.

"That's not necessary," he said as he followed her.

"I know it's not necessary." She pulled her smartphone out of her purse and started dialing.

"Who are you calling?"

"Delaney. You need to call Ethan and Sam. We can use everyone's help."

Nash wanted to keep this quiet. Didn't want to embarrass his dad. He'd done his best to keep his father's condition out of the media thus far.

At his hesitation, she prodded. "What's more important? Protecting your father's privacy or finding him safe?"

"Right. Call."

When they arrived at his father's house, the police were already there, cars parked on the street, lights flashing.

Sheriff Jim Cole greeted him. "All right. I've spoken to the home health aide. He's been missing now about forty-five minutes."

Ethan pulled up, and he and Sam jumped out of the car and ran over to where Nash, Shelby, and the deputies were gathered.

Jim led them over to the hood of his car where a map of the area was spread out.

"Can you think of somewhere your father might go? A favorite spot?"

Nash rubbed his forehead. "The hardware store. The high school football field. Ruby's." He shook his head. "I don't know."

"I called Ruby's. They haven't seen him," Ethan supplied.

Nash looked up. They were losing the light fast. It'd be fully dark soon. And the temperatures were dropping as fast as the light was fading.

"We'll find him, Nash." The sheriff clapped him on the shoulder. "All right." He turned to address his officers and the friends and neighbors who'd come out to help. "We all know what Carl looks like. He was wearing a pair of black sweats, tennis shoes, and a gray Atlanta Falcons T-shirt."

As Nash listened to the sheriff's instructions to the volunteers, a small, warm hand curled around his. Shelby gave his hand a squeeze and leaned into him. Her quiet support meant more to him than all the other volunteers' who stood at the ready to help.

～

THEY'D BEEN SEARCHING the neighborhood for over an hour, and still no sign of Nash's father. Nash and Shelby circled back to the house, partly to get an update from the sheriff, and partly to use the bathroom and get something to drink.

While Nash went to the bathroom, Shelby grabbed a couple of water bottles out of the fridge. Opening one, she wandered over to the sliding glass doors. "Where are you, Carl?" she muttered to herself. She couldn't imagine the hell Nash was going through right now. Odds were, they'd find his dad safe, if not cold and hungry. But there was always that small chance.

There were ravines in the area. Rocky ravines where she, Ethan, and Nash had played as kids. But in the dark, it would be easy to take a tumble.

A light in the backyard caught her eye—up high, at tree level—where the old tree house would be if it were still there. Her heart started pounding.

Nash joined her at the door, and she handed Nash the other bottle of water.

"Do you see that?" She pointed out the pale light.

"Holy shit. The tree house."

Yanking open the sliding glass door, he raced toward the

tree. "Dad! Carl!" He began climbing the wooden rungs bolted into the tree.

"Careful, Nash," Shelby called out as she craned her neck to watch him climb. "The wood looks pretty rotted."

She pulled out her smartphone and hit the flashlight app to help light Nash's way. He disappeared inside the tree house.

"He's here!"

She placed her hand over her racing heart. *Please let him be okay.*

She waited what seemed like a lifetime for further word.

"He's sound asleep."

"Thank God."

It took the fire department to get Carl down using a ladder. When he was back safely on the ground, he blinked at the crowd gathered around him, seemingly perplexed by the hullabaloo.

Nash, who'd been waiting impatiently for the fireman to carry Carl down, grabbed his dad by the shoulder and hauled him in for a hug. "Jesus, Dad. What were you thinking?"

"What was I thinking? Son, your mother and I have been looking for you for hours, so I went up in the tree house to see if you were hanging out with your friends."

Shelby caught Nash's pained look, and her heart ached for him.

As a fireman draped a Mylar blanket over Carl's shoulders, Nash just shook his head and led his father back into the house.

~

WITH THE HELP OF CRYSTAL, Nash got his father tucked into

bed. He had a few cuts on his hands where he'd apparently slipped climbing up into the tree house, but nothing serious. It definitely could have been worse. Much worse.

Crystal continued to apologize, clearly afraid she was going to lose her job. Nash did what he could to reassure her, but he didn't know what would happen tomorrow when she had to report everything to the home health agency.

He sent her home, told her to get some sleep.

Ethan, Sam, and Delaney were the last to leave after all the law enforcement, first responders, neighbors, and other volunteers had packed it in.

Just Shelby remained.

Nash collapsed on the sofa next to her and laid his head back against the cushion. "What a night." He closed his eyes for a moment, took a deep breath, then felt Shelby's hand close around his.

She'd been his rock tonight. Calm, steady, and supportive. And she'd been the one to find his father. He'd never be able to thank her enough.

Lifting his head, he brought her hand to his lips. "Thank you."

She raised her other hand to caress his cheek. "You're welcome." Then she leaned her head on his shoulder. "I'm so glad he's okay."

"Me too." He released a heavy sigh. "I think this is the sign I've been looking for."

"For what?"

He looked down at his lap, then back at her. "To make the decision to put my dad in a facility. Somewhere he'll be safe."

Shelby turned and knelt next to him, her searching gaze locked with his. "Do you think this is CTE?"

"I do. And so does Dr. Ibrahim, the specialist I see at Cornell."

"So, you retired."

"So, I retired." He scrubbed a hand over his face. "And yet, it could still be me someday."

"It could, but I think your odds are better than your father's."

"And why's that? Cause my head is harder?" He huffed out a laugh devoid of humor.

"Because you only had thirty-six college career sacks, and other than the hit that ended your career, you had the lowest sacks on record in the NFL."

He drew back. "How do you know that?"

He watched in fascination as a blush crept up her neck and into her cheeks.

She ducked her head then looked up at him, her eyes filled with . . . something. Admiration? "I kept stats on all your games."

"You did?" He couldn't have been more shocked. "Really? Why?"

She bit her lip, and God help him, but he wanted to bite that lip too.

"Shelby?"

"Because," she shrugged, "I followed your college and pro careers just like I followed your Pop Warner and high school careers."

He decided to let it go at that, but aside from being flattered, he wondered why she would have not only kept his stats, but memorized them as well.

"I should go. Let you get some sleep."

"I'll see you home."

"No. I'm fine. It's not that far. You stay here. With your

dad." She rose from the couch. "If you need anything, let me know."

"Thanks." He followed her to the door, and before she could open it, he took her by the shoulders and gazed down into her face. "Thank you, again."

"You've already said that," she said, a soft smile lifting the corners of her sweet mouth.

"I'll never be able to say it enough."

She licked her lips, and his gaze dropped to her mouth. Lowering his head, he grazed her lips, ever so soft, then retreated. "Goodnight, Shelby."

"Goodnight, Nash."

Opening the door, she walked out into the dark, chilly night. Nash couldn't help but wonder whether, if his dad hadn't gone missing, he'd be spending the night in Shelby's bed.

And violating university policy. A fireable offense.

NASH GROANED when his cell phone woke him from a deep sleep. Then he sat bolt upright. Where was his dad?

Dammit! He hadn't meant to sleep so soundly. Grabbing his phone, he looked at the number. Ethan.

Accepting the call, he strode down the hall to his father's room. Still in bed asleep. Thank God.

"What's up?" Nash asked, his voice soft so as not to wake his father.

"You, uh, you have company?" Ethan asked, a chuckle in his voice.

"No." He pulled his father's door closed. "Dad's still asleep. I'd like to keep it that way for a while longer."

"Turn on ESPN News."

"Don't tell me."

"Afraid so," Ethan confirmed.

"How the hell?" Nash pointed the remote at the TV, then selected ESPN.

ESPN's anchor spoke, a photo of his dad in an Atlanta Falcons uniform to her left. "The question many are asking today is whether Carl Taylor's condition is Alzheimer's or the result of all those hits he took throughout his career."

"Damn." Nash hit mute when they switched to a story about the upcoming heavyweight boxing match.

"Sorry, man. I thought you should know, so you could prepare."

"Thanks." He heard the toilet flush down the hall and knew his dad was awake. "Listen, Dad's up. I've got to go."

"Let me know what I can do."

"Yep." Trouble was, the kind of help he needed, Ethan couldn't give.

13

Nash rarely gave the Monday-morning quarterbacks much attention. Even so, he put on ESPN News for company as he set his messy house to rights after a busy two weeks on the road for away football games and caring for his dad when he was in town. He was aware from his coaches and staff that the commentators at last week's game were saying he needed to have his head examined after what could have been a suicidal play call on fourth and long with only two minutes left in a game where the Bobcats were down by a touchdown.

Thanks to Shelby's insistence, he'd gone with her odds on fourth down conversions against Savannah State deep in their territory.

It had paid off with a touchdown and a two-point conversion to win the game.

Two popular sports pundits were debating the call. The game had been broadcast on ESPNU, and they had footage of Shelby in the box with the coordinators. ESPN was calling her the Bobcats' secret weapon, which made Nash grin with pride.

After the story, he clicked off the TV and went in search of food, taking his phone into the kitchen with him. Opening up his email, he saw one from Kim, the team's PR person. Nothing unusual there, but when he opened the email, he stopped short. It was about his latest secret weapon. ESPN wanted to do a story on Shelby.

~

THE FOLLOWING WEEK, Ethan, Sam, and Delaney gathered on the sofa in Nash's living room awaiting the ESPNU segment on Sterling's new statistician.

Nerves had Nash reaching for another beer. He'd been interviewed more times than he could count, going back to his high school days, but today he was nervous for Shelby. A pre-recorded segment with vignettes from this year's football season, along with commentary from him and his coordinators, would be followed by a live interview of Shelby in the small recording studio in the Bobcats' stadium.

He collapsed onto the sofa, and Ethan gave him a slap on the shoulder with a laugh. "Relax, man. She's going to be great."

Delaney chimed in, "She's going to rock this interview," followed by Sam, "Girls rule!"

"Here it is!" Delaney said, picking up the remote and turning up the volume.

Nash sat forward on the edge of the sofa.

A recent headshot of Shelby flashed up on the screen next to the anchor's head as he started off the segment, "The Oakland A's had Paul DePodesta, and now the Sterling Bobcats have Dr. Shelby Wentworth."

"Woohoo!" Delaney clapped her hands. "She looks awesome!"

The anchor recapped the gutsy call Nash and his staff made at last week's game, complete with video of Shelby in the booth, looking adorable in her headset.

"Now we'll head over to Simone, who's got the Bobcats' not-so-secret weapon, Shelby Wentworth."

The scene switched to a beautiful blonde against the familiar backdrop of the Bobcats' studio. "We're here in the Bobcats' stadium with Dr. Shelby Wentworth, number-cruncher extraordinaire."

"Oh my god! Look at her!" Delaney clapped a hand over her mouth. "Sorry," she muttered behind her hand.

Yeah, look at her, Nash thought. She looked amazing. Confident.

"Shelby, let's start with, 'How'd this come to be?'"

She smiled, an easy, relaxed smile. Who knew she'd be such a natural in front of the camera?

"Well, Simone, I've always loved numbers, and I've always loved sports. It just made sense to combine my two loves in an effort to support the Bobcats' bid for the Division I FCS Championship."

"The coaches say you're a genius when it comes to numbers."

A laugh, and then a blush, "I don't know about that, but I will say I love what I'm doing. These are amazing athletes, and the coaching staff are some of the best people I've ever worked with. It's really easy to perform at your best when you're surrounded by the best."

The interview lasted about three minutes, and Nash must have held his breath the entire time. When it ended, he sagged against the back of the couch as Simone wrapped it up. "This may change the future of college football. All teams are going to want their very own Dr. Shelby Wentworth. Back to the ESPN studios."

Delaney brushed an imaginary tear off her cheek. "So proud. Our girl's all grown up."

Nash's chest filled with pride. And something else. Something that felt a whole lot like love.

~

SHELBY DROVE out to Nash's to meet up with the gang, her head in the clouds. Excitement. Satisfaction. Happiness. All feelings that had long been absent from her life now coursed through her.

The sports world was sitting up and taking notice of her skills. Skills she'd grown to doubt after years with Charlie. Nash had taken a chance on her, and she'd proven her value —to herself, to her team, and to him.

Turning into the driveway, she saw her "tribe" as Delaney called them, waiting on the front porch, all holding signs made out of her headshot like she was some kind of superstar. Tears welled in her eyes. She had a tribe. After years of feeling isolated, and then outright ostracized by Charlie's people, their support meant more to her than they could have ever known.

Brushing back the tears, she laughed and shook her head as she climbed out of the car. When she reached them, Delaney asked, "Can I have your autograph?"

Nash snorted. "You never asked for mine."

She swept her hand at him in dismissal. "Cause I don't want yours. I'm talking about my sister, here." She held out the photo sign and a Sharpie to Shelby. "Just sign it, 'To Delaney, my best friend in the whole world.'"

Nash rolled his eyes then winked at Shelby, and she felt that wink all the way down to her toes. She took the marker and did as Delaney asked.

"Come on." Nash held out his hand. "I've got a glass of champagne with your name on it."

She drew back in surprise.

"Your first interview on national TV—that's something to celebrate." He pulled her close, and leaning in, he murmured, "I'm so proud of you." Her face heated at the intimate contact, especially in front of the tribe, but it was the warmth around her heart that reminded her, once again, of the danger of falling for Nash.

ELATED BUT EXHAUSTED, Shelby said goodnight to her friends. It had been an amazing day, but having good friends to share it with made it one of the best days of her life. And then there was Nash.

"I have to thank you," she said to Nash as he picked up empty beer bottles.

"For what?" He stopped with his hands full and looked at her.

"For giving me the best job I've ever had. I've never felt so excited, so energized, by my academic work."

He set the bottle back down then stepped up behind her and closed the door.

Laughing, she turned to him. "But I was about to leave myself—"

She stopped short when she saw the heat in his eyes. "Stay." He set his hands on her hips, pulling her closer.

"Nash. We've been over this. I work for you. This isn't right." She'd already had a relationship at work that turned out to be the worst thing she'd ever done. She couldn't do it again. Even if it *was* with Nash and her body was singing a different tune.

"Okay, you're fired." He backed her up against the front door and leaned into her. She didn't know which was harder, the door at her back or the man in front of her.

"What about next week's game?"

He pressed kisses along her jaw. "I'll rehire you Monday morning," he said against her neck, sending delicious shivers dancing along her spine.

Giggling as he nuzzled her neck, her amusement quickly turned to lust when he nipped her earlobe. Her resolve began to fade as his hands glided up her ribcage, over her shoulders, then down her arms. That resolve disappeared altogether when he captured her wrists and lifted her arms above her head, pressing his erection into her.

They both moaned at the contact. "Shelby," he whispered, his breath tickling her ear. "Stay."

Then his mouth captured hers, silencing any protests and eliminating any coherent thoughts.

NASH HELD Shelby's wrists in one hand and slowly opened the silky blouse she'd worn for her interview. She'd looked so beautiful and poised on TV, in a blouse the color of pumpkins in the fields not far from his house.

He'd never seen her in anything silky, and yet, now he couldn't wait to shed her of it. As silky as the blouse felt beneath his touch, he knew the feel of her skin was even silkier.

Her breath caught as he cupped her breast.

He'd kept his hands to himself since the night his father went missing, but he couldn't do it any longer. He wanted her more than any other woman he'd ever known. Consequences be damned.

Releasing her wrists, he slipped the blouse from her shoulders then unzipped the back of her skirt and let it slide to her feet. She stood before him in nothing but flesh-colored bra and panties and a pair of borrowed heels from Delaney.

Desire surged through him, hot and impatient.

Wrapping his hands around her thighs, he lifted her. "Wrap your legs around me."

She whimpered when her core met his.

"Please tell me you're on birth control." He stared into her eyes, their amber depths glowing. She nodded. "You trust me?" his voice rough with barely suppressed desire.

"Yes."

"I want to feel you, Shelby. You, with nothing between us."

He made short work of the buttons at his fly, shoved her panties aside, then plunged into her.

"God, Shelby. I've wanted you like this since . . . forever."

He gazed down at her as her eyes flicked open. He'd never known a more beautiful woman in his life. Stephanie had been beauty-queen perfect. Perfect hair, perfect makeup, perfect nails. But Shelby didn't need any help. She was perfect just the way she was. Especially with the flush of passion on her face.

"You have?" she asked, her eyes wide with wonder.

"Yes." He pressed his lips to her forehead in a tender kiss, and she felt tears burn behind her eyes. It wasn't the three little words, but it was enough. For now.

Taking his face in her hands, she tugged his mouth

down to hers, pouring all of her unspoken emotion into a kiss so searing she expected to see scars tomorrow.

He filled her, inflaming her, as he began to move. Laying her head against the door, she rode the storm.

Holding her tight, he carried her away. Away from the previous year's hell. Away from the new problems this created for both of them. Carried her to the very brink of Heaven.

14

—————

They'd managed to make it to Nash's bed for round two. Now, with Shelby's warm body wrapped around his, he couldn't think of another place he'd rather be.

Which was a problem.

He'd originally hired her because he'd wanted to help her. He figured he'd give her a job for the remainder of the football season and she'd earn some extra money to get back on her feet. Instead, not only had he put them both in a precarious situation, she'd also proven herself invaluable to the team, and he didn't want to lose her.

Now he wanted a chance to explore where this could go. And the only way he could do that would be to fire her. Or ask her to quit.

Rock, meet hard place.

He closed his eyes against the pain that caused. Especially after she told him how much she loved the job. And if she quit, how would she be able to pay off her debts?

"I think I smell something burning," Shelby muttered, a

contented smile on her face. "What are you thinking about?"

"I'm pondering the imponderable."

She sat up. "What are we going to do, Nash?"

"I don't know." He sighed, then skimmed a finger along her cheekbone.

What if he gave her a choice—him or the job? What if she picked the job? How could he work with her, see her almost daily, and not have her?

"Truth or dare?" Nash asked, trying to take his mind off the clusterfuck he'd created.

"Truth."

"Who was the first person you had a crush on?" he asked as he stroked her hair.

"You."

He sucked in a breath as his heart performed a slow roll in his chest. Not the answer he'd expected. "Really? How come you never said anything?"

"Because I knew you didn't feel the same." She plucked at the edge of the blanket.

He sat up. "Whatever made you think that?"

She sat up as well. "Seriously? You're asking me that? How about senior prom?"

Nash scrubbed his face. *Oh. That.*

"When you asked Leandra Lucas instead of me? And then had the balls to run off my date on top of it?"

Shit. How had she found out about that?

"Who, by the way," she continued, "didn't bother to let me know he was breaking our date. He just didn't show up. I sat there in my hand-me-down dress for two hours waiting for the doorbell to ring, and it never did."

The icepick to his heart the image conjured left him breathless with regret and pain. He knew Rick "the Dick"

Clemons was a jerk, but he never thought he'd just stand Shelby up. He figured he'd made up some excuse for why he couldn't go.

She got up, began picking her clothes up off the floor, and put on her bra. She thrust her arms into the sleeves of her blouse then realized it was on inside-out. Yanking it off with a growl of frustration, she tried again.

"God, Shelby. I never thought he'd stand you up. I can explain."

"Where have I heard that before?"

"It's not what it seems." He threw the covers back, grabbed his jeans, pulled them on commando and gave them a quick zip.

"And the comebacks just keep getting better and better. Next you'll be saying it's me, not you."

Damn. He was, but only because it was the truth. He had to do something. She searched beneath the covers and came up with her panties then stepped into them. "Shelby, stop." Spinning around, she located her skirt in a heap by the door. Scooping it up, she drew it on, and as she zipped it looked around for her shoes.

"Dammit, Shelby. Stop." He took her by the shoulders and leaned down to make eye contact, but she kept looking away. Taking a chance, he pulled her into his arms. "I never meant to hurt you. You have to believe that."

She relaxed into him, but before he could breathe a sigh of relief, she sniffed. *Ah, man!* She was crying.

He was the world's biggest dick.

"I trusted you," she whispered against his bare chest. "You may not have had the same feelings for me that I had for you, but I trusted you. And you let me down."

He closed his eyes. And now he felt like he'd been kneed in the balls.

SHE PUSHED AWAY from his warm, bare chest and swiped at her tears. She swore that, after all the tears she'd shed over Charlie, she'd never cry over a man again. Let alone over a man who never felt that same for her that she had for him.

"Oh, Shelby." He kissed her hair. "Come here."

He pulled her over to the chest sitting at the foot of the bed and sat her down. Turning to her, he took her hands in his big calloused ones, his thumb caressing the skin there.

"When we were all fourteen, and Ethan and I were in the throes of puberty, we took notice of you as a girl for the first time. We realized we had to take action if we wanted to keep our three-way friendship intact. We made a pact. You were off limits to both of us. That way, there would be no rivalry between Ethan and me. And no awkward decisions for you to make."

"But—"

"We were both in love with you."

"You were?" Was he still, she wondered? Or had it only been a hormone-induced crush?

"Yes. And being the horny little teenagers we were, we both wanted you. Bad."

Definitely a hormone-induced crush. "Didn't I have any say in the matter?"

"No. Not when it came to best friends."

She huffed out a laugh. "Then what changed?"

"By senior year, I had it so bad for you. And after that kiss in Ethan's car, well, I thought maybe you wanted me too. And that couldn't happen. I couldn't break my promise to Ethan."

Shelby remembered that kiss like it was yesterday. No explanations required.

"So you asked Leandra to prom?"

"Yes. And if it makes you feel any better, the date sucked. I think she liked the *idea* of going to prom with me, but she didn't really like *me*. She just wanted to make Cade Newcastle jealous."

"Then why did you scare Rick away? Wasn't it enough that I didn't go with you? You had to completely destroy my senior prom?"

"After I asked Leandra to the prom, I overhead Rick talking with Cade in the boys' locker room. Cade bet Rick he couldn't get you to go to prom with him, and then Rick bet not only would you go to prom with him, but he'd be in your pants before the night was over. I couldn't let that happen."

She stood, her anger back. "Didn't you trust me to stand up for myself? Did you think I would fall for Rick's come-ons? Give me a little credit, Nash."

"You're right. Of course, you're right. It's just . . ." He stood, placed his hands on her shoulders. "I couldn't bear the thought of his hands on you. At all. Not even while you were dancing, let alone . . ." He shook his head.

"If he'd tried anything more than that, I would have kneed him in the nuts."

Nash laughed. "Yeah. You would have." Then his expression turned serious, and he cupped her face in his hands. "I'm so sorry, Shelby. I had the best of intentions—honor my pact with Ethan and protect you from a sleaze ball." He pressed his forehead to hers and closed his eyes. "Can you forgive me?"

Wrapping her hands around his wrists, she sighed. "Yes. Your loyalty is one of the things I love about you."

He pulled her mouth up to his, captured her lower lip in a gentle kiss, then released her. "Come back to bed, and I promise to make it up to you," he said with an irresistibly sexy grin.

And, God help her, she did.

"SHELBY. WAKE UP." He gave her a gentle nudge. "Wake up." She lay curled on her side, the sheet down around her waist, revealing creamy skin and sexy curves.

Damn, he hated to start a day with bad news. He'd much rather start it buried deep inside Shelby.

She groaned then rolled over, throwing her arm over her face, baring her beautiful breasts. He held back a groan of his own, then sat on the edge of the bed.

Sitting up, she pulled the sheet up to cover her chest. Thank God, because he was getting pretty distracted. "What time is it?" She ran her fingers through her hair.

"Seven-ten."

"What is it?" Then she tensed. "It's not your father, is it?"

He handed her one of his T-shirts. "No. But you're going to want to get dressed for this."

Tugging his T-shirt on—lucky T-shirt, he thought— she looked over at him as if waiting for him to drop the bomb.

"Kim Sacks from PR called me this morning. It seems your ex posted some pretty nasty and damning comments on ESPN's website in response to your segment. He's also taken to Facebook and Twitter."

Shelby stiffened and sat bolt upright. "Like what kind of comments?"

"Saying you ruined his career, that you falsified the data and then blamed it on him, reported him to the NIH to get back at him for having an affair."

Her face had gone white, and dammit it killed him to be the one to cause it.

"Don't worry, we'll fight it. Our lawyers will get ESPN to pull down the comments, contact Facebook and Twitter, get them to shut down his accounts."

Shelby looked away then back at him, gnawing on her lip, her eyes wide. Then she just shook her head. "You can't protect me from this," she whispered. "This isn't Tonya Jordan in the schoolyard or Rick trying to get into my pants."

"Shelby, the man is lying. That's defamation. We'll get our lawyers to take care of it." At her continued silence, he got an odd feeling, like when his opponent was about to run a fake field goal play. "He is lying, right?"

"Up to a point."

"Up to what point, exactly?"

~

SICK TO HER STOMACH, Shelby dragged in a breath. "He is right that I ruined his career, that I reported him. But I didn't falsify the data, and I didn't report him because he cheated on me." She hung her head and muttered, "I didn't find out about that until after."

"Dammit, Shelby. We need to know these things, so we can take evasive action if we need to." He paced away and scrubbed a hand down his face.

"I'm sorry, Nash. First, I didn't think he'd even see the segment, and second, I didn't think even he could sink this low."

Nash stood, hands on his hips. Prompting her, he said, "You reported him."

"Yes." She cleared her throat. She had been the one to

discover that her then-husband had falsified important research data.

"While analyzing data on our last study, I came across something that didn't look right. First, I thought it was an error, so I talked to Charlie about it. His answers didn't add up. Literally. So I looked over the raw data again." She tucked her hair behind her ear.

"Then, before confronting him, I carefully reviewed the raw data on previous papers and found the same issues."

"Why hadn't you seen it before?" Nash asked as he sat on the end of the bed.

"Because he'd been careful—at first—but then he'd become sloppy or cocky, or both. With each paper, the falsification grew bolder."

"In retrospect, I can see his progression. The more articles published with false data without discovery, the more arrogant he became. The more flagrant his data falsification, the more controlling he became, and the more demeaning he became."

"You said he often berated you in front of your colleagues. That he called you stupid. He knew, if anyone could discover his falsification, it would be you. So, he became more and more controlling, undermining both your self-confidence and your stature in the research community."

"Yes. And because over the years he'd made me question my skills, he made me doubt my own work."

It assuaged some of her guilt that, without hindsight, she wouldn't have caught the first few problem papers because the falsification had been so subtle.

"When I finally confronted him about it, he got defensive, then belligerent, then downright hostile and threatening."

"Of course he did. He was a bully. No different than Tonya or any other bully."

Squeezing her eyes shut against the pain, she recalled that fateful encounter.

"Everyone does it," he'd argued. "Don't think for one minute they don't. You think you're so high and mighty. You'd be nowhere without me and my reputation."

"A reputation you built on lies and false data," she'd responded. "All those papers, journal articles, and presentations, with my name on them." She'd felt sick. "And none of them were accurate."

His shame-faced defiant look had said it all.

Her whole career had been built on a lie.

"You report it, and you go down with me," he'd threatened.

"I'd rather have to rebuild my career than go on basing it on lies and false data."

Clenching her fists against the pain of that memory, she continued, "I told him if he didn't report it, I would. He refused, so, I called his bluff and reported it."

She sighed. "After a year-long investigation by Stanford and the National Science Foundation, all our journal articles were retracted, except for the first one, which was my Ph.D. dissertation. Charlie lost his job and was prohibited from receiving federal grant money." She snorted in disgust. "Our so-called friends and colleagues couldn't distance themselves fast enough."

She'd been acquitted, but that didn't matter. Her career, her life, would never be the same again. He may have been a pariah for cheating, but she was a bigger pariah for reporting it.

As if that weren't enough, Charlie had confronted her after he'd received the ruling on his appeal.

"You ruined my career."

"Your career? My career is ruined too," she'd pointed out.

Charlie had stepped into her, his expression nasty. "And whose fault is that? If you'd just kept your mouth shut you'd be—"

"I'd be what, Charlie? The ex-wife of a man who cheated on her instead of the ex-wife of a man who not only cheated on his wife but the whole scientific community?"

Their attorneys had had to step in to break it up.

The humiliation of that confrontation in front of faculty and students had sealed her fate. She couldn't stay at Stanford. It had been time to move on.

She shook her head at the memory. "I had been his doormat for so long."

"Until your integrity was at stake. Then you stood up. Fought back."

"And look where it got me." She threw up her hands. "It ruined my career. Sterling was the only university willing to give me a job after that."

He paused, pulling on his lower lip, clearly thinking. Probably wondering what he'd gotten himself into with her. "I know what it's like to start over, Shelby."

"Yes, but it wasn't your fault."

"And you think this was? On what planet is this your fault?" He leaned forward, adding emphasis to his words.

"I reported him. I gave the feds all the evidence they needed to find he falsified data—for years."

Nash rose from the bed and sat next to her, wrapping an arm around her shoulder.

"I think you're the bravest person I've met."

She shook her head.

"You stood up and did the right thing, knowing the

damage it would cause you. The grief, the heartache. Not many people would have done that, even if it *hadn't* meant sabotaging their own careers."

He pulled her into him, and he felt so good. So solid, supportive, and warm.

"And that's why you didn't come to our ten-year reunion."

"Partly."

Shelby felt a huge weight lift from her shoulders. Atlas shrugging off the world. Even so.

"Maybe it's best if I don't travel with the team this week."

"Oh, hell no. We're not going to let this asshole affect the way we do business." He stood up.

"Nash, the last thing I want is for this story to distract the team."

"All this is documented?"

"Yes. It's in the investigation records. And the *Chronicle of Higher Education* followed the whole humiliating story."

"Get dressed."

"Where are we going?"

"To meet with Kim. You're going to tell her the same story, and we're going to fight back."

15

———

Following a big win against Wofford on the road, and just when Nash thought PR had the story of Shelby's asshat ex under control, he got a text from Ethan:

TURN ON THE LOCAL NEWS.

Flipping on the TV, Nash sank to the sofa when he saw Tonya's face wearing a smug expression. She was being interviewed by Suzanne Davies, a local reporter.

"Sleeping with someone just to get a job. It's disgraceful. Sterling High should remove her Valedictorian title. Oh, and her Most Likely to Succeed superlative. Especially if that's how she succeeds." Tonya looked straight into the camera and smirked.

"You wouldn't know success if it came up and bit you on your fat ass." He clicked the TV off in disgust and threw the remote down. It bounced off the sofa cushion and hit the hardwood floor. The back came off, sending the batteries rolling in all directions. "Son-of-a—"

His phone rang. Looking at the screen, he saw it was Ethan and not some reporter.

"Did you catch it?" he asked without preamble.

"Only the end."

"It appears that Tonya has spotted your car at Shelby's late at night—"

"Talking about stats," Nash defended.

"And that she's seen the two of you holding hands and kissing in public. She went to the media with the story."

"That's bullshit. Shelby and I never kissed in public. Ever the vindictive little bitch." His phone beeped with another call. "It's Shelby, I've got to go."

"Call me later."

Nash switched over. "Shelby—"

"What are we going to do now?" she asked, panic clear in her voice.

"We'll handle it." He paced his living room.

"Handle it how?"

"I don't know. I'll come over so we can discuss it."

"No. People will see your car."

"Then you come here."

"I don't think that's a good idea either."

"Christ, Shelby. No one's going to see your car out here. Why not?"

"Because we have a way of ending up in bed together, and that's what got us into this mess in the first place."

True. "My office then. No one can fault us for meeting there."

"Fine. I'll see you at the stadium in half an hour."

She'd hung up. This was not going to end well. Either she had to give up a job she admittedly loved, costing him one of his best weapons, or he'd have to give her up, costing him his heart.

~

NASH STRODE DOWN THE HALL, a set of keys in hand. Shelby stood beside his door looking as if her world had come crashing down. *Dammit.* He unlocked the door to his office and let her in.

The minute they had privacy, she said, "I knew we shouldn't be doing this. And yet, I did it anyway." She threw up her hands. "Seems I can't learn from past mistakes."

"Mistakes?" Nash glared at her. "Is that what we are? A mistake?"

"Of course not, but this is my life, Nash! Not some game. I could lose my professorship over this. Again."

"I know," his tone more conciliatory.

She paced away. "Maybe if I agree to relinquish my position with the football team, they'll let me keep my assistant professor position."

He tossed his keys on his desk. "But you love this job."

"Yes. I do. But I don't have much choice do I? This is the job that prohibits our relationship, not my teaching job. Besides, it's only part-time. It's not like I could live off this job alone." She turned to face him. "It's either that, or we stop seeing each other."

"It's my fault." He released a humorless laugh. "This is what I get for trying to help. I never should have given you the job. I only did it—" He froze. *Holy shit.* What had he just done?

"Only did it for what, Nash?" When he didn't answer, she pushed. "Only gave me the job for what reason?" But the stricken look on her face told him she already suspected.

God, this was not the way he wanted this to come out. He thought a year or two from now, when she had her feet back under her and a successful career as a sports analyst, he'd tell her how it all started.

He sighed. He'd really stepped in it this time. "I hired you because Delaney saw you looking at the want ad at McGinty's. She guessed, and correctly, that you were having financial problems."

"You—" She stalked toward him, her eyes spitting golden fire. "You hired me out of *pity*? How dare you! How dare you, Nash. I'm not some charity case, someone to take pity on. Why would you do that? Why, Nash?" Her hands fisted at her sides.

"Seemed like a good idea at the time." *What the hell* had *he been thinking?*

"And now I'm paying for it. Again. Just like when I paid for reporting Charlie. No good deed goes unpunished," she muttered. Before he could respond, she continued. "Has this all been about pity? Poor little Shelby? I'll give her a job, take her to my bed. Throw her a bone? Give her a glimmer of hope?"

He reached out for her.

"Don't. Just don't." She crossed her arms over her chest.

Damn, but that hurt, especially when he was only trying to help. "Shelby—"

"No, Nash." She held up her hand, stopping him. "I can't do this."

"Do what? This conversation? The job? Us?"

"None of it, Nash." She turned and walked out.

❧

Hurt, anger, pain, and disappointment collided inside her. Shelby collapsed on her bed, face-down. She'd managed to get out to her car without losing it. She'd even managed to get in her apartment without running into Delaney. But she couldn't hold back anymore. She gave in to the emotions boiling inside her as tears flowed hot and bitter down her cheeks.

She was hurt that Nash felt so much pity for her that he'd hire her on that emotion alone. Did he make love to her for the same reason?

Then she was just as angry at him for giving her a job that she'd fallen in love with. And look where it'd had gotten them both. Her potentially without a job at all, and him with a scandal clouding his winning season.

The pain came from the heart that she didn't think could ever be broken again. How can you break something that is already so shattered, it shouldn't be possible to break anymore?

Finally, she was disappointed in herself. She'd been down this road before, and she'd allowed herself to do it all over again, knowing what the consequences could be.

Even if she could keep her teaching position, how could she face the ridicule of her colleagues and students? It was Stanford all over again.

It would be a toxic work environment, all of her own creation. And with no savings and no prospect for another position, especially now, she'd have nowhere left to go. Who would want her?

Even so, all that paled in comparison when she thought about never seeing Nash again. Never feeling his traitorous arms around her. Never hearing him whisper her name in the middle of the night.

Even after what he'd done, she still loved him. And probably always would.

Nash stared down the neck of his beer and sighed. What a clusterfuck.

McGinty's was quiet on a Tuesday afternoon. Thank God. He was in no mood to talk to anyone, but neither did he want to sit alone in the silence of his house. He knew Hugh would leave him be, so he'd pulled up a seat at the bar and ordered a Scotch ale.

He'd really screwed up this time. He'd screwed up his professional life and his personal life. He'd brought scandal to his team when the focus should have been on their undefeated season.

The athletic director had chewed him a new one, and rightfully so. Feeling like he was more of a distraction than an inspiration, he'd handed off practice to his offensive coordinator and taken off.

Taking another pull on his beer, he thought about the look on Shelby's face when she'd essentially told him goodbye. He was sorry he'd hired her, because if he had to choose between winning football games with her on his staff and having a relationship with her, he'd pick the relationship. But he may have ruined that too, and for the second time.

He glanced up at the television behind the bar and saw Shelby's picture on the screen. "Fuck." He looked around. No one else in the bar seemed to be paying any attention. Small favor. According to the closed captioning on the screen, ESPN had picked up on the story of his relationship with Shelby and was dragging up her past. His photo appeared next, followed by one of a man he assumed was her ex-husband.

As he watched the network that had recently interviewed her for her impressive skill with numbers rake her over the coals, he felt sick.

SHELBY COULDN'T WATCH ANYMORE. Flicking off the TV, she paced around her tiny still-unfurnished apartment. The extra money she'd been making she'd used to pay off her attorneys and credit cards. At least there was that.

Once again, she was shamed for a work-related relationship, this time in a very public way. They'd dredged up her past, airing all of her dirty laundry.

Her phone buzzed with yet another incoming text. So far she'd gotten numerous texts from Delaney, Sam, Ethan, and Nash, but she'd ignored them all. This one from Nash she couldn't ignore.

SHELBY. TEXT ME BACK AND LET ME KNOW YOU'RE OKAY. OR I'M COMING OVER.

He couldn't come over. The news media had staked out her house, and his presence would only add new titillating video, so she texted him back with *I'm okay*. Nothing more.

Feeling like a prisoner in her apartment, she paced. What a mess she'd made of her life, once again.

She had a part-time job she loved more than her regular job. But a job she'd acquired only out of pity from the man she loved. And now, not only did she have to choose between that job and the man she loved, she might also lose her teaching position with the university. The job that was her bread and butter.

The urge to get away, to escape, if only for a little while, surged through her. Away from the watchful eyes of the media, her colleagues, and her hometown. Away from Nash, where she could think and reevaluate her life.

Thanksgiving was Thursday, and her mother had been asking her to come visit her and her husband in Miami.

Maybe she'd splurge for a ticket and fly down, lick her wounds, and figure out where to go from there.

16

Damn, life sucked sometimes. And now was definitely one of those times.

First Shelby, and now this.

Nash stared out his windshield at the cold, steady rain and wished to be just about anywhere but here. After finally making the decision to move his father into a facility with memory care, this would be his first post-move visit.

He'd found an excellent facility in Decatur, east of Atlanta and a two-hour drive from Sterling. While it wasn't the most convenient location for Nash, it was the best-rated facility in the area, and that was more important.

At only fifty-six, Nash's father's condition had progressed significantly in the last few months. His caregivers had been unable to handle him anymore.

Shutting off the engine, he climbed out of the car, his reluctant feet taking him in the direction of the main entrance.

He checked in with the receptionist then walked around to the north wing where the dedicated memory care section was. It boasted additional security to ensure the memory-compromised residents didn't wander off. A staff member buzzed him in, and, taking a deep breath, he knocked on his father's door, unsure who he would find today.

Carl looked up, a frown on his face. *Uh oh.* What now?

On the TV, a local sports anchor was talking about Carl Taylor, a photo from his father's days with the Falcons on the screen. Seemed Nash and his loved ones were top stories this week, and not in a positive way.

His father pointed a finger at the TV. "They're talking about me. Saying I have Alzheimer's or Schizophrenia. That I've lost my marbles."

Nash scuffed his foot on the floor as anger and shame filled him. "Dad—" When Nash looked back at his father, a tear slid down his father's weathered cheek, and the anger and shame turned to pain. Like after taking a helmet to the gut, Nash felt sick.

His father, eyes filled with sadness, held Nash's gaze. "I don't have Alzheimer's or Schizophrenia. And you need to tell them."

"Dad—"

"I want them to know. I want them to understand, do you hear me?"

Nash wanted to argue with his father. He'd wanted to protect his father from the media, but by doing that, he'd only opened his father's condition up to conjecture and rumor, and sometimes the rumors were more painful than the truth. "Yeah, Dad, I hear you."

NASH HAD BEEN LOOKING EVERYWHERE for Shelby. She wasn't answering his calls or his texts. He had to talk to her. To explain to her about the job, and that, yes, he initially hired her because he wanted to help her, but she quickly proved herself vital to the team. And to tell her he and the Athletic Director had come up with a solution. One he hoped she'd like, if she was willing to give up her full-time teaching position.

He'd circled back to Ruby's for a quick bite to find Delaney, Sam, and Ethan sitting in a booth.

"Nash!" Ethan waved him over, and Delaney slid over to make room for him.

"Have you seen Shelby?" Nash asked, wasting no time with greetings.

"I saw her leave this morning with a suitcase," Delaney said. "I'm sure it hasn't been easy this week with all the news." Taking a sip of her iced tea, she eyed him over the rim of her glass.

"Leave?" Knowing how few belongings she had, he could imagine her moving out just that quick. "Did she say where she was going?"

"Miami."

To her mom's? Nash wondered. "For good?"

Delaney shrugged. "Just a visit."

"Doesn't her mom live in Miami now?" Ethan asked.

"Yep," Delaney supplied, popping the 'p' before giving Nash a mysterious smile. "I even have her address."

"You do?"

"Yep." Another popped 'p.' "But it depends on why you're looking for her."

"What do you mean?"

"I mean, are you looking for her for professional reasons or personal reasons?"

"Both."

"Wrong answer, big guy."

Ethan snorted then choked on his tea. Nash cut him a look.

"What do you mean 'wrong answer'?"

"Unless you're looking to apologize to her, I'm not telling you the address."

"Apologize? You're the one who asked me to help."

"I asked you to help her, not ruin her life."

Nash sighed. Delaney was right. Of course he had to apologize about the job. But he also had to convince her that he loved her.

"Look, I just need to talk to her, okay?" Everyone continued to look at him. "What?"

Delaney took her phone out and started tapping on the screen then looked up at Nash, eyes narrowed. "This better not be about the championship tournament and her mad number skills."

The eyes of the group were on him, judging him, waiting for him to speak. "I love her, okay?"

"Well, all right then." Delaney tapped on the screen once more, and Nash's phone buzzed with an incoming text. An address in Coconut Grove.

"It's about damn time," Ethan said.

"What do you mean? What about the pact?"

"What about the pact? Jesus, we were what, fourteen when we made that pact?"

"What pact?" Delaney and Sam asked.

Nash ignored the question, giving Ethan an incredulous look. "You mean to tell me you never gave a damn about that pact?"

"No. I gave a damn about that pact all through high school, but once you and Shelby left, you were adults, big enough to eat hay. And decide for yourselves if there was anything between you." He draped an arm around Sam's shoulders. "Besides, I've got my woman," he said with a big dopey grin.

Delaney was tapping away on her phone again, then his phone buzzed with another incoming text. He looked at the screen.

What are you waiting for?

The doorbell rang, and since her mother was wrist-deep in the turkey's cavity, Shelby answered it.

"Nash!" She couldn't have been more surprised if the President of the United States had been standing there. "What . . . ? How . . . ?"

"Delaney gave me your mom's address."

"Who's at the door, Shelby?" her mother called from the kitchen.

"A friend."

"I didn't know you had friends in Miami." Then her mother came out wiping her hands on a dishtowel. "Nash? Nash Taylor? Well, I'll be." She cut a glance at Shelby. "I hope you can stay for dinner."

"Thank you, Mrs. . ."

"It's Sutton now, but just call me Amy."

"Thank you, Amy."

"But—" Shelby tried to interject.

"Don't be rude, Shelby. Invite Nash in." Her mom headed back toward the kitchen. "Jerome should be home soon. He'll be thrilled to meet you, Nash."

Realizing she couldn't go anywhere, Shelby opened the door wider to let Nash in and closed the door behind him. Then she stood there, arms crossed.

"It's good to see you, Shelby."

No response.

"Why didn't you tell me you were leaving?"

"I didn't realize I had to."

"Is there somewhere we can talk?"

"What if I don't want to talk?"

"SHELBY . . ."

"Fine." He followed her across a cool terrazzo floor to the back of the house where room-length sliding glass doors opened into a lush tropical garden complete with a small pool. The mid-century bungalow reminded him of a vacation rental house his parents had taken him to when he was a little boy.

He shoved his hands in his pockets to keep from dragging her into his arms. "Your mom looks good. Happy."

"She is. She finally found a winner in Jerome."

"She certainly deserves it."

Shelby leaned against the back of a teak lounge chair and waited for him to speak.

"Look, I admit, at first I hired you because I wanted to help." At her scowl, he continued, "Jesus, Shelby, you didn't have any furniture. And your bumper was held up with duct tape."

He was met with another arm-cross. She wasn't making this easy. Not that he blamed her.

"But you proved you were worth far more than what I was paying you. I couldn't have won those games without you and your mad number-crunching skills. And not just your skills—your gut instincts. You have a knack for seeing things in the game that none of us can see."

"Is that the only reason you're here? To get me to come

back for the championship tournament? Because if it is, you've forgotten that I can't work for you anymore."

He wanted to reach out, pull her into his arms, but the distance she'd put between them was far more than the physical distance of four feet.

"That's not the reason I'm here." He gazed into her eyes, hoping to catch a glimmer of emotion. Some indication that what he had to say to her would be welcome. And most of all reciprocated. "Shelby, since the day I saw you in the schoolyard, your hair in messy pigtails, a hole in the toe of your canvas tennis shoe, you've had my heart."

Her mouth stretched into a thin line. "I don't want your pity."

He stepped into her then, pinning her against the lounge chair. "Dammit, Shelby. It's never been about pity." He grazed his fingers down her cheek. "It's been about admiration. Respect."

She shook her head, her tear-filled eyes wide.

"And affection."

"Nash—"

"Let me finish. Even that day when Tonya and her mob were ganging up on you, you had a glimmer of courage behind that fear. And watching as you grew—your self-confidence grew too—it was really something." He swiped a tear that fell. "Seeing your insecurity when you returned. Learning the reasons for it. I wanted to give you a kick in the pants, I wanted to see the old Shelby. The one who didn't take crap from the Tonyas or Charlies of the world. Now I'm asking you to come back with me and stand up for something you love. Don't let these people take that away from you."

"I see." She placed her hands on his chest and pushed.

THE HOPE BLOOMING in her chest had shriveled. Nash was asking her to come back and stand up for her job. Which meant only one thing. The game meant more to him than she did.

Even if the university's leadership let her continue to work for Nash, she couldn't do it anymore. She couldn't see him on a daily basis knowing she'd come in second. That he didn't love her. Her heart couldn't take another blow. It already felt so bruised and battered, it was a wonder it kept beating.

"I'm sorry you flew all this way on Thanksgiving. When I go back, it will be for my job in the mathematics department. If they let me keep it."

"Shelby, I'm not talking about the job, although I'd love to see you fight for that too."

"Then what *are* you talking about, Nash?"

"I'm talking about us." He stepped closer. "I'm talking about you and me."

"I don't understand." She braced her hand on the chair behind her because her legs suddenly wobbled.

"Look, if I have to choose between you and the championship, I choose you. But I'm hoping in this case that I can have my cake and eat it too."

Her heart stumbled when she realized what he was saying. "Nash, are you saying you want me *and* the win?"

"I'm saying I want *us* and the win. I want us to win together."

She threw up her hands. "Have you learned nothing from this week's events?"

"I have. And so has Patrick Gibson."

"Patrick? What does the Athletic Director have to do with this?"

"Everything, since if you say yes, he'll be your new boss."

"I—I don't understand."

"Pat has been so impressed by you that he doesn't want to lose you. In fact, he'd like to use your skills to benefit other sports. He wants to create a new position just for you —Director of Sports Analytics. You'll have to extend your number-crunching to other sports like baseball, softball, and lacrosse. You'll manage a new team of analysts and programmers who support athletics' decision-making by organizing, analyzing, and presenting information, and help the Bobcats put the best possible teams on their respective fields and then play their best games on those fields."

Shelby's mouth dropped. Too stunned to speak, she just stared at Nash.

"Of course, you'll have to give up teaching, at least full-time anyway. I'm sure you could teach a course here or there if you really wanted to." Nash's mouth split into a huge grin. "This solves the nepotism problem."

Then her eyes narrowed and he lost his grin. "Is this more pity?"

"No. Do you think Patrick would create a full-time position to manage a new team of employees out of pity?"

"I guess not."

He closed the gap between them and gathered her into his arms, resting his chin on the top of her head.

"You hurt me, Nash."

"I know. Seems like every time I try to protect you, I wind up hurting you."

"Then stop trying to protect me."

"Now that's the Shelby I know. But, I love you, Shelby.

And no matter what you say, that love makes me want to protect you. It always will. Can you live with that?"

Her eyes teared up again. "I suppose I'll have to. Because I can't live without you. I love you too, Nash."

He lifted her chin and brought his mouth down to meet hers in a kiss that touched her soul.

Her mom stepped out onto the patio and beamed at Nash and Shelby. "Looks like we have a lot to be thankful for this year."

"WE'RE IN THIS TOGETHER." Shelby clasped Nash's hand in hers. This wouldn't be easy for either one of them, but especially not for Shelby. The primary purpose of this press conference was to face the questions and rumors swirling about Nash's father's health. But questions about his and Shelby's relationship, her job, and the Bobcats' most recent win that would send them to the championship game would come up as well.

After Thanksgiving with Shelby's mom and Jerome, and a couple days of seclusion in a little bed and breakfast in Coconut Grove, he and Shelby flew back to Sterling for this press conference.

He couldn't help but remember another painful press conference three years ago when he had to face off a room of journalists to announce his retirement. That day he'd been alone. But not today. Shelby would stand by his side, facing her demons, as he would face his.

Nash lifted their clasped hands to his mouth, pressing a kissing on the back of her hand. They walked into the room, hand-in-hand, blinking at the flashing cameras.

Nash approached the podium, glanced down at Shelby then cleared his throat.

"Thank you for coming today. I'll get right to it. There have been rumors that my father, Carl Taylor, has Alzheimer's. I'm here today to put those rumors to bed."

With Shelby's warm hand in his, he could handle any question the reporters threw his way. He could handle anything life threw his way. He'd won something better than any championship. He'd won Shelby.

EPILOGUE

The roar of the fans was deafening. Nash searched the crowd for Shelby. The trophy presentation would begin shortly, and he wanted her there on the quickly assembled stage with him, the rest of his coaches, and his team. She'd been part of the win. But more importantly she'd become part of him.

Bobcats fans were chanting, "F-C-S! F-C-S! F-C-S!"

His phone buzzed. It had been buzzing with incoming texts since the clock ticked down the last second of the game. But there was only one text he wanted right now. One from Shelby. Pulling his phone out of his pocket, he got it.

Soaked from the Gatorade his players had dumped on him, it was a wonder the phone still worked.

I can't get through the crowd.

Dammit. Grabbing one of the many police officers on the field, he gave him a description of Shelby and asked him to find her and escort her back.

His players and coaches hugged, high-fived, fist-bumped, and back-slapped all around him, but he had only one thing on his mind. Shelby.

The announcer came on and said, "Please turn your attention to the stage for the trophy presentation."

The roar grew.

The NCAA President and FCS Committee Chair stepped forward.

"Coach! Coach! It's time!" His QB, Matt Castle, yelled.

"Nash!"

Nash spun to see the big burly police officer cutting a path through the crowd standing on the confetti-littered field with Shelby right behind him.

She finally reached him, and he wrapped his arms around her, burying his face in her hair. "Come on." He released her hand and pulled her up the stairs to stand beside him for the presentation.

After a quick speech from the NCAA President, he turned, "Coach Nash Taylor, it's my honor and privilege to present to you the Division I Football Championship Trophy. Congratulations on an extraordinary undefeated season."

Nash took the trophy and held it high to the cheers of the crowd, his players, and his staff. He'd reached the pinnacle of his coaching career, and, as meaningful as that was, it didn't mean as much to him as the woman standing next to him.

"I'd like to thank this incredible group of guys who have become a family, not just a team. I'd like to thank my coaching staff, and their wives and families, for their hard work and dedication toward achieving this goal. It sounds cliché, but that's why they become clichés—because they're true. I couldn't have done it without them. And then there's Dr. Wentworth." He reached for Shelby's hand and pulled her into his side. "Never underestimate the power of a woman, especially one with data." He leaned over and placed a kiss right on her lips and grinned.

Passing the trophy to his quarterback, he answered the network reporter's questions, but all he really wanted was to get Shelby alone.

After what seemed like a lifetime of questions, he saw his chance.

Pulling her through the crowd and down the stairs, he ducked behind the stage while the reporter interviewed his key players and coaching staff.

Gathering her into his arms, he lowered his mouth to hers for a gentle kiss then pulled back and gazed into her eyes.

"You did it, Nash! You won the championship! And with a team only three years old. I'm so proud of you."

"I'm proud of *us*." He kissed her again. "But winning all the championships in the world wouldn't compare to spending the rest of my life with you. You're my greatest win." Pulling the Gatorade-sodden white satin box out of his pocket, he went down on one knee. "Marry me, Shelby."

Tears filled her eyes, and a smile lit her face, then she threw her arms around his neck, knocking them both to the ground. "Yes!"

At the roar of the crowd, they both turned to see their images on the jumbotron. So much for privacy.

AWARD-WINNING AUTHOR
REBECCA HEFLIN

He has plenty to
learn about love.

STERLING UNIVERSITY
THE SERIES
BOOK THREE

She's just the
woman who can
teach him.

Educating
Dr. Mayfield

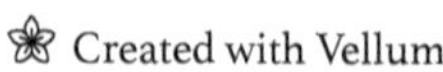 Created with Vellum

ACKNOWLEDGMENTS

I can't believe this is my eighth book! From my first published book in 2011 to my eighth published book in 2017, I have had the support of my husband, my family, and my friends. They say writing is a solitary effort, but there are always those standing in the background, celebrating your achievements, holding your hand when you stumble, and brainstorming with you through the plotting snags. I dedicate this, and all my books to you. I thank you all from the bottom of my heart.

QUOTE

"A loving heart is the beginning of all knowledge."
~ Thomas Carlyle

1

Green was not her best color.

Seated at a table in Sterling's one and only pub, Delaney Driscoll stared glumly across the table at her two best friends as they chattered about their upcoming weddings like two teenagers hopped-up on one-too-many energy drinks.

McGinty's Pub often played host to life's happiest and saddest events. It was where birthdays were toasted, engagements were announced, Sterling Bobcats wins were celebrated, and lives were remembered. It was only fitting that weddings should be planned there too.

Taking a swipe at the salt rimming her margarita, she stuck her finger in her mouth with a pout. She really needed to get over herself. Of course, she was ecstatic that her two best friends had found the loves of their lives. But, *come on.* Was it too much to ask that she find hers too?

"So, what do you think? Delaney? Earth to Delaney!" Sam snapped her fingers in front of her friend's face.

"Where were you?" Shelby asked, with a quizzical look.

"Oh. Sorry." She sighed then stuffed a fried pickle in her mouth.

Sam and Shelby exchanged glances.

"No, *we're* sorry. All this talk about our weddings must be boring you to tears," Sam said, a soft, understanding smile on her could've-been-a-model face.

Dr. Samantha Love, a psychology professor in the same college as Shelby and Delaney, had hit the news last year with a discovery the press called 'the love test'—a blood test that determined a couple's compatibility. One of the largest online dating services in the U.S. now offered the test as part of their premium package. And said 'love test' had found Sam's match in one Ethan Quinn, hunky literature professor and dean of their college. Now their wedding was just two months away—in April.

A whiz kid at statistics, Dr. Shelby Wentworth was a mathematics professor, first at Stanford, and then for a short stint at Sterling, before she became the Director of Sports Analytics for Sterling's athletics department. She and Sterling's head football coach, Nash Taylor, got engaged—on the football field, no less—after Sterling won its first NCAA Division I Football Bowl Subdivision Championship, thanks in part to Shelby's mad number-crunching skills. It was one of the most romantic proposals she and probably a million football fans had ever seen, thanks to an eagle-eyed cameraman who captured the moment, much to Nash and Shelby's chagrin.

Their wedding was coming up in June.

To make matters worse in the single department, Shelby, who had been Delaney's neighbor, moved out to Nash's farmhouse.

"Of course I'm not bored. I'm thrilled over both your weddings, it's just I have a lot on my mind." Like being the loving, supportive, not-jealous friend she should be . . . among other things. She absently stirred her drink with a finger.

Shelby reached over and squeezed Delaney's free hand. "Tell me about your curriculum submission. Have you heard anything yet?"

"No. It's with the curriculum committee. Ethan thinks there shouldn't be any issues since I've done such a thorough job of incorporating existing courses, adding the few it needs, and because it's a timely major."

Delaney had been dreaming of creating a new major in her program—Bachelor of Fine Arts in Romantic Fiction and Literature—and now her packet was completed and in the hands of the university's curriculum committee. She'd been working on it, in between teaching and conducting scholarly research, for months. She wanted Sterling University to offer this new degree program in the course catalog that would come out next spring. A couple of the course additions were already on the fall class schedule.

"Well, when the decision comes down from on high, we'll have to celebrate." Sam held up her martini glass in salute, and Shelby followed suit with her own margarita.

Delaney played along and lifted her glass. "To writing—and teaching—romantic fiction."

They clinked glasses then took sips of their drinks. This being her second margarita, Delaney was beginning to feel the effects. Maybe she should stop there.

Nah. She'd walked the five blocks here, anyway.

The door to McGinty's opened and in walked—*hel-lo*—Mr. Tall, Dark, and Brooding. She sat up a little bit straighter.

She'd always been attracted to the Mr. Darcys of the

world. The dark, forbidden men. The ones who so clearly needed the love of a good woman but didn't know it.

And this one fit the bill. Hair neatly cropped, the color of the mink stole her mom used to wear (before she went vegan), a strong chin with just a hint of stubble, and a body —clearly no stranger to the gym—that filled out the navy sweater he wore. Gray slacks. Conservative. And expensive, if she had to guess.

He walked over to the corner of the bar, away from the group huddled there watching NASCAR on the TV, and pulled up a barstool. Hugh McGinty, the pub's owner, approached and took his drink order. Scotch, neat. Shuddering, she wondered how anyone drank that, especially when good tequila was at hand.

She wondered if he was meeting someone. A woman, perhaps? Or a friend? She'd never seen him before, and with a population of sixteen thousand, including the students, it was rare to see someone in Sterling you didn't at least recognize. Was he new in town? Just visiting?

A comment from Shelby momentarily diverted her attention from Mr. TB&D to sigh over a picture of Shelby's wedding dress. A simple sleeveless, bateau-neck gown in white silk with three wide pleats across the front and a chapel-length train in the back. *Perfect.* "Oh, Shelby! It's lovely." Her enthusiasm returned. "When are we going to Atlanta to try it on?" The town of Sterling offered little in the way of wedding boutiques.

"Next weekend, if that's good for everyone. With the wedding only four months away, I've got to order it ASAP."

"That will be perfect. I can schedule my final fitting." Sam said as she checked her phone.

Delaney didn't bother checking her calendar. God knew

her weekends were free. Her weeknights, too, for that matter. "Works for me."

"Great! The guys will meet us for dinner later." Shelby entered the plans into her calendar.

Super. She'd be the fifth wheel. Again.

Delaney glanced back at the bar where Mr. TD&B sat. He had his drink in one hand, a magazine in the other. *Hmm.* Maybe he wasn't meeting anyone. Never one to pass up an opportunity, she chugged the rest of her drink. "Oh, look at that. I need another drink. Anyone else?"

Shelby and Delaney looked up from the bridal magazine they were studying.

"No, I'm good."

"Me too."

Delaney got up, maybe a tad too fast, given how the room spun. "Okey-dokey. I'll be back." Moistening her lips with a swipe of her tongue, she tossed her hair over her shoulder and made her way to the bar and the open spot next to him.

Signaling Hugh with her empty glass, she perched on the edge of the barstool, took a deep breath, turned her gaze on him, and stuck out her hand. "Hi, I'm Delaney Driscoll. You must be new in town." Although a bit tipsy, she thought she'd pulled that off with a dash of aplomb.

He shifted to look at her, put his magazine down, and held out his hand, albeit reluctantly. "Devon Mayfield." Distant. No smile.

But when his big warm hand wrapped around hers, she shivered. "Nice to meet you, Devon." *And you smell delish.*

"What was that?"

"What?" *Oh crap, did I just say that out loud?* Heat flooded her face. "Oh, I said, McGinty's food is delish."

He greeted her comeback with a muttered, "Good to know."

Hugh handed her another margarita. "I see you've met our Delaney here." He reached across and patted her on the cheek. "She's a good one, that's for sure."

The warmth of a blush crept into Delaney face at Hugh's words. Such a gem, that man.

Hugh continued, "You didn't have to come to the bar to order another drink. Why didn't you just signal Gabby? She would've taken your order."

"Pfft," Delaney said, with a wave of her hand. "I didn't want to bother Gabby. She's so busy." They all gazed in Gabby's direction, where she leaned against the register thumbing her phone.

Or not.

"Okay. Well. Thanks for the drink, Hugh," indicating— nicely, of course—that he should buzz off. Carefully lifting the full glass to her lips, she took a sip then turned back to Devon. "If you'd like, you can join my friends and me. We're just hanging out, talking about weddings." She winced. Nothing like wedding talk to entice a guy into joining you.

"Thanks, but I'm good here." He picked up his magazine as the now-busy Gabby brought him his dinner—McGinty's specialty—lamb stew.

Since he'd basically dismissed her, she said, "Alrighty, then. See ya 'round, *Devon.*"

What a snob.

She grinned.

Just like Mr. Darcy.

❧

DEVON SHOOK his head as he watched one Delaney Driscoll

weave her way back to her friends. Clearly, she'd already had one too many margaritas.

She dropped into the booth with an undignified plop and leaned over the table to whisper something to the women across from her.

They all lifted their gazes in his direction. Raising a brow along with his glass of scotch, he saluted them. Only one had the nerve to hold eye contact—the pretty blonde. She hefted her martini glass in return.

Feeling oddly self-conscious, he broke eye contact and turned his attention to the tantalizing aroma of lamb stew and the article in the latest issue of the *American Journal of Business Education*.

As the new dean for Sterling's College of Business, he'd had a mandate: to make the college one of the top ten business schools in the country by the end of his third year as dean. A tall order, but one he believed he could fulfill. They only had to move up six slots in the rankings. An achievable goal with the right leadership and teamwork.

Nestled in the hills of Northeast Georgia, the town of Sterling owed its existence to two things: granite and knowledge. Granite, because Sterling held some of the richest granite quarries in the world—if it was made of granite, it probably came from Sterling—and knowledge, because Sterling University—one of the Southern Ivy League schools, a.k.a. The Magnolia League—educated almost ten thousand students inside its hallowed halls and sent them out into the world to share that knowledge.

While researching the job offer, Devon learned that the university was founded in 1835 by wealthy granite quarry magnate and town founder Samuel Sterling. The university's arts department even offered classes in granite-carving, and of course its geology program was one of the country's best. Sterling had endowed the university with one million dollars and three hundred and fifty acres of land adjacent to the family home.

When the last of the Sterling line, Victoria Eliza Sterling-Pickard, died in 1974, she left the family home to the university for use as its main administration building, aptly named Sterling Hall.

Devon quickly discovered that if you lived in or around Sterling, you most likely either worked for the university or for one of the many granite quarries or monument-makers.

An outburst of giggles drew his attention back to the booth of three women. Attractive women at that, each in their own way. The cool blonde was polished and sophisticated—classic. The petite one with light brown hair was fresh-faced and casual—the quintessential girl next door.

But Delaney, with her golden-blond hair and curvy figure, was a bombshell. And when he'd responded to her introduction, he'd been momentarily stunned by the most arresting blue eyes he'd ever seen. No. Not just blue . . . sapphire.

He had to admit, she'd smelled nice too. Something sweet but light, like orange blossoms.

But he'd also been unnerved by that direct gaze. She'd looked at him like she could see right through his armor to the parts underneath that had been found lacking by those who should've loved him unconditionally.

The subject of his assessment snorted then burst into another fit of giggles.

Clearly ditzy, though. Not his type at all.

He liked smart, sophisticated women, with excellent manners and polished social skills. Someone with goals of her own and the determination and drive to meet them.

Delaney slapped the table with her hands, laughing—no, *guffawing*—at something her companions said.

Definitely not his type.

He needed a woman and a partner, someone who would support him and who would be an asset to him in the pursuit of his goals while she also pursued her own. Someone who would make a respectable first lady to the president of an Ivy League university. Preferably someone in academe.

And to that end, he ignored the women and returned to his journal article on business and computer science degrees and job satisfaction in a vain attempt to turn a deaf ear to the still-giggling threesome.

DEVON HAD JUST PAID his tab and was preparing to leave when two other men walked into McGinty's. He recognized one from the dean's meeting last week. Ethan Quinn, dean of the College of Arts and Sciences. He didn't know the other man, although he looked familiar.

After scanning the dining area, they made their way to the table of three women. The blonde rose from her seat, and Ethan gathered her into his arms, kissing her on the mouth. Well, that ended that. He'd thought to introduce himself to her at some point, strike up a conversation and see if she was interested. Clearly not.

The other man took the Girl Next Door's hand and pulled her in for a kiss as well, while the Blonde Bombshell looked on, a touch of envy evident in the pout.

Not only flighty, but an egg-timer on the final countdown. All the more reason to steer clear.

Devon picked up his magazine and headed for the door.

"Oh, Devon."

He turned to see Ethan waving him over. *Great.*

"Devon, let me introduce you," Ethan said as he stood. "Devon is the new dean of the College of Business. And this is Nash Taylor, head football coach."

Ah. That explains why he'd looked familiar. "You used to play for the Broncos." Devon stuck out his hand.

Nash nodded and shook it. "Nice to meet you. This is my fiancée, Shelby Wentworth," he said, as he gestured to the Girl Next Door.

"And, this is *my* fiancée, Samantha Love," Ethan continued, taking the Polished Sophisticate's hand.

Fiancée? Definitely off limits then. "Pleasure." So, that's the lay of the land. The weddings they were talking about were Bombshell's friends'.

"Oh, and I believe you two met—this is Delaney Driscoll," Samantha interjected.

"Yes. We met."

Delaney narrowed her eyes at him like she had his number.

"Settling in to life in Sterling?" Ethan asked.

"Yes. I'm closing on my townhouse in Georgetown Square next week."

"I used to live in Georgetown Square," Samantha said. "You'll love it. Very quiet. Nice neighbors."

"Good to know."

"We're putting together a little three-on-three basketball game tomorrow, and we just lost our third," Ethan said. "Care to join?"

"Sure. What time and where?" Devon asked. He needed the exercise, and a little competition couldn't hurt.

"Four o'clock at the Granite Park courts."

"I'll see you then. Nice meeting everyone." As he moved

to the door, he could feel a pair of eyes boring into his back. And he'd just bet those eyes were the color of the Mediterranean Sea.

His shoulder blades itched with the thought that she could see far more than he wanted her to.

2

———

The following Saturday, as Taylor Swift sang at full volume about never getting back together, Delaney put the finishing touches on her appearance. Not that there was anyone who would notice.

Grabbing her purse, she walked into the living room just as the doorbell rang. Swinging open the door, she invited Shelby in.

"You ready?" Shelby asked. But before Delaney could answer, Shelby continued, "Oh no. You're listening to Taylor Swift, and that can only mean one thing."

Shelby followed her into the kitchen. "Mason and I broke up. Again." Story of her life. She couldn't make a man stick if she stripped naked and rubbed herself in Elmer's Glue.

"I thought you broke up two weeks ago."

"We did." She put her coffee mug in the dishwasher. "But we got back together on Tuesday. And broke up again yesterday. Thus," she waved her hand in the direction of her iPod docking station, "the song."

Shelby shook her head. "Sounds like you should take Taylor's advice this time. You feel up to Atlanta?"

"Of course!" She put on a smile. "Are you kidding me? I wouldn't miss it." *What was a little salt in the wound when it came to her best friends' weddings?*

"Great. Sam's waiting in the car. The guys will join us later for dinner."

"Perfect." Just what she wanted—to be the tag along at a couples' dinner. A soon-to-be-*married* couples' dinner.

As they headed for the door, Shelby said, "I thought you didn't really like Mason because he stared at his own reflection too much."

"Beggars can't be choosers." Delaney locked up and tossed her keys into her purse with disgust.

Before she could take a step toward the car, Shelby took her by the shoulders and looked her in the eye. "You're not a beggar. Far from it. And you *should* be choosy. You deserve the best. Not some guy who's in love with his own appearance. It will happen. I know it."

"Yeah, well, care to run some numbers for me? Do the stats show it will happen before my eggs expire?"

"Listen to me. It will happen when you least expect it. Stop trying so hard. Focus on your career goals, the new major you've created, and the rest will fall into place."

"From your mouth to Cupid's ears," Delaney muttered, as she followed Shelby to Sam's waiting car.

THE PROVOST HAD APPOINTED Devon to the university's curriculum committee, contending the experience would provide useful information in pursuing his own college's goals. Since he wouldn't assume any teaching responsibilities until fall, he had the time to commit to the workload the committee position entailed.

So, bright and early Monday morning, he picked up the week's committee meeting packets that had been dropped off with his assistant and thumbed through them. An interesting mix of new courses, new majors, some new syllabi, and a few certificate programs.

To his mind, a college course or major needed to prepare a student for meaningful work in his or her chosen field. Impart skills that would be appealing to a potential employer. Some life skills courses were useful too, like etiquette, communication, and personal finances.

He frowned upon the so-called 'basket-weaving courses' that some students liked to take for an easy A. What good would Zombies in Popular Culture or The Science of Harry Potter do for someone seeking lucrative employment? Students needed structure and real-world experiences in their education. Not touchy-feely pop culture nonsense.

His own education had been very structured, almost militaristic in its formality. He'd attended an exclusive boarding school in Connecticut for the entirety of his primary and secondary education, and while it wasn't a military academy, his days were structured to the minute. From the time he'd wake up at 6 a.m. to lights out at 10 p.m., his day had been filled with everything from classes to study hall and physical education, as well as life skills training like financial management and budgeting, time management, and etiquette.

By the age of fifteen, he knew which fork to use with fish, how to balance a checkbook, budget for savings, and make informed financial decisions. Not that he had much money for any of those things. But what little he'd had, he'd handled judiciously.

Abandoned by his mother who'd left him with a wealthy man, presumably his father, who'd had little to nothing to do with Devon, he'd learned quickly to stand on his own two feet.

So, when it came time to go to college, Devon chose not to seek assistance from the man. Rather, he applied to the top business schools in the country, and was accepted into many, but selected Harvard when they offered him a full scholarship. He'd worked for a short time in a bookstore to cover his living and other expenses.

Money no longer an issue—he'd solved that problem when he'd created and sold two start-ups before he graduated—he could now do whatever he wanted for a living. And what he wanted was to impart his knowledge to the world's future business leaders and apply the business strategies he'd learned to institutions of higher education.

And while money was no longer his goal, respect was. Even if love wasn't in the cards for him, he would be respected. To that end, he had his sights set on moving up the ranks to provost and eventually president of a prestigious university, with a proper wife by his side.

Flipping to the last packet in the stack, he caught the name Delaney Driscoll, Ph.D.

He sat up. The Blonde Bombshell was a faculty member? Setting the packet aside, he searched for her profile on the university's website. It was her alright. The photo was unmistakably Delaney. Those eyes, that hair. And the smile. Nothing fake in that. It showed in her eyes.

He wondered what her life had been like to make her so open and . . . engaging.

Scrolling down, he read her *vitae*—Born and raised in Kansas. Attended Middlebury College in Vermont, earning her bachelor's degree in English lit, before heading off to the

University of Denver for both her master's and Ph.D. in English and creative writing respectively. Returned to Middlebury College following graduation to teach. A few years ago, she took a position at Sterling in their newly formed creative writing program.

Creative writing. Why didn't that surprise him?

Not that there was anything wrong with that. He enjoyed a good novel now and again. John le Carré and Tom Clancy came to mind.

But when he scrolled down to the list of courses Delaney taught, he rolled his eyes. Girl Power and The Young Adult Novel. "What the hell is that?" he muttered. The course readings included the *Twilight* novels and *The Hunger Games* series. "This is what she teaches?"

The next course on the list was Literature and Women's Sexuality. *Good Lord.* He skimmed the readings covered in the course: *Madame Bovary, Tess of the d'Urbervilles, Lady Chatterley's Lover, The Kadin,* whatever that was, and . . . "*Fifty Shades of Grey*?!"

"Did you say something, Dr. Mayfield?" Rachel, his assistant, popped her head in the doorway.

He cleared his throat in embarrassment. "No, Rachel. Thanks."

He scrolled back up to the photo of Miss Sexpot, and a vivid recollection of her curves and her scent accosted him. Maybe . . . "No." Not going there. He needed a wife, not a fling.

Even so, curiosity got the better of him and he opened the packet to see what she'd submitted. A new major in the creative writing program—BFA in Romantic Fiction and Literature. Gazing skyward, he muttered. "Figures."

THE UNIVERSITY'S curriculum committee had been at the March meeting's agenda for over an hour, voting to approve various new courses, a few certificates, and one new major. They'd also voted to deny a new course in engineering called The Science of Star Trek.

That one deserved a dose of scorn.

Devon looked at the next item on the agenda. Dr. Driscoll's new major. He glanced over at her, seated in a chair along the wall, wearing a suit that on most women would be modest, but on her, it all but screamed sexy secretary.

Dr. Morton Gregors, the committee chair, introduced the proposal, bringing Devon's attention back to the table.

A derisive snort came from the curmudgeonly Dr. Gordon. Out of the corner of his eye, he saw Delaney sit up, clearly affronted.

"Aren't those the books with long-haired shirtless men and busty women my cheatin' ex-wife was always readin'?" Dr. Gordon asked, a scowl on his florid face. His heavy accent belied a sharp mind, albeit with a sharp tongue to match.

"You're thinking of romance novels from the eighties," Angela Burton, chemistry professor, said waving her hand dismissively. "They've changed in the three decades since."

Dr. Gordon greeted her remark with a raised eyebrow. "I guess you *read* those rags?"

"I do, and I'm not ashamed to admit it," she said, with an indignant sniff.

"I think it's worthy of consideration," Dr. Adams, history professor, said. "We've certainly approved new majors for other degrees that may have been less marketable. Take the major we approved last year in the College of Journalism—Bachelor of Arts in Culinary Criticism."

Devon's head popped up from the notes he'd been reading. *Seriously?*

"At least there's a market for romantic fiction," Dr.
Adams continued.

A few nods followed.

"It's absurd." Dr. Gordon slapped the table.

Dr. Gregors held up a hand. "If we could dispense with
the judgments regarding one's choice of literature–"

"Hmph. Literature," Dr. Gordon muttered, receiving a
glare from Dr. Burton.

"As I was saying, the issue is not whether romantic
fiction is worthy of a read. It's whether this would be a legiti-
mate program of study to be added to our curriculum. Will
the granting of the degree prepare our students to enter a
lucrative job market, are there enough students interested in
such a degree, and is this is a defensible use of our
resources?"

"That's simple enough," Dr. Gordon chimed in. "It's a
total waste of resources." He folded his arms across
his chest.

Dr. Burton bristled at the opinion. "Dr. Gordon, are you
deeming romantic fiction unworthy because it is a female-
dominated industry? Literature written *by* women
for women?"

"There's that word again. *Literature.* I hardly think
romance novels are worthy of being included in that category with the likes of Hemingway, Fitzgerald, and Twain."

Dr. Burton crossed her arms over her chest, echoing his
body language. "Funny, no women included in that lineup."

Dr. Gordon answered with a contemptuous hand wave, a
scowl on his face.

Devon shifted uncomfortably in his seat. While he didn't
agree that the degree was a valuable addition to the Sterling

student catalog, he didn't approve of Dr. Gordon's rude and clearly biased tone.

If the responses to Dr. Gregors' key questions were 'yes,' then regardless of what one thought of the subject matter, it deserved the committee's consideration.

But he happened to think the answers to the questions were 'no.'

He cleared his throat, drawing the interest of the other committee members. "I realize this is my first committee meeting, and while I may not agree with some of Dr. Gordon's comments, I do agree that this proposed new major is not viable, strictly for practical reasons."

Now that he had their full attention, and the bickering had ceased, he continued, not risking a glance in Dr. Driscoll's direction. "Rising tides lift all boats. As you know, one of the criteria used to rank colleges and universities is their career placement."

"For those of you in colleges and programs—like the College of Business—that are part of the president's initiative to rise in the rankings, having a glut of dead-end majors ultimately impacts you, even if those degree programs are not in your college." He tapped the proposal packet with this finger. "This appears to be one of those dead-end programs."

Dr. Applebaum, from the College of Arts and Sciences, chimed in. "We have degrees in arts programs which might fall into the same so-called 'dead-end' category. Our graduates won't necessarily be *hired*, although certainly some will seek jobs in museums and galleries, but many will create art for sale. Are you saying our BFAs in sculpture or painting are dead-end degrees?"

Devon glanced around the table then looked back at Dr. Applebaum. "At least, if the graduate doesn't make it in the art world, he or she can teach sculpture or painting, or like you said, seek employment elsewhere in the art world. But who would hire someone with a BFA in Romantic Fiction to teach literature or work in a library?"

There were comments around the table, some nods of agreement, but also some skepticism.

"Sterling's motto is 'Preparing our students for today, tomorrow, and beyond,'" Devon continued. "It is the university's responsibility to give our students the tools they need to succeed in an increasingly complicated world. I hardly think Reading the Romance Novel is one of those tools."

An indignant sniff came from Delaney's direction.

"I can't help but believe that there is some degree of discrimination here," Dr. Burton stated.

"Perhaps, on the part of some of us," Dr. Gregors agreed, as he leveled a glare at Dr. Gordon. "But, be that as it may, Dr. Mayfield is right. There is not enough evidence here," he held up the proposal, "to convince me that this is a viable degree."

"Agree," Dr. Applebaum said.

"I make a motion to deny the proposal," Dr. Gordon said, raising his hand.

Devon sighed, disgusted to be the one to second the man's motion. "And I second the motion."

"All those in favor of denying Dr. Driscoll's proposal for a BFA in Romantic Fiction and Literature say *aye*."

Devon scanned the votes. All ayes except Dr. Burton.

"Those opposed."

Dr. Burton raised her hand, a frown on her face.

"Motion carries. This meeting is adjourned."

3

D elaney selected a pool cue from the rack and chalked the tip.

Hanging with her girls on a Thursday night at McGinty's was the highlight of what was an otherwise craptastic week. She intended to let off some steam and forget all about Devon Mayfield and the committee's narrow-minded view of education curriculum. With the exception of Angela Burton. Not to mention, Devon's apparent ability to turn otherwise open-minded professors on the curriculum committee, like Dr. Applebaum and Dr. Gregors, into his supporters.

"I mean, *come on*, the curriculum committee approved a certificate program in online video gaming just last year," she continued her complaints, as she picked up her margarita.

"I thought the point of tonight's activities was to take your mind off the subject." Shelby gathered up the balls and rolled them to the other end of the table. "What would Taylor Swift say?"

"Haters gonna hate." Delaney walked to the opposite end of the table.

"And what else would she say?" Sam added.

"Shake it off," Delaney muttered.

"Exactly," Shelby said, her voice emphatic.

"You're right. I won't bring it up again." Delaney placed the cue ball on the dot and bent over to break the balls. She popped up again. "It's just, without him rallying the troops, I think my proposal would have had more supporters. Dr. Applebaum could have been swayed, as well as Dr. Gregors."

Other than the crotchety old Dr. Gordon, there were plenty of head nods around that table. "You should have heard Devon calling the degree a dead-end." She threw up her free hand. "What does he know?"

Sam rolled her eyes and heaved a sigh. "You're right. But the question is: What are you going to do about it?"

"I don't know yet. But . . . something." This time she took her shot and sank a stripe in the far left corner. She missed her next shot—a bank—which was a tad over her skill level anyway.

Shelby stalked the table searching for an open shot. "I think you need to look at it from his perspective." Bending over the table, she cued up. "Four ball, side pocket."

"Shel, we don't need to call the pockets," Sam reminded her, leaning on her pool cue.

Shelby shrugged as the ball rolled in. "Habit."

Delaney put her free hand on her hip. "What do you mean, I need to see it from his perspective?"

"Now, don't get your knickers in a twist." Shelby crossed to the other side of the table. "He's a business professor—a Harvard MBA, Wharton, Ph.D.—you need to make your case with facts and figures. Data."

"Ugh." Delaney threw her head back. "You know me and numbers." She couldn't figure out her restaurant tab, much less run numbers on the romantic fiction industry.

"Yes, I do." Shelby sank two balls in one shot, both solid. "But you happen to have a friend who's very good with numbers."

"And running the pool table," Sam muttered.

"Sometimes I get lucky," Shelby said with a grin. "Anyway, I could help you." She stood, pool stick resting on the ground, and gazed across the table at Delaney.

Yeah. Shelby was a genius when it came to numbers. She could figure out a five-person restaurant tab, with tip, in her head. For that reason alone, Delaney worshipped her. Then there was the FBS Championship title that Sterling won earlier this year, thanks in part to Shelby's magic with numbers. "You'd do that?"

"Of course. What are friends for?"

"Ladies."

Delaney turned to see Nash and Ethan strolling over to the billiard tables looking handsome and happy.

Nash wrapped an arm around Shelby's waist and kissed her. Ethan followed suit with Sam.

And there Delaney stood, odd woman out. Again.

"Hi, guys." She nodded.

"We don't want to interrupt ladies' night out," Ethan said. "Just wanted to say hi."

"Yeah, we're meeting Devon for dinner," Nash explained.

Delaney shoved Nash, who didn't budge an inch. "How can you hang out with that jerk?"

Nash chuckled. "Jerk? I admit he's a bit stiff, but he's a nice enough guy."

"Apparently, Devon had a hand in throwing a monkeywrench into approving Delaney's proposed new major," Ethan supplied.

"Oh. Well, I'm sure you'll convince him otherwise." Nash bent his six-foot-four-inch frame to look her in the eye. "You can be very persuasive when you want something badly enough."

Delaney knew he was remembering her role in convincing him to fly down to Miami to apologize to Shelby when everything went FUBAR.

He straightened and, taking Shelby's hand, said, "See you later. Try not to run the table on these two."

Sam snorted. "Too late for that."

When Devon entered McGinty's, he spotted Nash and Ethan already at a booth. The place was busy for a Thursday night, but what did he expect? A pub in a college town was bound to be a popular hangout.

He nodded to a grad student from his college and took a seat next to Nash. He appreciated Nash and Ethan's attempts at befriending him. He didn't crave the company of others very often, but it had been nice to have a couple of guys to grab a meal with or go a few rounds on the basketball court.

Even so, he didn't expect to be best man at their weddings or anything.

After greeting the guys, he picked up his menu. He'd yet to have one of McGinty's juicy burgers, but he'd worked up an appetite on his run this afternoon.

The waitress took their drink order. The guys ordered a craft beer. When it was his turn, he said, "You know what, that sounds good. I'll have the same." Burger and beer. Not since his college days.

"You settled in?" Nash asked.

"Yes. I moved into the townhouse, learning my way around, and getting the lay of the land in the college as well."

"Well, if you need any help moving furniture or anything, we're happy to help."

"Thanks, but I think I'm good." But he appreciated the offer just the same.

A guffaw of laughter reached him. A guffaw he recognized immediately. Delaney was here?

"The women are back by the billiard tables." Ethan thumbed behind him, as if reading his mind. "Ladies night."

Shelby crossed his line of sight, but he didn't see Delaney. Probably for the best. Needless to say, she wasn't too happy with him or the committee right now.

Nash and Ethan eyed each other.

"What?" Devon prompted.

Ethan shook his head. "Not really my place."

"I see." Devon moved the salt-shaker out of the way then propped his elbows on the table. "Delaney told you about the committee's review."

"Yeah." Ethan lifted his hands. "But I've already done my part and approved it at the college level. I'm not going to interfere with the committee's consideration."

Devon nodded. "I know Delaney is your friend, so I appreciate that."

The waitress brought their drinks and took their dinner orders.

That frosty beer looked delicious. Devon picked up the mug and took a long, satisfying pull. At that moment, Delaney stepped into his line of vision and bent over the pool table, her curvaceous ass on full display in a pair of snug blue jeans.

And the beer went down the wrong pipe.

Coughing like he'd swallowed Lake Michigan, his eyes watered and he set the mug on the table, trying in vain to draw in a breath.

Nash pounded him on the back. "You okay?"

Devon couldn't respond as his throat continued to spasm. He picked up the napkin to wipe the tears from his eyes. *Jesus!*

Besides enduring the physical discomfort, he now suffered the humiliation of having nearby patrons gawking at him. When he cleared the tears from his eyes, he saw Delaney, one hand on her hip, pool cue in the other, glaring at him.

Perfect. Just perfect.

Why didn't he just charge admittance to the sideshow he'd become?

He threw his napkin on the table and rose. Still unable to utter a word, he raised his index finger, indicating to Nash and Ethan that he'd be right back, and then he bolted to the men's room, where he hoped he could regain control of both his spasming epiglottis and his composure.

DELANEY FOLLOWED Devon's progress to the back of the pub where the restrooms were. Maybe he choked on his own arrogance.

She winced at her uncharitable thought. He appeared to be in distress, and as much as she hated him, she hoped he'd be okay.

Sort of.

"Delaney? You going to take your shot?" Sam asked.

"Yeah." She bent over the table, lined up with the cue ball, then sighed and stood up. "Be right back."

"Don't do it, girlfriend," Sam warned.

"Do what?" Delaney asked, all innocence. "I've got to pee."

"Uh huh. I'm taking your turn," Shelby threatened.

"Fine. Maybe you'll actually make the shot."

Devon came out of the men's room, looking all emotionally unavailable, and she really wanted to rattle his chain. He stopped short when he saw her there. "Come to see if I'd choked to death?"

"No, not to *death*." She flashed him a cheeky grin. "But I wouldn't mind, say, a mild coma." She crossed her arms.

"Is there anything else you wanted besides gloating over my discomfort?"

"As a matter of fact, I wanted to tell you this isn't over. I'll be resubmitting my proposal."

"Fine. We'll review it per the committee's guidelines."

"Good. And just so you know, I won't give up without a fight."

"Clearly. But you should consider addressing some of the committee's concerns."

Struck by his constructive comment, she narrowed her eyes at him. "The committee's or yours?"

"Both. Goodnight, Dr. Driscoll. Now, if you don't mind, I'd like to see if my dinner has been served yet."

"Don't mind a bit." Delaney stepped aside, and Devon strode past her, leaving a spicy, masculine scent behind. And damn if it didn't make her knees go weak.

Damn knees.

4

—————

After spending most of his life in the Northeast, March in Sterling was a welcome change. The temperatures were still cool, but the warm sun on his back hinted at the promise of spring as Devon walked across campus, a hot coffee on his mind.

A sidewalk wound its way through a particularly picturesque section of campus, where moss-covered oaks likely offered a welcome respite from the hot sun in summer. The azaleas and dogwoods showed signs of the flowers to come.

Students sat at picnic tables scattered beneath the trees. Others sat on the ground, computers in their laps, while still others used their backpacks as pillows and stretched out for afternoon naps in spots of sun.

Perhaps because he grew up on a school campus, he felt most at home on one now.

He arrived at his destination—Uncommon Grounds, the campus coffee shop. Rachel had offered to get a coffee for him, but he wanted the fresh air, and to see more of the campus.

He queued up at the end of the line, checking out the chalk menu above the counter.

The offerings had a decidedly Southern twist, including praline coffee, with brown sugar and vanilla cream; pecan hot chocolate topped with whipped cream, maple syrup, and chopped pecans; and something called Moonlight and Magnolias—roasted chicory-root coffee blended with cinnamon and vanilla cream and topped with a dollop of chocolate whipped cream.

In deference to his sweet tooth, he decided on the praline coffee, and stepped up to a tattoo-covered barista to give his order. As he waited for his coffee, he spotted Delaney at a table in the corner, her laptop open. Probably reading *Fifty Shades of Grey*. He snorted. But just as he was about to turn his back on her, she dropped her head into her hand.

Was she crying over the committee's decision? Was something wrong? Did she get bad news?

Not his problem, he reminded himself.

Aw, hell. Did she just wipe a tear from her cheek?

The barista didn't bother calling his name, since he was still standing at the counter. He took his coffee and told himself to just keep walking out the door and back to Fisher Hall, which housed the College of Business. He had work piled on his desk that required his attention.

But somehow his feet took over and he found himself standing next to Delaney's table. She didn't seem to notice. Then she sniffed and lifted her head, startled by his presence.

"What?" she asked, a little defiant. She'd definitely been crying. "Come to criticize my proposal again? Didn't get in enough at the committee meeting?"

He cleared his throat. This is what he got when his feet

overruled his brain. "I couldn't help but notice you seemed upset."

She brushed another tear away. If there was one thing that broke through his thick skin, it was a woman crying.

He drew up a chair, without asking her permission. "Anything I can help you with?"

"No." Her chin lifted a hair.

He waited a moment to see if she was going to speak further. When she didn't, he decided it was best to leave her alone, and he started to rise.

"Eliot died." She sniffed again, as her eyes welled up.

Good Lord! Who was Eliot? A brother? A boyfriend? How to broach that subject? "I'm so sorry."

"I loved that cat!"

Cat? Eliot was a cat? "I'm sorry, did you say cat?"

"Yes," she blubbered. "T.S. Eliot."

He yanked a few napkins out of the dispenser on the table and handed them to her.

She blew her nose and wiped her eyes. "Thank you."

All this over a *cat*?

He'd never owned a pet. Never understood the purpose of sharing one's home with a furry creature that clawed up the furniture, pissed on the carpet, and shed all over everything.

He studied Delaney's face. Red-rimmed eyes, blotchy tear-streaked cheeks, runny nose. She shouldn't look the least bit attractive. Not many women would, under the circumstances, but for some reason she did. She looked . . . endearing.

"I've had Eliot since I was twelve."

Twelve? "I see." Even though he didn't. How old was Delaney? "And, how old was Eliot?"

"Seventeen."

Seventeen! That would make her twenty-nine. Six years younger than himself. The perfect age difference to his mind.

And why, exactly, should he care?

She sniffled. What should he say to comfort her? He had no experience with this sort of thing. "Well, sounds like he lived a long and happy life."

"Yes. He did." She dabbed at her eyes. "And I knew this day would come, but you're never ready, you know?" she asked, looking to him for confirmation of her feelings.

"I, uh, I know." Even though he really didn't.

"Did you have pets growing up?"

"No. Pets weren't allowed where I grew up."

"Oh. That's sad. And lonely." She gazed up at him with those big blue weepy eyes, and he almost regretted not having a pet.

"Have you, uh, provided for the animal's . . ." he continued, trying to choose his words carefully, "burial?" Perhaps he could call one of her friends for her, to help her with the arrangements. What does one do with a pet that has, er, well, croaked?

"My mother had him cremated."

"Already? When did he die?"

"Two days ago."

Two days! And she's still bawling about it? "And, your mother is here?"

"No. She's in Kansas."

He gave himself a mental headshake. "I don't understand." If the cat was here, how did her mother have him cremated in Kansas?

"Eliot lived with my mother because I couldn't have him in the university residence halls, and then I was moving, and then, well, then he was just too old to uproot and bring here."

"How long has it been since you've seen Eliot?" She's grieving a cat that didn't even live with her?

"Two years." She wiped her eyes with a napkin, leaving a streak of mascara behind. "And now I'm wracked with guilt. He died, without me there to hold him."

Annnd the weeping began anew.

He looked around, trying to figure out how to extricate himself from this . . . predicament.

"Is there someone I can call?"

"No. Thank you." She scrubbed her face again with the napkins, further streaking her makeup. "I'll be fine." She gave him a watery smile.

Maybe that was his cue to exit the scene. He nodded. "Do you have a mirror?"

"Yes, why?"

He pointed to his eyes, "You might want to, you know, clean up a bit."

"Oh. Yes." She laughed, and it was as if someone reached in and squeezed his heart. He'd made Delaney Driscoll smile through her tears.

"Well. I should go. I have to get back to work."

"Thanks for talking to me, Devon."

He nodded as he rose, coffee in hand, then hesitated. "You should know that it's nothing personal—my disapproval of your proposal, that is."

"Well, it feels personal, Devon." She gazed up at him with watery eyes. "Especially when the committee has already approved all the proposals that were submitted at the same time as mine. That feels personal. And when one of the reasons for denying the proposal was a blatant disdain for the subject matter. That feels pretty personal too."

Damn Dr. Gordon and his condescension. "The committee's decision is not personal," he reiterated. "*My* decision is not personal."

She rolled her eyes and snorted.

He simply nodded again, and with that high-tailed it out of there. Stepping outside, he took a deep breath. What a mess.

DELANEY BLEW HER NOSE AGAIN, as she watched Devon walk through the coffee shop door and out into the cool spring air. He was such a jerk. And then he did something nice. Like just now. Then he had to turn back into the jerk, as if 'nice Devon' had to have an expiration.

It's nothing personal. Easy for him to say. She'd put her blood, sweat, and tears into creating interesting, challenging, evocative courses for her students. And it was no different with the degree program she proposed.

She had been steadily submitting new courses to the curriculum committee in preparation for the new major. They'd approved them all. And now they balked at the major? What did they think she was doing when she submitted proposals like Reading the Romance Novel, Publishing Romantic Fiction, and the foundation courses, Writing the Romance Novel I and II?

Finding her compact, she opened it up to check out the damage. "Ugh." How humiliating. She looked like a psycho clown. After dipping a napkin in her glass of water, she dabbed at the streaks of mascara. Then she took the powder puff out and touched up her face with the powder. A swipe of lip gloss, and it would have to do. She had a class to teach in half an hour.

Gathering her laptop, notes, and purse, she packed them into her tote bag. She'd been researching the romantic fiction market, in preparation for her resubmission, when her computer wallpaper photo of Eliot had triggered another crying jag.

Devon Mayfield thought she was a flighty ditz. But she'd show him and the rest of the committee. With a little help from her number-crunching friend, Shelby. As Shelby and Sam pointed out, while she might be a liberal arts professor, she needed to argue her case in a language Devon would understand. She just needed Shelby to help her create those colorful pie charts and graphs. A skill totally foreign to her.

She'd discovered all kind of stats on the market. Stats that would impress a businessman like Devon. He thought writing romantic fiction was a dead-end career with no possibility of success. She'd show him.

In the end, she'd earn the curriculum committee's approval. With or without Devon's vote. And of course, that of crotchety old Dr. Gordon.

5

———

"So, I understand Sam is running another research study on her love test?" Nash asked, as he settled on the weight bench next to where Devon performed a set of arm curls.

Devon had run into Ethan and Nash in Granite Fitness during lunch, and they'd added him to their weight circuit.

Ethan wiped sweat from his face with a towel and stood ready to spot Nash as he bench-pressed. "Yeah. She's refining the assay to avoid the possibility of double matches like she had with me and a few other participants."

Devon listened to the conversation, unsure what they were talking about. "What sort of test is this?"

Ethan shook his head with a laugh. "Maybe a little background first, because it sounds rather clinical and impersonal. Let's see if I can get this right."

"Humans are often attracted to people who possess a particular set of genes called major histocompatibility complex, or MHC," he began. "MHC plays a critical role in the ability to fight viruses. Mates with dissimilar MHC genes produce healthier offspring with broad immune systems. It's an evolutionary thing, but Sam discovered its predictive value—like in whether couples will have long, happy relationships."

"Well," Ethan continued, as he took the barbell from Nash and set it in the stand. "Sam discovered a blood chemical, which she calls MHC-P1, that predicts MHC, and through her previous research, she's proven that couples whose MHC-P1 were on opposite ends of the spectrum, indicating their MHC genes were dissimilar, had longer, happier relationships—and healthier, more productive children."

Intrigued, Devon asked, "How did she prove this?"

"By taking blood samples, conducting interviews with, and administering compatibility questionnaires to, happily attached couples who have been together twenty years or more."

"Compatibility questionnaires like the ones online dating services use?" Devon set aside the dumbbell then took a gulp of water.

"Correct. She had a control group of some five thousand couples, married for at least twenty years. She gave them the questionnaire and took their blood. A high percentage of those who reported that they are happily married—or otherwise attached—showed strong chemical compatibility, similar to that of the questionnaires."

Nash prepared for another set of bench-presses, so Ethan paused in his explanation to spot him.

"She also had a cohort, to which both she and I belonged, of another five thousand single or divorced men and women who took the same questionnaire and blood test. She ran the tests against those individuals in the database, and when she found matches, she compared the chemical compatibility to the questionnaire compatibility. A statistically significant percentage of the time, when the blood chemistry inversely matched, the compatibility questionnaires matched as well."

"And you said the two of you were in the database. Were you a match?"

"Yes." Ethan guided the barbell to the stand again.

"But he also matched with another woman in town," Nash interjected as he rose from the weight bench.

Devon thought he saw Ethan shudder.

"So, what happened there?"

"Sam thinks that some people will have more than one match. After all, some people will have more than one successful relationship in their lives that ends through no fault of their own, like with the death of a partner. But later, they may find another partner with whom they spend the rest of their lives."

Interest piqued, Devon prompted Ethan. "And she's running this new study to refine the test?"

"Yeah. She's discovered a way to refine the levels of MHC-P1, but she needs to test the new assay against those individuals in the database whose results are from the original assay."

This could be the answer for him. Devon didn't have time to play the dating game. And the thought of going on an online dating site gave him hives. But a blood test? Efficient, scientific, *and* confidential.

He filed that possibility away for further consideration as talk turned to Nash's latest recruits, and they all headed for the treadmills.

∾

W ITH THE NEXT curriculum committee's meeting just a week

away, Delaney pulled up in front of Nash and Shelby's rambling farmhouse. Nash bought and fixed up the hundred-year-old farmhouse not long after he returned to Sterling to coach the football team, and Shelby moved in after Nash proposed.

Shelby sat in the porch swing, and waved at Delaney. "Come on up. I'm having a glass of lemonade. Want one?"

"Sounds good." Delaney climbed the steps, tote bag over her shoulder, as Shelby poured another glass.

"Nash is over in Decatur visiting his dad, so we have the afternoon to ourselves."

Nash's father, a former NFL quarterback, suffered from what they thought was chronic traumatic encephalopathy, or CTE, the result of years of quarterback sacks from defensive linemen the size of compact cars. Nash had moved him into a memory care facility last fall.

Delaney joined Shelby on the swing. "That's good. I need all the help I can get. With the exception of Dr. Burton, the committee members are a bunch of closed-minded old farts."

"We'll create a presentation that will knock their stodgy old socks off. First, let's talk about your approach, and then I can determine what data and graphs will wow the committee and make them wonder why they didn't just approve your major the first time around."

They talked things through while sipping refreshing lemonade then moved to Shelby's kitchen table. After another half hour of brainstorming, Shelby put the finishing touches on the colorful graphs, while Delaney watched in awe.

"You're a goddess. I don't know how you do that, but I'm thankful that you do."

Shelby clicked the mouse, moved some things around,

changed the color scheme, then nodded. "Well, I don't know how people write romance novels, so we're even." Shelby turned the laptop screen so Delaney could see it better. "That should do it."

Studying the screen to make sure she understood the various graphs, she sighed, "If this doesn't convince even my worst critics, I don't know what will."

~

THE FIRST WEEK OF APRIL, Devon checked the time on his watch. He had just enough time to walk back to his office, pick up his notes, and head to the curriculum committee meeting where he would no doubt encounter the persistent Delaney Driscoll.

Picking up his French press coffee, he gathered his trash and walked over to the receptacle.

A bulletin board hung on the wall with flyers of all colors and sizes, advertising everything from the film department's Noir Night, to an upcoming production of Shakespeare on The Green, featuring *Twelfth Night*. The drama department's flyer hung at the top, and just below it, another flyer caught his eye.

ARE YOU OVER 18 AND SINGLE?
PARTICIPANTS WANTED FOR A STUDY.
COMPLETE A COMPATIBILITY QUESTIONNAIRE
AND A BLOOD DRAW.
FOR MORE INFORMATION

And it listed Dr. Samantha Love and her email address and phone number.

Hmm. He'd put the conversation about the study on the

back burner, but it wouldn't hurt to sit down with her and ask a few questions. He glanced around to see if anyone was looking, then he tore off one of the tabs with her contact information, and stuck it in his pocket.

He surveyed the coffee shop once more, but no one seemed to notice him, so he headed for the door, an uncustomary spring in his step.

∼

DELANEY TRIED to steady the pounding of her heart. She hadn't been this nervous since her dissertation defense, but after the March curriculum committee meeting, she knew she had an uphill battle with this group.

The committee had discussed five new courses, revisions to three programs, and one new major. They were getting crankier with each proposal. And hers was dead last on the agenda.

She looked at the clock on the wall above the committee chair's head. Time was running out. They'd given her ten minutes to present her information in support of her proposal, but if they didn't get to her soon, she wouldn't have time for even half of it.

Feeling eyes on her, she looked up and caught Devon's gaze. He nodded then returned his attention to Dr. Burton who was discussing the merits of the new engineering curriculum.

Five minutes left in the meeting. Biting her lip, she wondered if they would extend the time.

A vote was called on the engineering proposal, which passed the committee.

Dr. Gregors, the committee chair, finally addressed

Delaney. Thank goodness. "Dr. Driscoll, your proposal is next." He glanced up at the clock, a frown on his face.

"Dr. Gregors, if I may," Devon interjected. "Given the lack of time, I move that we table Dr. Driscoll's proposal until the next meeting."

Shelby stiffened and glared at Devon. What the–? *You've got to be kidding me!*

"I agree," Dr. Gregors said, then turned to Delaney. "I apologize. I had no idea the discussion of Dr. Bellinger's program revision would take so much time."

Delaney's heart sank. Another month before she could make her case.

And Devon had proposed it.

"I second the motion," Dr. Applebaum said.

"So moved."

Dammit. She glared at Devon, but he was making a note on the agenda.

Great. Perfect. She rose on shaky legs, biting back tears, not waiting for the vote. Silly. It wasn't as if she had a cure for cancer. It was just a romantic fiction degree. But it was her dream.

Suck it up, Driscoll. It could be worse. They could have voted against you once again.

DEVON STRODE out of the conference room, late for his next meeting when Delaney stepped in front of him, hands on her hips, eyes twin blue flames.

"You're such a jerk. Why did you do that?"

"Do what?" He didn't have time for this.

"Move to table my proposal?"

"Because we were out of time, and because some of us

have other meetings, like the one I'm currently late for." He gave her a look to say, *is that it?*

"Fine." She threw up her hands. "I'll just wait *another* month." She stomped off then spun back to face him. "This is so frustrating! I have all the information the committee asked for. I have data, and graphs, and–"

"And you deserve the time to present the full measure of your argument without being rushed."

She opened her mouth, closed it, then spoke. "Wait. What?"

His statement took the fire right out of her anger, and he struggled to keep the smirk off his face. "Delaney, don't you want adequate time to present all the work you put into your presentation?"

"Of course, but–"

"Then you should be happy I moved to table, rather than letting the committee push through their review your proposal, possibly denying it again."

"I–"

"Now, I really do have to get to this meeting." He brushed past her and could feel the confusion emanating from her.

Outside in the bright sunshine, he barked out a laugh. Score one for the jerk.

~

WHAT JUST HAPPENED?

Delaney stared after Devon's retreating back. Did he just do something *nice* for her? Again, just when she's written him off as the world's biggest jerk, he goes and does something considerate.

The door to the conference room opened and Dr.

Gregors came out, followed by a couple of the other committee members. "Oh, Delaney. Thank you for your patience. Devon suggested we put your proposal at the top of next month's agenda to ensure you have adequate time for your presentation. See you next month."

He fell in line with his colleagues as they walked toward the glass doors in Devon's wake.

Well, crap. He did it again.

Hard to hold a grudge against a guy who ruined it with his devious thoughtfulness.

6

———

Restless and out of sorts, Delaney paused the TV show she was currently binge-watching. An empty Ben & Jerry's container sat on the coffee table, along with a half-eaten bowl of popcorn.

Eight o'clock on a Friday night and here she was, sitting at home and feeling sorry for herself. Her usual emotional eating go-tos weren't quite upholding their end of the bargain. Lonely and bored—a lethal combination when it came to sensible eating.

Ethan and Sam were having dinner at his mother's, while Nash and Shelby had gone to visit his father in Decatur.

But even if her friends weren't otherwise occupied, she really needed to get a life. She couldn't be that friend who tagged along on date night and showed up at couples' dinners solo.

Throwing her head back against the couch cushions, she groaned.

"Enough."

Dying for some human contact besides the characters

from eighteenth-century Scotland, she cleaned up the detritus of her pity party and headed for her closet and something that would make her feel skinny. Fat chance—pun intended—especially after a pint of B&J's Chunky Monkey.

Sighing, she pulled on her black skinny jeans—they were somewhat slimming—and a red halter-top that made her girls look good. Some strappy stilettos boosted her self-confidence, along with her height.

A pat of blush, some mascara, and a swipe of red lip gloss, and she was out the door.

Shortly after, she entered McGinty's to find a good-sized crowd, but still a little early for the college students who didn't get their nights started until later. A couple vacated their seats at the bar, and Delaney snagged one of them, then caught the bartender's eye and ordered her favorite, a margarita.

Sipping from the salty rim, she turned to watch the couples dancing to a DJ's beats on the pub's stingy dance floor. She'd like to dance. If only someone would ask her. Scanning the room, she waved to a couple of professors from her college who were over by the dartboards.

Turning back to the bar with the intention of ordering some potato skins to soak up the tequila, she noticed someone slide onto the still-empty barstool next to her.

"Hi."

She glanced up in surprise to see a nice-looking guy, maybe in his mid-thirties, smiling at her. "Hi."

She didn't recognize him. Hair the color of a California surfer's fell over his forehead, giving him a boyish appearance. He had gray-blue eyes, a firm jaw with a subtle five o'clock shadow, and full lips meant for kissing, which she had no intention of doing. Checking out his left hand for signs of marriage, she smiled at the empty left ring finger. No telltale tan line either.

"This looks like a happening place," he said, his eyes scanning the pub before coming back to rest on her face.

"I gather you're not from here."

"No. Just visiting. I had an interview at the university, and may be moving here fulltime."

"Oh? What college?"

"Business."

Thinking of Devon and his perpetual frown, she lifted a brow. "Really? You don't strike me as the stuffed-shirt type."

He laughed. A nice, masculine chuckle. "I get that a lot. I'm Curtis, by the way, Curtis Michaels. Maybe you could show me around town."

"Well, Curtis, I'm Delaney," she responded as she held out her hand. She intentionally left off the last name. She was lonely, not stupid. "And maybe I could." They shook hands. It was nice. No zing, but it might be fun to hang out with him for the night, dance a little.

"Delaney, can I buy you a drink?"

"Sure." The evening was looking up. Maybe he'd even ask her to dance.

DEVON KNEW the moment Delaney entered the pub in those snug jeans that hugged her luscious curves. And that red top. Damn, she oozed sex! He choked for a second time in Delaney's presence, the scotch burning its way down his esophagus. Drinking and Delaney were a dangerous combination.

"You okay?"

Giving himself a mental head shake, he struggled to

return his attention to the conversation he was having with one of his department chairs.

"Yeah. Wrong pipe." They'd finished up a day of final interviews and negotiations with a candidate from Boston College and sought out McGinty's to both decompress and toast their success.

A few minutes later, the very same candidate joined Delaney at the bar. Devon sat up. A pick up? Or a pre-planned meeting?

"Why the frown?" Cal, his colleague asked.

"Was I frowning?" He glared into his highball glass, as disgust and anger bubbled to the surface.

"Still are," Cal said on a laugh then rose from the booth. "I'm calling it a night. Karen's making my favorite tonight— beef stroganoff. Thanks for the drink. I'll see you Monday."

Devon just nodded. Cal didn't notice their Golden Boy flirting with the sexiest woman in the pub.

The *married-with-two-kids* Golden Boy.

Devon drained his glass, intending to leave, until Golden Boy led Delaney out onto the dance floor. As he pulled her into him for a slow dance, a new emotion filled Devon. A heretofore unexperienced emotion.

Jealousy.

Completely irrational jealousy.

Grinding his teeth, he watched as Curtis' hands slowly inched down Delaney's back. When one hand touched her derrière, she reached back and returned it to a more respectable location then smiled and wagged her finger at him.

Curtis shrugged, a look of feigned chagrin on his face.

Devon would like to punch that fake chagrin right off his smug face.

Irrational jealousy aside, a philandering dirt bag did not

fit the culture he sought to create in his college. Talk about 'don't shit where you eat'! The guy thought he could have a fling with another university professor then move his wife and family here? The same family he'd waxed poetic about only three hours earlier?

Oh, hell no.

The official offer letter had not been presented because it required the provost's approval, but as far as Devon was concerned there would be no official offer.

Delaney laid a hand on Curtis' chest and Devon's stomach roiled. Then, with a flirtatious smile she headed toward the ladies' room.

Curtis licked his lips, his eyes on Delaney's ass, displayed to perfection in the snug denim, then he scanned the bar as if looking for witnesses. He'd made a mistake in thinking he had the all-clear when he followed Delaney to the back of the bar.

Should Devon follow? Or should he leave the matter be? No matter what he thought of Curtis' behavior, he and Delaney were adults.

But, did Delaney know he was married? He'd like to think she wouldn't intentionally pick up a married man in a bar. So, if she didn't know he was married, she'd be hurt that he'd led her on.

Mind made up, Devon strode through the crowded bar. Coming around the corner to the hallway leading to the bathrooms, he stopped short.

Curtis had Delaney pressed up against the wall, one leg thrust between hers, kissing her. The vision of Delaney in another man's arms hit him like a sucker punch to the stomach. Through a red haze of anger and jealousy, Devon took out his cellphone and snapped a picture. Exhibit A in his decision not to hire Curtis.

Just as he'd decided to walk away, Delaney's hands shoved against Curtis' shoulders. "No! Stop it!" She wasn't trying to pull him closer, she was trying to get away.

"Come on, baby," Curtis said on a laugh. "You don't have to play hard to get with me. I know you want it." His hand slid up, groping her breast.

And Devon snapped. "Back off, asshole!"

∼

CURTIS BACKED AWAY, a smug expression on his face, his hands up in surrender, until he saw the source of the command. The jerk went from smug to horrified in a millisecond.

Delaney was just as shocked as Curtis to see Devon standing there, his jaw set, his eyes stony, but why Curtis' reaction?

Devon stepped in front of Delaney, putting himself between her and Curtis. "'No' means 'no.' And in this case, 'no' also means 'no job offer.'"

Job offer? Of course, she thought, the College of Business.

"You can't do that." Curtis stepped into Devon. "You've already made the offer."

Devon held up his phone. "I think your wife and family will have something to say in the matter."

Stunned, and a little sick, Delaney cried, "You're *married*?"

Curtis went white. "You wouldn't."

"Try me." Devon ground out.

"Bitch asked for it," he muttered.

Delaney gasped and staggered back. She'd done no such thing. She'd only wanted a dance and some conversation with a smart, nice-looking guy.

When she saw him standing in the hallway, she'd thought he'd come out of the men's room, but when he pushed her into the wall, she realized he'd been waiting for her.

"Get out, before I have Hugh toss your sorry ass out."

"I wouldn't want to live in this uptight town anyway." As Delaney watched Curtis stomp off, her knees suddenly went weak.

Devon glared after Curtis then turned to Delaney. "Are you all right?"

She nodded.

"No, you're not. You're trembling." He removed his suit jacket and draped it over her shoulders. Only Devon Mayfield would be at a pub on a Friday night wearing a suit and tie. The warmth of his jacket enveloped her, making her shiver in response. Then his sexy, spicy scent invaded her senses, and she drew in a deep, calming breath.

He rubbed her arms, warming her. "Come on. Let me see you home."

"I'm fine."

"Says every woman who's really not."

She took a step back, and her knee buckled. *Okay, so maybe not fine.*

Devon wrapped her hand into the crook of his arm and escorted her through the crowded bar as if escorting her to a ball. She ignored the *zing* his touch elicited.

Once outside, she took another deep, calming breath. *What a night.* She would have been better off staying home and polishing off another pint of ice cream.

"Where's your car?"

"I walked."

"You *what*?" he growled, as he turned to face her.

"It's safe."

"You mean like McGinty's is safe?"

She huffed out an exasperated sigh. "Fine."

"Come with me." He wrapped an arm around her waist.

"Where are we going?"

"I'm driving you home."

"But I only live five blocks from here." She pointed in the direction of her apartment. "We can walk."

"We'll apologize to the environment later," he muttered as he led her to a metallic silver car–

"A Tesla? Guess you don't need to apologize to the environment after all," she muttered.

He held open the car door for her, and she slid into the butter-soft leather seat. Classy, just like Devon. And environmentally friendly. Who knew?

How much did a college dean make anyway?

When they were both sealed inside the noise-cancelling passenger compartment, her pulse kicked up a notch. And not with fear. The quiet intimacy, the warmth of his jacket, and the scent of him formed a deadly mix, making her hyperaware of the man next to her.

No. Not fear. He might be a first-class jerk when it came to her curriculum proposal, but she knew in her bones he wouldn't turn into an octopus-with-a-dick like Curtis.

She felt his eyes on her. "What?"

"Your address?"

Licking her dry lips, she replied. "Oh. Right." She rattled off the address, and he backed out of the parking space.

It took all of about two minutes to reach her apartment. When he pulled up out front, she turned to him. "I was about to knee him in the family jewels when you showed up." She continued, "But thank you for stepping in."

She didn't know why she felt the need to explain herself to Devon, but she did. "I only wanted to dance. Not to . . ."

~

"Of course." He stared out the windshield, saying nothing more. The night's scene played on a loop in his head—Delaney in the arms of another man; Delaney unsuccessfully trying to shove the man off her. And every time the loop played, two emotions warred inside him: jealousy and anger.

Jealousy was a strange, new emotion for him. And he didn't care for it. As for the anger, any man worth his gentleman card would have been pissed to see an unwilling woman struggling against an unwanted embrace.

"He's joining the faculty at Sterling?"

Her question drew him back to the present. "Not anymore."

"Because of me?" her voice sounded small in the quiet car.

"No. Because of no one but himself."

"I didn't know he was married," she added.

"I gathered."

"And he has children?"

"Two. A three-year-old daughter and an eight-month-old son."

She pressed a hand to her stomach.

He finally allowed himself to look at her. "Are you sure you're okay?"

"Why wouldn't I be?"

"You were just . . . assaulted–"

She waved her hand, brushing off the seriousness of the night's episode. "It wasn't the first time something like that has happened, and I'm sure it won't be the last. Men see my body and think I'm all about sex. And that I'm more than willing to give that sex away. I'm used to it," she finished, with a resigned sigh.

He shifted in his seat to face her. "There's no excuse for that kind of behavior," he said. That Delaney believed that the Neanderthal behavior she apparently experienced on a regular basis was something to be shrugged off sickened him. She deserved so much more respect than that.

Not that Delaney was in any way . . . special to him. Of course, he would feel the same about any woman.

At least, that's what he told himself.

"You're right. But there will always be jerks out there just the same." Opening the door, she climbed out. "Well, thank you again."

"Delaney?"

She ducked her head inside the car. "Yes?"

"My jacket."

"Oh. Right. Thanks for that too."

He watched as she walked up to her door then turned to wave, signaling that he could go.

She closed the car door behind her, leaving the scent of her perfume behind.

Devon leaned his forehead against the steering wheel. Being in close contact with Delaney Driscoll was dangerous for his peace of mind.

7

———

As Sam laid out the items for his blood test, Devon read over the consent form.

It stated that participants would be notified if there was a match with someone in the database, provided the match had also agreed to be contacted. Good. He could get the results, and not have to go through the undignified process of an online dating site. He did have one very important question though.

"Are the individuals in your database only local?" So far he hadn't met anyone in Sterling who would meet his, er, professional needs. Delaney came to mind, but the needs she would meet were far from professional.

"No. I have participants from all over the country."

Convinced, he picked up the pen and scrawled his name across the bottom of the document.

"Ready?" she asked.

"Yes," he replied. She swabbed his finger with alcohol. "Ethan said the two of you were a match."

A shy smile lit her face and she blushed. Yet, she didn't strike him as the blushing type. "We were."

That was encouraging. Anyone could see they were the perfect partnership. Smart, successful, supportive. If he could find such a match, he could put the next step of his plan into action.

"How are you settling into your new position at the college?" Sam asked, as she wrapped a Band-Aid around his index finger.

"I'm still learning who hates who."

She laughed. "That's always a good first step in a new job, especially when that job involves managing people." She glanced up at him again, as if she had something else to say, then hesitated.

"What?"

She shook her head.

"Just say it."

"It's not really my place."

"But?"

"But. Delaney's proposal." She gathered up the trash. "She may not be scientific or data-driven like we are, but Delaney's smart. Her students adore her. And she's worked hard creating the major. She's done her research, not only on the best courses but on the romantic fiction market too."

Unsure what to say, he didn't respond. He'd tried, albeit unsuccessfully, to get Delaney off his mind all weekend, and here, Sam brings her up in conversation.

"Well, as I said, it's not my place. You need to log on to this website and take the compatibility questionnaire." She handed him a card. "This card has your unique code and password. Once you've completed the questionnaire, hit 'submit.' Your responses upload to my database with your unique code so I can match it to your blood test results."

Devon took the card from her and stuck it in his pocket. "I'll do it tonight."

"There's no rush. It will likely take me a year to complete enrollment on my study."

While she was in no hurry, Devon was. The sooner he found his mate, the sooner he could pursue his goals. And the sooner he could get Delaney off his mind.

THE FOLLOWING THURSDAY, Devon rubbed his eyes then gazed out the window to the Campus Quad three stories below. He'd spent the last several hours shuffling papers and responding to emails. His eyes deserved a break.

His butt likely deserved one too. A walk to Uncommon Grounds would fit the bill.

Just as he rose from his seat, an email popped up on his computer screen. He groaned and sat back down. Then his stomach did a backflip when he read the subject line: MATCH FOUND.

His hand hovered over the mouse. This could be it. But what if she lived in Oregon, or California, and had no desire to move to a small university town in Northeast Georgia? Or, what if she'd already found someone? Someone who wasn't her histocompatible mate because she'd given up? Sam warned that this could happen. That there were no guaranties.

He rose from his chair again and rounded his desk. It was lunchtime, and Rachel was probably out of the office, but he closed his door anyway. Returning to his chair, he pulled it up to the keyboard, took a deep breath, and opened the email.

DEAR DR. MAYFIELD,

We are pleased to inform you that your blood test results matched to an individual in our database. This individual agreed to the release of her name in the event of any histocompatible matches. You will find the information on this individual in the attached document, including her name, age, and contact information. If you desire to contact this person, or if this person chooses to contact you, this is not handled by the research team.

As always, if you have any questions, please feel free to contact the study investigator, Dr. Samantha Love.

The Study Team

He clicked on the attachment and quickly scanned it, sitting back in stunned silence. The name of his histocompatible mate: Delaney Driscoll.

~

"This can't be right. Can it? Tell me it's not right." Delaney held up a copy of the email she'd printed just this morning.

Sam smiled. Well, smirked really. "It's right. You and Devon Mayfield are a match."

"That's not what you were supposed to say." Delaney sank into the guest chair in Sam's office. "But. No." She shook her head. "It can't be."

Even as she said it, she couldn't deny the intensity of the chemistry between them. Even when he pissed her off, she wondered what it would be like to kiss him.

Nevertheless–

Sam stood and walked around her desk, perching on the

front edge. "I don't have to remind you I thought the same thing about Ethan—and it was *my* research."

Delaney stared up at Sam, still a little dumbfounded, but remembered Sam's reaction when she learned that, according to her love test, she and her now-fiancé were a match. She chose at first not to believe her own science, leading to an existential crisis of sorts.

Because if Sam believed in her science, it should follow that she would believe Ethan was her perfect histocompatible mate. And that, according to her research, histocompatible mates make the happiest relationships.

If she didn't believe Ethan was her perfect mate, it would bring into question her research. Her compatibility assay. Her reputation. Not to mention her very career.

Delaney really wanted to be supportive of her friend by supporting her science, but believing that the broody, Darcy-like Devon Mayfield was her perfect match was a bridge too far. Even if Mr. Darcy was her favorite literary character.

And even if, like Mr. Darcy, he did surprisingly nice things sometimes.

She glanced up at Sam who was patiently waiting for her to accept the results and move on.

But–

"You know I love you and respect your work, but this," she lifted the now-crumpled email, "I just can't go there." Even if he is the hottest thing she'd seen in a very long time.

Sam shrugged and rose to walk back around her desk. "Suit yourself."

"Does he know?"

"If not yet, he will soon. His email went out the same time yours did."

Delaney closed her eyes and groaned. "He'll think this is

some kind of set-up. Maybe a way to get back at him for his opposition to my proposal."

"Yeah, because finding his perfect mate is the ideal revenge," Sam replied, her voice laced with sarcasm.

~

"No offense, but this is preposterous." Devon pointed to the email he'd summarily laid on Sam's desk.

"Déjà vu," Sam muttered to herself.

"What?"

"Nothing." Sam shook her head. "And none taken. Been there," she said with a grin. "No one else knows but you and me. And Delaney, of course. What the two of you decide to do with the information is up to you, but you'll see it's right in the end."

"A foregone conclusion then?" He eyed her. "She's your friend. Correction, she's your *single* friend. Who's to say you two didn't cook this scheme up?"

She glared at him. "Okay, now I'm offended."

He rubbed his brow. "You're right, that was insulting. I apologize."

"And for what possible purpose would we cook up such a scheme?" Sam continued.

"To get her married off, of course." He threw up his hand as if to say, 'Isn't it obvious?'

"Devon, this isn't Regency England. People marry whomever they choose to. Even my test results can't *make* you marry someone you don't believe is a match for you."

"Believe?"

"Yes. If you don't believe the results, there is nothing I, or Delaney for that matter, can do."

"You're talking as if I should believe in the results like

children believe in Santa Claus, the Tooth Fairy, or the Easter Bunny. Is this science, or is this make-believe?"

"Oh, it's science. But not everyone believes in science. Even when the evidence is irrefutable."

Irrefutable?

He'd been restless and out of sorts since that first day Delaney introduced herself in McGinty's, unable to focus on his plan both for the college and for his life, but especially his love life. He snorted. *Love life?* Where had that come from?

Devon Mayfield didn't do love. Or, if he was brutally honest with himself, love didn't do him.

"If it makes you feel any better, she's not thrilled either."

His head snapped up. "What?"

"She's in the same boat as you—floating down Denial River."

He snorted. "Denial?"

"Yes. She doesn't want to believe you're her match, either."

Delaney didn't want *him*? Good. Fine. It was for the best.

Rejection wasn't a new emotion for him. He'd already experienced it from the one person in the world who should love and accept him without reservation.

Then why did learning about Delaney's rejection make his chest tighten?

THE FOLLOWING MORNING, after a night spent tossing and turning, Devon slipped into Delaney's classroom planning to confront her afterward with the test results. Nip this thing in the bud.

While Sam said Delaney wasn't happy about the results

either, he wanted to see for himself and clear up any potential for confusion on her part. They were not a perfect match, science be damned.

He closed the door at the back of the classroom with a soft click and slid into an empty seat in the last row.

Delaney stood at the front of the compact theater-style classroom, an open book in one hand as she paced. With her blond hair pulled back into a high ponytail and her pin-up girl body displayed to perfection in a colorful dress that wrapped around her curves and tied at the waist, she made it difficult for him to remember his mission this morning.

The guys whose faces he could see stared at her, lust written all over their faces. And he had an irrational desire to blindfold them all.

But he also noticed that every female student was engaged in the discussion. Not a single laptop screen displayed solitaire, Instagram, or Twitter. They were opened to word-processing programs filled with notes.

Delaney caught sight of him and frowned before continuing her lecture. "When Othello enters the bedchamber, he doesn't know whether to kill Desdemona or go all *Fifty Shades* on her."

The class laughed, and a student raised her hand. "Why doesn't he just wait to see if Desdemona cheated on him?"

"What would be the fun in that? Then there would be no tragedy, and I wouldn't be torturing you with a play Shakespeare wrote over four hundred years ago."

The class laughed again.

"All right, time's up. Don't forget, your papers are due next Monday."

A collective groan spread through the thirty-some-odd students as they packed up their laptops and books. A few walked down the steps to talk with Delaney. She smiled, her blue eyes alight with pleasure. Nodding, she listened intently to what a petite brunette was saying, then Delaney giggled and pulled her in for a hug. Clearly her students admired and respected her, and the feeling was mutual. Delaney stepped back then lifted her closed hand for a fist bump.

Before everyone exited, Delaney called for their attention.

"Congratulate Bethany here. She just received a small private grant to attend Oxford University this summer for a special program on Jane Austen."

Bethany's fellow classmates clapped and cheered, as she waved them off, blushing.

Devon waited for the last of the students to exit then made his way down the steps to the lectern.

Closing her laptop, Delaney tucked it into a tote bag that read: THE PAST, THE PRESENT, AND THE FUTURE WALKED INTO A BAR. IT WAS TENSE.

"Slumming, Dr. Mayfield?"

"What?"

"I never thought you would deign to enter the world of literature."

He snorted. Guess he deserved that. "I like Shakespeare. Even if I don't always understand it."

"Was that a self-deprecating remark?"

He shoved his hands in his pockets and shrugged.

"Well, what can I do for you?"

Now that she stood in front of him, he hesitated to broach the subject. "I don't suppose you received an email yesterday?"

Delaney shouldered the tote bag and turned to him. "And what email would that be?"

Devon sighed. So this was how she was going to play it.

"The email from Sam that said," he pulled a hand out of his pocket and waved the piece of paper between them, "we're a match."

"Oh, *that* email." She put a finger to her chin in feigned thought. "Come to think of it, I think I saw something like that in my junk mail."

Junk mail? "So, you don't–"

"Believe it? No."

He nodded. "Good."

Her head snapped up as she narrowed her eyes at him. "Good?"

"Yes. I mean, Sam is your friend, so I'm sure you have a great deal of confidence in her science, but I wouldn't want you to get the impression that we were headed for the altar or anything."

"The altar?" She gave a rueful laugh. "Don't flatter yourself, Dr. Mayfield. You're not my type."

"And what type is that?" he asked, unable to keep the defensive tone out of his voice.

She tilted her head as if considering him as a potential mate. His back itched between his shoulder blades as he got the distinct impression that she found him lacking. An all-too-familiar feeling.

"Men with a heart." She breezed past him, her perfume enveloping him in a cloud of sweet seduction.

"That went well," he muttered as he watched her climb the steps. "So glad we understand one another."

Even so, his heart felt like lead in his chest.

8

———

The following Friday evening, Delaney stretched out on a blanket, legs crossed at the ankles, hands behind her back propping herself up. Next to her, the lovebirds held hands or cuddled on their own blankets. She'd hear the occasional smooch, further deepening her morose thoughts.

Good thing tonight's Shakespeare on the Green was *Twelfth Night* and not *Hamlet*. Otherwise, the tragedy might tempt her to follow Ophelia's lead and drown herself in the nearest brook.

If she had to match with someone in Sam's database, why'd it have to be Devon Mayfield?

She could admit a touch of split personality disorder when it came to Devon Mayfield. He tried her patience, challenged her views, kept her constantly off-balance with his Dr. Jekyll/Mr. Hyde act all rolled into one sexy package. And wasn't that just the problem?

Too damn sexy for his own good. Or hers, for that matter.

Popping a grape into her mouth, she grimaced at the

sour taste. *Perfect.* Even the grapes were souring from her mood. Well, she thought, as she lifted her cup of wine, if the grapes didn't make her feel better, maybe their fermented juice would.

The Green, the former site of the Sterling estate's tennis courts and croquet green, sat on the southwest corner of campus enclosed by a wall of six-foot Burford holly hedges. Several years ago, when a wealthy donor gave the university a generous gift to build a small amphitheater that could be used for performances by the school's drama, music, and dance departments, they'd torn up the tennis courts, graded the land, and built the amphitheater.

The university also rented out the venue for concerts and other theatrical productions, creating a funding source to support the College of Arts and Sciences' programs. The venue had become a popular spot for entertainment all through the spring, summer, and fall months.

"There he is," Ethan said, drawing Delaney's attention. *There who is?*

She got her answer when she looked up to see the source of her aggravation standing behind them, a bottle of wine in one hand, his other in the pocket of his khaki pants and a frown gracing his face. Nothing new there.

And didn't the man own a pair of jeans?

"Join us," Ethan said, indicating Delaney's blanket. *What the–?*

Ethan had invited Devon to the play then expected Delaney to share her blanket with him?

She caught Sam's eye, but she shrugged at Delaney's incredulous expression.

"Thanks, I'll just sit over here." He nodded to a spot a few paces to Delaney's left, where he'd have to sit on the grass.

Sighing, she moved over, giving him room between her and the lovebirds. "Come on, there's plenty of room." She patted the blanket.

"You sure?"

"Yes. You can't sit on the grass. You'll get your pants dirty." She released a sigh that said, *Silly man, don't you know grass stains are a bitch to get out?*

"Thanks." He stretched out next to her, careful to hug the edge of the blanket.

Rolling her eyes, she said, "I won't bite, you know."

"No, I don't know."

She snorted. "I never thought you'd come to a Shakespeare play," Delaney prodded. "You know, with your hatred of literature and everything." She gave him a broad smile.

"I never said I hated literature. I told you, I like literature and Shakespeare as much as the next person."

"So you say. You just don't like romance."

"I never said that either." He sounded exasperated. "I just don't think there is any value in a major for romance writers."

"Tell that to the more than nine thousand members of Romance Writers of America. Did you know that romance novels share more than thirty-four percent of the U.S. fiction market? That–"

"Wine?" Ethan held out a cup of the merlot they'd been drinking, interrupting Delaney's tirade. She cut a glance his way, and he gave a subtle head shake. She huffed. *Fine.* So now wasn't the time.

Devon took the cup and nodded his thanks.

"There's crackers, cheese, and fruit too." Sam supplied, also giving Delaney a look that said, *Don't swat at the hornet's nest.* "We'll set out dinner during intermission."

"Sounds good." He rose to his knees and reached for a small plate, loading it with appetizers.

Eyeing his plate, Delaney asked after he'd stretched out again, "Hungry?"

He glanced up at her, the corner of his mouth curving, flashing a tiny dimple in his cheek, then he set the plate between them. "I thought you might like something as well."

"Oh. Thanks." Well, that was . . . thoughtful. Dammit.

Musicians dressed in sixteenth-century garb entered the stage playing flutes, and a hush fell over the audience.

"It's starting," Delaney whispered.

The Duke Orsino entered, attended by his lords, and recited the famous opening line: "If music be the food of love, play on."

Delaney closed her eyes and let the words wash over her. One of her favorite Shakespeare plays, *Twelfth Night* tells the story of Viola, who is in love with Orsino, who is in love with Olivia, who is in love with Viola's male disguise, Cesario. This love triangle is complicated by the fact that neither Orsino nor Olivia knows that Viola is, in fact, a woman pretending to be Cesario.

It's the stuff of a perfect romantic comedy.

But, as the play progressed, Delaney found herself distracted by the man lying on the blanket next to her. Even with hundreds of other people around her, the arrangement felt intimate, especially since night had fallen.

His cologne, the now-familiar warm, spicy scent, drifted her way on the breeze. They both reached for something on the plate at the same time, and their hands touched, sending a jolt up her arm. He must have felt it too because he jerked his hand back. "You first," he whispered, his voice holding a rusty quality to it.

"No. I'm good." She directed her attention back to the stage.

Later, she adjusted her position, and her hand landed directly on top of Devon's. Another now-familiar jolt ran up her arm, and she sat up, resisting the urge to shake her hand as if shocked. "Sorry."

As Sir Andrew, Sir Toby, and Maria headed off to watch Malvolio make a buffoon of himself, a court jester stepped forward to announce a fifteen-minute intermission, and Delaney breathed a sigh of relief. She needed to distance herself from the infuriating, superior, and—*dammit* —appealing Devon Mayfield. ASAP.

"Bathroom," she muttered, as she headed off in that direction. Any port in a storm, even if that port was a Porta-Potty.

DEVON WATCHED Delaney pick her way around lawn chairs and blankets, picnic baskets and coolers, until the darkness swallowed her up.

What had he been thinking? He should have turned down Ethan's invitation to join them. Naturally, Delaney would be with them.

Hyperaware of the woman next to him, he couldn't concentrate on the play. Shakespeare was difficult enough to follow when given his undivided attention, but with Delaney's scent and warmth, not to mention her sultry giggles when a comedic line was recited, he'd become completely lost.

He might as well have been watching a play performed in Polish.

Then there were Delaney's silky legs, displayed to

perfection in the deep pink dress she wore, and her dainty feet with their bright purple toenail polish.

As the audience prepared to dine on cold fried chicken, sandwiches, or salads, lights flickered on across The Green. Camp lanterns, battery-operated candles, flashlights, and cell phones provided light.

"Devon, what would you like?" Sam interrupted his thoughts. "We have a cold salmon-and-cucumber salad, Shelby's homemade potato salad, Ruby's cold fried chicken, a green salad, and for dessert, Delaney's chocolate pie."

He should have guessed a dessert as sinful as chocolate pie would come from Delaney. Sin on a plate, just like her. "I'll take a little of everything, thanks."

Delaney breezed past him, her orange-blossom scent driving him nuts. When she sat back down on the blanket, her skirt floated up, giving him a flash of smooth thigh and bright pink panties, and he nearly groaned out loud.

She crossed her legs yoga-style, draped her dress over her lap, and reached for a plate, before kneeling and helping herself to the green and salmon salads. He almost swallowed his tongue when her delicious ass hovered near his face.

If this damnable play didn't end soon, he'd have to make an early exit in order to avoid embarrassing himself with his physical reaction.

THE ACTORS CAME out for their curtain calls as the audience stood and applauded, a few 'bravos' coming from the crowd. *Thank God.* Not that the performance had been bad—it had been quite good. That is, when he could actually concentrate on it.

But sitting in close proximity to Delaney for over two and a half hours was akin to dangling a carrot in front of a starving rabbit, but not letting the creature have it.

The empty wine bottles, leftovers, dirty dishes, blankets, and lawn chairs had been packed away, and the patrons began making their way to their cars or bicycles.

"Not too bad for small-town living, right, Devon?" Ethan asked.

"I had a good time. Thanks for the invitation."

"Any time. Delaney, can we walk you to your car?"

"Oh, I walked. Thanks, though."

Walked? Again?

"We'll give you a lift then," Ethan continued.

"I'm fine. Really."

"Del, I don't think so," Sam shook her head.

"I'll see that she gets home," Devon interjected. Why, he didn't know. Except he couldn't allow a woman to walk home alone at night, even if the town seemed safe. At Delaney's frown, he continued, "I insist."

"Thank you, Devon," Sam said. "I feel better."

He nodded and cut a glance at Delaney. If looks could kill . . . Maybe he should be concerned for his own safety instead.

Indicating that he would follow her lead, he waited for her to say her goodnights and then fell into step beside her. The temperature had dropped, and clouds scudded across the dark sky. Delaney shrugged into a sweater and pulled it tight, crossing her arms over her body.

They walked in an uncomfortable silence across The Green toward downtown Sterling.

Clearing his throat, he broke the silence. "What's with you and walking?"

"It's good for the environment, and it's healthy. But don't

worry, it's just a few blocks. You won't be stuck escorting me for too long."

Heaving an exasperated sigh, he said, "It's no hardship."

Her head snapped in his direction, a look of surprise on her face.

"Despite what you may think of me, Delaney, I have no ill feelings toward you."

"As long as I'm not trying to drag you to the altar or implement a major in romantic fiction." She shook her head.

They walked in silence for a time. A light rain began to fall.

"Perfect," Delaney muttered.

"You cold?" Devon asked, cutting a glance her way.

"I'm fine."

He rolled his eyes. "Come here." He put an arm around her shoulder and tucked her up against him. She stiffened then snuggled closer into his warmth wrapping an arm around his waist, and his brain momentarily short-circuited at the contact.

A few tense minutes later, she stopped in front of her apartment complex, and stepped away from him. "This is me."

He hadn't paid much attention when he'd previously dropped her off—he'd still been seeing red over Curtis' animalistic behavior. The apartments were attractive, with red-brick façades, black shutters, and red doors giving them a Georgian aesthetic, not uncommon in the Deep South.

"You're dismissed, Dr. Mayfield." She smirked. "You have fulfilled your obligation to see me home."

"My obligation isn't over until I see you to your door."

She tilted her head, her hair damp from the rain. "This isn't the inner city, Devon."

"Even so." He held out his hand for her to precede of him.

They arrived at her doorstep. "Mission accomplished," she said, with a sharp heel-click and a salute.

She'd accented her front door with clay pots filled with a riot of colorful flowers. A doormat with a yellow-brick-road graphic read: YOU'RE NOT IN KANSAS ANYMORE. Remembering her bio on the university's website, he couldn't help but smile at that.

When he looked up, her eyes held his, and the air between them crackled. He had the inexplicable urge to kiss her. Absurd. This hadn't been a date. And she'd made it clear that the sooner they parted, the better.

"Goodnight, Delaney."

Delaney inserted her key in the lock. "Goodnight, Devon."

He hiked back through the rain, the memory of Delaney's curves keeping him warm all the way back to his car.

The quaint downtown area streets were closed to vehicular traffic, and tents lined both sides, artists displaying everything from paintings to jewelry and pottery to quilts. They'd gotten a lucky break with the weather, after a week of cold, drizzly rain.

But with the passing of the rain, spring had sprung in all its glory. The trees lining Main Street sported bright green leaves, tulips and hyacinths vied for space in the planters along the sidewalks, and the air was warm and fragrant.

Devon didn't generally have an interest in art festivals, but with weather too inviting to stay indoors, it was as good an excuse as any to enjoy the fresh air and bright sunshine.

The scent of funnel cakes, mixed with grilling meats, kettle corn, and roasted nuts, created an appetizing cornucopia of smells.

He nodded to an acquaintance from the university, side-stepped two dogs who greeted one another like long-lost friends, and then caught a glimpse of a curvy blonde in a spring-green dress up ahead. He'd recognize that body anywhere. The feel of it pressed against his side last Friday night was indelibly imprinted on his memory.

She meandered along, stopping at tents, talking with the artists, her smile so bright, she competed with the sun. In one hand she held a bag, and in the other an ice cream cone, her purse over her shoulder. In that moment, she looked young and innocent. But as the breeze flirted with her skirt, the image the glimpse of bare leg conjured was far from innocent.

He finally caught up to her and couldn't decide whether to leave her be or acknowledge her.

When she turned and spotted him, she made the decision for him.

"Delaney."

"Devon." She nodded then took another lick of her melting ice cream cone, and dear God, he felt it like a hot dart to the groin.

He hadn't spotted her friends. "Are you here alone?"

"Yes. You?"

"Yes."

Awkward pause. He cleared his throat. "You, uh, mind if I join you?"

She shrugged. "Sure."

He fell in beside her, interested in what artists drew her attention. "Where are your sidekicks?"

She grinned at the moniker. "Shelby and Nash are visiting Shelby's mother in Miami, and Sam and Ethan left for a conference in San Francisco where Sam is speaking."

She stopped in front of a tent displaying delicately wrought jewelry pieces, some with tiny gemstones, others with pearls. He could see her wearing many of the items on display. They suited her blatant femininity. After a few minutes of browsing, she complimented the artist and they moved on. She'd polished off the ice cream cone and paused to toss the napkins in the trash.

Next stop—a tent displaying breathtaking photos of faraway places he hoped to someday visit. The next—a tent with enormous colorful canvases painted with broad, confident strokes.

"Which do you prefer, photographs or paintings?" he asked, as they stood in front of a red, orange, pink, and yellow abstract piece that reminded him of a sunset.

She considered the question a moment before responding. "While I appreciate the skill and talent of a painting, I prefer photographs. They capture the beauty in the world for that one moment in time. Nature photographers, especially, don't get to pick their compositions. They see it in the blink of an eye and have to capture it before it's gone." She'd responded to his question without looking at him, staring at the sunset painting.

Very astute. "I agree. I have some walls in my new home in need of some art. Perhaps I'll purchase something here today."

"You should. Support the arts and the artists who create them."

He pointed to her bag. "Is that what you're doing?"

"Yes. And because I like what I see." She exited the tent, and he followed.

She stopped in front of a portraitist, the subject of his drawing a little girl squirming in a chair a few feet away. "Mom, can I see it yet?"

"Not yet. Sit still. The sooner you sit still, the sooner he can finish, and the sooner you can see it."

The artist showed skill. He'd managed to capture the precocious little elf in just a few strokes of charcoal.

The mom paid, handed her little girl the drawing, and thanked the artist.

"How about you, ma'am? Would you like a portrait?" he asked Delaney, an expectant look on his bearded face.

"Sure," she said with a shrug. "Why not." Sitting in the chair, she flipped her hair back and cast a flirtatious grin over her shoulder, looking both sultry and innocent at the same time.

The artist made quick work of the drawing, capturing the alluring dimple in her right cheek, the curve of her upper lip, the arch of her eyebrows. But more than that, he captured her sunshine.

When the artist revealed the final drawing to her, she clapped her hands and laughed. "I love it. Thank you."

She dug in her purse and handed him the fee plus a large tip.

"Thank you, ma'am. Much appreciated."

Delaney gave Devon a shoulder nudge. "Your turn."

"What?" Devon glanced up from the drawing, startled. "No."

"Oh, come on." She indicated the chair. "Support the arts and the artists who create them," she said with a smirk.

"Fine." Sighing heavily, Devon sank to the hard metal folding chair, feeling incredibly self-conscious as the artist worked to render his likeness in charcoal, Delaney standing over the artist's shoulder with a sly smile on her face.

A few short, uncomfortable minutes later, the artist handed him the drawing.

Devon stared at the portrait of himself. *Hmm.* Did he really look like that?

"Wow! He captured you perfectly. All broody and grumpy." Delaney gave him another shoulder nudge.

"I'm not broody. I don't brood."

"The gentleman doth protest too much, methinks," she admonished with a wink.

He examined the picture with a critical eye. *Huh.* Maybe she was right.

~

DEVON HANDED money to the artist.

A fifty! Holy cow. Delaney's mouth dropped open, and the artist's eyes nearly bugged out of his head. "Thank you, sir."

Devon nodded then rolled up his drawing, binding it with a rubber band from the grateful artist.

As they walked away, she leaned in and whispered, "You do realize you just gave the man a fifty, right?"

"Of course."

Well then. Big spender.

Dressed in navy slacks and a white button-down, Devon was his usual buttoned-up self.

"Can I ask you a question?"

He tensed next to her. "Yes. I think."

"Don't you own a pair of jeans?" She thought she caught a glimmer of a smile, but she must have been mistaken.

"I'm sure there's a pair somewhere in my closet. Why?"

"You should wear them sometime. You always look so . . . unapproachable."

His steps faltered, and his eyebrows shot up, but that was the extent of his reaction.

She paused in front of a tent displaying what appeared to be hand-drawn book covers of literary classics like *Jane Eyre, Anna Karenina, A Christmas Carol, Huckleberry Finn,* and, her favorite, *Pride and Prejudice.* So unique.

"These are beautiful." She reverently touched a framed

print. Most appeared to be of the original first edition covers. The artist had clearly done his or her homework. They'd look wonderful in her office.

Peering at the price tag, disappointment sank in. Pricey. Not that she could blame the artist. The work was detailed, and no doubt time-consuming. Even so. While she could appreciate the time, energy, and skill that went into the drawings, she couldn't afford even one of them.

"See something you like?"

Delaney turned and gazed into the smiling eyes of a woman in bohemian dress with long flowing gray hair.

"Everything?" Delaney laughed. "Are these yours?"

"Yes."

"You do exquisite work."

"Thank you."

"You enjoy the classics?"

"Yes. And I enjoy researching the first-edition covers and bringing them back to life." She handed a brochure to Delaney and Devon.

"Well, you've done an amazing job. I wish I could afford one for my office."

The artist smiled. "I understand."

Delaney felt Devon's presence and glanced over her shoulder. He wore a frown as he studied the brochure. Probably bored stiff.

"Maybe another time," Delaney said as she exited the tent, Devon right behind her.

"It's early, but I skipped lunch. How about some dinner?" He stopped in front of a kettle corn vendor, and the scent made her stomach growl.

"Dr. Mayfield, are you asking me to dinner?"

"Yes. But it's not a date."

She laughed. "Heaven forbid."

He smiled. Or at least she thought it was a smile. A slight lift of the right corner of his mouth. Or maybe it was a twitch. Probably a twitch.

"To what do I owe this honor?" Delaney prodded.

"No honor. Just an olive branch."

"Oh? What for?"

"I think we got off on the wrong foot."

"You mean first by you voting against my proposal, and second by insulting me with your insinuation that I'm a gold digger? Does this mean you've changed your mind about my curriculum proposal?"

"Not unless you change it for me. But that doesn't mean we can't be friends."

"Oh." A strange man Devon Mayfield was. "Sure." She shrugged. They'd spent this much time together without killing each other. Maybe they could get through dinner.

Devon held open the door of Ruby's, indicating she should precede him.

"You said 'friends.' But friends support one another. Stick up for one another. Don't vote against their friends' hopes and dreams."

Ruby's was doing a brisk business with patrons from the art show. The lunch counter resembled something out of the 1950s. Red vinyl stools, Formica countertop, stainless-steel trim. An old jukebox stood in the corner, playing Frankie Valle. The booth, with its red vinyl upholstery beckoned for the cast of *Happy Days*.

As they waited for the besieged staff to help them, Devon continued, "Hopes and dreams? Delaney, think about this logically. The curriculum committee can't just approve a new degree because it's someone's hope or dream."

Delaney rolled her eyes. "That's not what I'm saying."

"There's not enough data to support approving the degree program."

Mandy, one of the servers, looked harried as she carried a tray weighed down with food across the black-and-white-checkered linoleum floor. The tantalizing aroma of Ruby's meatloaf reached Delaney's nose and nearly made her faint from hunger.

The server paused in her bustling from one table to the next. "Busy today. If you don't mind grabbing a couple of menus, you can take that corner table." She nodded in the direction of a table that still showed signs of recent bussing.

"Thanks." Delaney picked up the menus, and Devon indicated she should precede him. Despite his grumpiness and unapproachability, his manners were always impeccable.

Delaney tossed her bag onto the red vinyl bench and slid in, while Devon took the bench opposite her and studied the menu.

She didn't need to look—she'd have Ruby's chicken pot pie, and she'd enjoy every creamy, carb-filled bite.

Lisa, another waitress, walked past, a slice of chocolate cake the size of a microbus on her tray, and Delaney nearly whimpered.

"Would you like a slice of cake?" Devon asked. Her gaze shot to his face, and his eyebrows were lifted.

She shrugged. "Life's too short not to have dessert."

Mandy came to take their order. "Ladies first." Devon gestured to Delaney.

They placed their orders.

Circling back to the conversation, Delaney said, "I'll have you know, Dr. Mayfield, that I am gathering . . . *data* to prove to you and the committee that this is a viable degree. And I'm going to knock your socks off."

He lifted a brow. "Great." He sat back to allow Mandy to set their drinks on the table.

Taking a sip of her diet soda, she continued, "I'm going to take you and the committee to school and educate you on the romantic fiction market."

That got a grin out of him, a fleeting one, before he sobered, but it looked good on him.

"Looking forward to it."

10

Delaney dug into her chicken pot pie with gusto. It surprised him that he liked that she didn't fret over calories like so many other women. Her confidence in her curves made her even more enticing.

Setting her fork on her plate, she tilted her head. "So, how'd you end up in a small town in Northeast Georgia?"

"My story isn't very interesting." Especially since he had no intention of telling the whole thing.

"Come on." She reached across the table and nudged his arm. "We have to make polite conversation, otherwise it'll just be two people who happen to be eating at the same table."

"All right, I'll give you the condensed version. I grew up in Connecticut, attended boarding school, did my undergrad and master's at Harvard, then a Ph.D. at Wharton. Taught for a few years, became a department chair, then took the job at Sterling."

She snorted. "You haven't told me anything I couldn't find on your bio." Eyeing him, she took a bite of the pot pie, and his eyes honed in on her mouth as she licked some of the creamy sauce off her lips.

Smirking, she pointed at him with her glass. "Let me guess. Preppy, over-priced boarding school where you played Lacrosse, excelled at math and science courses . . ." She narrowed her eyes and tilted her head, as if studying him. "Class president and . . . oh!" She snapped her fingers. "Class valedictorian."

Damn. She was good. "Not bad, but not entirely correct. I played basketball."

"I could see that. Then what?"

He shrugged. "I earned an MBA from Harvard, before moving on to the Wharton School of Business where I earned a Ph.D. in Management with a specialization in strategy at the age of twenty-eight. I taught for seven years then became a department chair at the age of thirty-three, before accepting the position here."

"Quite the over-achiever." She propped her chin in her hand. "You don't strike me as an academician. Rather, I see you as the CEO of some multinational corporation, making a bajillion dollars, collecting your golden parachute before moving on to the next multinational corporation. Wash and repeat."

"Money's not an issue."

She lifted a brow. "Member of the Lucky Sperm Club? Do tell."

Wiping his mouth with his napkin, he took a sip of Ruby's sweet iced tea then gazed across the table into Delaney's sapphire-blue eyes, filled, to his surprise, with interest. He didn't mind talking about his business accomplishments. But 'family' was off limits.

"In undergrad, I started a company purely out of necessity. That personal necessity became an online textbook exchange for college students, where they could offer their used text books to other students in need of those same books. Sort of like an eBay for textbooks."

"I sold the company to the largest textbook supplier in the country for a tidy sum. The company figured college students were going to find a way to get their hands on discount textbooks, so why not profit from that too."

"Well, that explains the Tesla," Delaney muttered.

"Then, in grad school, I started another tech company, an idea that came to me as part of my master's thesis. The company was a web-based platform for bringing guest lecturers from around the world into classrooms, at a fraction of the cost to physically bring these same speakers in. The platform saved the schools from paying travel expenses, which for some of the heavy hitters, could break the bank, what with first class airfare, private cars, and hotel suites, in addition to a hefty honorarium."

He continued, "What started as a platform for the technical side of the guest lectures—things like satellite uplinks and video equipment—turned into a full-service company that handled the honorarium payments, the scheduling, and any materials needed for the lecture."

He slid his plate out of the way. "I later sold that company before earning my Ph.D. to an innovative education technology and services company for more zeroes and commas than I'd ever imagined possible."

"So, I repeat. Why academia?"

"I'm lucky. I can do whatever I want. And what I want to do is shape the minds of the world's future business leaders, and since I have more money than I could ever spend, I took what I learned both in the classroom, and in the real world, and became a professor at Wharton."

"You're an interesting man, Dr. Mayfield."

That simple statement from Delaney warmed him from the inside out.

"And a contradictory man." She tilted her head.

"How so?"

"You dress like you should be on Wall Street, yet you're a dean at a small university. You drive a Tesla yet live in a modest townhome in Georgetown Square. You are opposed to my proposal, yet you go out of your way to ensure that I have time to make my argument in its support."

"As I've said before, it's nothing personal. And it's only fair that you should be given the opportunity to defend your idea."

She pushed her plate aside.

"Are you having cake?"

"If you'll split it with me."

"Is it worth the extra mile I'll have to run tomorrow?"

"So worth it," she said with a wink.

~

"Let me guess, you walked."

"Of course. Why would I drive five blocks downtown to walk around an art festival?" They'd stepped out of the bright lights of Ruby's and into the falling dusk.

The festival vendors had packed up for the night, their tent flaps closed, and the crowds had thinned.

"We seem to be making a habit of this."

"What's that?" She turned to look up at him.

"Me escorting you home." He gazed down the street toward her apartment complex, hands in his pockets, as if disinterested.

"You really–"

"Don't have to?" The corner of his mouth lifted. "I know.

But I'm going to regardless." Placing his hand low on her back, he guided her around the sign advertising Ruby's specials then walked beside her.

The air had cooled with the setting sun. A star winked on in the cloudless sky. They strolled along, Devon in no apparent hurry to ditch her at her door. They strolled in silence, but a comfortable one. Maybe they'd actually succeeded in establishing a truce of sorts.

She'd had a surprisingly nice time, and in some ways, this non-date felt . . . like a date. One of the better ones she'd had in recent memory, at that.

Devon was smart, he had impeccable manners, and he treated her with respect—something she hadn't experienced from a man in a very long time, unless she counted Nash and Ethan. Grudgingly, of course, she had to admit that maybe his opposition to her proposal wasn't personal.

They'd arrived at her door, and she turned to Devon. "Thank you. I know this may shock you to hear me say it, but you're not so bad."

He shook his head with a brief chuckle that she felt down to her toes. "I'll take that as a compliment. You're not so bad yourself." Then his demeanor changed. Not the serious, broody demeanor she'd grown accustomed to, but something intense and yet a little uncertain. "In fact," he stepped closer to her. "I'd like to kiss you."

"Oh," she replied on an exhale. In her experience, men didn't ask. They just assumed. Then took. "I, I think I would like that." Her knees quivered as his gaze dropped to her mouth.

$\sim$

CUPPING HER FACE, he closed the distance between them

until they were only a breath apart and the air around them hummed with electricity. Instead of 'the love test,' Sam should call it 'the lust test,' because there was definitely a lot of *that* between him and Delaney right now.

He bent forward and put his mouth on hers, tentative at first, gauging her response.

Ho-ly hell. Her lips parted, and his tongue tangled with hers, and a throaty moan escaped—he had no idea whose.

Spicy sweet.

One hand curled into his shirt, then her purse and shopping bag hit the ground, landing on his foot, as her other hand wrapped around his neck.

The kiss exploded, going from a mere flame to a blazing inferno in seconds.

Delaney pressed her body against his, and he groaned in both pleasure and agony. His hands skimmed up her rib cage until they encountered those voluptuous breasts. He'd dreamed about her breasts. Then again, what red-blooded male wouldn't have? Her hardened nipples bore into his chest, and he took command of the kiss, backing her up against the brick wall of her apartment building.

A car horn blared as someone peeled out, bringing them to their senses, and they broke apart.

Wide blue eyes, filled with confusion, stared at him in search of answers.

He had none to give. He bent to pick up her purse and shopping bag and handed them to her. "I hope that wasn't fragile."

She just shook her head.

"Goodnight, Delaney."

~

Hands to her lips, Delaney shut the front door behind her and leaned against it for support. That had come out of the blue. Of course, she'd felt the sexual tension all evening, but she hadn't realized the feeling was mutual. And who knew the buttoned-up Dr. Devon Mayfield could kiss like that?

A kiss she had felt all the way down to her toes.

A kiss that could never, ever happen again.

Ever.

More's the pity, since that kiss had rocked her world.

Since the day she'd introduced herself in McGinty's, she'd wanted to push Dr. Mayfield outside the bounds of his control. And she'd succeeded. In a big way.

Pushing off the door, she wandered through her apartment in a hot-kiss-induced daze. Through the kitchen, skimming her hand across the countertops, into the dining room, around the table, along the hallway to her bedroom. Her lonely bedroom.

It had been far too long since she'd wanted someone like she wanted Devon Mayfield. Was it because he posed such a challenge with his polished manners and his impeccable dress?

She groaned. Why did she fall for the emotionally unavailable men? The men who looked hot as hell on the outside but were cold as ice on the inside?

Collapsing onto her bed, she remembered the feel of his mouth on hers. But *was* Devon cold as ice on the inside? Or did his reserved demeanor camouflage a passion lurking just beneath the surface of that implacable façade?

No man could kiss like that and be cold.

Flopping onto her back, she stared up at the ceiling.

This. Was. Not. Happening.

She was not crushing on a man who held the future of

her life's work in his hands. A man who would likely never support her proposal.

A man who'd kissed her like he never wanted to let her go.

Yeah. This was so happening.

11

———

On Monday, Delaney entered the creative writing department's main office to check her mail. As she sorted through the junk mail, academic journals, and invitations for speaking opportunities, Carolyn, the department's receptionist, walked by.

"Oh, Delaney. I was going to email you. You have a package." She moved behind her desk and lifted a sizeable brown paper-wrapped package.

What could that be? She hadn't ordered anything.

"A good-looking guy dropped it off. He your boyfriend?"

Delaney ignored the question.

"He left a card. I taped it to the package."

Curiosity aroused, Delaney accepted the parcel. "Thanks."

"Aren't you going to open it?"

Not here. Carolyn had a reputation as a gossiper, and Delaney had no intention of providing fodder for the gossip mill. "Later. I'm late for a meeting."

Carolyn released a disappointed sigh, and Delaney beat a hasty retreat to the relative privacy of her office.

She placed the package on top of her desk and stared at it, hands on her hips. Biting her lip, she reached for the envelope taped to the front, grateful to see the seal had not been broken by Miss Meddlesome.

She opened the envelope and pulled out a mono-grammed card with the initials DWM. Scrawled in bold masculine script:

CONSIDER THIS A FURTHER EXTENSION OF THE OLIVE BRANCH.
DEVON

Surprised by his gesture, she set aside the card and tore into the paper. Surprise turned to shock when she discovered the framed *Pride and Prejudice* poster she'd coveted at the art festival.

She dropped into the guest chair in front of her desk, hand to her mouth. He kept her constantly off balance. Every time she pegged him as the biggest jerk in the world, he did something nice.

And after spending Saturday with him, and that kiss at her door, she'd begun to think his jerkiness wasn't inten-tional. That maybe there was a reason for his Darcy-like broodiness, and it wasn't just arrogance or condescension.

"Hey Del, wanna join us for lunch?" Shelby said, as she walked into Delaney's office with Sam right behind her.

"What's this?" Sam leaned over the poster to get a better look. "Nice. It's perfect for your office."

"Did you get that at the art festival we missed?" Shelby asked, joining Sam in her examination of the artwork.

"Um, no."

"Your mom send it you?" Sam turned to her with a ques-tioning look.

"Guess again." Shelby picked up the card and handed it to Sam.

Sam gazed down at the card then up at Delaney. "Devon? As in Devon Mayfield, hater of romantic fiction?"

"That would be the one," Delaney mumbled.

"Huh. Maybe he wants to make amends." Shelby took the card and returned it to Delaney's desk. "Or maybe he wants to get in your pants," she continued on a laugh.

"Shelby." Sam placed her hand on Delaney's shoulder. "Or maybe he's come to the conclusion that my test is right."

Delaney's head snapped up. That couldn't be it. Could it?

"Oh, that's right! You two matched!" Shelby sat on the corner of the desk, crossing her khaki-clad legs.

"Love and hate are but two sides of the same coin," Sam pressed. "There's definitely a lot of chemistry between you two."

"I'll say." Shelby examined her nails. "That night at the play I thought I might need a fire extinguisher in case you two spontaneously combusted."

Delaney snorted and folded her arms across her chest. "The only reason we would have spontaneously combusted *that* night was from extreme annoyance." Now, *Saturday* night. Well, that was a different story. A fire extinguisher might have come in handy. Or maybe a fire *hose*.

Uncomfortable with this line of conversation, Delaney sought to change the subject. "Seriously, why do you think he bought this for me?"

"I don't know. Why don't you ask him," Shelby said, looking over Delaney's shoulder.

"He's standing behind me, isn't he?"

"Yup." Rising, she said, "Oh, is that the time? Sam, don't you have a meeting to go to?"

"You're making your getaway is what you're doing."

"Retreat is the better part of valor." And with that, Shelby and Sam high-tailed it out of her office.

"Ladies." Devon nodded then leaned on the door jamb, hands in his pockets as he waited for Sam and Shelby to leave. "I see you got the poster." Damn, he looked good enough to eat in a pearl-gray suit and charcoal tie. But, he needed to add some color to his wardrobe. He dressed so conservatively.

Delaney stood then started fidgeting with the paper the artist used to wrap the print. "Yes." She kept her back to him as she put the card back in the envelope.

"Don't you like it?"

She finally faced him. "I love it. You knew I would. It's just," her voice trailed off.

He pushed off the door jamb and stepped into her office, making it feel small and . . . steamy.

"It's just what?" His gaze captured hers and held.

"You shouldn't have."

"You liked it. I wanted you to have it. Nothing more."

"And Saturday night?"

He frowned and rubbed his chin. "Yeah. That was more."

"I don't know how I'm supposed to feel about that. And this." She pointed to the poster.

"Then you've got company."

His response surprised her. He always seemed so sure of everything.

She shook her head. "I don't know what to say."

"How about 'thank you'?"

"For the kiss or the poster?"

"The poster." The corner of his mouth lifted. "But, I should say thank you for the kiss." His eyes locked on her mouth, and she resisted the urge to lick her lips.

Her heart stuttered. She'd never been thanked for a kiss, and it was, well, sweet.

"If you have a hammer and nail, I can hang it for you."

Again . . . surprise!

"Uh, sure." Delaney walked over to the filing cabinet against the wall and, opening a drawer, pulled out the hammer. She had to rummage a bit for a nail. "Will this do?"

Devon had removed his suit jacket and laid it over the arm of her guest chair. Taking the nail from her, his fingers touched hers and she'd have sworn she'd felt a spark.

His eyes shot to her face, revealing that he'd had a similar reaction. "Yes. Now where would you like it?"

"On that wall." She pointed to the wall behind her guest chairs.

Devon stepped back, gauging the center of the wall. "Hand me the poster."

Delaney brought him the poster, careful not to touch his hands when she transferred it to him.

Holding it up, he asked, "How's this height?"

"Down and to the right just a little. Perfect."

He marked the spot with the nail. "Take this," he said, referring to the poster.

In order to do that, she'd have to reach across his body. She bit her lip, hesitating.

"Delaney?"

Taking a deep breath, she moved in, reaching up. Her breast brushed his arm for a second, and they both froze.

Clutching the poster like a life raft, she backed away,

avoiding his gaze, while he focused his attention on hammering the nail into the wall, using a tad more force then seemed necessary.

She leaned the poster against the chair, so she wouldn't have to hand it back to him, and under the guise of checking the positioning, walked behind her desk. Rather than studying the poster, she studied Devon's broad shoulders and tight ass as he stretched to hang the picture. He wore suits more often than not, but he wore them so well.

She tilted her head in admiration.

"How's that?"

"Huh?"

"Is it straight?"

She blinked, refocusing on the cover of *Pride and Prejudice* that now hung on her wall. "Oh. Yeah. Perfect."

He stepped back, examined his handiwork, then handed her the hammer, careful not to touch her this time.

"So, what now?"

"What do you mean?" he asked with a frown.

"We've kissed. You gave me a gift. You hung said gift. Have we declared a ceasefire? Signed a peace treaty? What?"

"Depends."

"On what?"

"On you."

"I don't follow."

"For my part, I'd say we've signed a peace treaty, but if I vote against your proposal again, I fear another declaration of war."

She crossed her arms over her chest and narrowed her eyes at him. "You won't. Because the presentation I have is going to knock your socks off."

He pulled his jacket back on, buttoned it, then adjusted

the sleeves. "So you've said. We'll see." As he walked out, he cast a glance over his shoulder, an uncharacteristic grin on his face.

Annnd the jerk was back.

12

———

Why had he come? Oh yeah, because Ethan, who had become a valued friend, had invited him. *Friend.* A first for him.

Devon stood in an out-of-the-way corner, scotch in hand, watching the festivities. Sam and Ethan wandered through the crowd hand-in-hand, greeting guests and accepting congratulations.

Sam made a beautiful bride, but she wasn't the woman who'd caught his attention the moment she walked down the flower-strewn aisle. No, it had been a curvy blonde in peach silk. She wore her hair up in some elaborate twist, tendrils curled around her face and along her neck. She resembled a character out of some Jane Austen novel. But she was far too sexy for the proper manners of Regency England. And what he wanted to do with her probably wouldn't have been considered Regency appropriate either.

Scanning the reception tent, his gaze landed on the object of his fantasies. She had a smile for the elderly gentleman talking with her. She often wore a smile, and he found himself looking forward to seeing it. Then he recalled how that mouth tasted, the scent of her perfume, the feel of her pressed against him. Maybe her smile wasn't the only thing he looked forward to.

Shaking his head at the nonsense of the thought, he sighed, wondering how long before he could politely exit the love fest.

He nodded at Nash and Shelby as they walked by. He'd never felt so out of place, but with his newfound friends in pairs, he often felt like the fifth wheel. He gathered Delaney felt the same way.

Maybe they could do something about that.

∼

As the bride and groom made their way to the dance floor for their first dance as Mr. Dr. and Mrs. Dr. Quinn, a familiar sense of longing washed over Delaney. With a *soupçon* of jealousy.

She was so happy for Ethan and Sam. They made an amazing couple, inside and out.

But.

Her heart ached a little too.

The wedding tent on the grounds of the quaint white country church was decked out with white fairy lights, cream-colored linens, centerpieces of peach peonies, white roses, and dusty miller. Beautiful. Elegant. Understated. Just like Sam.

Scanning the room for someone to talk to, her gaze landed on Devon, standing by a potted palm near the bar, one hand in the pocket of his suit trousers, the other holding a drink. Looking uncomfortable with the festivities.

She hadn't seen him since he'd hung the poster in her office.

A glass of wine sounded good, so she turned her steps in that direction just as "All of Me" morphed into "Shut Up and Dance," and the wedding guests applauded the bride and groom.

Waiting her turn at the bar, she glanced over at Devon. The Widow May Carpenter, Sterling's last living debutante, had him cornered, probably telling him all about her latest brush with death. According to May, she'd been near death for about five years now. Yet, when they called for the single ladies to make a grab for the bridal bouquet, she was always there hoping for another chance at love.

Delaney couldn't fault her for that. If only she could have a *first* chance at love.

After ordering a sauvignon blanc, she took pity on Devon and joined the conversation. "Mrs. Carpenter! You're looking lovely in lavender."

"Oh, Delaney! This old thing? It's at least a decade or two old," she said, a blush tinging her leathery cheeks. She was ninety if she was a day.

"Well, on you it looks fresh as a daisy."

Mrs. Carpenter patted her on the cheek. "Thank you, dear." Then she scanned the room, on the hunt for fresh meat. Finding her prey in the form of Mr. Greybow, the officiant, she made her way through the crowd.

"Thank you," Devon said, acknowledging Delaney's good deed.

"You're welcome." She raised her glass to her lips. "Now you owe me," she joked, sending a flirtatious smile his way, just to see if she could shake that cool-as-a-cucumber demeanor.

"Oh, is that the way it is?"

"Yes. And I know the perfect way for you to repay your debt."

"Vote to approve your new major?"

"Well, that too. But I was thinking of something more immediate. And perhaps less painful for you."

Setting her drink aside, she plucked his from his hand and set them both on an empty tray behind them.

"Hey," he protested.

Taking his hand, she pulled him toward the dance floor.

"Oh, no." He dug in his heels. "I don't like to dance."

Dropping his hand, she spun to face him, hands on her hips. "What do you mean you don't like to dance? Everyone likes to dance."

"No, they don't."

"You mean you *can't* dance."

"No. I can dance. I just don't like to."

"Well, get over it." She grabbed his arm and tugged, thinking he was going to stand his ground and not budge. Instead, he reluctantly followed her out to the dance floor.

"Let's bust a move," Delaney said when they found an open spot.

Before she could get in her first hip waggle, the song changed from fast to slow. Stifling a groan, she turned to him with a sheepish expression. It was one thing to ask Devon to shake his groove thing. It was another thing entirely to get up close and personal in a slow dance.

Memories of The Kiss flooded her with warmth and want.

Just as she'd been about to let him off the hook, his hand encircled her waist and reeled her in.

"Where do you think you're going?" Devon asked, his broad hand warm and firm on her back, his other hand clasping hers.

∼

"You don't . . . I mean, we don't–"

"Relax. You dragged me out here, now let's see this thing through."

Delaney's luscious curves fit him to a T. The smell of her perfume tickled his nose and sent heat straight to his groin.

He'd been watching her all evening, from the moment she walked down the aisle in her bridesmaids dress the color of the ripe peaches Georgia was famous for. He'd watched her flirt with the elderly Dr. Vanderkirk, a former dean of the College of Business. She'd brought a very pregnant Kara Blakely, wife of the mathematics department chair, what looked to be a glass of cranberry juice. She'd made a lonely old woman feel beautiful, and saved him in the process.

Everywhere she went, she brought sunshine.

And he'd come to realize his life could use a little sunshine.

Delaney was the slab of cherry pie topped with whipped cream that you shouldn't be eating. The wife he'd had in mind was the celery stick you *should* be eating instead.

After a few turns, Delaney sighed and relaxed into him. And damn, if it didn't feel good. Too good. He remembered how she felt pressed against him, her lips soft, warm, and willing under his. And he wanted more. So much more.

The truth was, she scared him. Made him feel things he'd never felt for anyone before. Things like compassion, warmth, and caring—things that made him weak and vulnerable, made him need and opened him up to rejection. Not a position he relished. Maybe if he'd grown up with a nurturing mom or a supportive father, those feelings wouldn't seem so alien to him now.

Her free hand slid up his spine and back down and his

knees nearly buckled. The hand he clasped in his gave a slight squeeze.

Before he could consider it, he pressed his lips to her temple, and she sighed, shifting his thoughts to making her sigh for other, more erotic reasons. Wondering how she would sound as he kissed and nipped his way down that voluptuous body of hers.

Damn. If he didn't put a stop to this fantasy, he'd be hard-pressed—no pun intended—to exit the dance floor without alerting Delaney and everyone else to his predicament.

Then she turned her mouth into his neck, and her hot breath against his skin solidified his growing erection.

Sweet Jesus.

The way she was pressed up against him, she had to feel what she was doing to him.

The song ended, and Delaney took a step back. His undoing came when she glanced at his crotch, licked her lips, and raised her wide-eyed gaze to his. The air crackled with so much electricity he expected all the wedding guests to spontaneously combust.

"Thank you for the dance, Devon."

And then she was gone.

Way to go, Devon. Now she thinks you're not only an asshole, but a horny teenager.

DELANEY TOSSED the peach-and white-rose bridal bouquet onto the dresser as she stepped out of her stilettos. If she had a dime for every wedding bouquet she'd caught in the last two years, she could pay off her car and take a vacation to Hawaii.

Slipping off the full-length chiffon bridesmaid's dress, she reached into her closet and pulled out her fluffy white robe. She needed the comfort and assurance the robe offered. Belting it, she sank onto the bed behind her and began taking the pins out of her hair.

Earlier, on the dance floor with Devon, when she'd felt his lips on her temple, followed by that unmistakable bulge, she'd come close to grabbing his hand and hauling him off to some secluded spot outside the wedding tent for a hot, quick romp. The thought of making Devon Mayfield lose control, and in a public place, made her shiver in anticipation.

Then common sense took hold. *Thank God.*

Sex with Devon was a bad idea. The worst. Even if Sam's test said they were a match. And even though his kiss was the greatest thing since milk chocolate . . .

Not only were they at odds over her proposal, if she fell for him and his broodiness, she'd never forgive herself. After a failed six-month relationship two years ago, she'd sworn off her Kryptonite—emotionally unavailable men.

If she wanted a serious relationship, Devon Mayfield was *not* the man. She wasn't Elizabeth Bennet, and he wasn't Fitzwilliam Darcy.

She thought about what Shelby had said. *Stop trying so hard.*

That's what she intended to do. Focus on her career, and give Mr. Tall, Dark, and Brooding a wide berth. The only contact she planned to have with him was during the curriculum approval process. No more bumping and grinding on the dance floor, no more dinners at Ruby's or picnic dinners on The Green. Or hot kisses outside her front door.

Devon Mayfield was off her to-do list.

Her mind made up, she decided a long, hot bath was in order. Maybe it would calm the sexual frustration she'd been feeling since their slow dance together. Who was she kidding? Since The Kiss.

A few candles, a glass of wine, maybe a chocolate or two, and she'd be right as rain.

Mostly.

Flipping on the bathtub faucet, she dug around in the cabinet for bath salts and candles. Coming up with lavender bath salts and a couple of vanilla candles, she set the scene. While the bathtub filled with hot water and the bathroom filled with the scents of lavender and vanilla, she headed to the kitchen and the open bottle of chardonnay in the fridge. Holding it up to the light, she saw it was more than half full. Perfect.

Uncorking it, she poured a glass then hurried to check the water level.

A quick sip, and then she set the glass on the edge of the tub. Twisting up her hair, she secured it with a clip and shucked her robe.

Easing into the hot water, she sighed. Leaning back, she clasped the wine glass, closed her eyes, and . . .

The doorbell rang.

"Oh, come on! You can't be serious." Who the hell could that be?

It was only about nine-thirty, so it wasn't late. It could be her neighbor, Jenny Stevens, whose husband was currently overseas serving his country.

"Oh God. What if it's bad news?"

Climbing out of the tub, she wrapped her robe around her, not even bothering to dry off. Just in case, she grabbed the baseball bat she kept by her bed.

She reached the door and peered through the peephole.

And there stood Mr. TD&B himself. Looking über hot in his suit pants, *sans* jacket and tie, sleeves rolled up over his forearms, his white shirt open at the neck.

Did he come to finish what they'd started? Her resolve began to crumble like dry cornbread.

Chewing on her lip, her hand poised at the deadbolt, she debated with herself. Should she open it? It was clear she was home. The lights were on in the living room and the kitchen. He could think she was in the shower—or bath— which, technically, she had been.

But.

Maybe something was wrong. She peeked again. He did have a frown on his face. But then again, when didn't he?

Compassion won out over common sense and she opened the door.

"Devon. What's wrong? Why are you here?"

He gave her a sheepish look. "I, uh, I came to apologize."

13

———

T his had been a mistake. A colossal mistake.

Clearly Delaney had been in the shower. Or the bath.

Devon scrubbed his hands over his face attempting to wipe the vision of Delaney, her body slick with water and suds, from his imagination. He nearly groaned aloud.

Her hair hung in damp ringlets along her neck, and her wet robe clung to her curves, especially her breasts, free and unhindered by a bra, their nipples pebbled against the fabric. He knew those breasts would feel heavy in his hands. The scent of lavender assaulted him.

"Apologize? For what?"

He cleared his throat. Get it together, man. Or you'll be apologizing for much more than your behavior on the dance floor.

"For my inappropriate behavior on the dance floor, and even more for my . . . reaction."

Her brow puckered, whether in anger, or just in thought, he couldn't tell. Then she cinched the tie on her robe tighter, folded her arms across her chest, boosting her breasts even higher. He was making her uncomfortable. Again. Which was not his intention.

"It's okay." She looked up at him with those breathtaking baby blues.

The silence grew as the tension went from a five to a ten on the Richter scale. *Speak, man! Say something, anything.*

"Well, I'd better go, and let you get back to your . . ." He waved his hand in the general direction of her damp hair and robe. The robe that clung to her breasts like cellophane to a ripe melon. He swallowed hard. "Bath."

He turned to go.

"Devon?"

Damn. So close. "Yeah?"

"Did you really, um, want me tonight?"

This time he did groan out loud. He took a deep breath and responded. "Yes."

She nodded her head.

That's it?

As she put her hand on the door to close it, she looked him in the eye and said, "Ditto."

The door closed with a soft click, yet the honesty of her answer left him so stunned he couldn't move.

Delaney Driscoll was proving to be the most interesting woman he'd ever met. And the most frustrating.

Adjusting himself with a wince, he headed down the sidewalk to his car unable to get the vision of a naked and willing Delaney off his mind. He'd just reached the parking lot when Delaney's door opened again. He turned at the hopeful sound to see her silhouetted by the light, and damn if his mouth didn't water.

"Do you still? Want me, I mean?"

Oh God, yes! "Delaney." He'd intended for her name to

come out as a warning, and instead it came out gruff and wanting.

"Do you?" she asked again.

He closed his eyes. God help him. "Yes." When he opened his eyes, she held out her hand to him and opened the door wider.

Sweet Jesus. If there was a hell, he was going straight there. But by God, he would enjoy every minute of the reason for that trip.

~

DEVON HESITATED, and Delaney gave herself a mental forehead slap. *What was she thinking?* This had disaster written all over it. In ALL CAPS. Then he was on the move, stopping just short of her personal space. His eyes burned hot as his gaze captured hers.

Oh, what the hell. She was never very good at keeping to-do lists anyway.

Stepping into her, he reached back and closed the door. She stared up at him, her throat dry, her heart threatening to tap dance out of her chest. Apparently his wasn't far behind, given the thudding of the pulse in his throat.

His big, warm hands settled on her waist, and his eyes honed in on her lips.

Oh yes. Kiss me again. Please.

He tilted her chin up and she closed her eyes.

"Are you sure about this?"

She opened her eyes and nodded, trying to read his mood. Then he bent his head and captured her lips with his. Wrapping her arms around his neck to keep from sliding to the floor, she opened her mouth to him. Their tongues tangled and groans escaped them both.

Adjusting the angle, he backed her up against the door, his hands gliding up her rib cage, just below her breasts, which yearned for his touch. He parted her legs with one of his own and ground into her, his impressive erection pressing against her belly.

Sweet Lord! It had been far too long. Her fingers curled into his thick hair, holding his mouth to hers.

But he withdrew, his breath coming in harsh pants. He stepped back, leaving her bereft. "I'm behaving no better than Curtis." He scrubbed a hand through his already-mussed hair. And Devon Mayfield with messy hair was a sight to see.

"There's one big difference."

"What's that?" he asked, confusion skittering across his face.

"I didn't want Curtis." She reached out for his waistband and gave a tug, drawing him back toward her.

DAMN. Those big blue eyes held his as she nibbled on her lower lip. She let go of his belt and they stood, not touching, only an inch of space between them. Her breasts rising and falling with each raspy breath, her hands went to the belt of her robe, loosening the tie, and then she opened it and let it slide from her shoulders and onto the floor.

Speechless, Devon held his breath at the sight. Perfection.

Creamy skin, still rosy from the heat of her bath, begging to be touched. And her breasts far exceeded his imagination. Large, pink-tipped nipples beckoned for his mouth. He lifted his hands, covering her, and her head fell back against the door.

"Beautiful." Bending forward, he brought a nipple to his mouth, circling it with his tongue, taking pleasure in her throaty moan. He moved to her other breast as her breath came out in a velvety sigh.

Raining kisses up her neck, his teeth found her earlobe and nipped, drawing another moan from her.

He slid a hand down her belly until he reached her core, sliding a finger inside her. Her eyes closed as he stroked her, her breathy pants heating his cheek.

"Devon," she cried out. She grasped his shoulders like a woman on the edge, as her release hit her.

He continued to stroke her through the aftershocks, pressing kisses to her temple.

"Too many clothes," she finally muttered, as her eyelids fluttered open and her hands began working on the buttons of his shirt. She tugged it out of his pants and drew it off his shoulders.

The look on her face nearly brought him to his knees. Pure unadulterated lust. Her hands skimmed his chest on their way south. He groaned in anticipation of them reaching their destination and almost exploded when she cupped his erection through his slacks.

She glanced up at him from beneath her lashes, a saucy smile on her face. Damn, but everything about her screamed sex. And he was more than willing to oblige.

"Bedroom?" he rasped. "Where's your bedroom?"

Taking his hand, she led him through her apartment in all her naked glory. It could have been furnished in leather and fur for all he'd noticed. He had his eyes on Delaney's delicious derrière and beautiful legs, his mind already several steps ahead, imagining those legs wrapped around his waist as he drove into her.

When they'd reached the dimly lit bedroom, she

returned to finish the job she'd started and unbuckled his belt. Making quick work of it, she unbuttoned his waistband, tugged the zipper down, and plunged her hand into the opening. Her hot little hand made contact with his erection, and whatever doubts he'd had about this encounter vanished.

He grabbed her wrist and pulled her hand out of his pants. "Hold on, Delaney, or this will be over before we start."

Scooping her up, he laid her on the bed and gazed down at the sexiest body he'd ever seen. In his life. Ever.

A gift of voluptuous curves wrapped in smooth, silky skin, adorned by eyes so blue they rivaled the summer sky, a sultry mouth meant for kissing, and a wealth of blond hair. And at the center of all that beat the heart of a woman that captured his imagination in a way no other woman ever had.

Slipping out of his shoes and socks, he then pulled his slacks and boxer briefs off. Her eyes never left his, until she glanced down and licked her lips before her eyes flicked back up to his face.

He wanted to take all night to get to know every honeyed inch of her, but he was screaming for release. Crawling onto the bed, he covered her, and then froze. "Tell me you have condoms."

"Bedside drawer."

Thank God. Reaching for the drawer, his body gliding along hers, hot skin to hot skin, his hand actually shook as he pulled a foil packet out of the box. Rolling on the condom, he then settled himself between her thighs and pressed into her, watching her face for any sign of discomfort. He slid into her with a long slow move and stopped, gritting his teeth.

"What?" Delaney asked at his hesitation.

"You feel so damn good."

With that, she wrapped her legs around him. "So do you."

Before he could embarrass himself by coming too soon, he slid her lower beneath him so he towered over her, propping himself up on his forearms, and picked up the pace. Delaney matched him thrust for thrust, her throaty cries driving him toward his release. She cried out just as he exploded into a million pieces.

As his breath slowed its frantic rhythm, Devon knew it would be a long time, if ever, before he had sex that good again.

"Oh. My. God. I have never—that is to say-"

He rolled off her and propped himself up on an elbow and brushed the hair out of her face. "Spit it out, Delaney. You've never been one to mince words."

She ducked her head against his chest. "I've never . . . come . . . like that . . ."

He pulled back to gaze into her eyes. "Never?"

"Well, I mean I've had orgasms. Of course I've had orgasms." She waved her hand as if that was a given, especially since he'd given her one against her front door minutes earlier. "Just not, you know, during intercourse."

A grin split his face, and he kissed her forehead. "It's all in the angle."

Devon Mayfield grinning was like the sun emerging from behind a dark cloud. "The angle?"

"Yeah, and it just so happens I was a very good student of geometry."

"Well, props to your teacher."

He chuckled.

She blinked, stunned. Devon Mayfield—the man who could give Mr. Darcy a run for his money in the brooding department—actually laughed. Her heart rolled over, and a warning bell sounded in her head. *Don't do it, Delaney. Don't fall for him. He'll break your heart into a million and one pieces.*

Still basking in the glow of two orgasms, she ignored the bell.

Devon rose from the bed and headed for the bathroom. She pulled the covers over her and admired his mighty-fine backside. Who knew buttoned-up Dr. Mayfield looked like that under those designer suits.

When he came back to the bedroom, he had a towel around his waist. "I interrupted your bath."

She rolled to her side and propped her head in her hand. "I'm not complaining."

"Good to know."

"So, geometry." She lifted a brow.

He nodded. "Angles."

"Got any more talents you'd care to share with the class?"

"As a matter of fact, I do."

She threw the covers back, and with a flick of his hand the towel dropped to the floor.

"There's one in particular, but first things first." He crawled up the bed, settling between her legs and grinning up at her before putting his mouth on her.

"Oh God."

Maybe she'd underestimated the importance of geometry.

14

After two rounds of the best sex he'd ever had, Devon's mind turned to the awkward post-sex dilemma. Should he stay or should he go?

His first inclination was to get up, get dressed, and get the hell out of Dodge. However, Delaney's warm, luscious curves pressed up against him, beckoned him to stay. The arm he had wrapped around her waist felt like lead. Indolent and sated, he could barely move, even if he'd wanted to.

"I smell smoke," Delaney muttered against his neck, where she was currently nestled. Her warm breath raised gooseflesh as he remembered the way her mouth felt on other parts of him.

Jesus. Twice in a row wasn't even enough.

"Smoke?"

"Yeah. You're thinking too hard."

He snorted. Right now, his brain was the only part of him functioning. But as she slid her leg along his, another part of his anatomy sprang to life.

"Don't make this a thing," she said, as she rose to her forearm and tucked her hair behind her ear. It was no use trying to tame her thoroughly sexed hair, but Delaney was a woman completely comfortable with her sexuality.

"A *thing*?"

"Yeah, you know, 'Do I leave or do I stay?'" She gazed down at him, and heaven help him, he craved her lips on his again. "It's okay. Whatever you feel comfortable with."

"Now there's a trap if I've ever heard one."

She sat up, dragging the sheet with her and covering those magnificent breasts. "Devon, I enjoy your company–"

He chuckled. "Company? Is that what they're calling it these days?"

She shook her head with a laugh. "But I understand if you feel the need to leave."

Who *was* this woman? She wasn't begging him to stay? He took in the smooth skin of her shoulders, the tumble of blond hair, the sapphire-blue eyes that gazed at him patiently waiting for his decision, and for some inexplicable reason, he wanted to know Delaney in more than just the biblical sense.

"Do you have any of that wine I saw in the glass beside the tub?"

She nodded.

"I'll take a glass."

Smiling, she rose from the bed, unashamed of her nakedness, and headed for the kitchen.

By the time Devon entered the kitchen, Delaney had pulled on her robe, opened the bottle of wine, and poured two glasses.

She took a sip of hers and handed him his. "Hungry?"

"Famished."

"I have some sliced Gouda, salami, and crackers. Oh, and a jar of Kalamata olives."

"An antipasto plate, then?"

She chuckled. "Of sorts."

Devon had on his suit pants, his shirt untucked, the cuffs rolled up, his feet bare, and she could've eaten him up instead. Sex on a stick was what the disheveled Devon Mayfield was.

"Can I help?"

"No. I've got it. We'll eat in the dining room." She pointed around the corner with her wine glass.

Devon took his glass and followed her direction.

She pulled the items out of the fridge then took a platter down from the cabinet above her and began arranging slices of cheese and salami on it. Then she grabbed the crackers from the pantry and scattered several alongside the toppings. Next, she opened the olives and put a few in a small bowl then set the bowl on the platter.

Rounding the corner into the dining room, she saw Devon standing in front of a bookcase holding a framed photo.

"Your mother?"

"Yes." She set the platter on the table and went back to the kitchen for some napkins and small plates.

When she returned, he'd placed the photo back on the shelf and picked up one of her and her mother, along with the man Delaney considered her grandfather.

At the sound of the plates touching the table, he turned. "Looks good."

"It might not be gourmet fare, but it'll do in a pinch."

They sat across from one another and dug in. Hot, steamy sex really worked up an appetite.

Devon popped an olive into his mouth then pointed at

the photo of her mother. "Tell me about her, this woman who cared for Eliot all those years while you were away."

He remembered her cat's name? *Aww.*

Around a mouthful of cracker topped with cheese and salami, Delaney said, "Well, Carly Driscoll is a trust-fund baby but was black-balled when she got pregnant with me outside of wedlock and then refused to name the father, much less marry him."

She sipped some wine, ate an olive, then continued. "So she packed up and took her trust fund and baby girl to Kansas—Wichita at first. Then she bought some land about fifty miles outside of town and built an artist commune."

She got an eyebrow lift out of him over that tidbit of information, but he didn't interrupt. "My mother loved art, of all kinds, not to mention the artists who created it. I'm certain my father was a starving artist."

"You don't know who your father is though?"

"Nope."

"And that doesn't bother you?"

"Not really." She propped her chin in her hand. "By the time I was seven, the artist commune had filled to capacity, so I had a large family. I never wanted for love or attention."

"You've never thought about trying to find him?"

"No. Why would I? What is there to be gained by it? It's not going to change who I am." She shrugged.

His brow furrowed at that statement, and she wondered if he thought she was being shortsighted, but before she could ask, he continued with his questioning.

"And your mom's family?"

"Never met them. Although I've seen photos of them in newspapers."

"How's that?" he asked, a look of confusion on his face.

She sighed and rolled her eyes. "My mom's family owns the privately-held Driscoll Luxury Hotel Chain."

Devon sat back in his chair. "Seriously?"

"Yeah, why? You know it?"

"Do I *know* it? It was one of the companies we studied in a course on privately and closely held corporations. They have award-winning hotels all over the world."

"That's them."

He shook his head. "How is it that your grandparents never met you?"

"I was a bastard child of some lowly artist. As far as they were concerned, they wrote me and my mother off the moment they learned I was conceived." She lifted a shoulder. "If it weren't for the fact that the trust fund was under the control of a private manager, they would have done their damnedest to take that from her too."

Swirling the wine in her glass, she continued, "I never felt like I missed out on anything. My mother is a bit flighty, but she always put me first."

"And school? Were you educated on the commune?"

"No. I attended a small private school that employed the Sudbury teaching method."

"Sudbury? I'm not familiar with it." He layered another cracker with smoky Gouda and salami then handed it to Delaney.

Such a gentleman. "Thanks."

Taking a bite, she chewed for a minute and washed it down with a sip of wine. "Under the Sudbury method, students have complete responsibility for their own education, and the school is run by a direct democracy in which students and staff have an equal vote. There was no set curriculum or courses, and students were not separated into age groups."

"And you actually *learned* something?" he asked, incredulous.

Poor Devon. She could understand his shock over that revelation.

"Oh, I thrived in the free-form environment. But college, with its structured curriculum and courses proved to be a shock." She lifted a shoulder. "I adjusted quickly, especially once I landed on my major—creative writing and literature."

He pointed at her with his wine glass. "Middlebury College, right?"

"Right. How'd you know that?"

He stopped chewing, as if he hadn't meant to blurt that out. "I looked up your bio the day I received your degree proposal."

"Huh." She let that percolate a moment. Devon Mayfield had checked her out.

"So, BOARDING SCHOOL," she said, clearly remembering their conversation in Ruby's. "That explains why you're always so buttoned up."

"What do you mean?"

"Nothing but suits for work, I've never seen you in jeans, your hair is always perfect. You know, buttoned up. Unapproachable."

Unapproachable? That's the second time she'd used that word to describe him.

"If I'm so unapproachable, why did you *approach* me at McGinty's that day?"

"I needed another drink," she said with a hand wave and some chagrin.

"Uh huh," he replied, unconvinced that was the only reason.

She ran a finger around the rim of her glass. "True confession—I've always had a thing for unapproachable men. You know, the Mr. Darcys of the world." She lifted her gaze to his. "I want to see if I can ruffle their perfectly preened feathers."

"And you think you ruffled my feathers?" He dropped his gaze to her mouth.

"Yes." She licked her lips. "And tonight I loved watching you lose control."

Heat settled low in his belly at her bold statement. And damn if he didn't enjoy the hell out of losing control with her.

Delaney rose from her seat, pulling loose the ties of her robe, leaving it to hang open. Climbing onto his lap, she straddled him. "And I'm going to enjoy watching you lose control again." She plunged her fingers into his hair, as she claimed his mouth with hers.

Gliding his hands up her ribs and around to her breasts, he growled with pleasure. Yeah, he thought, as she plundered his mouth with her own. Turned out losing control with Delaney was the most enjoyable thing to happen to him in a long time.

Maybe ever.

DELANEY ROLLED over in bed and cracked open an eye. She felt well-used and thoroughly relaxed. Guess three rounds of sinful sex did that to a girl. Glancing over at the empty bed, she sighed in disappointment. Devon must have left at first light so he wouldn't have to do the walk of shame.

Then she smelled it—coffee. Bless him, at least he'd made coffee before he'd left.

Rising, she wrapped her robe around her and tied it then gathered her hair into a twist and secured it with a clip she'd tossed onto the bedside table. First coffee, then a shower. Then maybe she could face the repercussions of last night's amazing sexscapade.

Stumbling into the kitchen, in an oxytocin-induced haze, she grabbed a coffee mug and filled it to the rim. Then she spotted the note in handwriting she now recognized as Devon's.

DELANEY,

IT WAS NOT MY INTENTION TO SNEAK OUT, BUT I HAD A SESSION SCHEDULED WITH A PERSONAL TRAINER THIS MORNING, AND I DIDN'T WANT TO WAKE YOU.

I'LL CALL YOU LATER.

D

SHE COULDN'T SUPPRESS the teenage-like giggle. "He'll call me later."

Uh oh. If that didn't sound smitten, she didn't know what did.

15

———

A few days later, Delaney, Sam, and Shelby gathered around the table in Shelby and Nash's kitchen to look at one another's candid wedding photos. The professional photos wouldn't be ready for another week.

Sam and Ethan would take their honeymoon next month—two weeks on the island of St. Lucia, after a conference where he was the keynote speaker.

Wistful sigh.

Salt-rimmed glasses stood at the ready for the pitcher of margaritas Shelby had whipped up. And to soak up the alcohol, a platter of munchies.

Shelby poured the drinks, as Sam reached into a tote bag and pulled out her iPad. "Before we start on the photos," Sam said, setting the tablet on the table and turning it on, "what's up with Devon?"

Delaney choked on her margarita.

Shelby and Sam glanced at Delaney then at each other.

"He still opposing your major?"

Oh. Whew. Sam wasn't asking, 'What's up with Devon?' as in 'What's going on with *her* and Devon?'

"Yeah."

Then Delaney felt Shelby's eyes on her. "Are you wearing new blush?"

Uh oh. "No."

"Lipstick?"

"No." Shifting uncomfortably in her chair, Delaney reached for a bacon-wrapped date, but Sam smacked her hand.

Delaney's gaze shot to Sam's face. "What?"

"Not until you spill."

"Spill what?"

Lifting her hand and indicating Delaney's face. "This."

Delaney caved under the pressure of Sam and Shelby's silent interrogation technique. "I slept with Devon."

It was Shelby's turn to choke.

Sam just stared at her, bug-eyed. "No way. You *hate* him."

Delaney lifted her shoulder in a chagrined shrug. "Hate is such a strong word," she muttered, swiping salt off the rim of her glass and sticking her finger in her mouth with a wry grin.

"Oh my God!" Shelby and Sam exclaimed at the same time.

Then Shelby leaned over the table and whispered, "How was it?" as if there was someone else there to overhear their conversation. In fact, Nash and Ethan were in Atlanta for a Braves baseball game.

How was it? How was she supposed to answer that? She tapped her finger against her lips, as if in thought. "It was . . . fucking fantastic!"

Sam and Shelby looked at one another again then burst out laughing.

"You go, girl!" Sam said, lifting her hand for a high-five.

Delaney slapped her hand. It felt good to have that off her chest. She'd been dying to talk to her best buds about this.

"Once?" Shelby asked.

"Definitely not." Delaney reached for the date she'd wanted earlier.

"Whoa! Then how many?"

Delaney began counting silently on her fingers before giving up. "You know me and math. But a lot."

"More than a couple?" Sam pressed.

Delaney nodded.

"More than several?" Shelby cajoled.

"Yeah, I'd say more than several." Delaney knew she was wearing a silly grin.

Shelby waggled her fingers. "Details. When? Where? How?"

"Shel, if you don't know the *how* yet, I'm deeply disappointed in Nash," Delaney said, and laughed.

Sam snorted and prodded Delaney to spill.

"Well, it was the night of your wedding."

Sam's eyes grew wide. "Seriously?"

"Yeah." Delaney told them about the sexy slow dance, about Devon coming over afterward to apologize, and how one thing led to another. "And let me tell you, if Devon Mayfield is hot perfectly coifed, he's beyond smokin' with bedhead." In fact, Devon Mayfield with bedhead and a satisfied smile is the hottest thing she'd ever seen.

"So what now?" Sam asked, a concerned expression on her face.

Good question. But Delaney didn't want to think beyond the great sex, so she shrugged. "We're just having fun."

Shelby glanced over at Sam then back at Delaney. "Honey, it's all fun and games until somebody's heart gets broke."

"Meaning mine," Delaney muttered. "I'm going into this with my eyes open." *Well, that sounded convincing.* "Look, I appreciate your concern, but–" she cut her eyes in Sam's direction, "test results notwithstanding, I have no illusions about Devon falling madly in love with me. We're just . . . I don't know, having fun."

"Yeah. You keep saying that," Sam pointed out.

"And by 'having fun' you mean 'having wild, uninhibited sex,' correct?" Shelby asked.

Delaney smiled and waggled her eyebrows. "Still waters run deep, if you know what I mean."

"Just . . . be careful." Shelby's gaze held nothing but support. "I don't want to show up at your apartment to find you listening to Taylor Swift singing about tears on her guitar."

Sam snorted. "Seriously. Or worse, bad blood."

Her friends knew her all too well.

SEVERAL DAYS after his sexual encounter with Delaney, Devon came to a stop at one of the town's few red lights, next to an electric-blue convertible Mini Cooper with the windows down and music blaring. He glanced over to see Delaney gyrating in her seat to some guy singing about 'funking you up.'

Why didn't the Mini Cooper surprise him?

She swung her head from side to side, that blond hair swirling around her, while tapping her hands to the beat on her steering wheel. Then she threw her head back and blurted out the lyrics, several notes shy of perfect pitch.

And he smiled. He couldn't help himself. Delaney inhaled life. And life, in turn, filled her up. He could take a lesson from her on that.

She finally looked over at him, momentarily froze, then laughed and waved as she hit the gas.

The car behind him beeped, and he realized the light had turned green.

The Mini Cooper turned into the Piggly Wiggly parking lot on the other side of the intersection.

As he drove past, he couldn't resist looking for her. Spotting that blond hair and that curvaceous derrière in snug jeans, he chuckled and shook his head. His car's collision-avoidance system activated, braking just inches from the bumper of the car that had stopped in front of him.

Gripping the steering wheel and taking a deep breath, he admonished himself, "Keep your eyes on the road, Mayfield, and off Delaney's delectable ass."

~

DELANEY'S PHONE CHIRPED, signaling an incoming text. Setting aside the student paper she was grading, she picked up her phone and smiled when she saw Devon's name.

COLLEGE MIXER TUESDAY NIGHT 7:00.

Biting her lip, she texted him back.

IS THAT A NEWS FLASH?

A few seconds later her phone chirped.

NO, THAT'S A DATE.

She snorted.

COCKY MUCH? I MAY HAVE PLANS.

The three dots appeared on her screen signaling that he was typing a response, and then another chirp.

AND IF I SAY PLEASE?

She rolled her eyes.

I'LL THINK ABOUT IT.

His reply came seconds later.

GOOD. I'LL PICK YOU UP AT 6:30.

"Pfft." She set her phone aside. She wouldn't even dignify that with a response.

They'd been sleeping together a few times a week, sometimes having breakfast together when he stayed the night. She enjoyed listening to the trials and tribulations of being a college dean, and he understood when she vented about a helicopter parent or gushed about a particularly bright student.

Initially, they'd seemed worlds apart, but in truth, they shared the same world and related to one another's experiences pretty well.

The one topic they didn't talk about was her degree proposal. The last thing she wanted was for Devon—or anyone else, for that matter—to think that she'd use sex to get what she wanted. So, with the curriculum committee meeting less than a week away, she continued to revisit and revise her presentation, and avoided raising the issue with Devon.

The other topic she was avoiding? What she would do if Devon voted against her proposal again.

FINISHED up with the last of the urgent emails, Devon sat back in his office chair, rubbing the ache in his neck. Too much computer work today. He should take a walk, work out the kinks from sitting too long, maybe walk over to Uncommon Grounds for some caffeine.

Who was he kidding? He only wanted to walk over to the coffee shop in the hopes of running into Delaney. He'd left her bed just this morning and he already missed her.

He smiled, recalling her car dance. Sexy, adorable, kind-hearted, smart Dr. Delaney Driscoll. What was that song she'd been dancing to?

Rising from his chair, he poked his head out of his office door to see if Rachel was at her desk. No sign. He returned to his computer and typed in a snippet of the lyrics blaring from Delaney's car speakers. Google came up with Bruno Mars' "Uptown Funk." That sounded about right.

Opening a streaming service, he typed in the name of the song and hit play when it came up. Catchy beat. He could see why Delaney couldn't sit still to it. He turned up the volume.

His foot tapping, his knee bouncing, he kept time with the rhythm. Unable to sit still, he stood up and moved his hips, fingers snapping. Chin bouncing, he did a little spin, bent his knees and bounced to the beat.

He'd had basic ballroom dance lessons as a reluctant teenager in boarding school. He could handle most social dance situations, from a waltz to a foxtrot, but this was . . . liberating. Swinging his head side to side mimicking Delaney, he spun around with a hip shake, arms over his head, and froze.

Leaning against the door frame, a cup of coffee in each hand, a gift bag dangling from her wrist, stood Delaney, a broad smile across her face.

She giggled. "Gotta love Bruno." She pushed away from the door and walked into his office.

He scratched his nose, as heat flooded his face. "How long have you been standing there?"

"Long enough."

He closed his eyes. The one time he cuts loose, he's busted.

"I loved it." She held out a coffee cup. "I thought you might need an afternoon pick-me-up. After all, we didn't get much sleep last night," she added with a wink.

No argument there.

Taking the proffered coffee, he walked around her, looked outside his door once again, then closed it behind him.

She lifted a brow. Standing there in a white skirt and a fitted blouse the color of her eyes, Delaney was the only afternoon pick-me-up he needed.

Lifting her hand, she said, "This is for you."

Setting his coffee aside, he took the bag. "It's not my birthday."

"I wouldn't know whether it was or not, since I don't know your birthday."

"It's next Tuesday."

"Really? We'll have to celebrate."

"Or not," he muttered. Pulling the pinstriped tissue from the bag—nice masculine touch—he peered inside to find a dress shirt. "Purple?"

"Yeah. To loosen up a little, put some color in your life. You can wear this with your pearl-gray suit and charcoal striped tie."

She patted his chest, but before she could remove her hand, he took it, and, moved beyond words, lifted it to his mouth and kissed it.

Gifts were an uncommon occurrence in his life. Carter sent obligatory gifts to the school every year for his birthday, usually practical items like laptop computers or tablets for his schoolwork. But those had stopped on his eighteenth birthday. Then there were the occasional gifts from co-workers, like when he moved on in his career, but nothing like this.

That Delaney took the time to pick out a shirt, considered what he should wear it with, and gift wrap it meant more to him that any other gift ever had.

The music changed to a slow song full of regret, and he plucked the coffee from her hand, setting it on the desk next to his, and took her into his arms. He began to sway to the music—as Bruno, was it?—sang about what he should have done when he had his girl. With his chin on her head, the scent of orange blossoms, the warm soft body pressed to his, he felt . . . content.

Delaney's hands skimmed along his back, easing the tension and removing all thoughts of faculty hirings, departmental budgets, and college rankings.

The song ended and Delaney withdrew, smiling up at him. He bent his head to kiss her. Just a quick peck—after all this was a place of employment—but a peck wasn't nearly enough. As his tongue grazed hers, she moaned and leaned into him, her hands going to his shoulders.

The kiss heated and, just as he considered bending her over his desk to see what she had under that flirty little skirt, she pulled back, her gaze cloudy with desire. Patting his chest, she said, "As much as I would like to take you up on that," she glanced down at his erection, "I have a class to teach in fifteen minutes."

Repressing a groan, yet thankful she had come to her senses before he did something altogether inappropriate, he nodded.

Her hand grazed across his chest as she retrieved her

coffee. "But, if you should find yourself in my neighborhood, say around sixish, I'll be home . . . trying on my latest Victoria's Secret purchase."

This time he did groan. "Lace?"

"*Lots* of lace," she said with a saucy wink.

He was a sucker for Delaney in lace. "I'll bring the wine."

16

As Devon stood talking to the chair of the management department, he kept an eye on Delaney as she circulated among faculty, staff, grad students, and administrators. The sapphire-blue dress matched her eyes and complimented her blond hair. It was conservative in cut, but nothing on Delaney would ever look anything but sexy.

She greeted students, faculty, and staff alike, with a radiant smile that made her eyes sparkle like the gemstones he often compared them to. Never met a stranger either. She knew what to say to break the ice and how to step away from a conversation without making the person feel slighted.

While she didn't have the polish he'd always thought he'd wanted in a wife and partner, she had something he'd come to value more—sincerity.

And she'd avoided any public displays of affection, lending credence to his introduction of her as a friend. A friend with closet benefits, since they had yet to go public with their . . . whatever this was.

But was that all she was? Did he want more? Did he

want to take her hand in public, wrap his arm around her waist and stake his claim to her, putting the rest of the men in the crowd on notice?

She approached him, a glass of wine in her hand. "I thought you might like something to drink."

"Thank you." He took a sip of the crisp, cold chardonnay. "Mm. I haven't had a chance to get something. Every time I head for the bar, someone stops me to talk."

"That's because you're the dean. Did I tell you how handsome you look in that purple shirt?"

"You like it? It was a gift."

"Well, someone has good taste," she said with a wink.

They looked up to see the provost, Dr. Chamberlain, moving in their direction.

"I'll just go get a bite."

"No. Stay." He wrapped an arm around her waist then leaned in to whisper in her ear, "I want you in my bed tonight."

~

Delaney shivered when Devon's warm breath caressed her ear, and then she heated at his remark. "Is it hot in here? Cause it feels hot in here to me."

He'd just staked his claim in a very public way.

Devon smiled at the provost. If it weren't for the heat in his eyes, Delaney would think he hadn't heard her.

"Dr. Chamberlain, you know Dr. Driscoll, professor of creative writing and literature?"

She didn't know what to make of Devon's PDA, in front of the provost no less. But she liked it. More than she should.

"Yes, Delaney. We met at the holiday party."

"Dr. Chamberlain," Delaney took his hand.

"Please, call me Ken." He patted Devon on the shoulder. "You're doing great work in your first hundred days, and I'd like to talk with you about another of the president's initiatives."

"Of course."

"Would you excuse me?" Delaney nodded at the provost as he dove into his topic. Devon's hand reluctantly slid from her waist, but the heat of his eyes on her as she walked away warmed her to her toes.

She could get used to this.

She'd never considered being in a relationship with another academic, having shared interests, shared lifestyles, and a depth of understanding between them about their daily lives that she wouldn't get with someone outside academia.

Maybe that's why they'd matched.

She wouldn't go there.

Regardless of that match, she held no illusions when it came to a long-term relationship with Devon. She'd enjoy it while it lasted.

And deal with the heartbreak that would surely follow when it ended.

～

"Are you going to do bad things to me?" she murmured against his lips.

"I'm going to do *very* bad things to you." He nipped her lower lip, as his thumb rubbed her hard nipple.

"Good." She sighed into his mouth.

"Keys," he murmured.

"Hmm?"

He stepped back. "Unless you want to give my neighbors a show, I need my keys."

"Oh. Right." She stepped back while he pulled his keys from his pants pocket.

No sooner did he have the door unlocked than he gave her a gentle shove into his townhome, where she promptly dropped her handbag to the floor and dove at him.

He caught her against him, his mouth claiming hers again, as he kicked the door shut behind them.

She'd ached for him all evening at the mixer, especially after she'd looked up several times to find his eyes on her. "Clothes," she panted.

"Don't care," he growled.

Backing her into the kitchen, lips against hers, he unbuckled his belt as he went. He stopped in front of an island. "Turn around," his voice a throaty snarl.

She complied, as a frisson ran down her spine.

"Bend over." He pulled her skirt up, baring her bottom. Sliding her panties down her legs, he steadied her as she stepped out of them. She gazed back over her shoulder to see him rip open a condom packet and roll it on, and she shivered in anticipation. He stepped up behind her and entered her in one smooth thrust.

The things he did to her—for her—were the stuff of every woman's fantasy.

His hand reached around her, stroking her body, and she gave herself over to him, promising her heart she could protect it, but knowing it was far too late for that.

DEVON SKIMMED a hand over her smooth round ass, buried deep inside her, where it seemed he always longed to be.

Delaney Driscoll had spoiled him for every other woman. His plan to settle down with a proper wife no longer mattered.

She backed into him, her four-inch heels putting her at just the right height for him, and thoughts of proper wives and career plans evaporated.

He pulled almost all the way out before sliding back in. She let her head fall with a groan. "Devon."

"I've got you. Hang on."

She gripped the counter as he picked up the pace, driving harder and faster with every thrust. He reached around and resumed his stroking until he felt her tense then let go as she cried out with her release.

He followed her over with a mind-numbing orgasm.

As his breathing struggled to return to normal, he covered her back with kisses.

She reached around for his hand and gave it a squeeze, and the wall around his heart did something he never thought possible. It cracked.

Pulling out, he lifted her up and turned her to face him. Cupping her jaw, he studied her. "I didn't hurt you, did I?" He shook his head. "I'm s–"

"Don't you dare, Devon Mayfield." Her eyes flashed blue fire. "Don't you dare apologize for giving me the best sex of my life." As quickly as it ignited, the fire in her eyes extinguished, leaving a soft smolder behind, and she touched his cheek. "I love what you do to me. Don't hold back. Don't ever hold back."

God, she unraveled him. Made him feel things. Things that collided and merged, like lust and tenderness, hope and fear, want and need, until he didn't know which was which anymore. Gathering her close, he touched his lips to hers, softer, sweeter this time. The heat banked, for now.

"How about we take this to my bedroom where I can love you slow and easy this time?"

"I like the sound of that."

DEVON DRIFTED INTO CONSCIOUSNESS, wrapped around a warm, soft woman, his hand proprietarily cupping a perfect breast, and he felt ... content. Satiated. Happy.

Interesting.

As he lay there listening to Delaney's even breathing, that happiness expanded into something . . . more. More with a capital "M."

When he took the time to think about it, the last few weeks had been some of the happiest. For the first time in his life, he had friends, good friends in Nash and Ethan, and even Sam and Shelby.

Delaney sighed in her sleep. And, not only did he have good friends, he had . . . what? What did he have with Delaney? Friends with benefits didn't seem to cover it. Fuck buddies—not one of his favorite terms—especially as it applied to Delaney, didn't seem to cover it either.

So, what was this? Extreme like? Intense fondness? Powerful affection?

One thing he knew it couldn't be—love.

He thought about Sam's test and the results. Could Sam be right? Were he and Delaney a perfect match?

Possibly.

But love didn't enter into it.

Devon Mayfield was not built for that emotion. It just wasn't in his DNA. Clearly, since he'd been abandoned first by one parent then rejected by another presumed parent.

But, even without love, couldn't he and Delaney form an

attachment to one another? Could she be the partner he'd been looking for? Would she be happy with a relationship that fell short of love?

He closed his eyes and let sleep overtake him, and dreamed of a life with Delaney.

DEVON KNOCKED on Delaney's door, a bottle of red in hand.

Shortly after, she opened the door, and he almost dropped said bottle of red. Dressed in a slinky black dress and black stilettos, her blond hair a tumble of waves, she took his breath away.

"Happy birthday!" She tossed colorful confetti all over him and her front stoop.

He laughed and shook his head. "I don't think I've ever been the recipient of birthday confetti before."

"Well then, it's high time." She took his hand and led him into the kitchen where delicious aromas reminded him that the sandwich he'd grabbed for lunch was long gone.

"I didn't know you cooked." He set the bottle of wine on the counter and pulled her in for a kiss.

She shrugged. "Not much. My mother says pick one thing and do it well. Pot roast is the one thing I do well in the kitchen."

He nuzzled her neck, eliciting a sexy gasp. "I can think of another thing you do well in the kitchen," he said, recalling a certain encounter of the hot kind in his kitchen that didn't involve food.

"Keep that up and dinner will have to wait."

"Promises, promises."

She patted his shoulder and he released her. "Wine?"

"Definitely."

As he uncorked the bottle, he watched her move around her little kitchen, admiring how her derrière looked in that black dress as she opened the oven door and bent over to check on the roast.

He opened a cabinet, found a couple of wine glasses, and poured the wine before spotting a bakery box from Sterling's local bakery, Sweet Tooth. Handing her the glass of wine, he nodded toward the box. "Is that what I think that is?"

A sly grin spread over her face as she lifted the glass to her lips. "Depends. What do you think it is?"

"A birthday cake?"

"Can't put anything past you, can I?" She walked over and lifted the lid to reveal a miniature chocolate confection for two decorated with the words 'Happy Birthday.'

Huh. Today he celebrated his thirty-fifth birthday, and in all those thirty-five years, no one had ever given him a birthday cake.

And damn, but that simple gesture touched him to the core.

"Thank you." Pulling Delaney in, he captured her mouth with his, tasting the dark fruit of the wine on her lips. She sighed then leaned into him, her curves pressed to the harder planes of his body, and his heart swelled.

He struggled to remember what his life was like before Delaney, and that scared the hell out of him.

Withdrawing, she lifted her gaze to his, her blue eyes warm. "I have something else for you."

"Tell me you're wearing black lace underneath that dress."

"You'll have to find out for yourself." She slapped a hand to his chest as he reached for her, determined to find out. "But that's not it."

He groaned and rolled his eyes. She slayed him with her brazen sexuality.

She went into the dining room and returned with a splashy birthday gift bag stuffed with colorful tissue and held it out to him with a flirtatious wink. He shook his head and took the bag from her.

Maybe it held something lacey for her to model. Not that she'd be wearing it for long . . .

He pulled the paper out of the bag, and in the bottom was a framed photo of the two of them at last week's BBQ at Nash and Shelby's house. Lifting the photo from the bag, his throat tight, he stared at the gift. Delaney sat on his lap, an arm draped around his shoulder, a big smile on her face.

But what surprised him most was the smile on his face. He looked . . . happy.

He had no photos, no mementos of Christmases past, no keepsakes from family vacations, nothing. Not even a photo of his mother.

Now he had this.

Beyond words, he wrapped an arm around Delaney's waist and vowed to show her how much this—and she— meant to him.

17

———

A few days later, Devon headed for his car in the faculty parking lot after a long day, looking forward to a glass of scotch, the latest John le Carré novel, and a quiet evening in.

Delaney and Sam were helping Shelby with wedding stuff—something about birdseed bags, whatever that was about. He'd see her later. He opened the back door of his car, tossed in his laptop case, then shut the door and turned around to find Nash and Ethan standing there, grins on their faces.

"A little birdy told us that you just had a birthday," Ethan said, clapping Devon on the shoulder.

Delaney.

"So, since the girls are busy with wedding things, we thought a boys' night out was in order," Nash added.

"Thanks, but that's not necessary." Devon waved them off.

Not taking no for an answer, Nash continued, "Of course it's not necessary. It's fun. And besides, that's what friends do."

"I'll drive." Ethan indicated his car parked across from Devon's.

Devon hesitated a moment, but in the face of their determination, he sighed and fell into line with Nash and Ethan. So much for a quiet evening at home.

Two hours later, Devon found himself at a trendy tapas bar in midtown Atlanta, a twelve-year-old scotch in his hand and the table loaded with plates of baby back ribs, tenderloin mac 'n' cheese, flatbread pizza, and something called pork cheek tacos.

Ethan raised his glass of scotch, and Nash followed suit with this beer. "To the birthday boy!"

"And a good excuse for ribs and beer," Nash added.

Devon lifted his glass in toast, ridiculously moved by Ethan and Nash's acceptance and camaraderie. They dug into the fare, content to eat in a comfortable silence until they'd taken the edge off their hunger. Then talk turned to their women and Nash's upcoming wedding.

"You nervous?" Ethan asked.

"Nah." Nash spooned more mac 'n' cheese onto his plate. "What do I have to be nervous about?"

"Second marriage and all that?" Ethan added.

"This is Shelby we're talking about. My best friend."

"Glad to hear it. I'd hate to have to kick your ass if you left her standing at the altar."

Nash snorted. "Not gonna happen. Not me leaving Shelby at the altar. And not you kicking my ass."

Devon could feel Ethan's eyes on him. He looked up while Ethan took a bite of ribs, chewed a minute, then washed it down with his drink. Pointing at Devon with the now-clean bone, he said, "You know, you've been awfully happy these last few weeks."

"Yeah," Nash nodded then wiped his mouth with his

napkin. "You've loosened up since we first met. You're more, I don't know . . . relaxed."

"Maybe it's the laid-back atmosphere of Sterling." *Or maybe it's all the scorching sex he'd been having lately.*

"Could be," Ethan said, helping himself to more of the flatbread pizza. "Or, it could be a pretty blonde with a sunny personality."

Nash glanced over at Ethan then back at Devon. "I'm going with the pretty blonde theory."

Great. Now they were going to talk about his . . . relationship . . . with Delaney. *Fine.*

"All right." Wary, he propped his elbows on the table. "You got me."

Ethan pointed his thumb at Nash. "What Dad's trying to say here is, what are your intentions with regard to our girl?"

His intentions? "Beg your pardon?"

Nash's gaze turned to Devon, making his shoulder blades itch. "Look, man. You're our friend. And so is Delaney." Nash leaned back in the booth.

"But?" Devon gestured with his scotch for Nash to continue.

"Don't be the guy," Ethan said instead.

"What guy?" Devon asked, afraid of the answer.

"The guy that rips out Delaney's heart." Ethan leaned over the table.

Devon took offense to Ethan's remark. He would never intentionally rip anyone's heart out, let alone Delaney's.

"I know you won't intentionally break her heart, but–" Nash said, before Devon could speak up in his own defense.

"But," Ethan interjected, "You could do it just the same."

"Delaney's heart is bigger and more open than anyone's I know. Don't be the guy that damages it," Nash said.

"Were you one of those guys?" Devon asked, pinning Nash with his gaze.

Nash looked away, a chagrinned expression on his face. "Uh, yep. Not intentionally. I did something stupid. Something I thought would help Shelby. Something I knew would piss her off and didn't tell her precisely because I knew it would piss her off. When that help got us both in hot water and I let it slip, there was hell to pay. And then I thought I'd lost her."

Devon directed his attention to Ethan. "And you?"

Ethan held up his hands. "No. In my case, it wasn't me. Let's just say mine is a tad hardheaded and it took a while to bring her around to my way of thinking."

"Just," Nash slapped a hand on the table to make his point, "don't be that guy."

So, if Devon broke Delaney's heart, his name would likely be mud around here, and he could lose the only real friends he'd ever had. And that included Delaney.

As she slathered cream cheese on her bagel, Delaney gazed across the glass and chrome breakfast table in Devon's townhouse. She'd been spending more time at his place the last few days.

He had a sexy case of bedhead, a shadow of stubble along his strong jaw, and a contented look on his face as he sipped his coffee and flipped through Sterling's humble local paper, the Sunday edition of *The New York Times* sitting at his elbow.

She'd certainly changed her tune these last few weeks. Gone from despising him for his refusal to support her degree proposal to loving him for his ability to challenge her. Make her work for what she wanted, fight for it even. And he'd made her a better person for it.

She paused with the bagel halfway to her mouth. *Whoa! Rewind the tape. Love?* Did she just admit to herself that she'd fallen in love with Devon? Taking a bite of the cinnamon raisin bagel, she pondered this latest turn of events.

Let's see, did she have all the signs?

Happiest when she was with him. *Check.*

Missed him when they were apart. *Check.*

Thought of him frequently throughout her day. *Check.*

Loved waking up with him, going to sleep with him, and sitting across the breakfast table from him. *Check, check, and check.*

Trembled at his touch. *Double check.*

And the biggie, do anything to make him happy. *Check.*

She sat back, chewed her bagel, and smiled. Maybe Sam's test was right. Maybe Devon *was* her perfect histo-compatible mate after all. She'd just reached across the table to touch his arm when he picked up *The New York Times* and opened it to the front page.

"I love you, Devon."

All the color drained from his face, a stricken look as if he'd just learned someone had died, and her words hung in the air, either unwelcome or unheard.

"Devon? Devon, what's wrong?"

DEVON BLINKED, unable to believe the headline: BILLION-AIRE CARTER LIVINGSTON DEAD AT THE AGE OF 64.

He anxiously skimmed the story, picking up words and

phrases like 'cancer,' 'survived by' . . . 'three children, five grandchildren.'

Emotion clogged his throat. Anger? Resentment? Rejection?

But grief? No. Not grief. How could he mourn someone he'd never really known? Someone who'd never cared enough to know him?

He dropped the paper to the table like it had bitten him.

"Devon, please, tell me what's wrong." Delaney knelt by his chair, her blues eyes filled with concern.

And without thinking, he said, "My father died."

"What?"

She stood and picked up the paper, reading it, searching for a clue to what had sent his world spiraling out of control.

"I don't understand. Carter Livingston is your father?"

"Yes . . . No." He scrubbed a hand through his hair. "I don't know." Leaping from his chair, he paced the floor.

His own father had been sick, for months, according to the article, and he hadn't known. No one had bothered to get in touch with him. Collapsing on the sofa, he buried his face in his hands.

He'd always held out hope that one day Carter would contact him, would ask to meet him, would acknowledge Devon as his son. He didn't expect Christmas cards and birthday gifts, just recognition. Not for the money, or even for the name, but . . . because he was proud to call him son.

And now that would never happen.

He choked out a mirthless laugh. As if his little fairytale would have ever come true.

The sofa dipped, and Delaney's hand glided down his back in an attempt to soothe him, to assuage the hurt that could never be assuaged.

He'd always known he'd been unworthy of love. His

mother's. His presumed father's. Even Delaney's. And this turn of events confirmed it.

Love didn't exist in Devon's world.

He pulled away from Delaney, capturing her wrist. She'd been so patient, waiting for him to explain. But he couldn't. Not to her. Not to anyone.

Shame, bitterness, and isolation filled him.

"I can't do this," he said, his voice calm, quiet. He set her hand on her lap and released it.

"Okay. We don't have to talk about it right now–" Her understanding tore at him.

"No. I mean I can't do this at all." He forced himself to look into her eyes, eyes that held compassion and sorrow. "I can never give you what you need. What you deserve." His quiet, painful confession hurt more than he'd ever expected. "I can't love you. Ever."

Her eyes filled, first with pain, and then with tears.

She reached for him, but before she could touch him and crumble his resolve, he rose from the sofa and, turning, walked out the front door, closing it quietly behind him.

Yeah. He'd become that guy.

STUNNED, Delaney sat on the sofa, staring back at the front door.

What had just happened?

One minute she was telling him she loved him, and the next he'd walked out of his own house, leaving her. Rising, she crossed her arms, hugging herself, thinking that if she could just wrap up tight enough her heart wouldn't crash to the floor and shatter into a million pieces.

Vision blurred by tears, she saw the newspaper lying on

the table. Swiping away the tears, she walked over and picked up the paper to read the story that had so shaken Devon's world that he told her he could never love her, trying to piece things together. He'd said his father died, but his response hadn't been clear as to whether *this* Carter was his father.

"Livingston is survived by his wife, Melinda, his three children, Michael, Stuart, and Charlotte, and five grand-children ..."

Devon wasn't listed.

She shook her head, a single teardrop splattering on the article.

Pressing a hand to her chest, where her heart thudded painfully with the weight of Devon's words, she couldn't help feeling sorry for the grown man whose little boy's heart had been broken today just as he had broken hers.

18

———

A week after Devon learned of Carter's death, and six lonely, hellish days later, Rachel knocked on his office door. "There's a Robert Stone here to see you."

Devon glanced up from the blank computer screen he'd been staring at for who knows how long. "Who?"

"He's says he's an attorney."

Attorney? His first inclination was to ask Rachel to tell him he wasn't in the market for an attorney, but a glimmer of . . . something gave him pause. "Send him in."

A short, stout man with thinning hair and glasses followed Rachel into Devon's office, his face dour. The man glanced around then stepped up to Devon's desk and reached out a hand. "Devon Mayfield? Thank you for seeing me without an appointment."

Devon shook his hand. "Have a seat."

"I don't have much time, as my return flight out of Atlanta is in four hours." He reached into his brief case and pulled out a sheaf of papers.

"I'm here on behalf of the Livingston estate."

Devon froze in the process of clearing a spot on his desk. "I beg your pardon?"

"Mr. Livingston left a bequest in your name." He cleared his throat. "The other family members were present at the reading of the will on Friday, but the family attorneys thought it best to meet with you alone."

"I'm sorry, but I don't follow." Devon's heart hammered in his chest.

"I'm sure you can understand the delicacy of the matter, what with Mrs. Livingston and the children ignorant of your existence." The gentleman placed the papers on the desk, facing Devon.

"What? How?" His breath left in a whoosh.

"I just need you to sign here, here, and here," he said, pointing to pages flagged with tabs. "If you'd like, you can fill out the paperwork for direct deposit of the bequest into the account of your choice," he continued, as he fished around in his brief case, before pulling out another form and placing it on top of the other papers.

Devon finally found his voice. "Mr. Stone, are you saying Carter Livingston left me something in his will?"

The attorney finally smiled. "I guess you could say that."

DELANEY HAD DROWNED her sorrows for over a week, and while she knew getting over Devon would be a long time coming, it was time to get back to the business of life, even if that life had lost most of its joy. Shelby and Nash's wedding was less than a month away, and the last thing she wanted was to be the Eeyore of the group before such a happy event.

Her mother taught her to own her feelings, to wallow in her sorrow when it came, but then to move past it as best she could because life was too short to waste it feeling sorry for herself.

She tossed her sheets in the wash and turned it on. Her weeklong pity party had resulted in a pile of dirty laundry, an empty refrigerator, and a few extra pounds, which she'd have to lose in order to fit into her bridesmaid's dress.

Many times over the last week, she'd considered texting Devon, sending a sympathy card or flowers, but she had no clue what to say. She knew he was hurting, and as if it wasn't enough that she carried the burden of her own broken heart, she carried the burden of his broken heart as well.

From what she could piece together, Devon was either illegitimate and Carter Livingston never acknowledged him, or Carter never knew Devon existed.

Her plants near death, she turned her attention to watering and fertilizing them, even as her chest ached.

Delaney had noticed that Devon had no photos in his townhome, save the photo she'd given him for his birthday. His home otherwise lacked the typical memorabilia of life—birthday party photos, graduation photos, or even prom photos. There were no photos of his mom, his dad, or his siblings. It's as if he arrived on the planet all alone and lived the last thirty-five years that way.

Pausing mid-pour, the watering can fell from her fingers as she stifled a sob for the lonely child who no doubt believed himself unworthy of love and thus incapable of feeling that emotion for someone else.

But she knew better. She knew that if he allowed himself to, he could love. He just needed a nudge in the right direction. Or maybe a shove.

DEVON BRACED himself for Delaney's appearance. He'd been both dreading and anticipating this day since he'd walked out of his own home, leaving Delaney behind.

When he'd returned later that morning, Delaney was gone, as were some of the telltale signs of her involvement in his life. The one thing she'd left behind—the photo she'd given him for his birthday.

She walked into the conference room looking poised and professional. And beautiful, as always. The sapphire-blue dress she'd worn to his college mixer was paired with a black jacket and a single strand of pearls around her neck.

She didn't meet his gaze, instead greeting Dr. Gregors and handing him a thumb drive for her presentation.

God, he missed her. He'd barely slept in the last week and half, and when he did sleep he woke sweaty, entangled in the sheets. His life lost all color the moment he'd walked away from her. He had to fix it, he just didn't know how. How could he fix their relationship if he didn't even know how to love?

She stood at the front of the room, remote control in her hand, and, clearing her throat, glanced around the room, her eyes never meeting his.

Delaney didn't know who her father was and she didn't let that negatively impact her life. It was high time he got over himself. There's nothing he could do to change the past, but there was something he can do to change his *future*. For the better.

DELANEY ADVANCED to her last presentation slide, listing the various career options for her proposed degree, in addition to the obvious, which was romance author.

"While becoming a successful published romance author is the primary purpose of the degree, it also prepares graduates for positions in the lucrative romantic fiction market as editors and agents. I conducted a survey among twenty-five editors with the top five romantic fiction publishers." Delaney pointed to the fancy bar graph Shelby created for her. "The results showed their unequivocal support for hiring graduates with the proposed degree and for accepting interns in the program."

"Thank you, Dr. Driscoll," Dr. Gregors said, nodding. "That was a very informative presentation. I learned a great deal about the romantic fiction market and the career opportunities available."

Delaney heaved a sigh of relief and took a seat in the chairs along the wall reserved for guests. She had yet to make eye contact with Devon. As she'd scanned the committee members during her presentation, she always stared at a spot above his head. Cowardly, maybe, but she couldn't bear to look into his deep brown eyes, afraid she'd crumple into a heap of heartache.

"Let's open it up for discussion," the chair continued.

"I, for one, don't need any further discussion," Dr. Gordon said.

Delaney resisted an eye roll. The man reminded her of the Grinch. The only thing missing was the green skin. No wonder his ex-wife had cheated on him.

"I am opposed to approving a degree program for the writing and publication of smut about women of loose morals."

She sucked in a breath. Dr. Gordon had been a vocal critic of her proposal from the very beginning, but he'd never made it so personal.

Out of the corner of her eye, she saw Devon rise then

smack his hands on the table. "That's it." He glared at Dr. Gordon. "I'll ask you to keep this conversation civil. There is no cause to insult an entire genre of fiction simply because your late wife read it and you think that's why she had an affair."

A few snickers followed.

"I can assure you, there is likely another reason for her affair." Devon pointedly stared down Dr. Gordon, until he looked away with a *harrumph.*

"I do have concerns over the cost of the guest lecturers," Dr. Gregors interjected. "With travel expenses and honoraria, this is a pricey proposal. But I do think it adds to the interest and value of the curriculum."

As part of the new major, Delaney planned to invite guest lecturers to speak to students, including top romance writers, agents, and editors. Dr. Gregors was correct, the expense could be enormous, and while she'd applied for a grant from the National Endowment for the Arts, it wouldn't be nearly enough. She was actively seeking private funding, but no one had come through yet. Even the services of the company Devon had started and sold would cost her money she didn't have.

Devon sank back into his seat. "I know that I have been opposed to Dr. Driscoll's proposal. Unlike Dr. Gordon, my primary concern was the usefulness of the degree, whether it prepared our students to enter the work force with the tools they need to succeed, and whether there was a market for the degree."

Delaney held her breath. Although the newest member of the committee, Devon's opinion appeared to carry a lot of weight with the others.

He nodded at the screen and her last slide. "The data Dr. Driscoll has presented on the romantic fiction market, the top five publishers, as well as the smaller publishers that have emerged as a result of the impressive romantic fiction market share in the publishing industry, has changed my mind."

Delaney's throat clogged with tears. He caught her gaze, but his face remained an unreadable mask.

"I support the proposal to add a Bachelor of Fine Arts in Romantic Fiction and Literature. And I know a company that could help with the guest lecturers, greatly reducing the associated expense."

Delaney pressed a hand to her mouth to hold back a sob.

Even if the committee voted against her proposal in the end, Devon Mayfield had restored her faith, if not her heart.

19

"Devon!"

He turned to see Nash and Ethan hot on his heels in the Granite Fitness parking lot.

Shit. Maybe they'd come to make good on their promise to kick his ass for hurting Delaney. He unlocked his car, tossed his gym bag in the back, then turned to face the two men he'd learned to call friends, prepared to accept whatever they dished out.

"Haven't seen you around lately," Nash said.

That's it?

"I've been tied up with a business matter and the hiring of a new department chair." And avoiding the people who had come to matter most to him.

"We're having a bachelor party for Nash," Ethan added. "Low key, just a few friends, some juicy steaks, and a bottle of fifteen-year-old scotch I picked up for the occasion."

Devon nodded, but Nash and Ethan just looked at him. "What?"

"You in or not?" Nash prodded.

"Am I in?" Devon asked, confused.

"No, we're just telling you about the party, but you're not invited." Ethan laughed then sobered. "You know that, right? That you're invited?"

Devon scratched his chin. No. He didn't know that. "Aren't you two going to do something, kick my ass . . . something?"

"What for?" Nash's brows lifted in surprise.

"Delaney."

Ethan shouldered his gym bag. "You two are adults. I think you can work out your own problems without the two of us interfering."

"I became that guy—the one who broke Delaney's heart," Devon continued. Maybe he wanted his ass kicked. Maybe it would alleviate some of the guilt.

"So fix it." Nash folded his arms over his chest.

Devon scoffed. "Easier said than done."

Nash glanced at Ethan then back at Devon. "Let me ask you something." At Devon's nod, he continued, "You miss her?"

"Yes."

"You think about her all the time?"

"Yes."

"You want her back?"

"Yes."

"Then do yourself a favor. Let Delaney in. You won't find a more loving, accepting heart than hers. She doesn't know how *not* to love. Whether it's her friends, her flighty mother, or her students. It's in her DNA." Ethan smiled. "It's a rare trait."

A rare trait indeed. Something both of his parents lacked. But that didn't necessarily mean he lacked it as well, did it? Delaney had taught him that.

"Damn, man. That was beautiful," Nash said, staring at

Ethan like he'd just revealed the secrets of the universe. Then he slapped Devon on the back. "So, you in?"

"We aren't going to join hands and sing 'Kumbaya' or anything, are we?" Devon asked.

Ethan slapped him on the shoulder. "Nah. I thought we'd recite poetry instead."

Devon cracked a smile. "I'll be there."

Nash and Ethan headed for the gym.

"Oh, and Devon?" Nash called.

"Yes?"

"Groveling doesn't hurt."

THE NEXT DAY, Devon jumped into his car determined to find Delaney and convince her that Sam's love test was right.

His groveling plan had been delayed by some important business he needed to attend to. Business related to the bequest from his father. But everything was in place, and now he could face Delaney, on his knees if he had to, and beg her to take him back.

Heart in his throat, he pulled into Delaney's parking lot, ignoring the possibility that Delaney might say no.

DELANEY HAD GOTTEN HER WISH—HER Bachelor of Fine Arts in Romantic Fiction and Literature had been approved— but the victory now rang hollow.

Oh, she'd celebrated with Shelby and Sam at McGinty's. She'd received congratulations from Ethan and a few of her colleagues, but what she wanted more than anything was to thank Devon for his part in the committee's approval.

But she needed a plan. Which is where today's lunch-date-slash-strategy-session with her BFFs came into play. She'd just piled her hair on top of her head in a messy chic twist when her doorbell rang. She'd planned to meet Shelby and Sam at Ruby's, so unless they'd changed the plans, she couldn't imagine who was at her door.

Peering through the peephole, she blinked in confusion. Devon! And he looked a little rough around the edges, like he hadn't slept in days.

Well, join the club.

Taking a deep, cleansing breath, she opened the door, playing it cool, even though her insides were melting. "Hi."

"Hi." He stood, hands in the pockets of his khaki slacks, appearing awkward and unsure of himself. "Can I come in?"

She opened the door wider, indicating her acquiescence, and when he brushed past her, she closed her eyes and inhaled his scent, pressing a hand to her stomach where a hive of bees had taken up residence.

Closing the door, she faced him. "Can I get you something to drink?"

"No, thank you." His gaze held hers and her knees turned to Jell-O.

After several uncomfortable seconds, she cleared her throat. "How are you doing?"

"I've been better." He glanced down at the floor, a sad smile on his face.

"Yeah, I'm really sorry about your, um, Carter." She didn't know whether to refer to him as his father or not.

"Thanks, but that's not what I meant." He took a step toward her, and her heart took a hopeful leap inside her chest.

"No?" Her question came out in a breathy whisper.

He moved closer. "No." Closer still.

"Then what?"

He stood toe-to-toe with her, his gaze locked on hers. "I think you know."

She shook her head and realized she was crying when a tear spilled over onto her cheek.

He reached out his hand, capturing the tear with his thumb. "I've missed you." He cupped her face, and she closed her eyes as she leaned into his open palm. "I'm so sorry, Delaney. Can you ever forgive me?"

When she opened her eyes, she read the anguish on his face.

But–

She needed to know whether he could open his heart to her. To love. To let her see not just his strengths, but his weaknesses too.

She took his hand then let it fall by his side. "First, I need you to talk to me." Tapping his chest with her finger, she continued, "I need you to let me in. I need to know who you are, warts and all."

HE KNEW there would be a price to pay in winning Delaney back, and that price would be laying open his soul, revealing his shame. That he'd been unworthy of even his parents' love.

Delaney led him over to the sofa. She took a seat and faced him full on, so there would be no hiding. She listened intently, without interruption, while he laid it all out there. Every painful detail.

"When I was three years old, my mother left me with a man she claimed was my father, and I never heard from her again. That man, Carter Livingston, already the CEO of a

Fortune 500 company at age thirty-five, had little time or patience for me."

He stood, pacing her living room, unable to look her in the eye for fear of what he'd see—pity. Derision, even. "To his credit, though, he took responsibility for me, even if he never acknowledged his paternity."

"He hired a nanny until I was ready for kindergarten then shipped me off to boarding school for the entirety of my primary and secondary education. I, along with a few other kids, even remained on campus during the holiday and summer breaks, especially after Carter married and had three children. He provided my tuition and boarding at the school, gave me an allowance for clothing and other essentials, along with the occasional obligatory birthday gifts. Other than that, I never saw or heard from the man."

He finally looked across the room and into her face, expecting to see pity there, but instead, he saw understanding and acceptance.

"So, you see, I've never had a role model for love or relationships. In fact, when I signed up for Sam's research study, I was looking for a business partner, not a romantic one. A business partner kept me safe. A romantic one risked yet another rejection. And after being rejected by both my parents, I couldn't take another rejection. Especially from you."

"Oh, Devon."

She rose and came to him, pressing her lips to his in an achingly tender kiss, then gazed into his eyes. His soul. "It's his loss, you know. Your father missed out on a relationship with a smart, successful, compassionate man. Someone any father would be proud to call son."

He wrapped his arms around her, breathed her in. "Delaney, you make me want things I never thought were possible. Especially for me. And in the four months I've known you, you've taught me so much. But I have so much more to learn." He dropped his arms and took a step back. "I'm not sure I know what love is."

"It's a verb," she said, matter-of-fact.

He barked out a laugh. "I'm serious."

"So am I." She took his face in her hands and searched his eyes. "My mother always says love is something you do, not just something you feel."

He nodded then reached out for her hands. "I admire your determination and your persistence, and that you don't let adversity extinguish your love of life." He shook his head and smiled. "The cliché 'when life throws you lemons, make lemonade' was written for you." He gathered her close. "I love going to sleep with you at night and waking up next to you in the morning. If all those things are love it must mean . . . I love you, Delaney."

"I love you, Devon."

His heart swelled beyond its capacity. Content to just hold her, he closed his eyes, felt her heart beat. "Oh. I have something for you." Devon reached into his pocket and pulled out a folded, slightly crumpled piece of paper then handed it to her.

Brow furrowed, she took the paper then lifted her gaze to his face.

"Open it." He held his breath while Delaney read the letter, her expression going from curiosity to confusion to surprise.

"I don't–" She shook her head and her eyes flew to his. "You created a fund . . . for me?"

"For your degree program. That way you can afford to bring in the best in the business for your guest lectures, travel to the annual conference for romance writers, and the program will sustain for as long as you want it to."

"But, where–?"

"Did the money come from? Let's just say, I had a little help from . . . my father."

"So, he acknowledged you posthumously?" she asked, confused.

"No. Not exactly." He scratched his chin. "There was no remorseful note, no paternity test results. But I've decided it doesn't matter. I've never had a family. But you, Nash and Shelby, and Ethan and Sam are my family now."

"You're right about that. But you're wrong about something else. You know exactly what love is and how to give it."

"There's a saying in business—no risk, no reward. I guess the same thing applies to relationships."

"Yeah? And what else does that saying apply to?" She gazed up at him with so much tenderness, that the last of his armor fell away.

"Love?" He lifted his eyebrows.

"Good answer."

Placing his hands on her hips, he reeled her in. "By the way, I didn't support your proposal because I'm in love with you."

"And I didn't accept your apology because you supported my proposal."

"Good to know."

EPILOGUE

The lovely old barn by the river was dressed for a summer afternoon wedding.

Delaney, a bridesmaid once again, had fulfilled her duties, and the afternoon reception was hers to enjoy.

Shelby made a beautiful bride, and Nash a handsome groom. As they recited their vows, Delaney had teared up. She always cried at weddings. Nothing new there. But mingled with the tears of happiness were tears of envy.

Two weddings in as many months. How much could a single woman take? Glancing down at her silk ice-blue sundress, she thought that it at least didn't look like a bridesmaid's dress.

She surveyed the barn, searching for Devon's dark brown hair among the guests. They'd only been officially dating for a month, but they'd been heading in that direction since the day they met four months earlier, albeit with a few detours and bumps in the road.

He was the most maddeningly stubborn, rigid, arrogant man she'd ever met. And she loved him unconditionally.

And he loved her. But would she ever walk down the aisle to see him standing at the other end waiting for her?

Patience was not her strongest virtue.

Sighing, she sipped from her glass of champagne as couples danced, laughed, and kissed. Where was he? He'd disappeared just when she wanted to dance. Likely on purpose.

She smiled when her gaze landed on Shelby and Nash, slowly swaying to an up-tempo song, like they were dancing to their own music, oblivious to everyone else around them.

It would soon be time to cut the cake and toss the bouquet. She'd caught so many bouquets in the last few years, and what had it gotten her? Nothing. This time, she refused to join the fray. Let someone else catch it. Maybe they would have better luck.

Hands grabbed her waist, startling her.

"Ever the bridesmaid, never the bride?" Devon spun her to face him, and she felt like throwing the champagne in his handsome face. "But what a beautiful bridesmaid you make." He kissed her on the lips. "Maybe that's the problem. Did you ever consider that? You're too beautiful a bridesmaid." He wore a mischievous grin. He loved to tease her, but today his jest hit bone.

Taking her glass from her hand, he set it on the table behind her and pulled her out onto the dance floor just as Etta James belted out the opening notes of "At Last."

She knew Devon wasn't fond of dancing, so the fact that he gathered her into his arms and began to sway touched her and made up for the unintentional jab. One arm around her waist, his other hand clasping her hand to his heart, he pressed his lips to her temple, reminiscent of the first time they'd danced. She sighed and leaned into him.

"Keep that up and we won't make it through this song

before I carry you off to a private corner for a make-out session."

"Promises, promises," she muttered against his neck.

She felt him smile against her hair. Closing her eyes, she lost herself in the feel of his arms around her, the length of him pressed to her. All too soon, the final notes of the song trailed off, and the DJ announced the cake-cutting.

Taking Devon's hand, they walked over to the linen-draped table displaying a confectionary creation almost too pretty to cut. Shelby and Nash did the honors then happily shoved cake into each other's faces, laughing like kids. Delaney rolled her eyes. Only Shelby wouldn't have minded have icing smeared all over her face on her wedding day.

The cake was sliced and served to the guests, then the DJ called for all the single ladies to step forward for the bouquet toss. Delaney planted her feet. Beyoncé's "Single Ladies" blared from the speakers.

"Aren't you going?" Devon asked, his brows lifted in question.

"No." She folded her arms across her chest.

"Isn't it a tradition?"

"Some traditions should be broken."

He gave her a little nudge. "Oh, go out there. Are you afraid you won't catch it?"

She turned and poked him in the chest. "For your information Dr. Mayfield, I've caught every bouquet thrown at me these last two years, and it's gotten me nowhere."

"Maybe this time is different," he said with a shrug.

"Come on ladies, don't be shy," the DJ encouraged. "Any other single ladies out there?"

"Yes!" Devon called. "This one." He pointed his finger at Delaney.

Mortified, she hissed at him. "Stop!"

He gave her a none-too-gentle push into the crowd of single ladies waiting for their chance to catch the bridal bouquet in the hopes of being the next to marry. Including the ancient widow, May Carpenter.

Delaney turned and gave him the evil eye, eliciting a laugh in response. God, she loved his laugh, all the more because it was so rare, but she'd heard more of it lately.

Shelby stood on the stage, grinned over her shoulder, then hurled the bouquet of blue hydrangeas and baby's breath over her shoulder.

Instinct kicked in and Delaney jumped for the bouquet as it sailed in her direction. Coming down with it, she tossed Devon a chagrined smile.

As Queen's "Another One Bites the Dust" opened, the DJ cajoled the single men in the crowd to step up for the garter toss. Amid whistles and catcalls, Shelby sat on a linen-covered chair, while Nash knelt in front of her and reached under her skirts for the garter. Shelby blushed then smacked his hand, as he'd obviously gotten fresh. Slipping the garter off her leg, he gave her a wink, and the females in the crowd audibly sighed.

Delaney looked around for Devon and was stunned to see him on the dance floor standing among the single men.

Nash turned his back on the crowd, pulled the garter back like a rubber band and launched it off the stage. Devon reached up and pulled the garter in like a fly ball in center-field. Delaney's mouth dropped open.

Amid pats on the back, Devon made his way to her. "You might want to close your mouth. I hear the flies can be murder around here in the summer."

Her jaw snapped shut.

"Come. I believe it's tradition for the single man who caught the garter—that would be me—to put it on the leg of the single woman who caught the bouquet—that would be you."

Speechless, she followed him up the steps to the stage and the waiting white linen-draped chair. Shelby and Nash stood hand-in-hand, big grins on their faces.

Delaney swallowed hard, scanned the crowd, all eyes on her. Ethan and Sam stood in front.

"Madam," Devon said, as he indicated for her to take a seat. Since her bridesmaid's dress was short, Devon didn't have to fumble beneath yards of fabric. He lifted her ankle and slowly, sensually, slid the blue lace garter up her leg, as the wedding guests shouted their encouragement. His warm hands glided up her bare legs, sending a frisson along her spine. Delaney's face burst into flames when his hands reached her thigh with a soft caress.

"While I'm down here–" Devon began, stirring up the audience even more with his innuendo.

Just as Delaney was about to smack his hand away, he reached into his pocket with his free hand and pulled out a little blue velvet box. Gasps arose from the crowd, and then they fell silent.

"Delaney, I realize we've only known each other four months, and most of that time was spent on opposite sides of an issue, but I can't think of another person I'd rather be on opposite sides of an issue with than you. Will you marry me?"

Barely able to see through the blur of her tears, she laughed, clutched his hand, and said, "Yes."

Sam's test had been right after all.

The guests applauded as Devon slid the beautiful

sapphire ring onto her finger. "Blue like your eyes," he whispered.

"It's perfect."

He took her hands and pulled her to him, kissing her lips. "Soon to be a bride instead of a bridesmaid."

ABOUT THE AUTHOR

 Rebecca Heflin is an award-winning author who has dreamed of writing romantic fiction since she was fifteen and her older sister sneaked a copy of Kathleen Woodiwiss' Shanna to her and told her to read it.

Never quite sure what she wanted to be when she grew up, Rebecca didn't attend college until age 30, and earned her bachelor's in literature, before going on to complete her law degree.

Ever the late bloomer, Rebecca finally turned her attention to fulfilling her dream of writing, and published her first novel at age 48. When not passionately pursuing her dream, Rebecca is busy with her day-job at a major state university.

She and her husband are also co-founders of a non-profit organization, which raises money to help cancer patients and their families.

Rebecca's pen name is an abbreviated version of her great-great grandmother's name: Sarah Anne Rebecca Heflin Apple Smith. Whew! And you wonder why she shortened it.

Rebecca writes women's fiction and contemporary romance, and she is a member of Romance Writers of

America (RWA), Florida Romance Writers, RWA Contemporary Romance, and Florida Writers Association. Rebecca and her mountain-climbing husband live at sea level in sunny Florida.

Sign up for Rebecca's newsletter for all the latest news on upcoming releases, appearances, and contests.

www.rebeccaheflin.com
rebecca@rebeccaheflin.com

ALSO BY REBECCA HEFLIN

THE PROMISE OF CHANGE

RESCUING LACEY

DREAMS COME TRUE SERIES

DREAMS OF PERFECTION, BOOK 1

SHIP OF DREAMS, BOOK 2

DREAMS OF HER OWN, BOOK 3

www.ingramcontent.com/pod-product-compliance
Lightning Source LLC
Chambersburg PA
CBHW072159130726
47910CB00011B/1574